Geronimo Stilton

3 in 1

PAPERCUTZ

Geronimo Stilton

#1
"The Discovery
of America"

#2
"The Secret
of the Sphinx"

#3
"The Coliseum
Con"

#4
"Following the
Trail of Marco Polo"

#5
"The Great
Ice Age"

#6
"Who Stole
The Mona Lisa?"

#7
"Dinosaurs
in Action"

#8
"Play It Again,
Mozart!"

#9
"The Weird
Book Machine"

#10
"Geronimo Stilton
Saves the Olympics"

#11
"We'll Always
Have Paris"

#12
"The First Samurai"

#13
"The Fastest Train
in the West"

#14
"The First Mouse
on the Moon"

#15
"All for Stilton,
Stilton for All!"

#16
"Lights, Camera,
Stilton!"

#17
"The Mystery of the
Pirate Ship"

#18
"First to the Last Place
on Earth"

#19
"Lost in Translation"

GERONIMO STILTON
3 in 1 #1

GERONIMO STILTON
3 in 1 #2

GERONIMO STILTON
3 in 1 #3

THEA STILTON #1
"The Secret
of Whale Island"

THEA STILTON #2
"Revenge of
the Lizard Club"

THEA STILTON #3
"The Treasure of
the Viking Ship"

THEA STILTON #4
"Catching the
Giant Wave"

THEA STILTON #5
"The Secret of the
Waterfall in the Woods"

THEA STILTON #6
"The Thea Sisters and
the Mystery at Sea"

THEA STILTON #7
"A Song for the
Thea Sisters"

THEA STILTON #8
"The Thea Sisters and the
Secret Treasure Hunt"

Geronimo Stilton

3 IN 1 #5

By Geronimo Stilton

THE FASTEST TRAIN IN THE WEST
THE FIRST MOUSE ON THE MOON
ALL FOR STILTON, STILTON FOR ALL!

PAPERCUTZ
New York

GERONIMO STILTON 3 IN 1 #5
Geronimo Stilton names, characters and related indicia are copyright, trademark, and exclusive license of Atlantyca S.p.A.
All rights reserved. The moral right of the author has been asserted.

Based on an original idea by Elisabetta Dami

"The Fastest Train in the West"
© 2012 Edizioni Piemme © 2018 Mondadori Libri S.p.A. for PIEMME, Italia
International rights © 2012 Atlantyca S.p.A.
© 2013–for this work in English language by Papercutz
Original Title: Il treno più veloce del Far West
Text by Geronimo Stilton
Editorial Coordination by Patrizia Puricelli
Artistic Coordination by BAO Publishing
Story by Michele Foschini
Script by Leonardo Favia
Illustrations by Ennio Bufi
Color by Mirka Andolfo
Cover by Marta Lorini

"The First Mouse on the Moon"
© 2013 BAO Publishing. © 2018 Mondadori Libri S.p.A. for PIEMME, Italia
International rights © 2013 Atlantyca S.p.A.
© 2014–for this work in English language by Papercutz
Original Title: Il primo topo sulla Luna
Text by Geronimo Stilton
Story by Michele Foschini
Script by Leonardo Favia
Illustrations by Ennio Bufi
Color by Mirka Andolfo
Cover by Ennio Bufi and Mirka Andolfo

"All for Stilton, Stilton for All!"
© 2013 Bao Publishing, published in Italy by arrangement with Edizioni Piemme
International rights © 2013 Atlantyca S.p.A.
© 2014–for this work in English language by Papercutz
Original title: Uno per tutti, tutti per Stilton!
Text by Geronimo Stilton
Story by Michele Foschini and Leonardo Favia
Script by Leonardo Favia
Illustrations by Federica Salfo
Color by Mirka Andolfo
Cover by Ennio Bufi and Mirka Andolfo

© Atlantyca S.p.A. – Corso Magenta, 60/62, 20123 Milano, Italia – foreignrights@atlantyca.it
© 2022 for this Work in English language by Papercutz. www.papercutz.com
www.geronimostilton.com
Special thanks to Anita Denti and Alessandra Berello

Stilton is a name of a famous English cheese. It is a registered trademark of the Stilton Cheesemakers' Association.
For more information go to www.stiltoncheese.co.uk

Translation — Nanette McGuinness
Lettering and Production — Ortho, Big Bird Satryb/Zatryb
Original Production Coordinators — Beth Scorzato, Jeff Whitman
Assistant Managing Editor — Stephanie Brooks
Original Editors — Robyn Chapman, Michael Petranek
Jim Salicrup
Editor-in-Chief

ISBN: 978-1-5458-0902-0
Printed in China
July 2022

Papercutz books may be purchased for business or promotional use.
For information on bulk purchases, please contact Macmillan Corporate and Premium Sales Department at (800) 221-7945 x5442.

Distributed by Macmillan
First Papercutz Printing

THE FASTEST TRAIN IN THE WEST

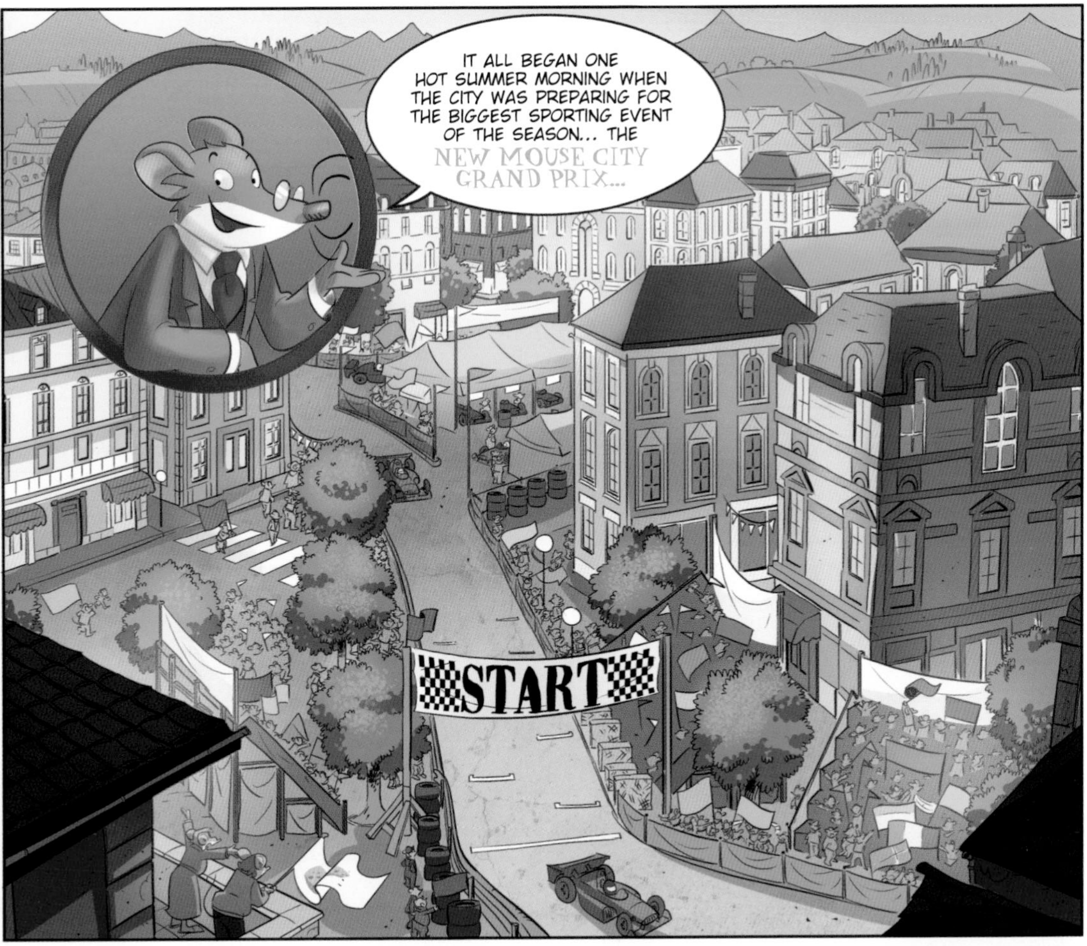
IT ALL BEGAN ONE HOT SUMMER MORNING WHEN THE CITY WAS PREPARING FOR THE BIGGEST SPORTING EVENT OF THE SEASON... THE NEW MOUSE CITY GRAND PRIX...
START

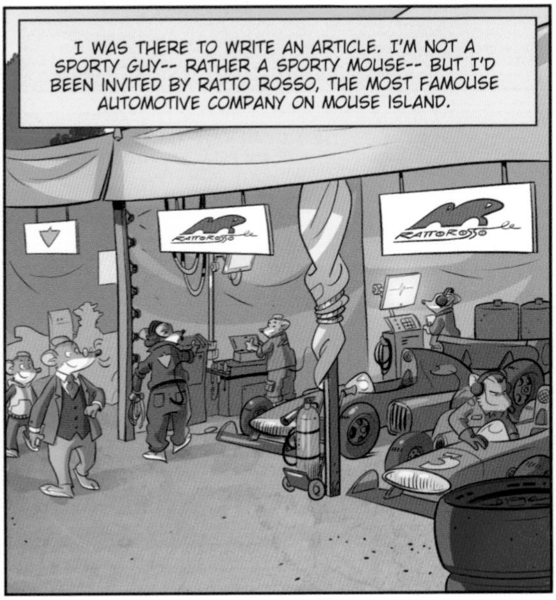
I WAS THERE TO WRITE AN ARTICLE. I'M NOT A SPORTY GUY-- RATHER A SPORTY MOUSE-- BUT I'D BEEN INVITED BY RATTO ROSSO, THE MOST FAMOUSE AUTOMOTIVE COMPANY ON MOUSE ISLAND.
RATTOROSSO
RATTOROSSO

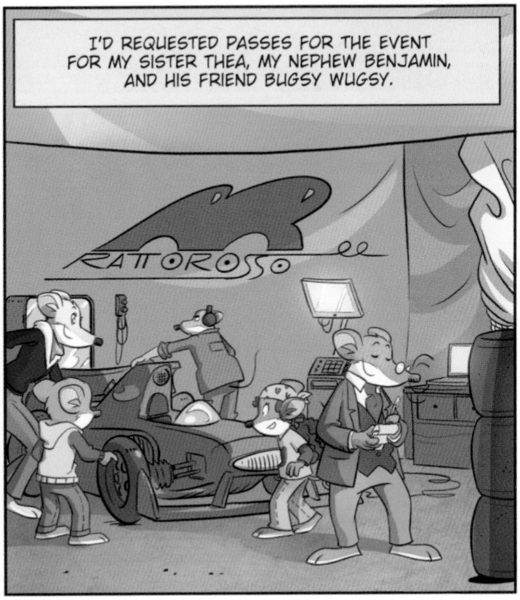
I'D REQUESTED PASSES FOR THE EVENT FOR MY SISTER THEA, MY NEPHEW BENJAMIN, AND HIS FRIEND BUGSY WUGSY.
RATTOROSSO

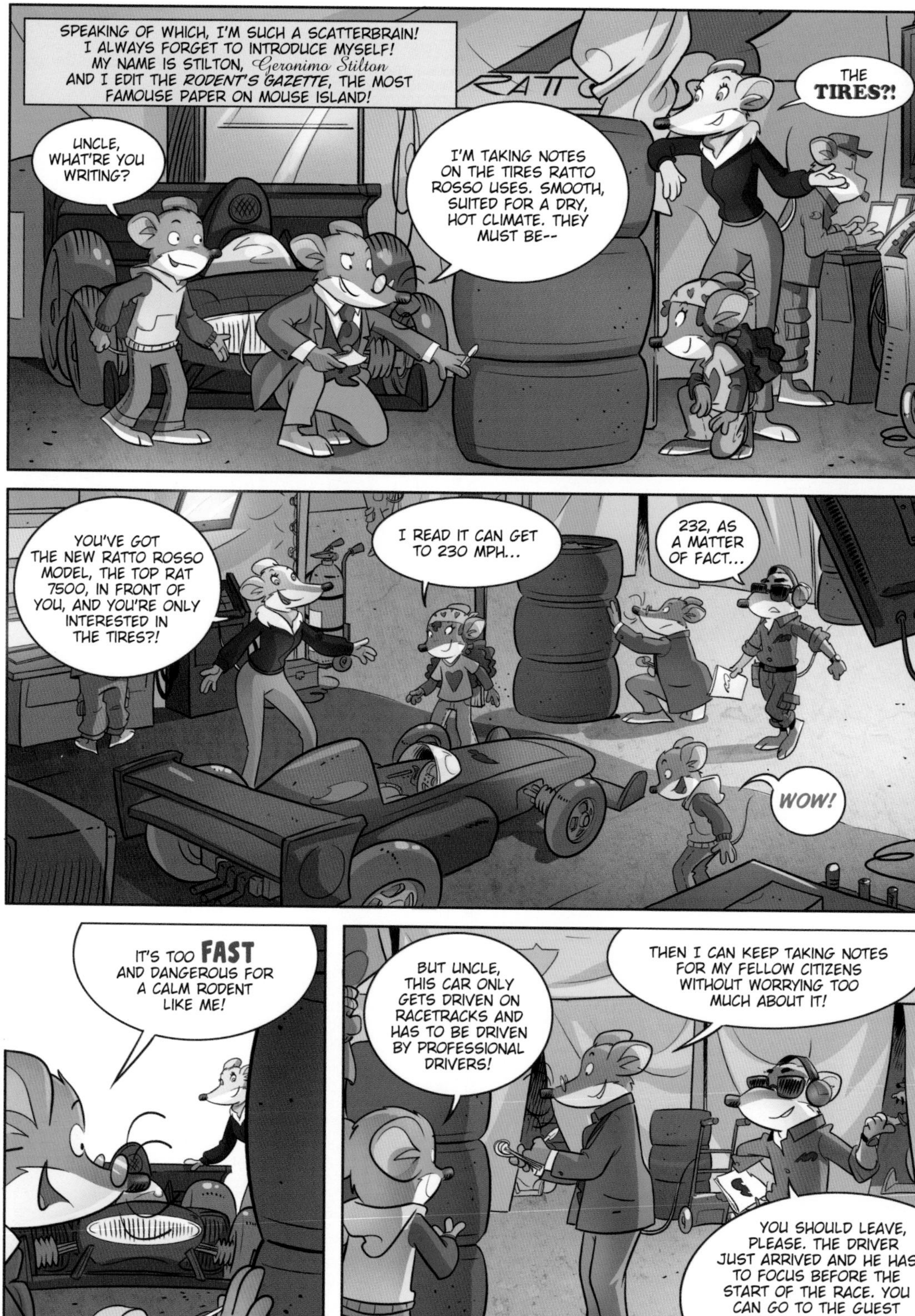
SPEAKING OF WHICH, I'M SUCH A SCATTERBRAIN! I ALWAYS FORGET TO INTRODUCE MYSELF! MY NAME IS STILTON, Geronimo Stilton AND I EDIT THE RODENT'S GAZETTE, THE MOST FAMOUSE PAPER ON MOUSE ISLAND!
UNCLE, WHAT'RE YOU WRITING?
I'M TAKING NOTES ON THE TIRES RATTO ROSSO USES. SMOOTH, SUITED FOR A DRY, HOT CLIMATE. THEY MUST BE--
THE TIRES?!
YOU'VE GOT THE NEW RATTO ROSSO MODEL, THE TOP RAT 7500, IN FRONT OF YOU, AND YOU'RE ONLY INTERESTED IN THE TIRES?!
I READ IT CAN GET TO 230 MPH...
232, AS A MATTER OF FACT...
WOW!
IT'S TOO FAST AND DANGEROUS FOR A CALM RODENT LIKE ME!
BUT UNCLE, THIS CAR ONLY GETS DRIVEN ON RACETRACKS AND HAS TO BE DRIVEN BY PROFESSIONAL DRIVERS!
THEN I CAN KEEP TAKING NOTES FOR MY FELLOW CITIZENS WITHOUT WORRYING TOO MUCH ABOUT IT!
YOU SHOULD LEAVE, PLEASE. THE DRIVER JUST ARRIVED AND HE HAS TO FOCUS BEFORE THE START OF THE RACE. YOU CAN GO TO THE GUEST REFRESHMENT STAND.

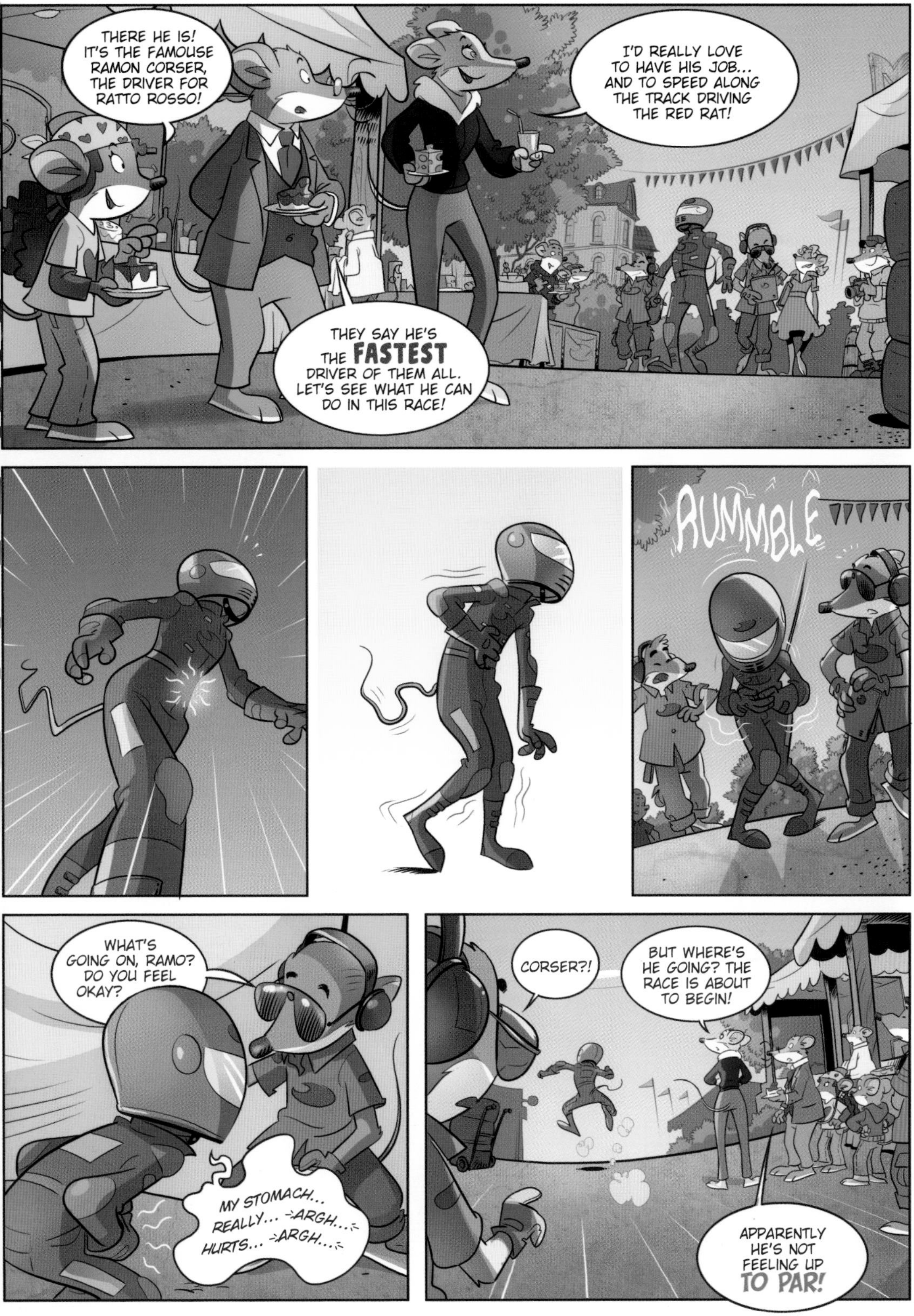
THERE HE IS! IT'S THE FAMOUSE RAMON CORSER, THE DRIVER FOR RATTO ROSSO!
I'D REALLY LOVE TO HAVE HIS JOB... AND TO SPEED ALONG THE TRACK DRIVING THE RED RAT!
THEY SAY HE'S THE **FASTEST** DRIVER OF THEM ALL. LET'S SEE WHAT HE CAN DO IN THIS RACE!
RUMMBLE
WHAT'S GOING ON, RAMO? DO YOU FEEL OKAY?
MY STOMACH... REALLY... ARGH... HURTS... ARGH...
CORSER?!
BUT WHERE'S HE GOING? THE RACE IS ABOUT TO BEGIN!
APPARENTLY HE'S NOT FEELING UP **TO PAR!**

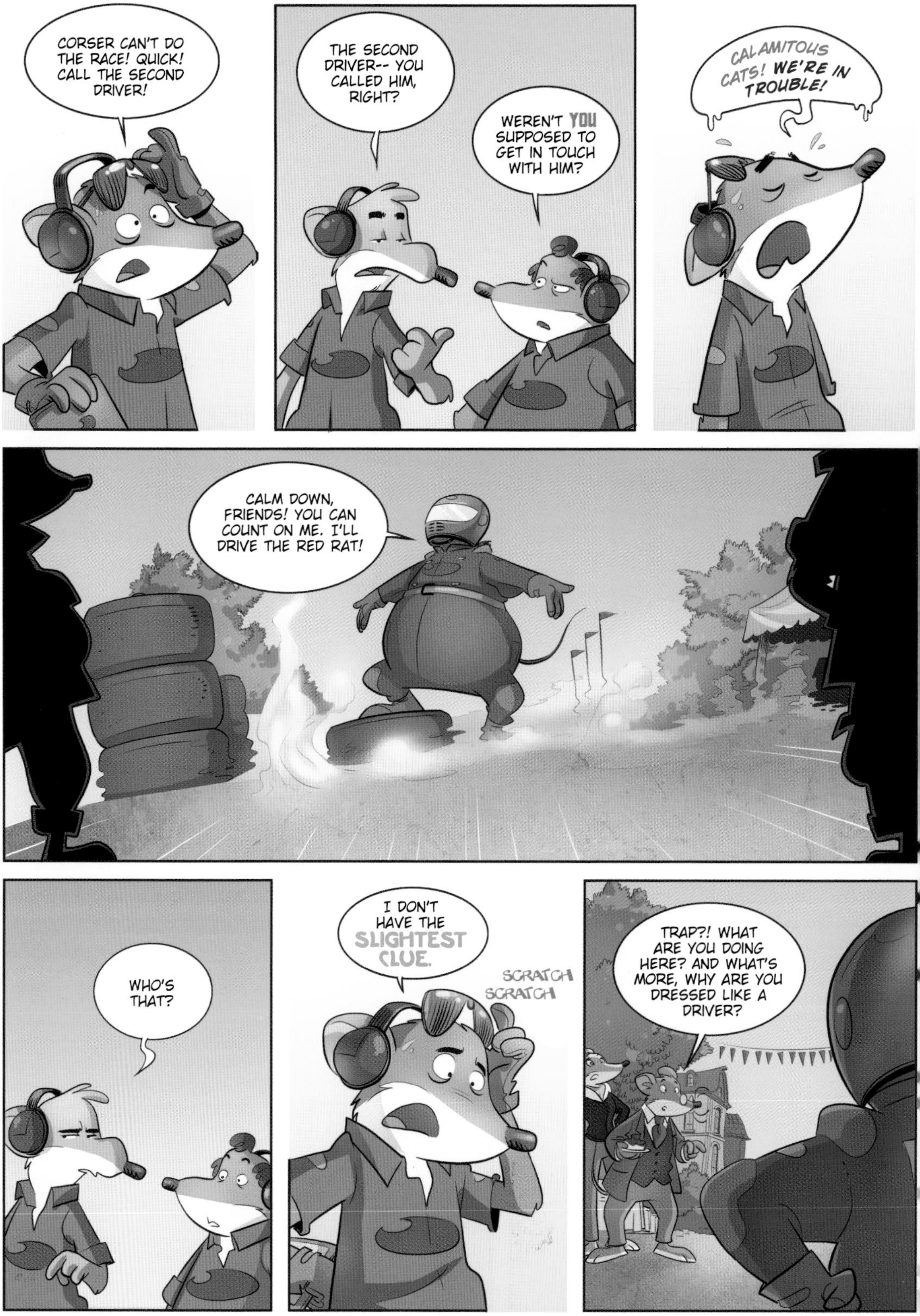
CORSER CAN'T DO THE RACE! QUICK! CALL THE SECOND DRIVER!
THE SECOND DRIVER-- YOU CALLED HIM, RIGHT?
WEREN'T YOU SUPPOSED TO GET IN TOUCH WITH HIM?
CALAMITOUS CATS! WE'RE IN TROUBLE!
CALM DOWN, FRIENDS! YOU CAN COUNT ON ME. I'LL DRIVE THE RED RAT!
WHO'S THAT?
I DON'T HAVE THE SLIGHTEST CLUE.
SCRATCH SCRATCH
TRAP?! WHAT ARE YOU DOING HERE? AND WHAT'S MORE, WHY ARE YOU DRESSED LIKE A DRIVER?

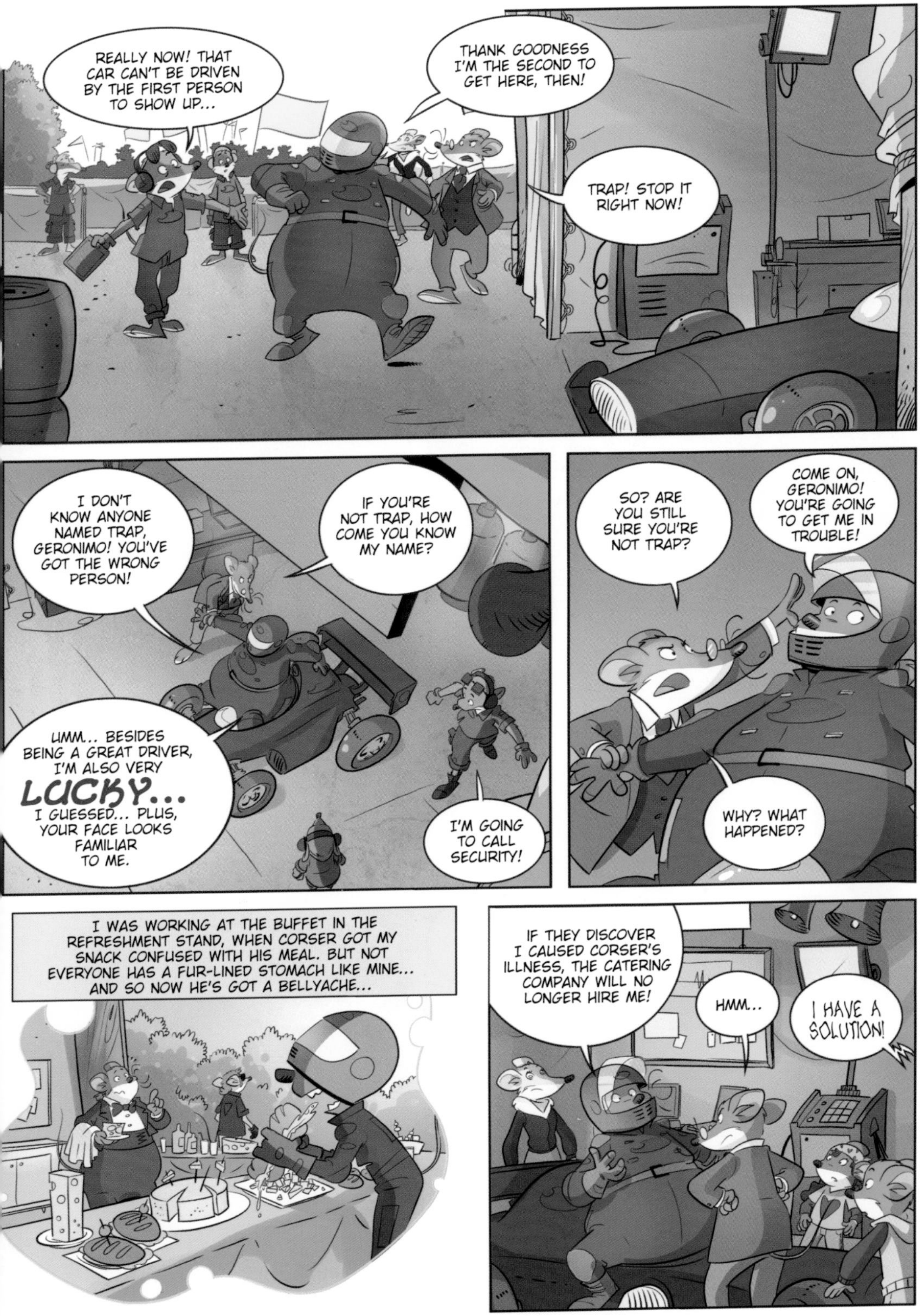
REALLY NOW! THAT CAR CAN'T BE DRIVEN BY THE FIRST PERSON TO SHOW UP...
THANK GOODNESS I'M THE SECOND TO GET HERE, THEN!
TRAP! STOP IT RIGHT NOW!
I DON'T KNOW ANYONE NAMED TRAP, GERONIMO! YOU'VE GOT THE WRONG PERSON!
IF YOU'RE NOT TRAP, HOW COME YOU KNOW MY NAME?
UMM... BESIDES BEING A GREAT DRIVER, I'M ALSO VERY LUCKY... I GUESSED... PLUS, YOUR FACE LOOKS FAMILIAR TO ME.
I'M GOING TO CALL SECURITY!
SO? ARE YOU STILL SURE YOU'RE NOT TRAP?
COME ON, GERONIMO! YOU'RE GOING TO GET ME IN TROUBLE!
WHY? WHAT HAPPENED?
I WAS WORKING AT THE BUFFET IN THE REFRESHMENT STAND, WHEN CORSER GOT MY SNACK CONFUSED WITH HIS MEAL. BUT NOT EVERYONE HAS A FUR-LINED STOMACH LIKE MINE... AND SO NOW HE'S GOT A BELLYACHE...
IF THEY DISCOVER I CAUSED CORSER'S ILLNESS, THE CATERING COMPANY WILL NO LONGER HIRE ME!
HMM...
I HAVE A SOLUTION!

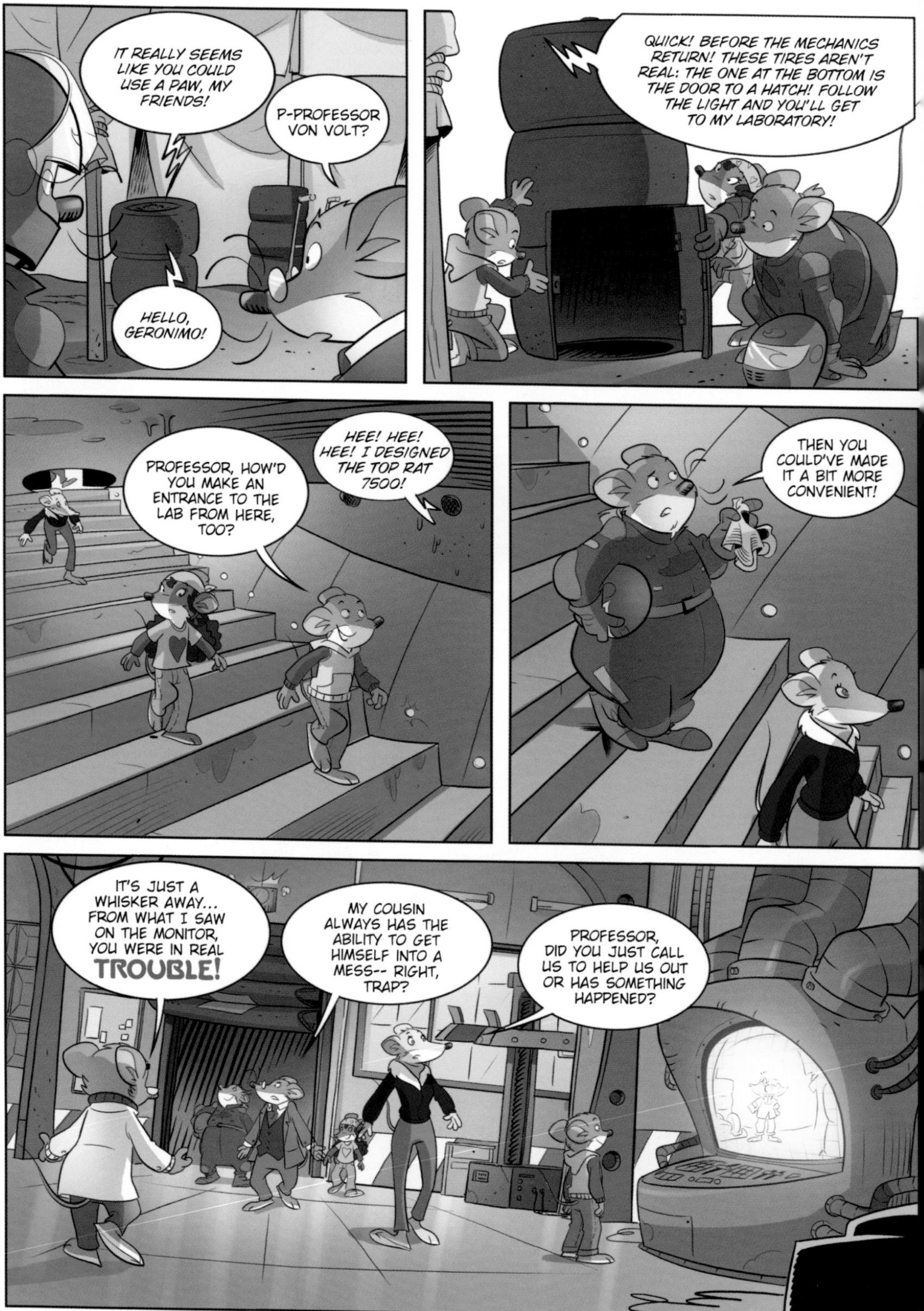
IT REALLY SEEMS LIKE YOU COULD USE A PAW, MY FRIENDS!
P-PROFESSOR VON VOLT?
HELLO, GERONIMO!
QUICK! BEFORE THE MECHANICS RETURN! THESE TIRES AREN'T REAL: THE ONE AT THE BOTTOM IS THE DOOR TO A HATCH! FOLLOW THE LIGHT AND YOU'LL GET TO MY LABORATORY!
PROFESSOR, HOW'D YOU MAKE AN ENTRANCE TO THE LAB FROM HERE, TOO?
HEE! HEE! HEE! I DESIGNED THE TOP RAT 7500!
THEN YOU COULD'VE MADE IT A BIT MORE CONVENIENT!
IT'S JUST A WHISKER AWAY... FROM WHAT I SAW ON THE MONITOR, YOU WERE IN REAL TROUBLE!
MY COUSIN ALWAYS HAS THE ABILITY TO GET HIMSELF INTO A MESS-- RIGHT, TRAP?
PROFESSOR, DID YOU JUST CALL US TO HELP US OUT OR HAS SOMETHING HAPPENED?

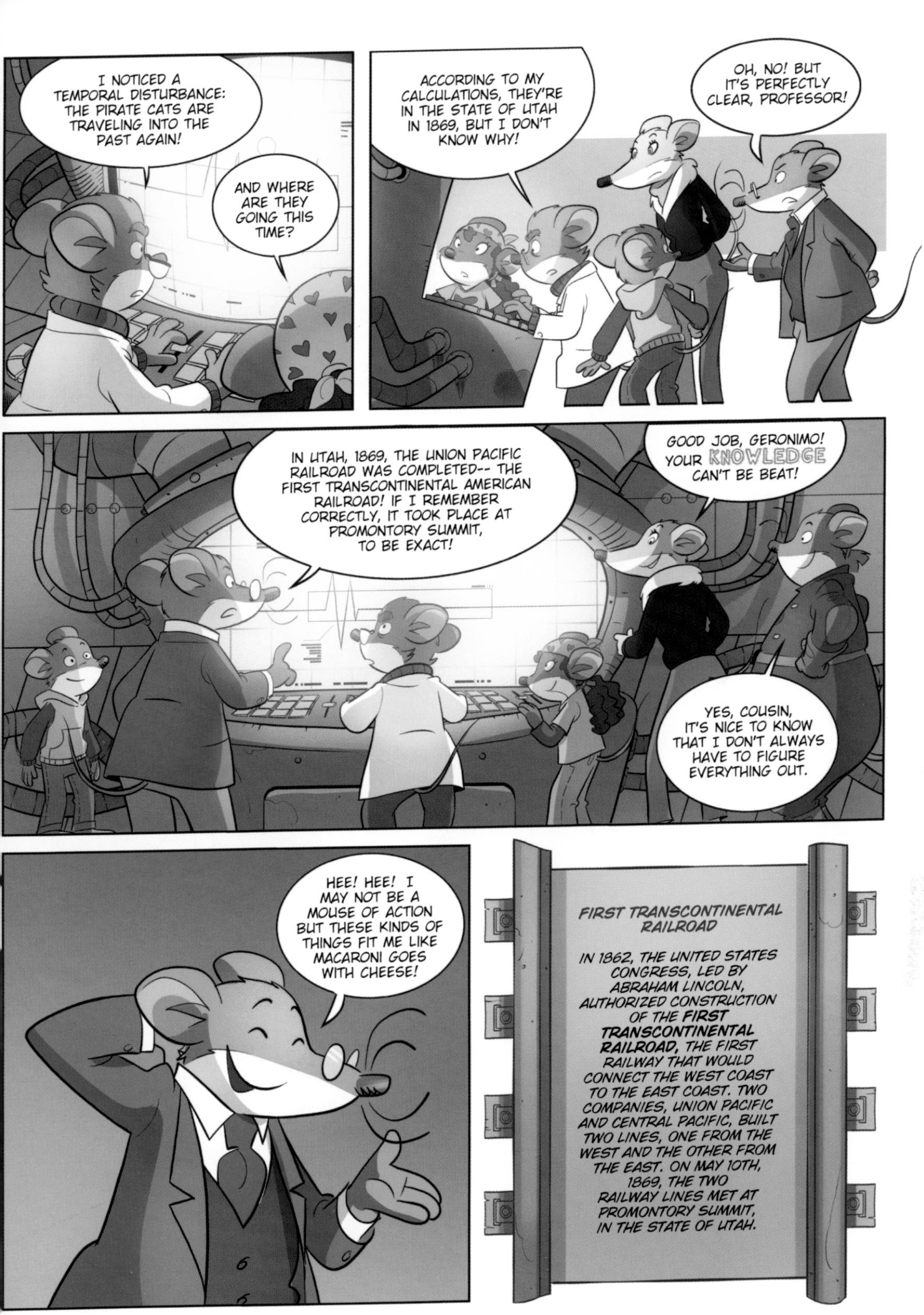
I NOTICED A TEMPORAL DISTURBANCE: THE PIRATE CATS ARE TRAVELING INTO THE PAST AGAIN!
AND WHERE ARE THEY GOING THIS TIME?
ACCORDING TO MY CALCULATIONS, THEY'RE IN THE STATE OF UTAH IN 1869, BUT I DON'T KNOW WHY!
OH, NO! BUT IT'S PERFECTLY CLEAR, PROFESSOR!
IN UTAH, 1869, THE UNION PACIFIC RAILROAD WAS COMPLETED-- THE FIRST TRANSCONTINENTAL AMERICAN RAILROAD! IF I REMEMBER CORRECTLY, IT TOOK PLACE AT PROMONTORY SUMMIT, TO BE EXACT!
GOOD JOB, GERONIMO! YOUR KNOWLEDGE CAN'T BE BEAT!
YES, COUSIN, IT'S NICE TO KNOW THAT I DON'T ALWAYS HAVE TO FIGURE EVERYTHING OUT.
HEE! HEE! I MAY NOT BE A MOUSE OF ACTION BUT THESE KINDS OF THINGS FIT ME LIKE MACARONI GOES WITH CHEESE!
FIRST TRANSCONTINENTAL RAILROAD
IN 1862, THE UNITED STATES CONGRESS, LED BY ABRAHAM LINCOLN, AUTHORIZED CONSTRUCTION OF THE FIRST TRANSCONTINENTAL RAILROAD, THE FIRST RAILWAY THAT WOULD CONNECT THE WEST COAST TO THE EAST COAST. TWO COMPANIES, UNION PACIFIC AND CENTRAL PACIFIC, BUILT TWO LINES, ONE FROM THE WEST AND THE OTHER FROM THE EAST. ON MAY 10TH, 1869, THE TWO RAILWAY LINES MET AT PROMONTORY SUMMIT, IN THE STATE OF UTAH.

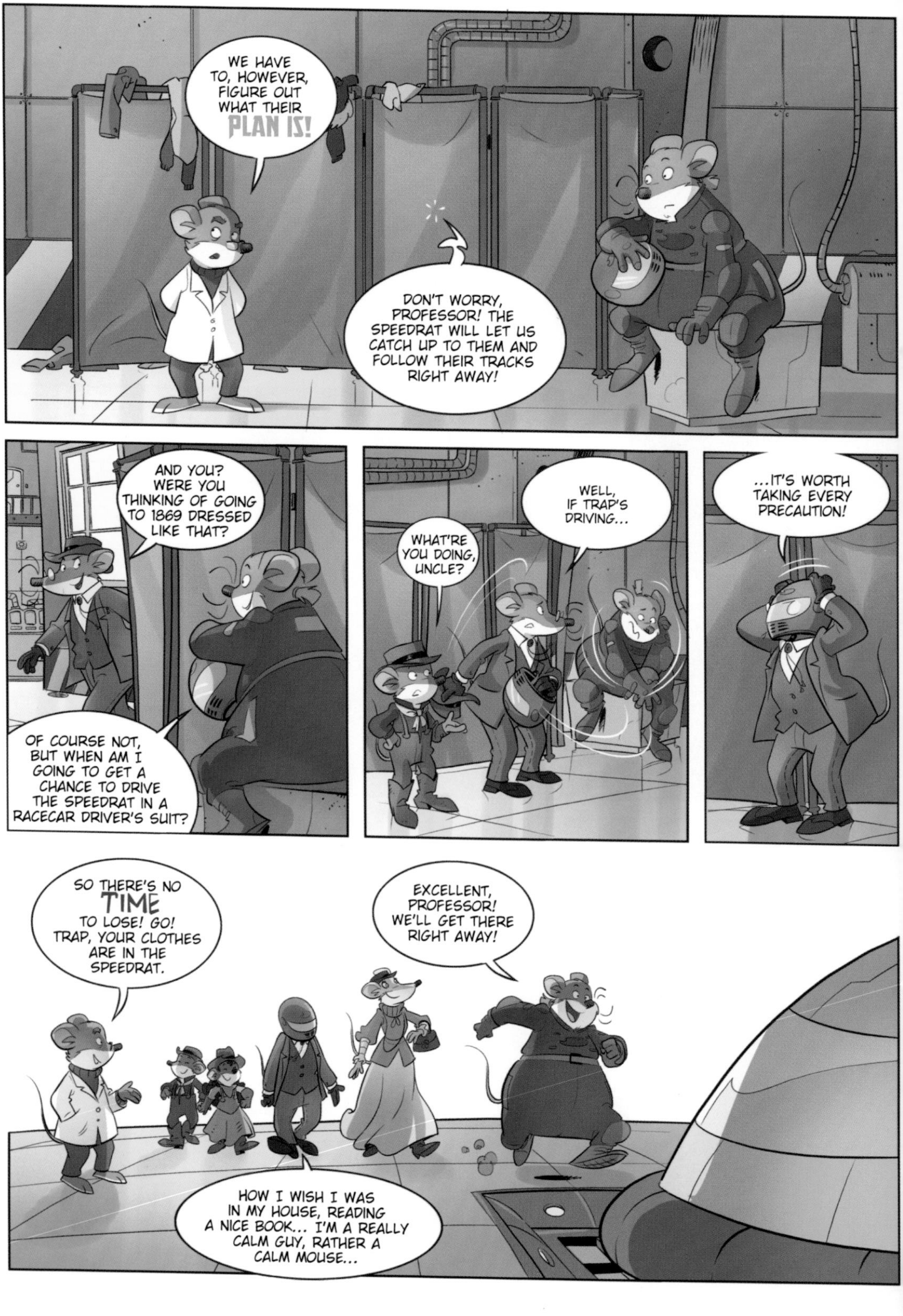
WE HAVE TO, HOWEVER, FIGURE OUT WHAT THEIR PLAN IS!
DON'T WORRY, PROFESSOR! THE SPEEDRAT WILL LET US CATCH UP TO THEM AND FOLLOW THEIR TRACKS RIGHT AWAY!
AND YOU? WERE YOU THINKING OF GOING TO 1869 DRESSED LIKE THAT?
OF COURSE NOT, BUT WHEN AM I GOING TO GET A CHANCE TO DRIVE THE SPEEDRAT IN A RACECAR DRIVER'S SUIT?
WHAT'RE YOU DOING, UNCLE?
WELL, IF TRAP'S DRIVING...
...IT'S WORTH TAKING EVERY PRECAUTION!
SO THERE'S NO TIME TO LOSE! GO! TRAP, YOUR CLOTHES ARE IN THE SPEEDRAT.
EXCELLENT, PROFESSOR! WE'LL GET THERE RIGHT AWAY!
HOW I WISH I WAS IN MY HOUSE, READING A NICE BOOK... I'M A REALLY CALM GUY, RATHER A CALM MOUSE...

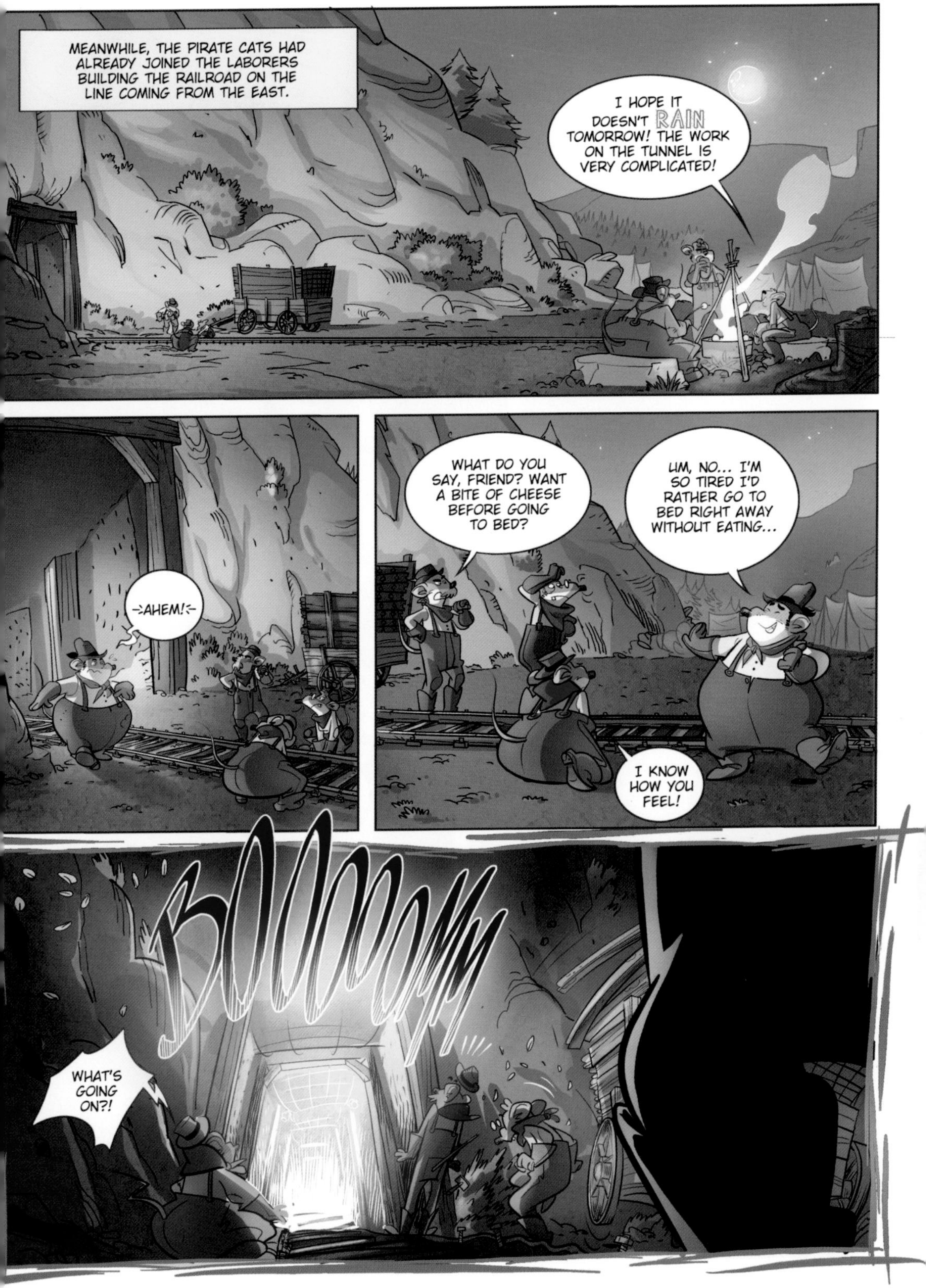
MEANWHILE, THE PIRATE CATS HAD ALREADY JOINED THE LABORERS BUILDING THE RAILROAD ON THE LINE COMING FROM THE EAST.
I HOPE IT DOESN'T RAIN TOMORROW! THE WORK ON THE TUNNEL IS VERY COMPLICATED!
AHEM!
WHAT DO YOU SAY, FRIEND? WANT A BITE OF CHEESE BEFORE GOING TO BED?
UM, NO... I'M SO TIRED I'D RATHER GO TO BED RIGHT AWAY WITHOUT EATING...
I KNOW HOW YOU FEEL!
BOOOOOM!
WHAT'S GOING ON?!

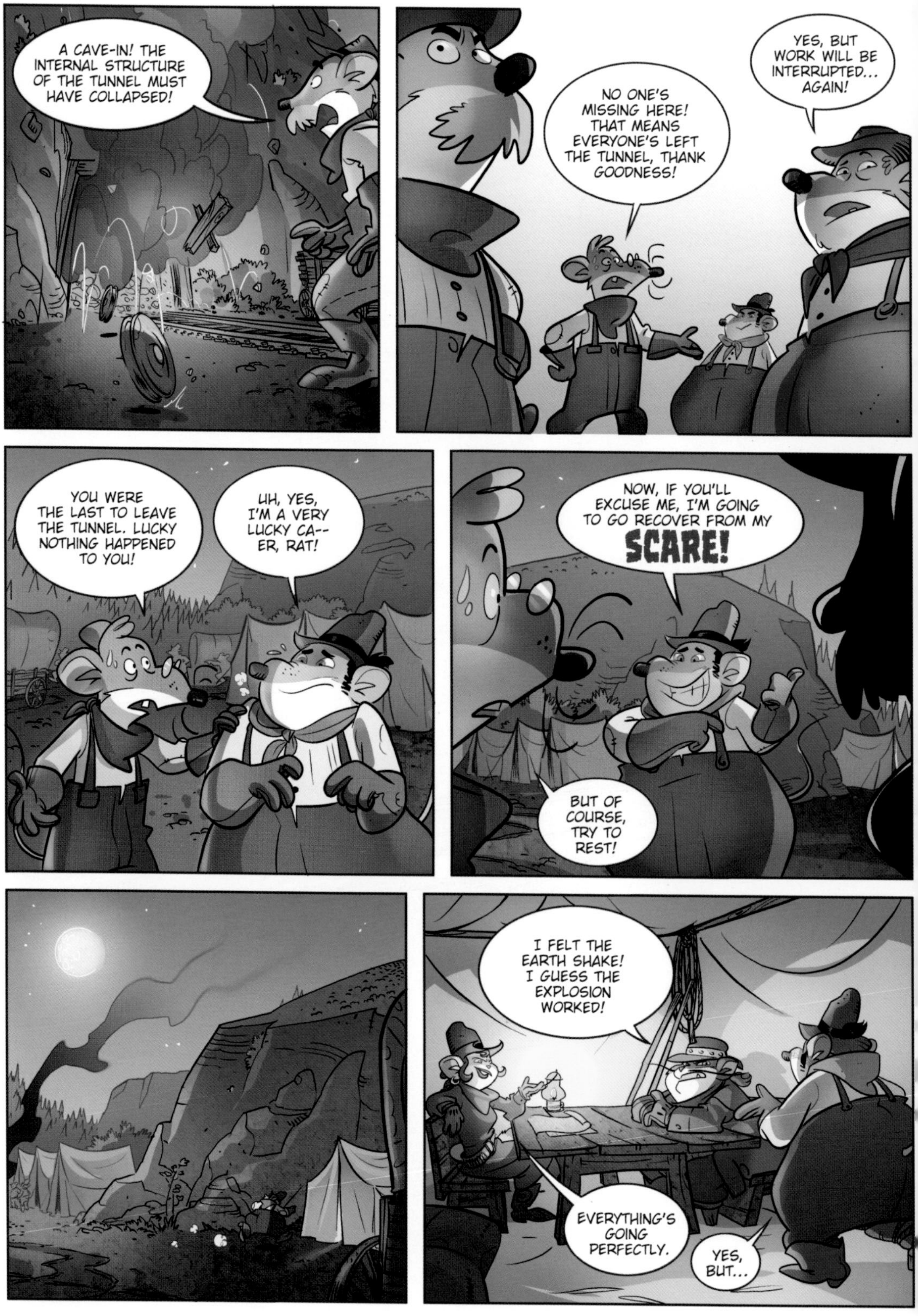
A CAVE-IN! THE INTERNAL STRUCTURE OF THE TUNNEL MUST HAVE COLLAPSED!
NO ONE'S MISSING HERE! THAT MEANS EVERYONE'S LEFT THE TUNNEL, THANK GOODNESS!
YES, BUT WORK WILL BE INTERRUPTED... AGAIN!
YOU WERE THE LAST TO LEAVE THE TUNNEL. LUCKY NOTHING HAPPENED TO YOU!
UH, YES, I'M A VERY LUCKY CA-- ER, RAT!
NOW, IF YOU'LL EXCUSE ME, I'M GOING TO GO RECOVER FROM MY
SCARE!
BUT OF COURSE, TRY TO REST!
I FELT THE EARTH SHAKE! I GUESS THE EXPLOSION WORKED!
EVERYTHING'S GOING PERFECTLY.
YES, BUT...

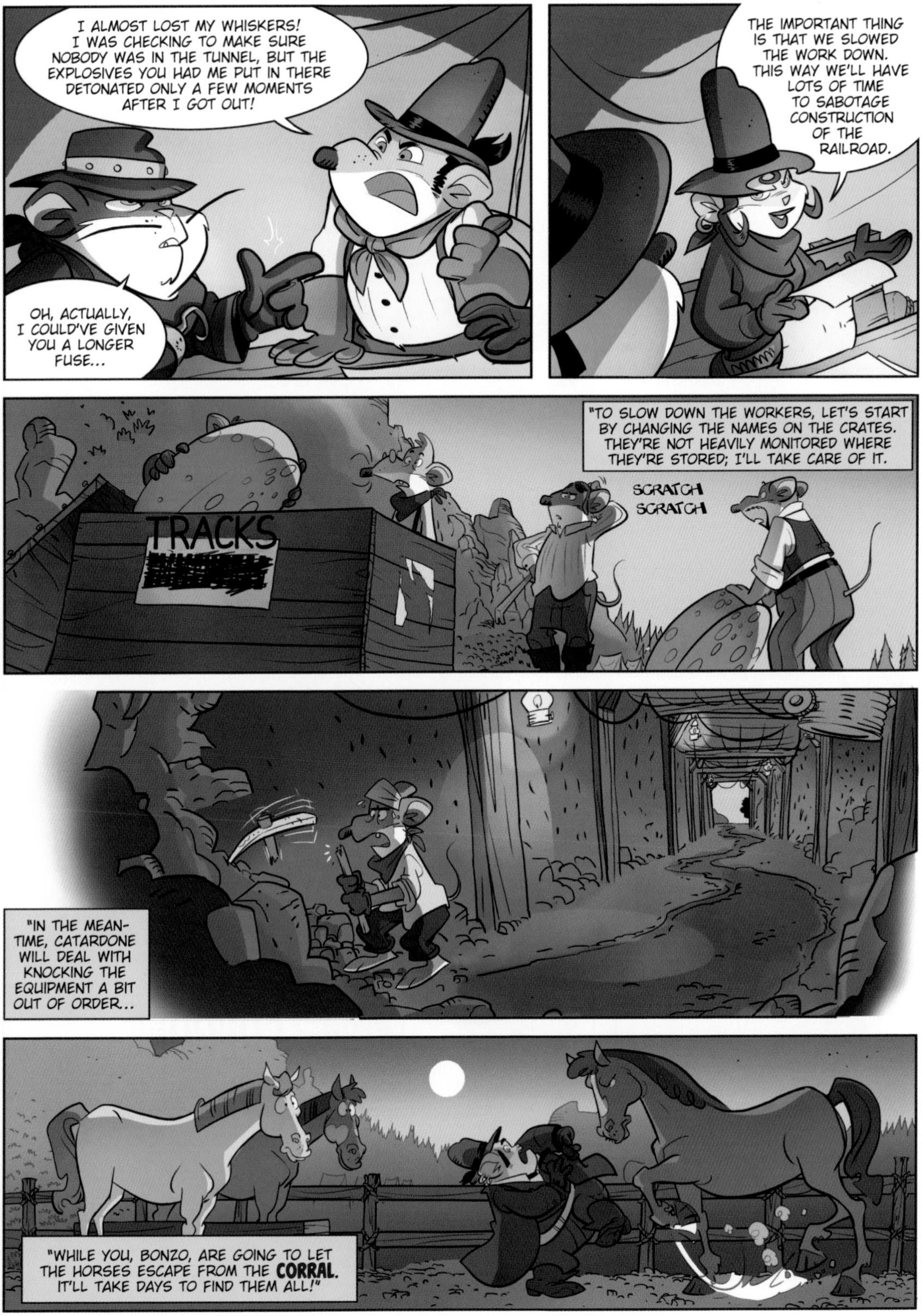
I ALMOST LOST MY WHISKERS! I WAS CHECKING TO MAKE SURE NOBODY WAS IN THE TUNNEL, BUT THE EXPLOSIVES YOU HAD ME PUT IN THERE DETONATED ONLY A FEW MOMENTS AFTER I GOT OUT!
OH, ACTUALLY, I COULD'VE GIVEN YOU A LONGER FUSE...
THE IMPORTANT THING IS THAT WE SLOWED THE WORK DOWN. THIS WAY WE'LL HAVE LOTS OF TIME TO SABOTAGE CONSTRUCTION OF THE RAILROAD.
"TO SLOW DOWN THE WORKERS, LET'S START BY CHANGING THE NAMES ON THE CRATES. THEY'RE NOT HEAVILY MONITORED WHERE THEY'RE STORED; I'LL TAKE CARE OF IT.
TRACKS
SCRATCH SCRATCH
"IN THE MEAN-TIME, CATARDONE WILL DEAL WITH KNOCKING THE EQUIPMENT A BIT OUT OF ORDER...
"WHILE YOU, BONZO, ARE GOING TO LET THE HORSES ESCAPE FROM THE CORRAL. IT'LL TAKE DAYS TO FIND THEM ALL!"

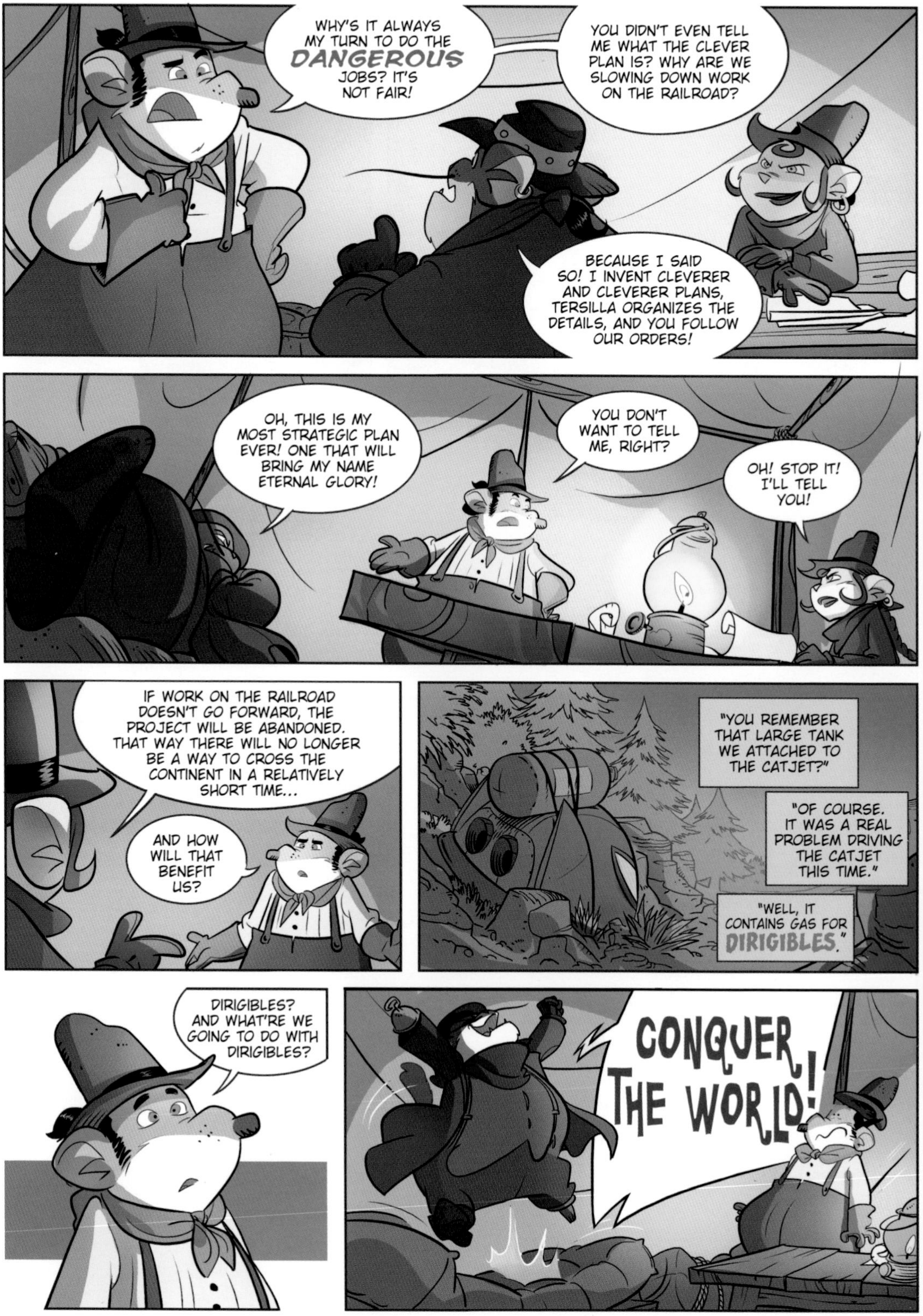
WHY'S IT ALWAYS MY TURN TO DO THE DANGEROUS JOBS? IT'S NOT FAIR!
YOU DIDN'T EVEN TELL ME WHAT THE CLEVER PLAN IS? WHY ARE WE SLOWING DOWN WORK ON THE RAILROAD?
BECAUSE I SAID SO! I INVENT CLEVERER AND CLEVERER PLANS, TERSILLA ORGANIZES THE DETAILS, AND YOU FOLLOW OUR ORDERS!
OH, THIS IS MY MOST STRATEGIC PLAN EVER! ONE THAT WILL BRING MY NAME ETERNAL GLORY!
YOU DON'T WANT TO TELL ME, RIGHT?
OH! STOP IT! I'LL TELL YOU!
IF WORK ON THE RAILROAD DOESN'T GO FORWARD, THE PROJECT WILL BE ABANDONED. THAT WAY THERE WILL NO LONGER BE A WAY TO CROSS THE CONTINENT IN A RELATIVELY SHORT TIME...
AND HOW WILL THAT BENEFIT US?
"YOU REMEMBER THAT LARGE TANK WE ATTACHED TO THE CATJET?"
"OF COURSE. IT WAS A REAL PROBLEM DRIVING THE CATJET THIS TIME."
"WELL, IT CONTAINS GAS FOR DIRIGIBLES."
DIRIGIBLES? AND WHAT'RE WE GOING TO DO WITH DIRIGIBLES?
CONQUER THE WORLD!

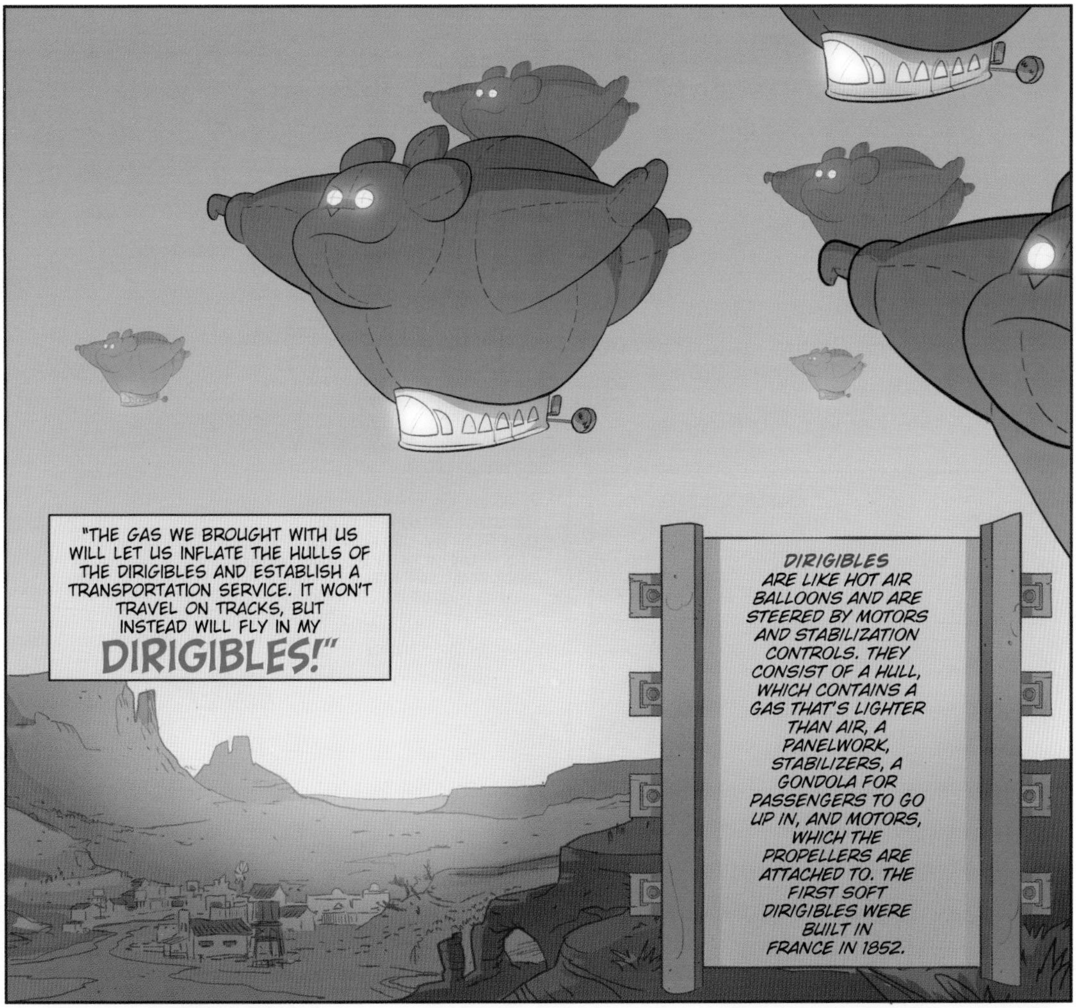
"THE GAS WE BROUGHT WITH US WILL LET US INFLATE THE HULLS OF THE DIRIGIBLES AND ESTABLISH A TRANSPORTATION SERVICE. IT WON'T TRAVEL ON TRACKS, BUT INSTEAD WILL FLY IN MY DIRIGIBLES!"
DIRIGIBLES ARE LIKE HOT AIR BALLOONS AND ARE STEERED BY MOTORS AND STABILIZATION CONTROLS. THEY CONSIST OF A HULL, WHICH CONTAINS A GAS THAT'S LIGHTER THAN AIR, A PANELWORK, STABILIZERS, A GONDOLA FOR PASSENGERS TO GO UP IN, AND MOTORS, WHICH THE PROPELLERS ARE ATTACHED TO. THE FIRST SOFT DIRIGIBLES WERE BUILT IN FRANCE IN 1852.

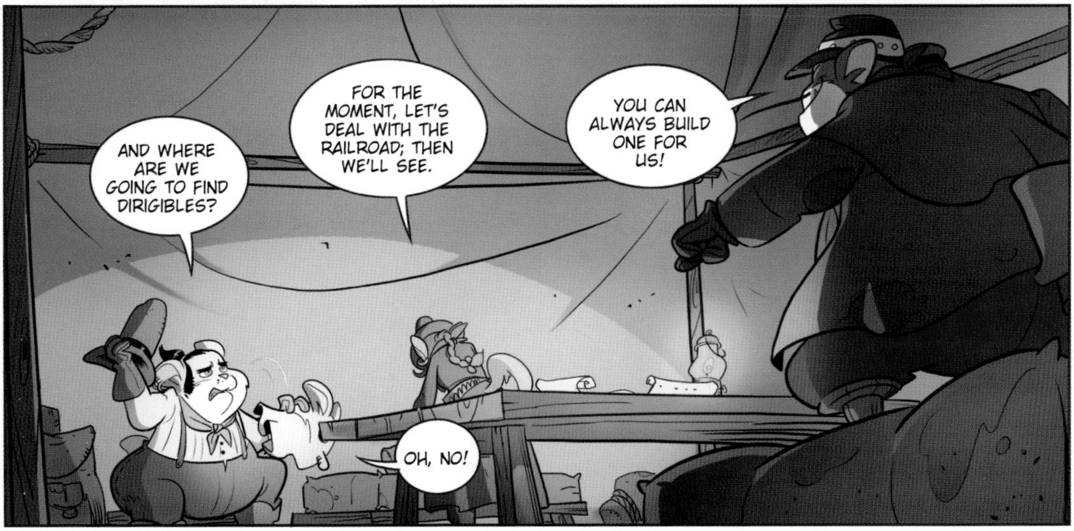
AND WHERE ARE WE GOING TO FIND DIRIGIBLES?
FOR THE MOMENT, LET'S DEAL WITH THE RAILROAD; THEN WE'LL SEE.
YOU CAN ALWAYS BUILD ONE FOR US!
OH, NO!

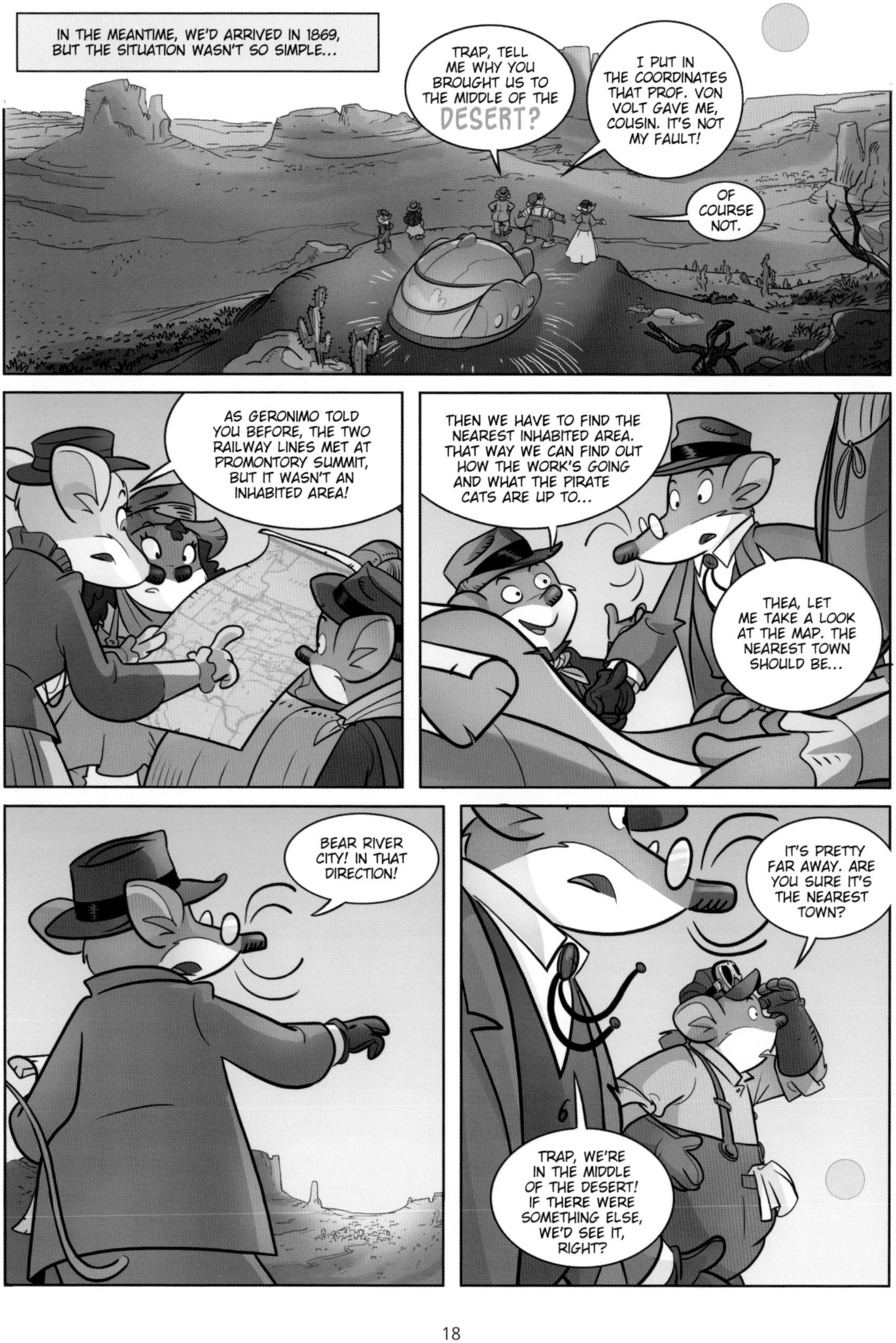

IN THE MEANTIME, WE'D ARRIVED IN 1869, BUT THE SITUATION WASN'T SO SIMPLE...
TRAP, TELL ME WHY YOU BROUGHT US TO THE MIDDLE OF THE DESERT?
I PUT IN THE COORDINATES THAT PROF. VON VOLT GAVE ME, COUSIN. IT'S NOT MY FAULT!
OF COURSE NOT.
AS GERONIMO TOLD YOU BEFORE, THE TWO RAILWAY LINES MET AT PROMONTORY SUMMIT, BUT IT WASN'T AN INHABITED AREA!
THEN WE HAVE TO FIND THE NEAREST INHABITED AREA. THAT WAY WE CAN FIND OUT HOW THE WORK'S GOING AND WHAT THE PIRATE CATS ARE UP TO...
THEA, LET ME TAKE A LOOK AT THE MAP. THE NEAREST TOWN SHOULD BE...
BEAR RIVER CITY! IN THAT DIRECTION!
IT'S PRETTY FAR AWAY. ARE YOU SURE IT'S THE NEAREST TOWN?
TRAP, WE'RE IN THE MIDDLE OF THE DESERT! IF THERE WERE SOMETHING ELSE, WE'D SEE IT, RIGHT?

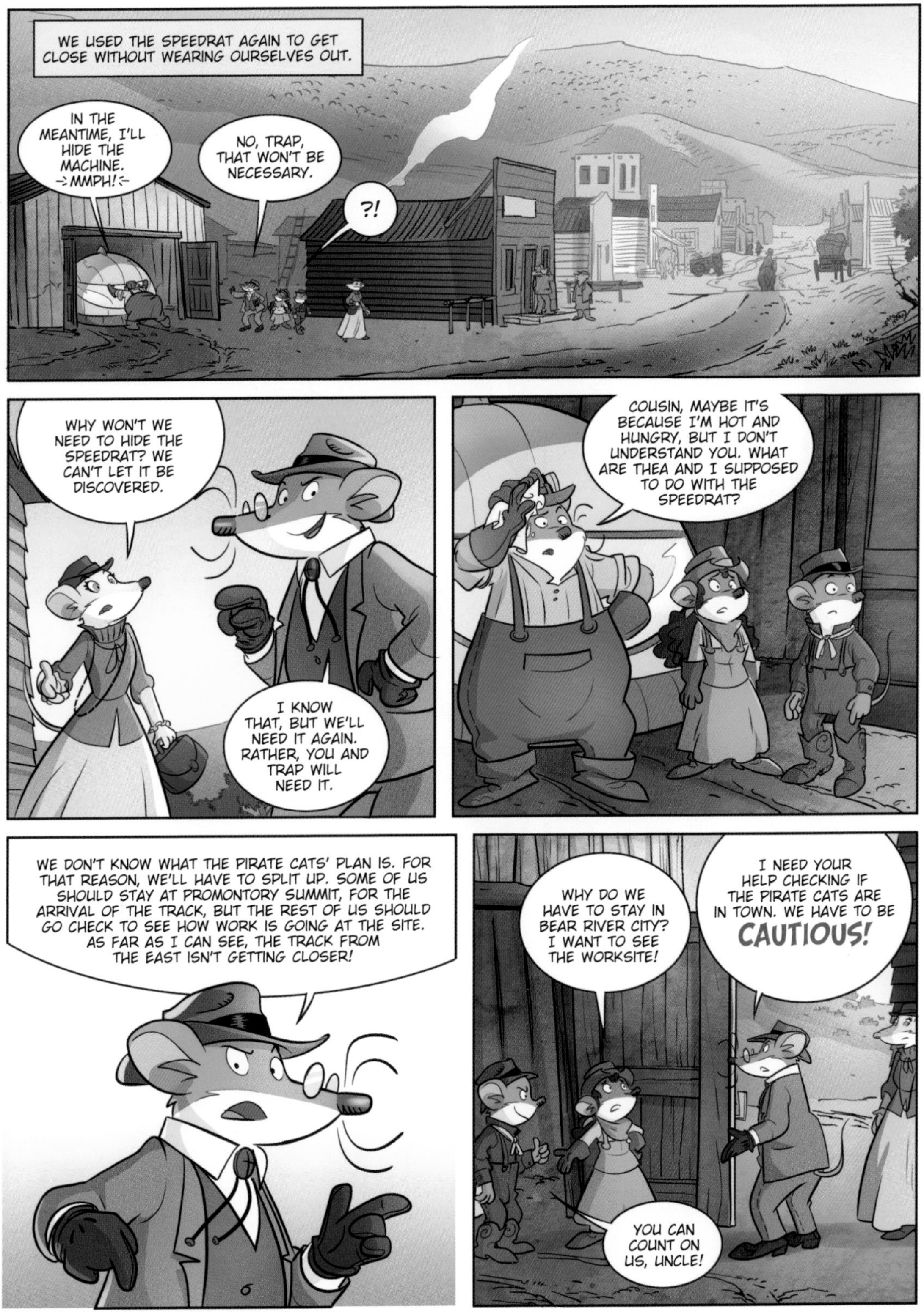
WE USED THE SPEEDRAT AGAIN TO GET CLOSE WITHOUT WEARING OURSELVES OUT.
IN THE MEANTIME, I'LL HIDE THE MACHINE. MMPH!
NO, TRAP, THAT WON'T BE NECESSARY.
?!
WHY WON'T WE NEED TO HIDE THE SPEEDRAT? WE CAN'T LET IT BE DISCOVERED.
I KNOW THAT, BUT WE'LL NEED IT AGAIN. RATHER, YOU AND TRAP WILL NEED IT.
COUSIN, MAYBE IT'S BECAUSE I'M HOT AND HUNGRY, BUT I DON'T UNDERSTAND YOU. WHAT ARE THEA AND I SUPPOSED TO DO WITH THE SPEEDRAT?
WE DON'T KNOW WHAT THE PIRATE CATS' PLAN IS. FOR THAT REASON, WE'LL HAVE TO SPLIT UP. SOME OF US SHOULD STAY AT PROMONTORY SUMMIT, FOR THE ARRIVAL OF THE TRACK, BUT THE REST OF US SHOULD GO CHECK TO SEE HOW WORK IS GOING AT THE SITE. AS FAR AS I CAN SEE, THE TRACK FROM THE EAST ISN'T GETTING CLOSER!
WHY DO WE HAVE TO STAY IN BEAR RIVER CITY? I WANT TO SEE THE WORKSITE!
I NEED YOUR HELP CHECKING IF THE PIRATE CATS ARE IN TOWN. WE HAVE TO BE CAUTIOUS!
YOU CAN COUNT ON US, UNCLE!

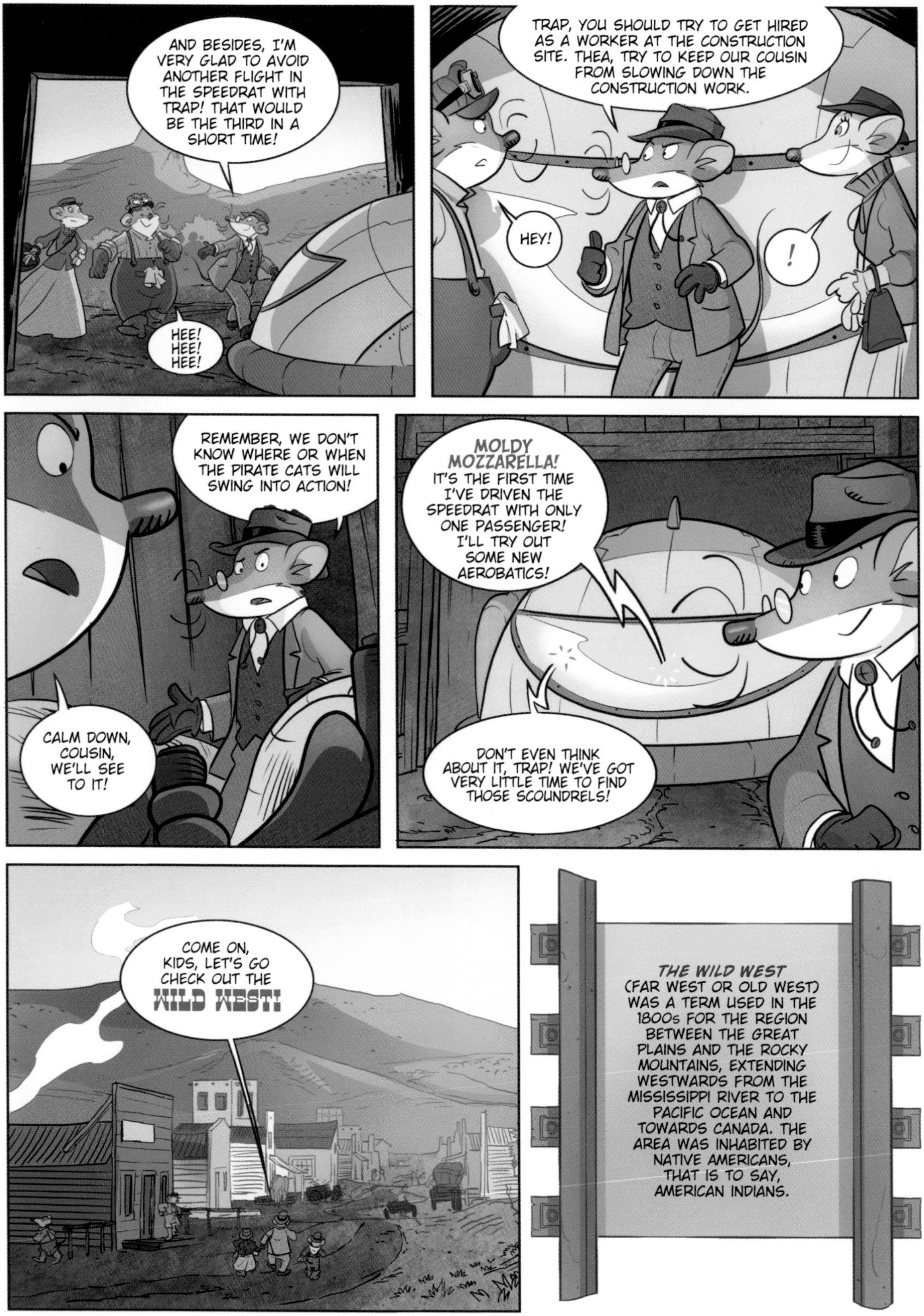
AND BESIDES, I'M VERY GLAD TO AVOID ANOTHER FLIGHT IN THE SPEEDRAT WITH TRAP! THAT WOULD BE THE THIRD IN A SHORT TIME!
HEE! HEE! HEE!
TRAP, YOU SHOULD TRY TO GET HIRED AS A WORKER AT THE CONSTRUCTION SITE. THEA, TRY TO KEEP OUR COUSIN FROM SLOWING DOWN THE CONSTRUCTION WORK.
HEY!
!
REMEMBER, WE DON'T KNOW WHERE OR WHEN THE PIRATE CATS WILL SWING INTO ACTION!
CALM DOWN, COUSIN, WE'LL SEE TO IT!
MOLDY MOZZARELLA! IT'S THE FIRST TIME I'VE DRIVEN THE SPEEDRAT WITH ONLY ONE PASSENGER! I'LL TRY OUT SOME NEW AEROBATICS!
DON'T EVEN THINK ABOUT IT, TRAP! WE'VE GOT VERY LITTLE TIME TO FIND THOSE SCOUNDRELS!
COME ON, KIDS, LET'S GO CHECK OUT THE WILD WEST!
THE WILD WEST (FAR WEST OR OLD WEST) WAS A TERM USED IN THE 1800s FOR THE REGION BETWEEN THE GREAT PLAINS AND THE ROCKY MOUNTAINS, EXTENDING WESTWARDS FROM THE MISSISSIPPI RIVER TO THE PACIFIC OCEAN AND TOWARDS CANADA. THE AREA WAS INHABITED BY NATIVE AMERICANS, THAT IS TO SAY, AMERICAN INDIANS.

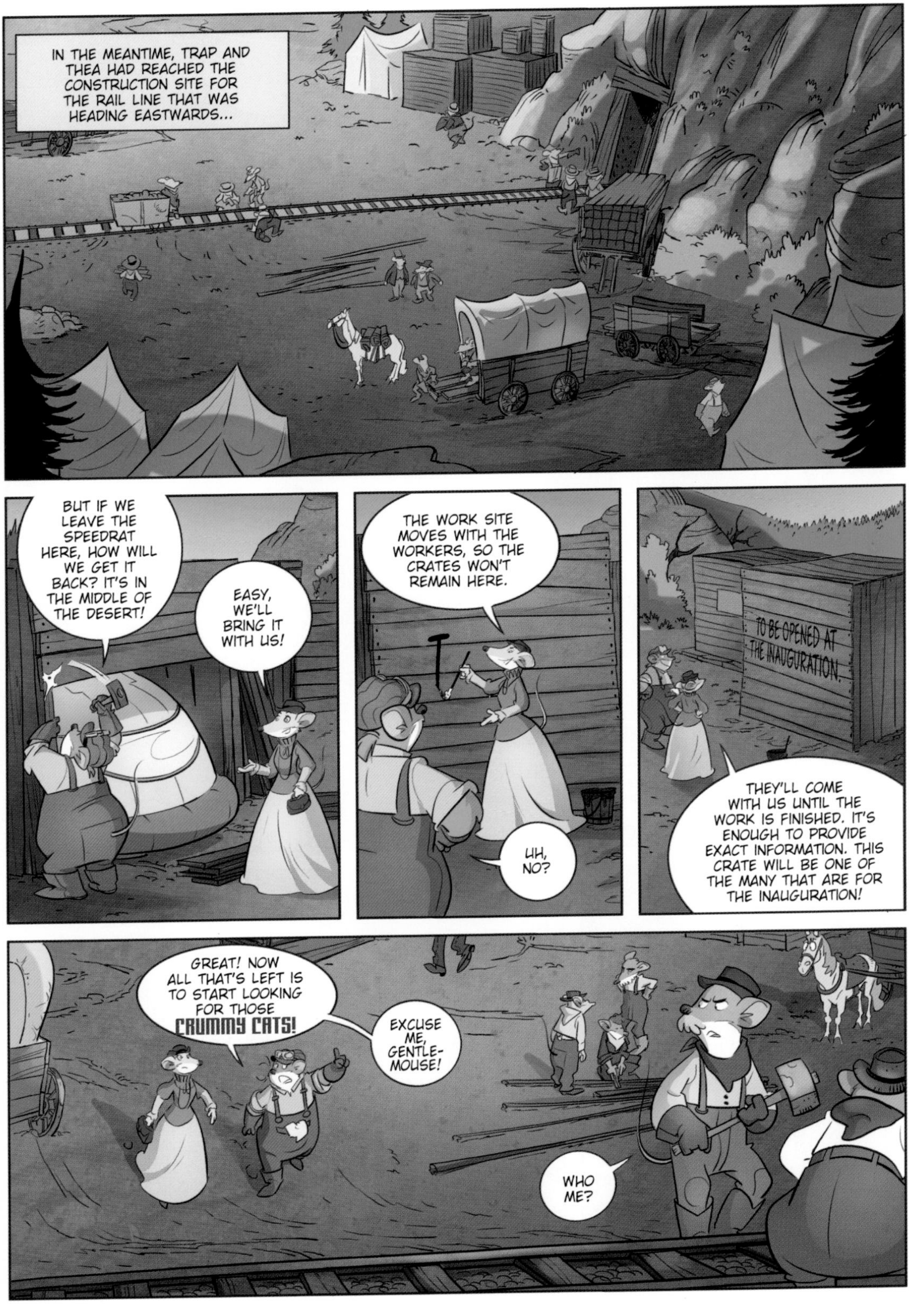
IN THE MEANTIME, TRAP AND THEA HAD REACHED THE CONSTRUCTION SITE FOR THE RAIL LINE THAT WAS HEADING EASTWARDS...
BUT IF WE LEAVE THE SPEEDRAT HERE, HOW WILL WE GET IT BACK? IT'S IN THE MIDDLE OF THE DESERT!
EASY, WE'LL BRING IT WITH US!
THE WORK SITE MOVES WITH THE WORKERS, SO THE CRATES WON'T REMAIN HERE.
UH, NO?
TO BE OPENED AT THE INAUGURATION.
THEY'LL COME WITH US UNTIL THE WORK IS FINISHED. IT'S ENOUGH TO PROVIDE EXACT INFORMATION. THIS CRATE WILL BE ONE OF THE MANY THAT ARE FOR THE INAUGURATION!
GREAT! NOW ALL THAT'S LEFT IS TO START LOOKING FOR THOSE CRUMMY CATS!
EXCUSE ME, GENTLE-MOUSE!
WHO ME?

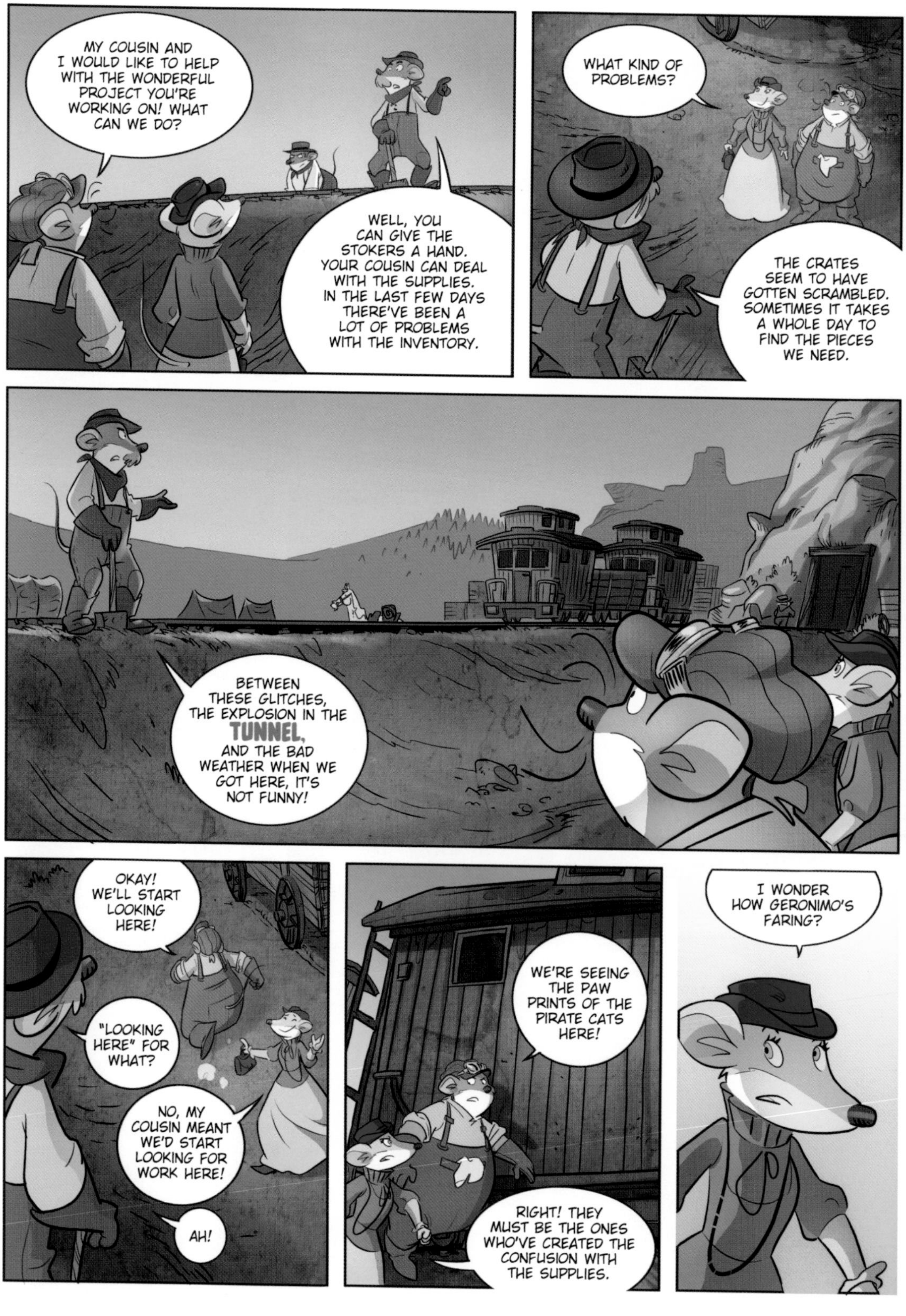

MY COUSIN AND I WOULD LIKE TO HELP WITH THE WONDERFUL PROJECT YOU'RE WORKING ON! WHAT CAN WE DO?
WELL, YOU CAN GIVE THE STOKERS A HAND. YOUR COUSIN CAN DEAL WITH THE SUPPLIES. IN THE LAST FEW DAYS THERE'VE BEEN A LOT OF PROBLEMS WITH THE INVENTORY.
WHAT KIND OF PROBLEMS?
THE CRATES SEEM TO HAVE GOTTEN SCRAMBLED. SOMETIMES IT TAKES A WHOLE DAY TO FIND THE PIECES WE NEED.
BETWEEN THESE GLITCHES, THE EXPLOSION IN THE TUNNEL, AND THE BAD WEATHER WHEN WE GOT HERE, IT'S NOT FUNNY!
OKAY! WE'LL START LOOKING HERE!
"LOOKING HERE" FOR WHAT?
NO, MY COUSIN MEANT WE'D START LOOKING FOR WORK HERE!
AH!
WE'RE SEEING THE PAW PRINTS OF THE PIRATE CATS HERE!
RIGHT! THEY MUST BE THE ONES WHO'VE CREATED THE CONFUSION WITH THE SUPPLIES.
I WONDER HOW GERONIMO'S FARING?

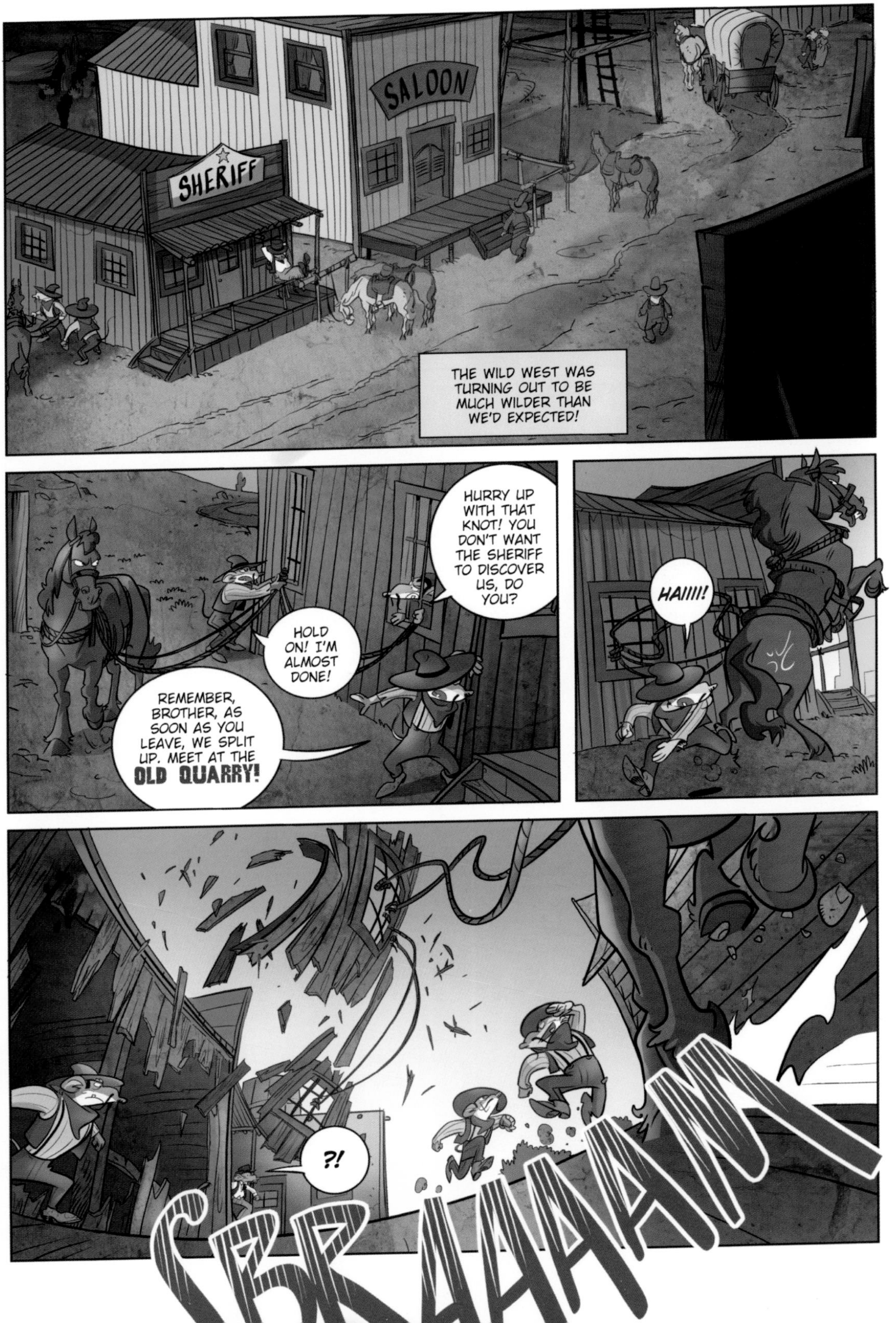
SALOON
SHERIFF
THE WILD WEST WAS TURNING OUT TO BE MUCH WILDER THAN WE'D EXPECTED!
HURRY UP WITH THAT KNOT! YOU DON'T WANT THE SHERIFF TO DISCOVER US, DO YOU?
HOLD ON! I'M ALMOST DONE!
REMEMBER, BROTHER, AS SOON AS YOU LEAVE, WE SPLIT UP. MEET AT THE OLD QUARRY!
HAIIII!
?!
CBRAAAAM

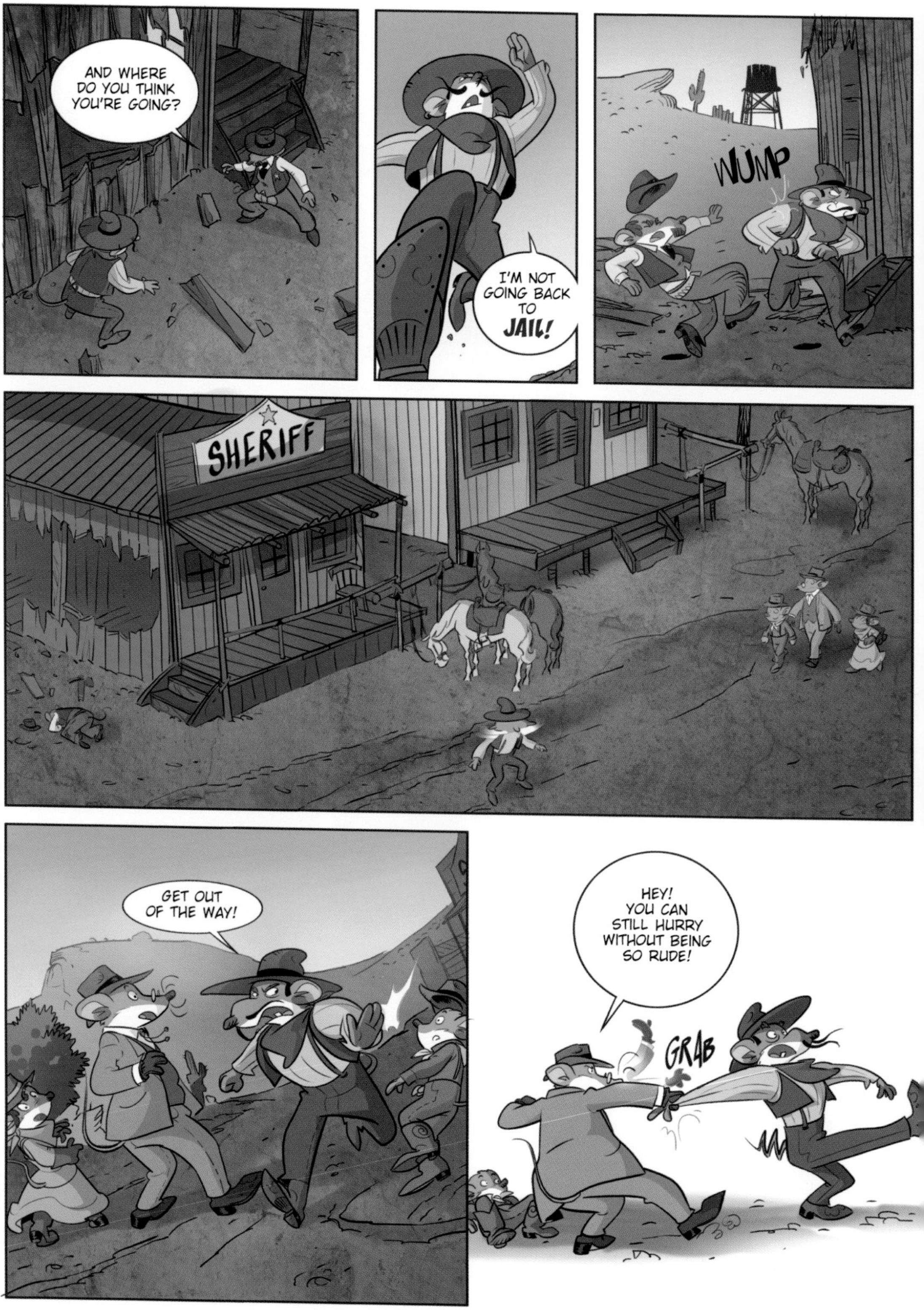
AND WHERE DO YOU THINK YOU'RE GOING?
I'M NOT GOING BACK TO JAIL!
WUMP
SHERIFF
GET OUT OF THE WAY!
HEY! YOU CAN STILL HURRY WITHOUT BEING SO RUDE!
GRAB

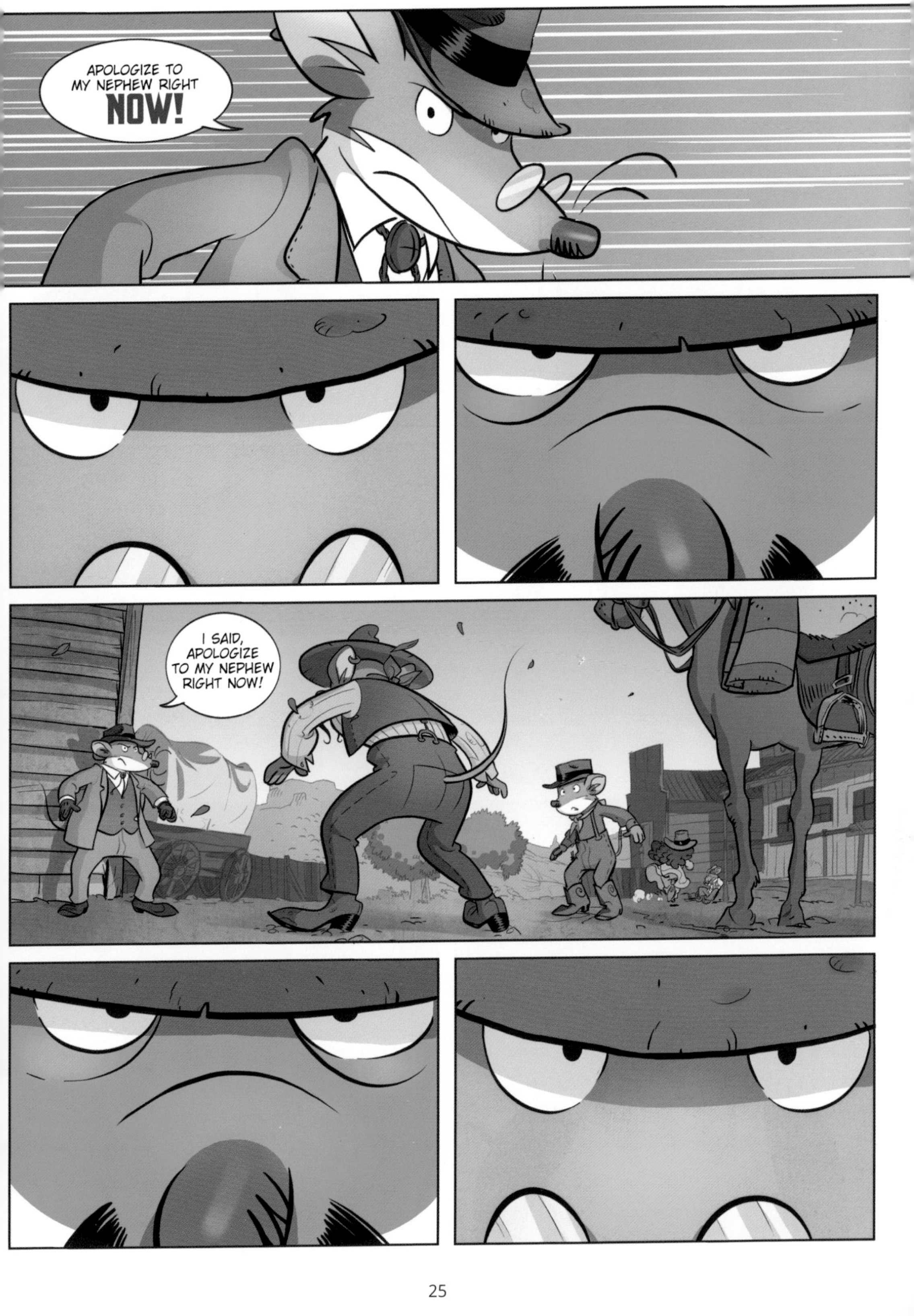
APOLOGIZE TO MY NEPHEW RIGHT NOW!
I SAID, APOLOGIZE TO MY NEPHEW RIGHT NOW!

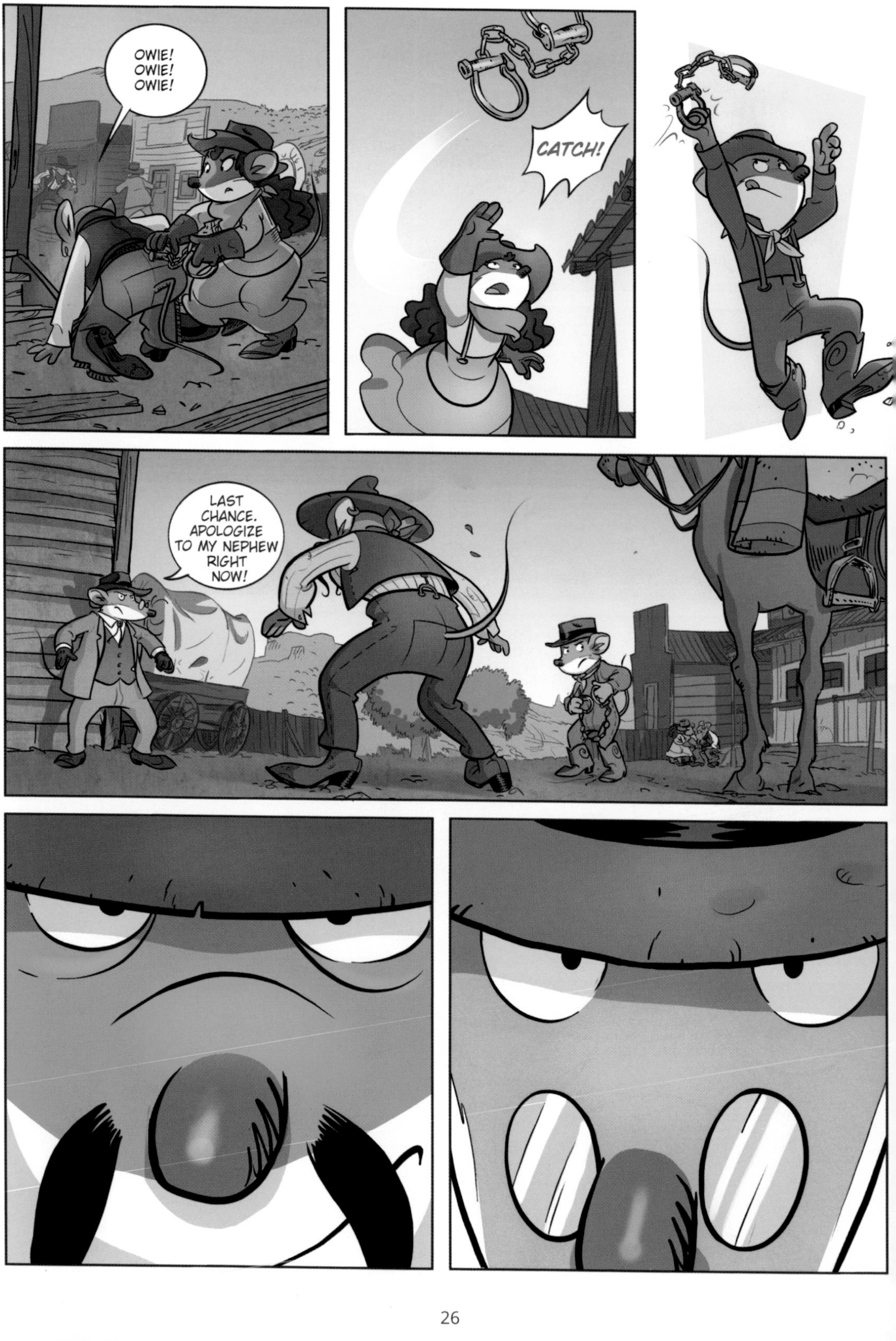
OWIE! OWIE! OWIE!
CATCH!
LAST CHANCE. APOLOGIZE TO MY NEPHEW RIGHT NOW!

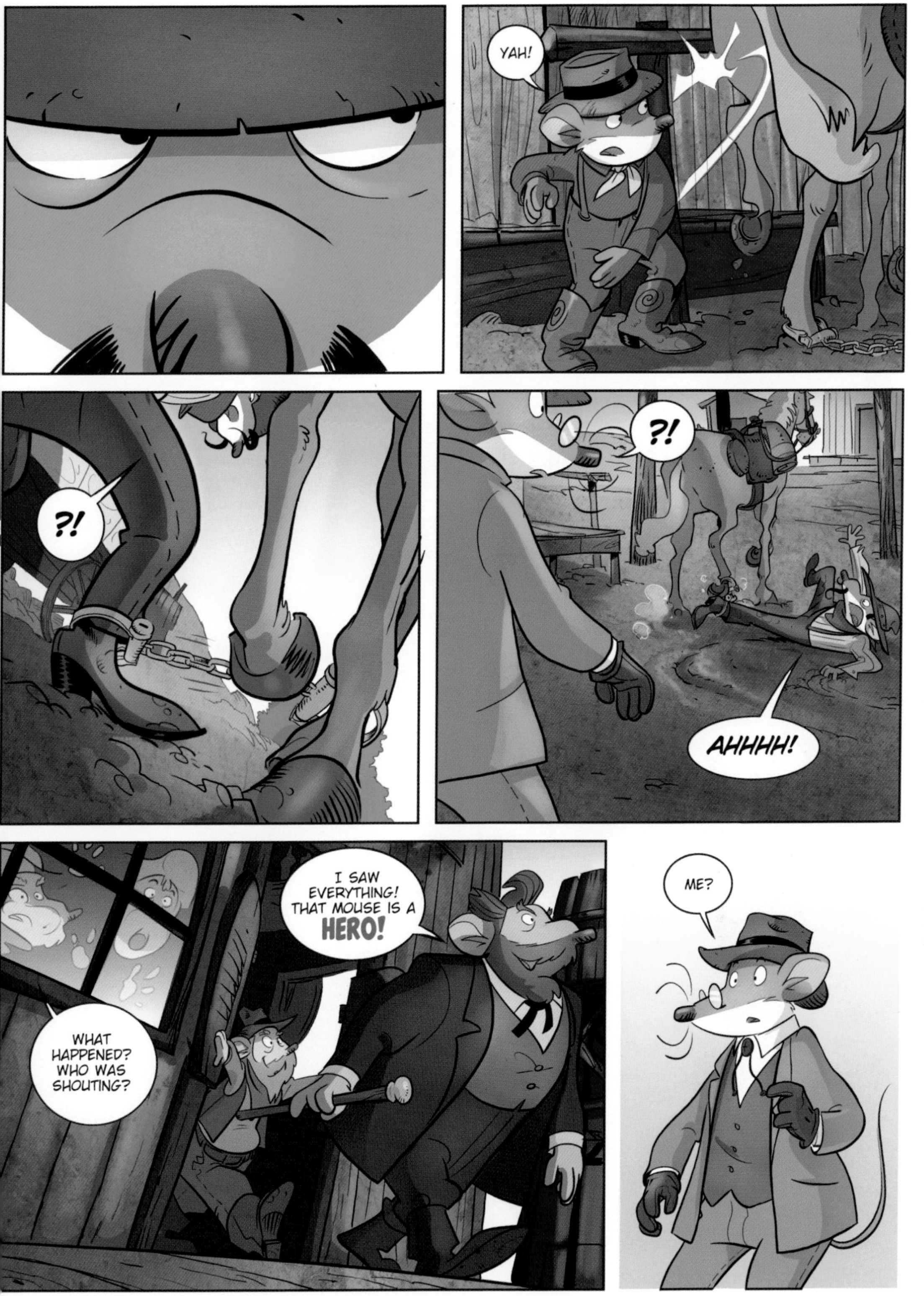
YAH!
?!
?!
AHHHH!
I SAW EVERYTHING! THAT MOUSE IS A HERO!
WHAT HAPPENED? WHO WAS SHOUTING?
ME?

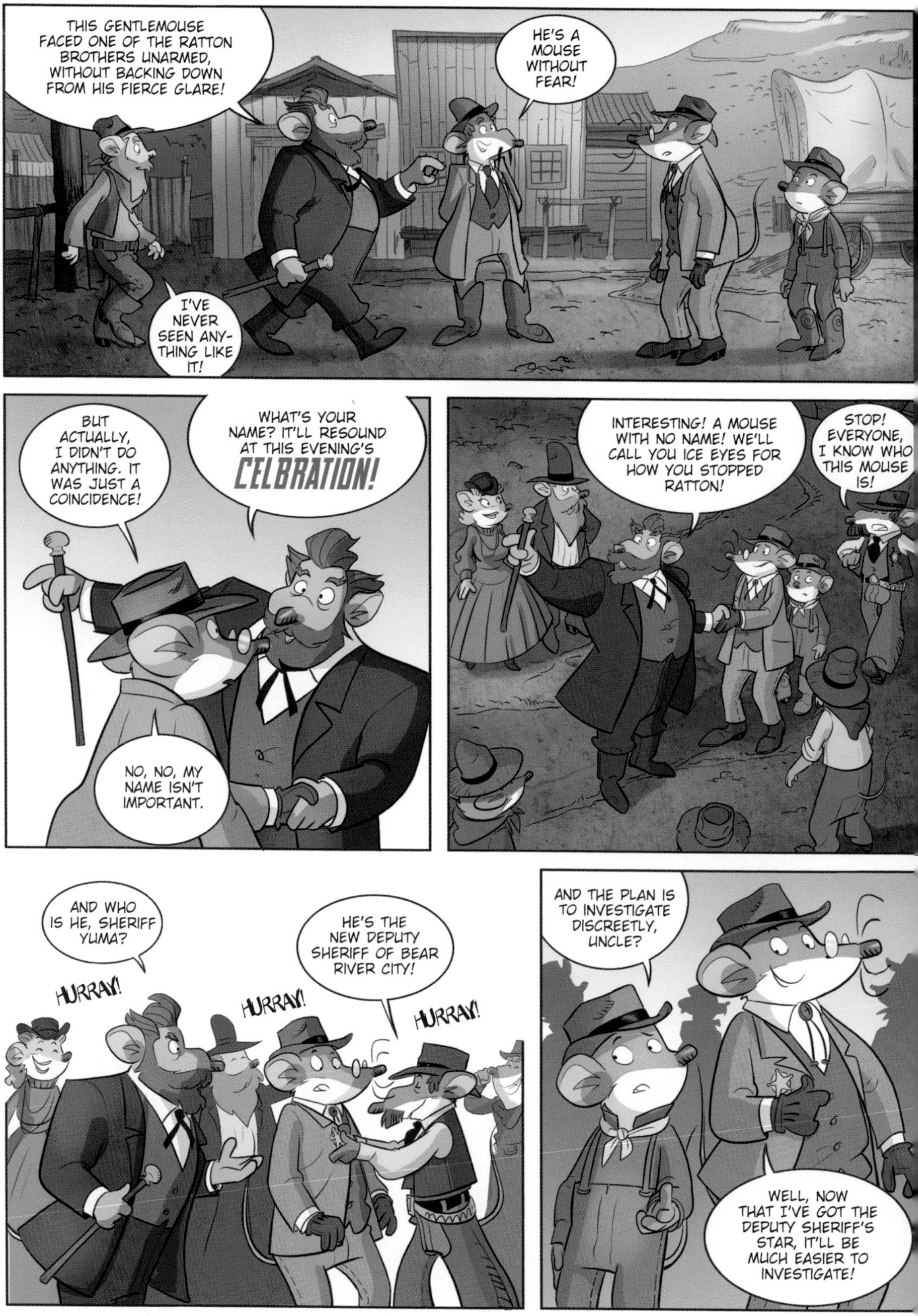
THIS GENTLEMOUSE FACED ONE OF THE RATTON BROTHERS UNARMED, WITHOUT BACKING DOWN FROM HIS FIERCE GLARE!
HE'S A MOUSE WITHOUT FEAR!
I'VE NEVER SEEN ANY-THING LIKE IT!
BUT ACTUALLY, I DIDN'T DO ANYTHING. IT WAS JUST A COINCIDENCE!
WHAT'S YOUR NAME? IT'LL RESOUND AT THIS EVENING'S CELBRATION!
NO, NO, MY NAME ISN'T IMPORTANT.
INTERESTING! A MOUSE WITH NO NAME! WE'LL CALL YOU ICE EYES FOR HOW YOU STOPPED RATTON!
STOP! EVERYONE, I KNOW WHO THIS MOUSE IS!
AND WHO IS HE, SHERIFF YUMA?
HE'S THE NEW DEPUTY SHERIFF OF BEAR RIVER CITY!
HURRAY!
HURRAY!
HURRAY!
AND THE PLAN IS TO INVESTIGATE DISCREETLY, UNCLE?
WELL, NOW THAT I'VE GOT THE DEPUTY SHERIFF'S STAR, IT'LL BE MUCH EASIER TO INVESTIGATE!

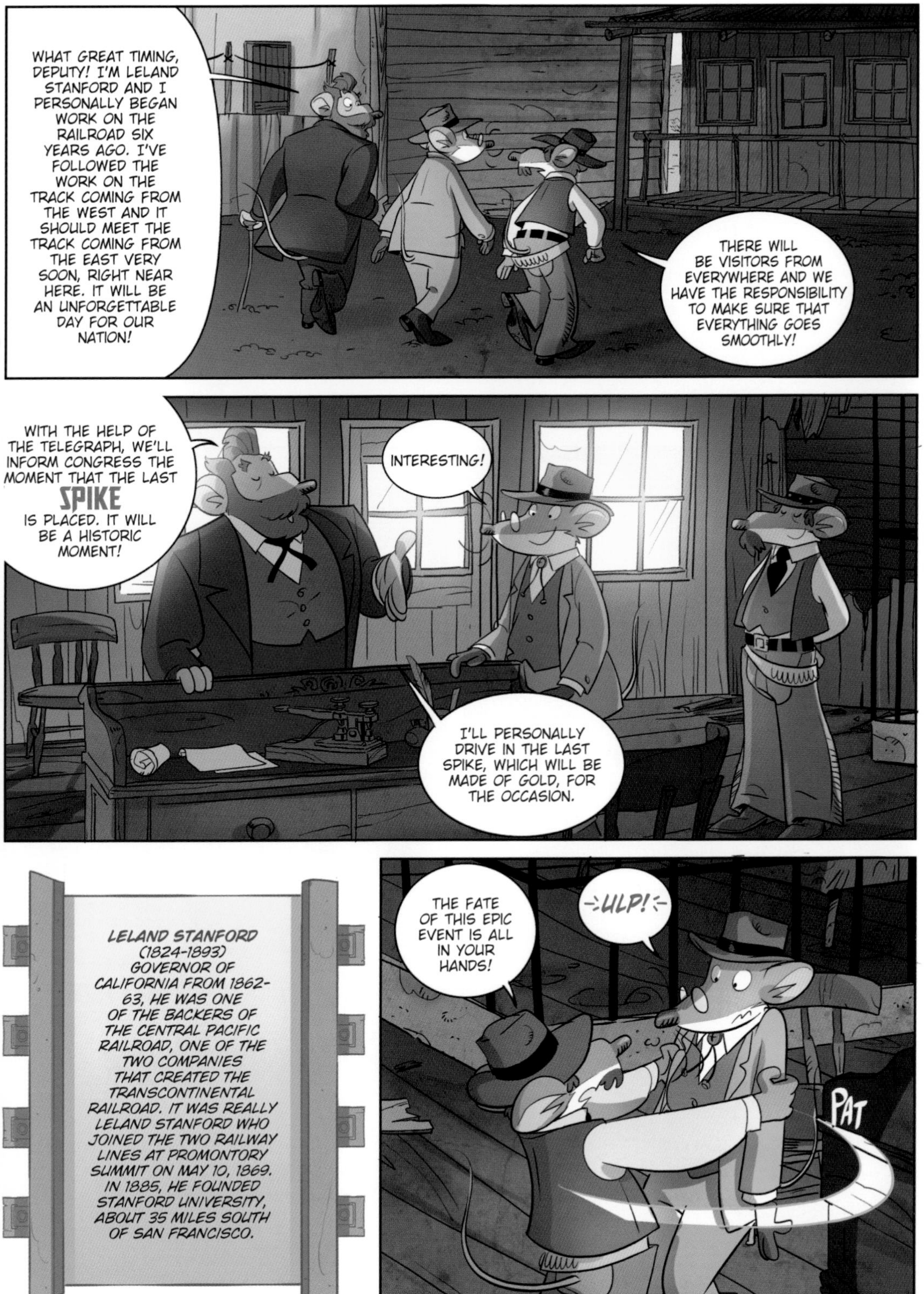
WHAT GREAT TIMING, DEPUTY! I'M LELAND STANFORD AND I PERSONALLY BEGAN WORK ON THE RAILROAD SIX YEARS AGO. I'VE FOLLOWED THE WORK ON THE TRACK COMING FROM THE WEST AND IT SHOULD MEET THE TRACK COMING FROM THE EAST VERY SOON, RIGHT NEAR HERE. IT WILL BE AN UNFORGETTABLE DAY FOR OUR NATION!
THERE WILL BE VISITORS FROM EVERYWHERE AND WE HAVE THE RESPONSIBILITY TO MAKE SURE THAT EVERYTHING GOES SMOOTHLY!
WITH THE HELP OF THE TELEGRAPH, WE'LL INFORM CONGRESS THE MOMENT THAT THE LAST SPIKE IS PLACED. IT WILL BE A HISTORIC MOMENT!
INTERESTING!
I'LL PERSONALLY DRIVE IN THE LAST SPIKE, WHICH WILL BE MADE OF GOLD, FOR THE OCCASION.
LELAND STANFORD (1824-1893) GOVERNOR OF CALIFORNIA FROM 1862-63, HE WAS ONE OF THE BACKERS OF THE CENTRAL PACIFIC RAILROAD, ONE OF THE TWO COMPANIES THAT CREATED THE TRANSCONTINENTAL RAILROAD. IT WAS REALLY LELAND STANFORD WHO JOINED THE TWO RAILWAY LINES AT PROMONTORY SUMMIT ON MAY 10, 1869. IN 1885, HE FOUNDED STANFORD UNIVERSITY, ABOUT 35 MILES SOUTH OF SAN FRANCISCO.
THE FATE OF THIS EPIC EVENT IS ALL IN YOUR HANDS!
ULP!
PAT

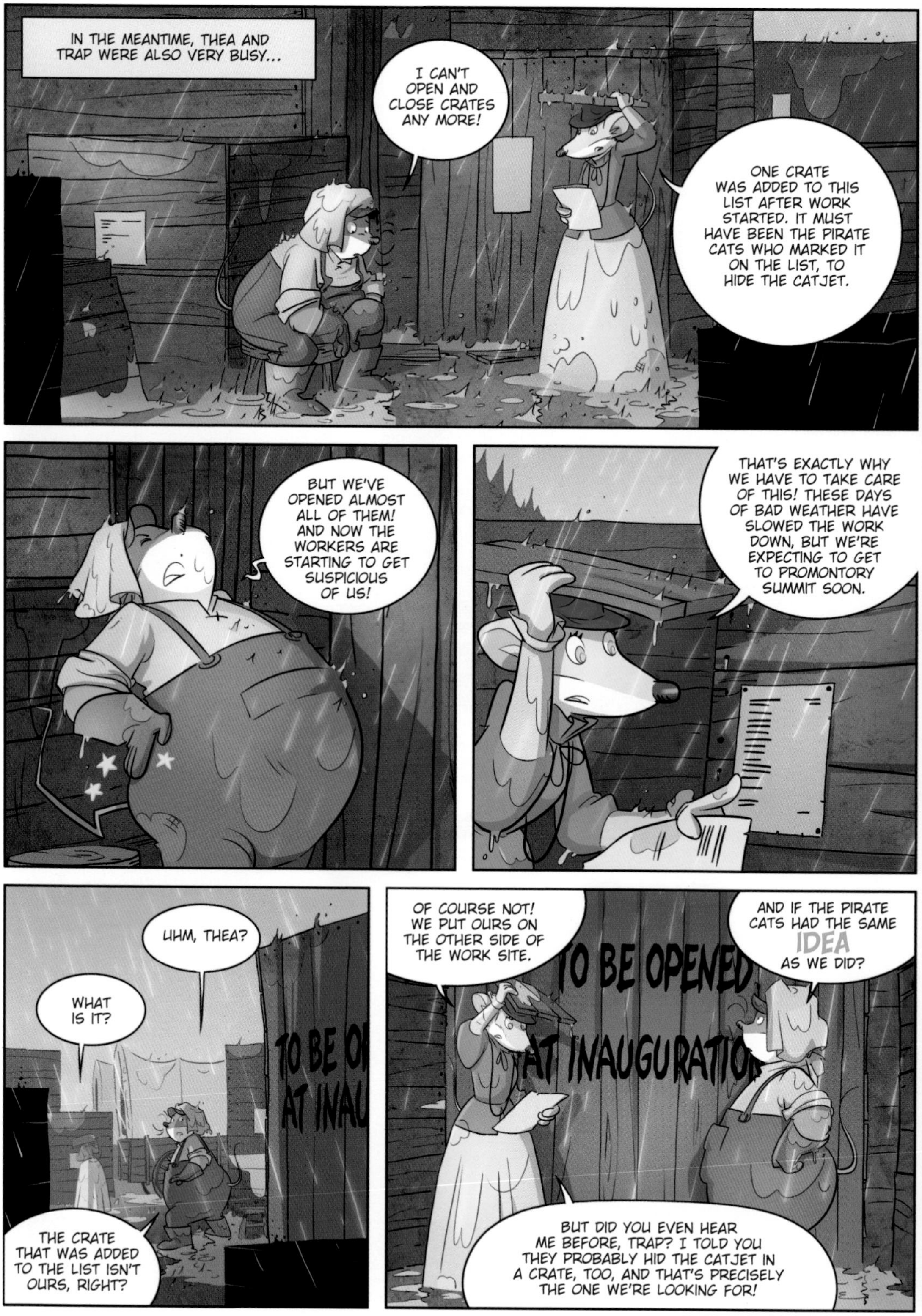
IN THE MEANTIME, THEA AND TRAP WERE ALSO VERY BUSY...
I CAN'T OPEN AND CLOSE CRATES ANY MORE!
ONE CRATE WAS ADDED TO THIS LIST AFTER WORK STARTED. IT MUST HAVE BEEN THE PIRATE CATS WHO MARKED IT ON THE LIST, TO HIDE THE CATJET.
BUT WE'VE OPENED ALMOST ALL OF THEM! AND NOW THE WORKERS ARE STARTING TO GET SUSPICIOUS OF US!
THAT'S EXACTLY WHY WE HAVE TO TAKE CARE OF THIS! THESE DAYS OF BAD WEATHER HAVE SLOWED THE WORK DOWN, BUT WE'RE EXPECTING TO GET TO PROMONTORY SUMMIT SOON.
UHM, THEA?
WHAT IS IT?
THE CRATE THAT WAS ADDED TO THE LIST ISN'T OURS, RIGHT?
OF COURSE NOT! WE PUT OURS ON THE OTHER SIDE OF THE WORK SITE.
AND IF THE PIRATE CATS HAD THE SAME IDEA AS WE DID?
TO BE OPENED AT INAUGURATION
BUT DID YOU EVEN HEAR ME BEFORE, TRAP? I TOLD YOU THEY PROBABLY HID THE CATJET IN A CRATE, TOO, AND THAT'S PRECISELY THE ONE WE'RE LOOKING FOR!

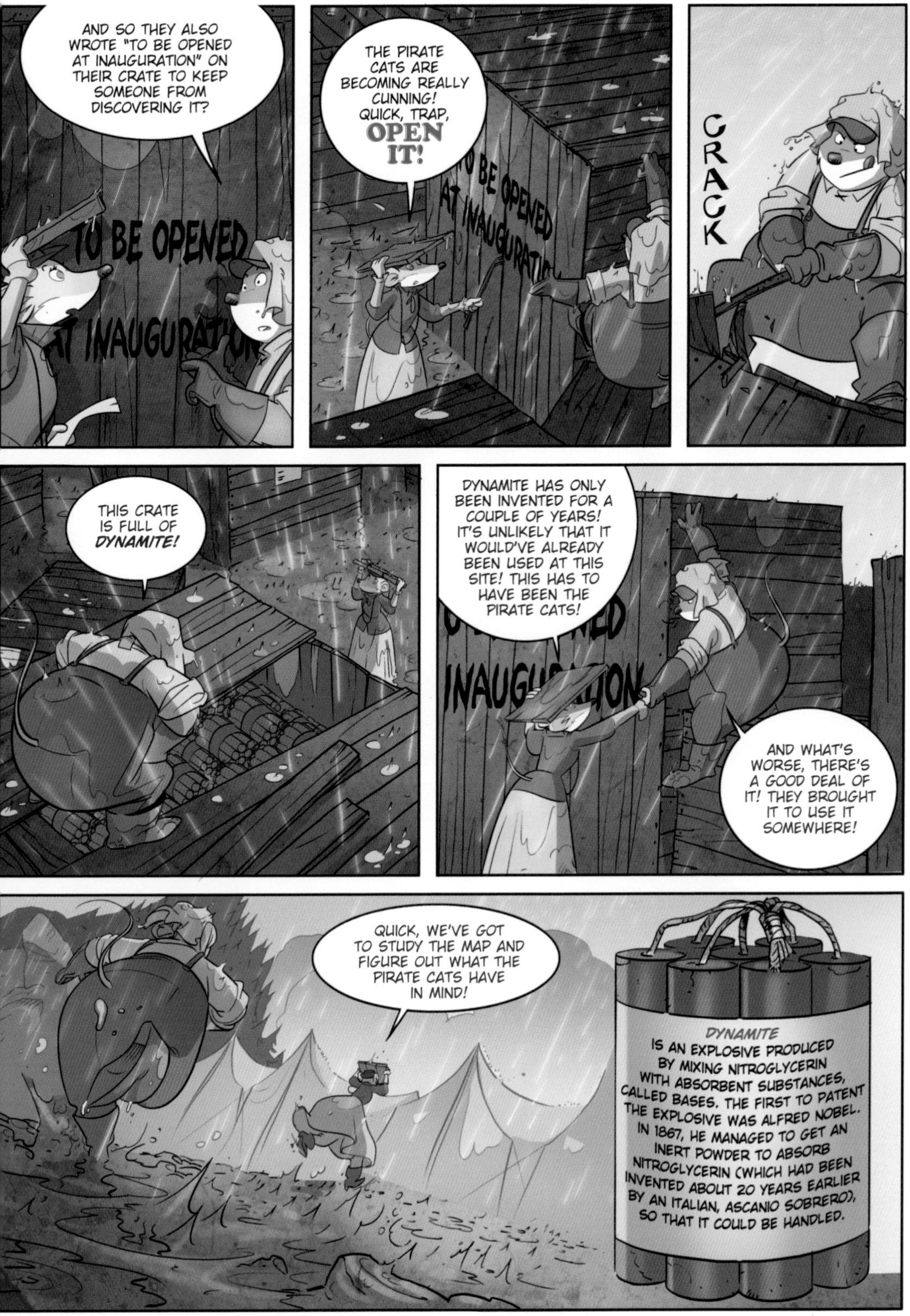

AND SO THEY ALSO WROTE "TO BE OPENED AT INAUGURATION" ON THEIR CRATE TO KEEP SOMEONE FROM DISCOVERING IT?
TO BE OPENED AT INAUGURATION
THE PIRATE CATS ARE BECOMING REALLY CUNNING! QUICK, TRAP, OPEN IT!
CRACK
THIS CRATE IS FULL OF DYNAMITE!
DYNAMITE HAS ONLY BEEN INVENTED FOR A COUPLE OF YEARS! IT'S UNLIKELY THAT IT WOULD'VE ALREADY BEEN USED AT THIS SITE! THIS HAS TO HAVE BEEN THE PIRATE CATS!
AND WHAT'S WORSE, THERE'S A GOOD DEAL OF IT! THEY BROUGHT IT TO USE IT SOMEWHERE!
QUICK, WE'VE GOT TO STUDY THE MAP AND FIGURE OUT WHAT THE PIRATE CATS HAVE IN MIND!
DYNAMITE
IS AN EXPLOSIVE PRODUCED BY MIXING NITROGLYCERIN WITH ABSORBENT SUBSTANCES, CALLED BASES. THE FIRST TO PATENT THE EXPLOSIVE WAS ALFRED NOBEL. IN 1867, HE MANAGED TO GET AN INERT POWDER TO ABSORB NITROGLYCERIN (WHICH HAD BEEN INVENTED ABOUT 20 YEARS EARLIER BY AN ITALIAN, ASCANIO SOBRERO), SO THAT IT COULD BE HANDLED.

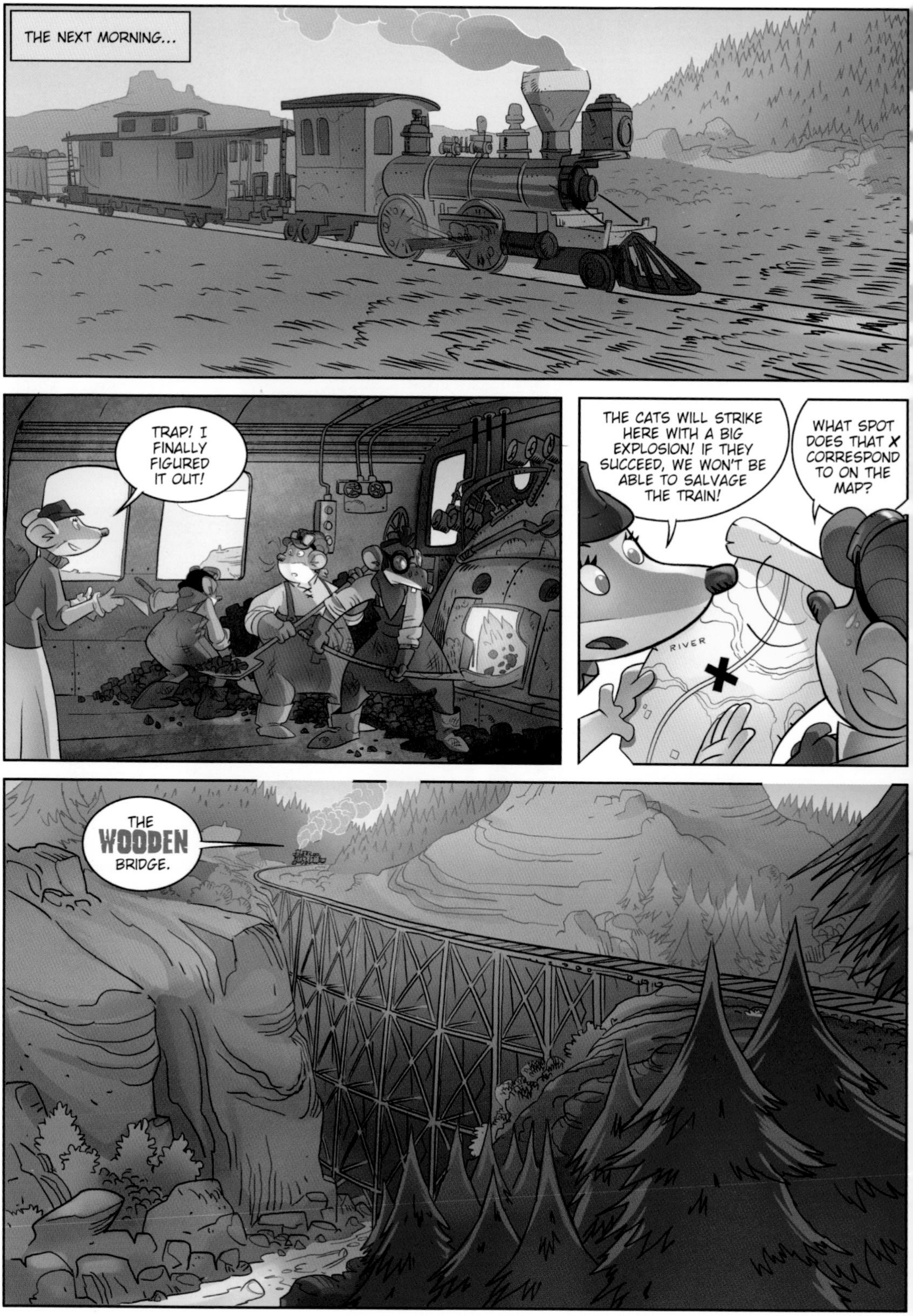
THE NEXT MORNING...
TRAP! I FINALLY FIGURED IT OUT!
THE CATS WILL STRIKE HERE WITH A BIG EXPLOSION! IF THEY SUCCEED, WE WON'T BE ABLE TO SALVAGE THE TRAIN!
WHAT SPOT DOES THAT X CORRESPOND TO ON THE MAP?
RIVER
THE WOODEN BRIDGE.

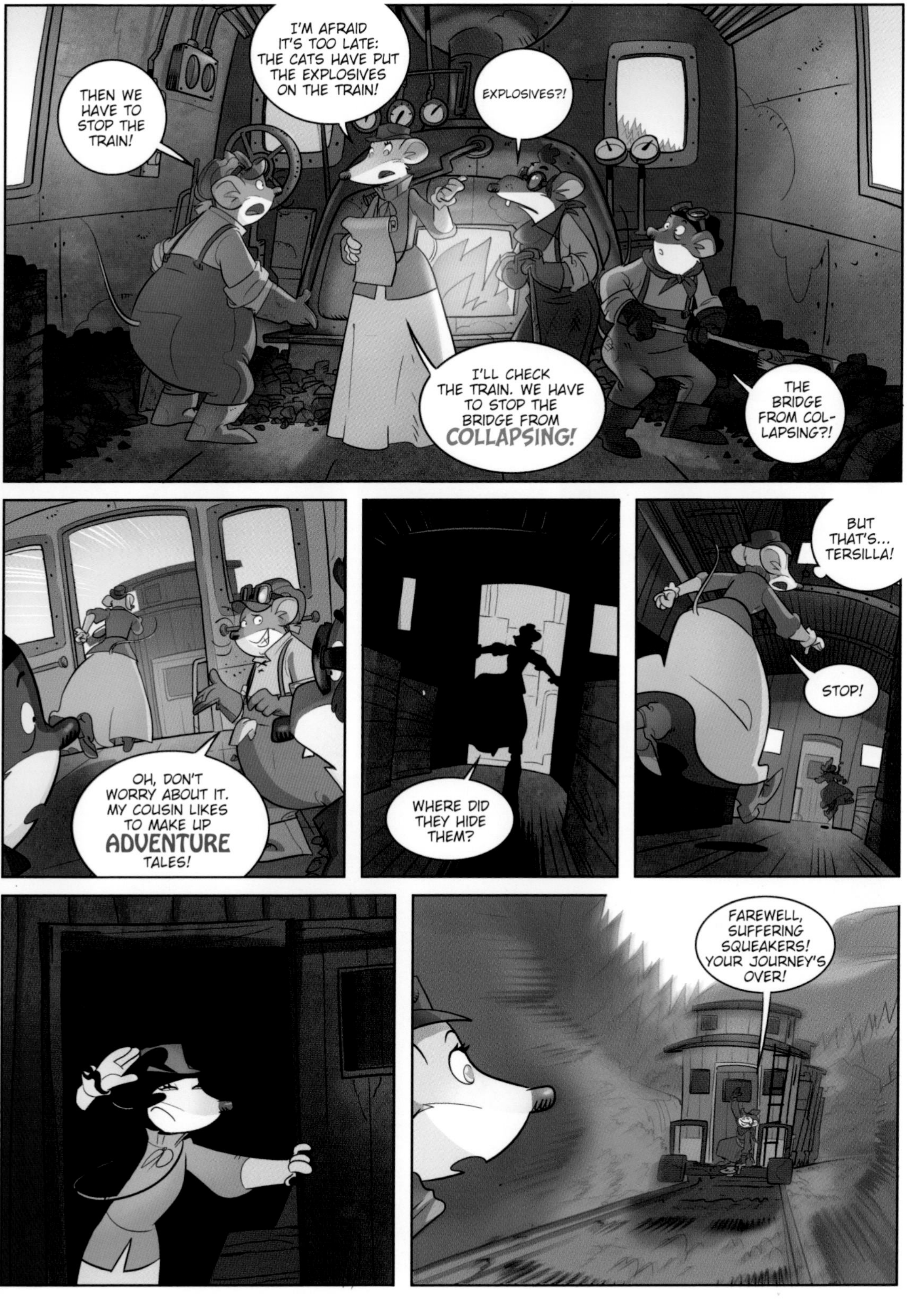
THEN WE HAVE TO STOP THE TRAIN!
I'M AFRAID IT'S TOO LATE: THE CATS HAVE PUT THE EXPLOSIVES ON THE TRAIN!
EXPLOSIVES?!
I'LL CHECK THE TRAIN. WE HAVE TO STOP THE BRIDGE FROM COLLAPSING!
THE BRIDGE FROM COL-LAPSING?!
OH, DON'T WORRY ABOUT IT. MY COUSIN LIKES TO MAKE UP ADVENTURE TALES!
WHERE DID THEY HIDE THEM?
BUT THAT'S... TERSILLA!
STOP!
FAREWELL, SUFFERING SQUEAKERS! YOUR JOURNEY'S OVER!

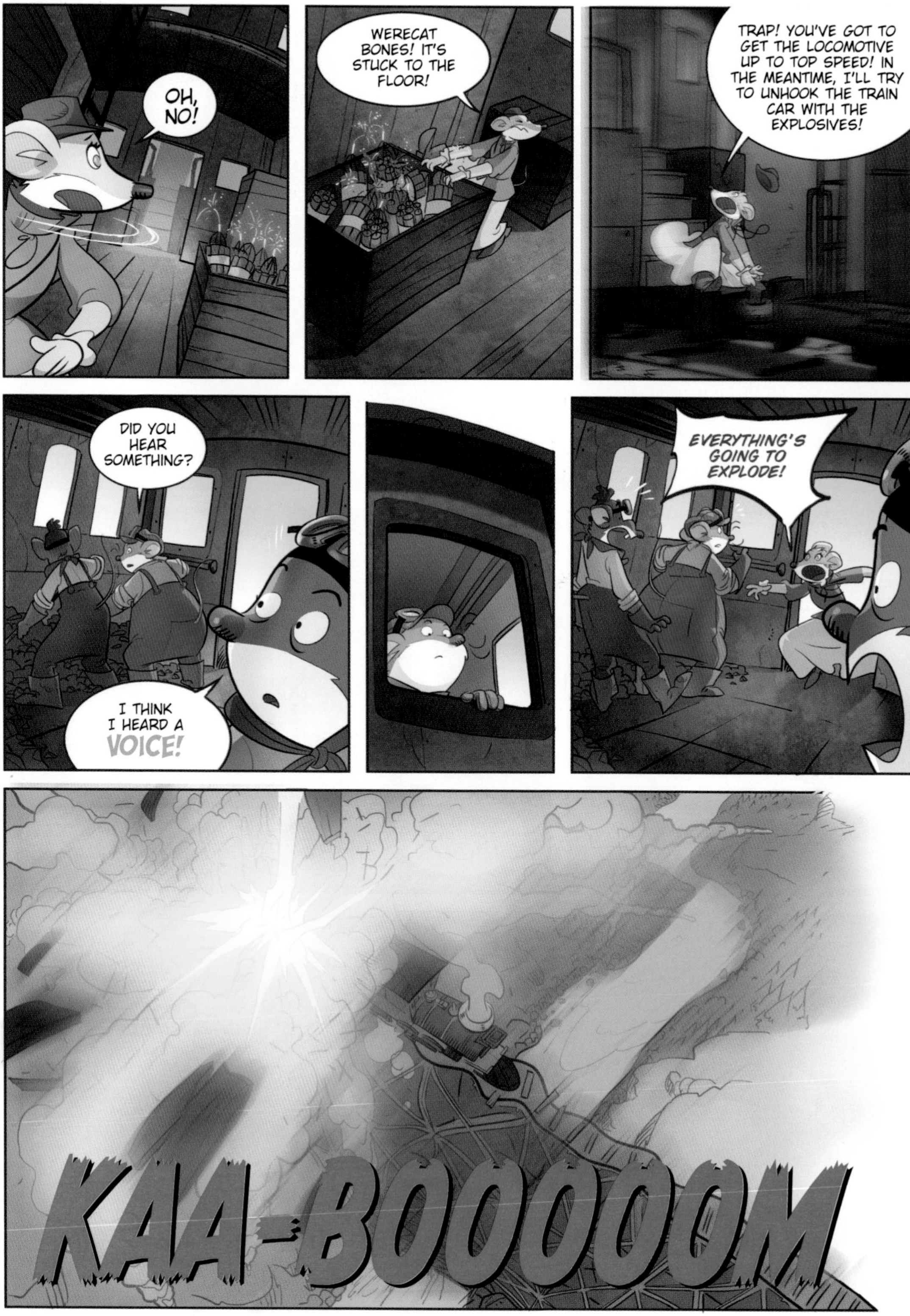

OH, NO!
WERECAT BONES! IT'S STUCK TO THE FLOOR!
TRAP! YOU'VE GOT TO GET THE LOCOMOTIVE UP TO TOP SPEED! IN THE MEANTIME, I'LL TRY TO UNHOOK THE TRAIN CAR WITH THE EXPLOSIVES!
DID YOU HEAR SOMETHING?
I THINK I HEARD A VOICE!
EVERYTHING'S GOING TO EXPLODE!
KAA-BOOOOOOM

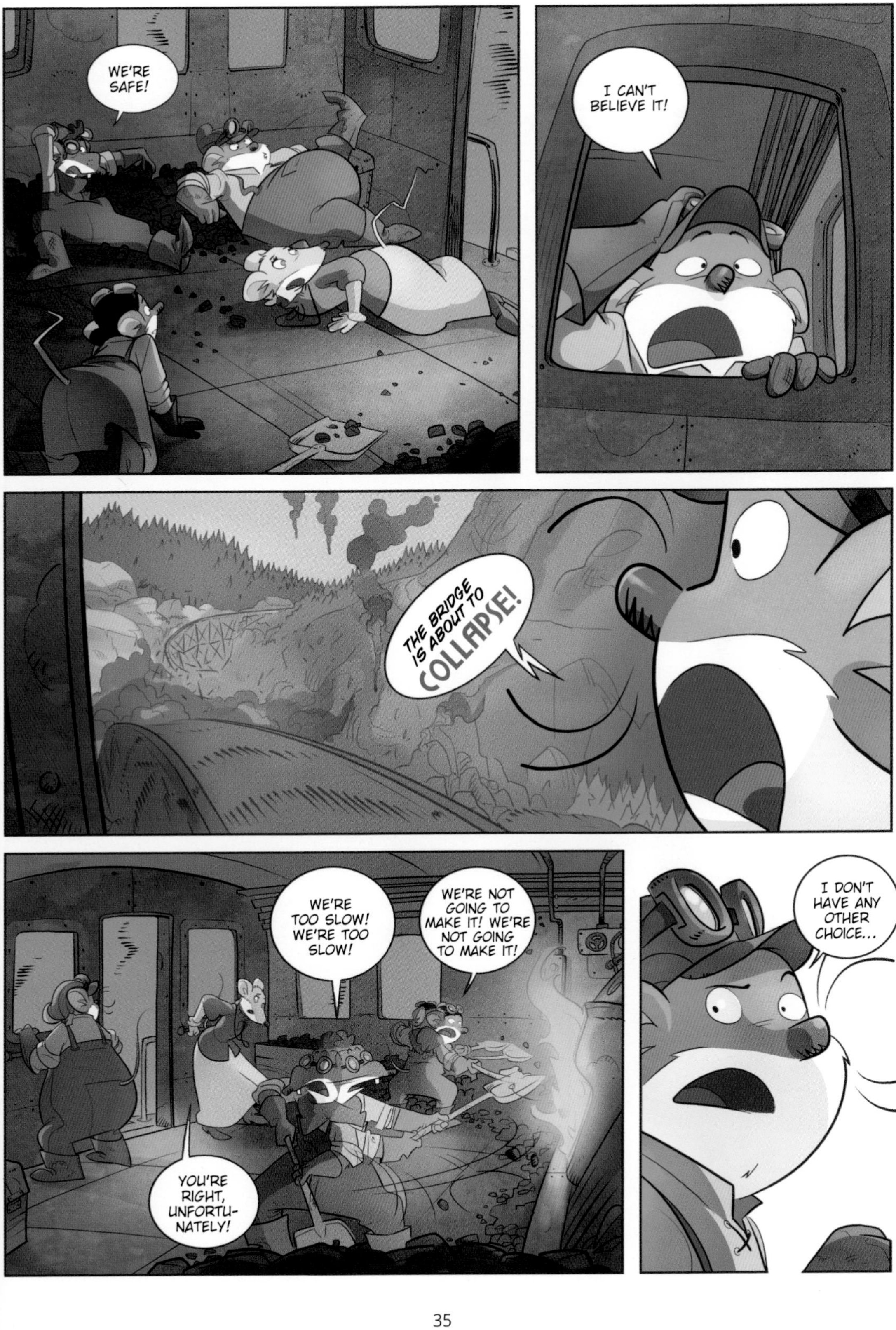
WE'RE SAFE!
I CAN'T BELIEVE IT!
THE BRIDGE IS ABOUT TO COLLAPSE!
WE'RE TOO SLOW! WE'RE TOO SLOW!
WE'RE NOT GOING TO MAKE IT! WE'RE NOT GOING TO MAKE IT!
YOU'RE RIGHT, UNFORTU-NATELY!
I DON'T HAVE ANY OTHER CHOICE...

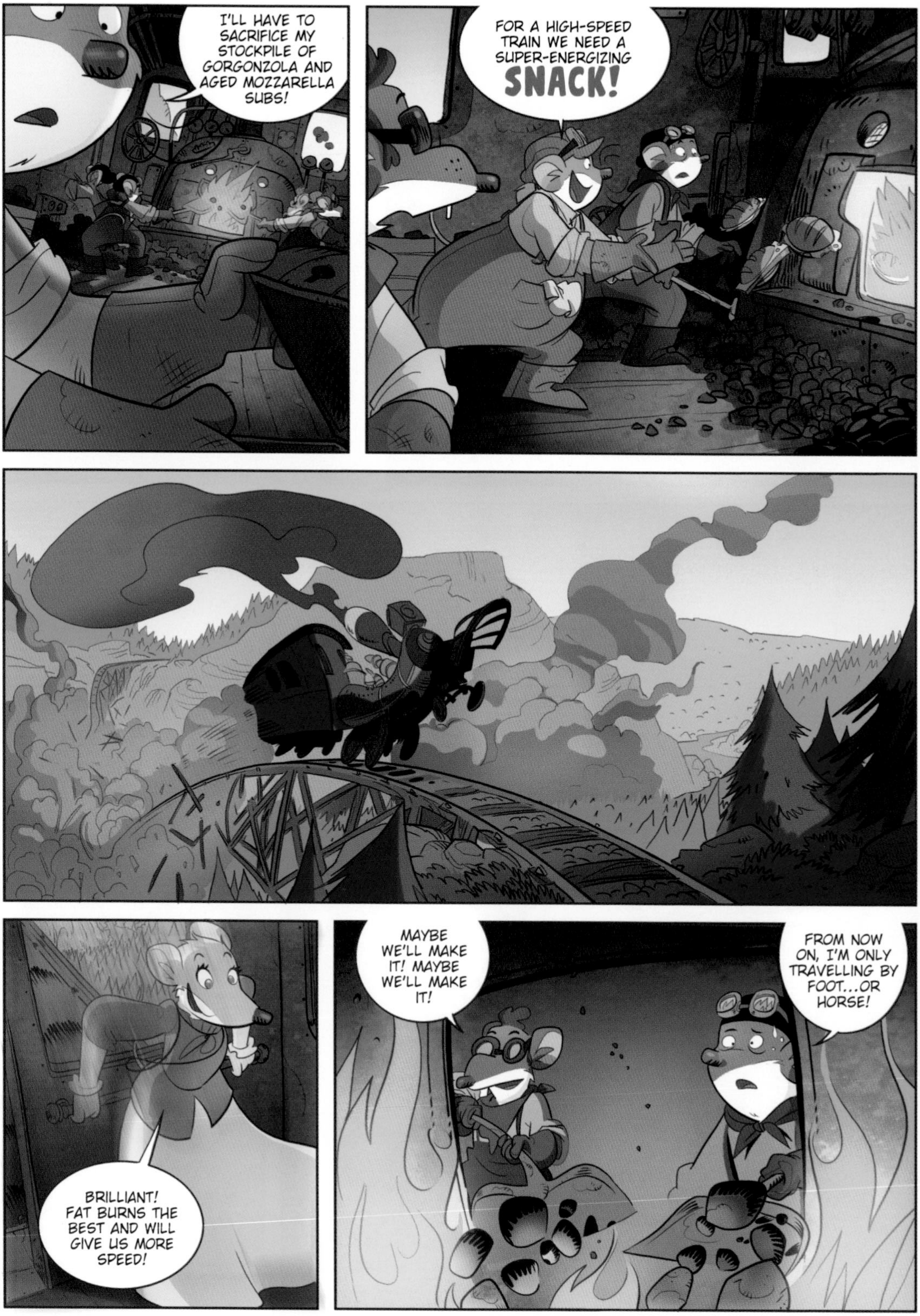
I'LL HAVE TO SACRIFICE MY STOCKPILE OF GORGONZOLA AND AGED MOZZARELLA SUBS!
FOR A HIGH-SPEED TRAIN WE NEED A SUPER-ENERGIZING
SNACK!
BRILLIANT! FAT BURNS THE BEST AND WILL GIVE US MORE SPEED!
MAYBE WE'LL MAKE IT! MAYBE WE'LL MAKE IT!
FROM NOW ON, I'M ONLY TRAVELLING BY FOOT...OR HORSE!

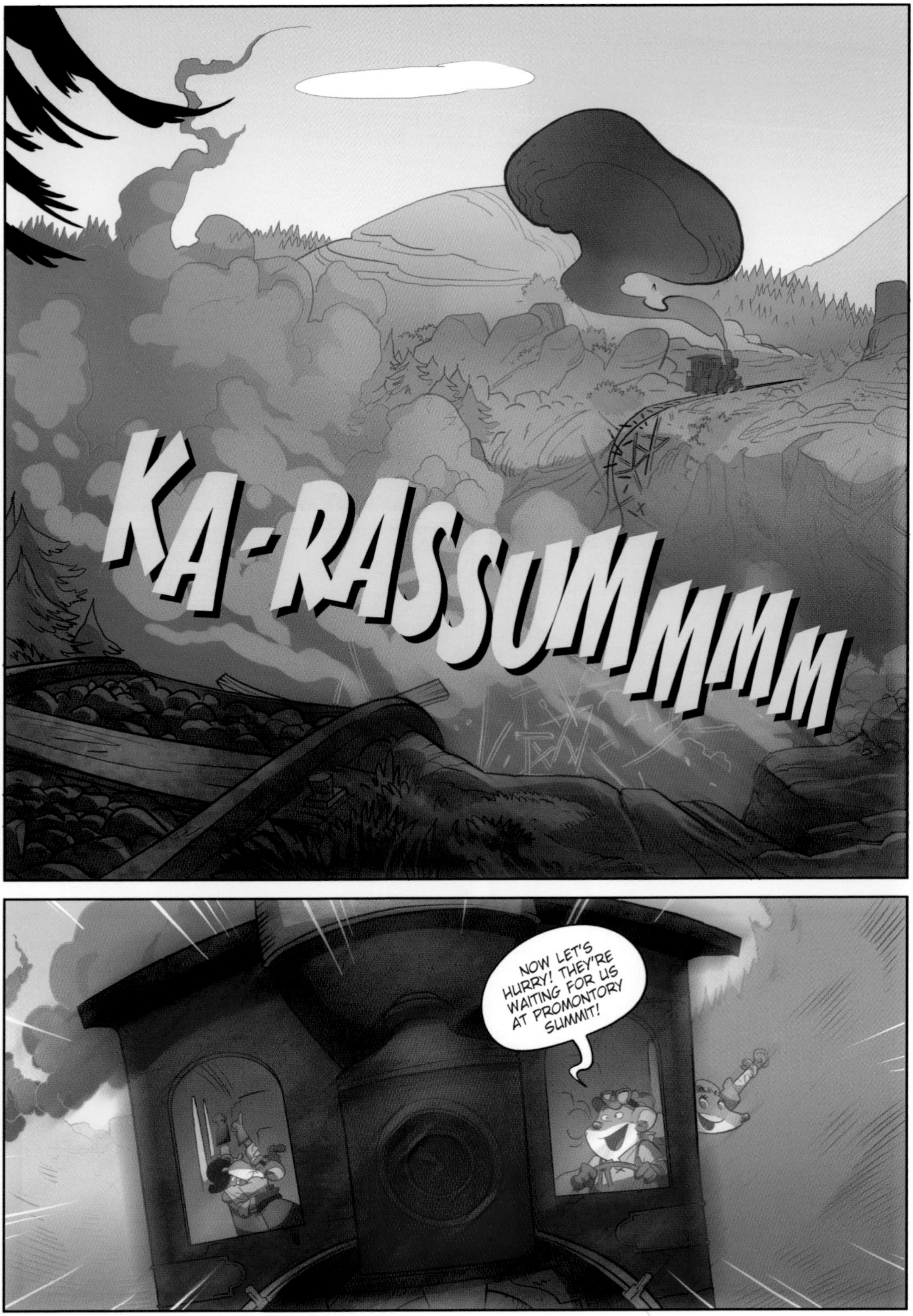
KA-RASSUMMMM
NOW LET'S HURRY! THEY'RE WAITING FOR US AT PROMONTORY SUMMIT!

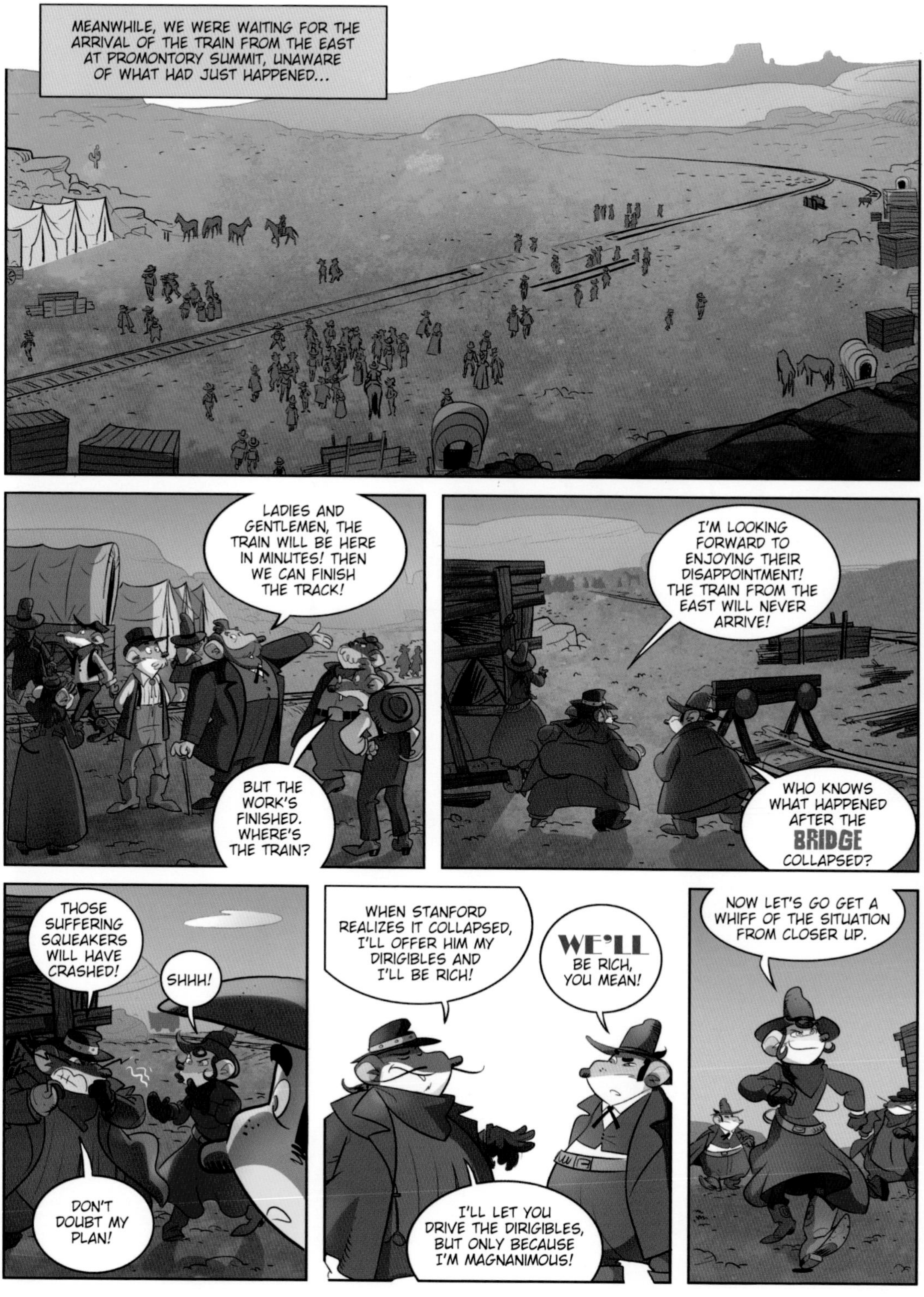
MEANWHILE, WE WERE WAITING FOR THE ARRIVAL OF THE TRAIN FROM THE EAST AT PROMONTORY SUMMIT, UNAWARE OF WHAT HAD JUST HAPPENED...
LADIES AND GENTLEMEN, THE TRAIN WILL BE HERE IN MINUTES! THEN WE CAN FINISH THE TRACK!
BUT THE WORK'S FINISHED. WHERE'S THE TRAIN?
I'M LOOKING FORWARD TO ENJOYING THEIR DISAPPOINTMENT! THE TRAIN FROM THE EAST WILL NEVER ARRIVE!
WHO KNOWS WHAT HAPPENED AFTER THE BRIDGE COLLAPSED?
THOSE SUFFERING SQUEAKERS WILL HAVE CRASHED!
SHHH!
DON'T DOUBT MY PLAN!
WHEN STANFORD REALIZES IT COLLAPSED, I'LL OFFER HIM MY DIRIGIBLES AND I'LL BE RICH!
WE'LL BE RICH, YOU MEAN!
I'LL LET YOU DRIVE THE DIRIGIBLES, BUT ONLY BECAUSE I'M MAGNANIMOUS!
NOW LET'S GO GET A WHIFF OF THE SITUATION FROM CLOSER UP.

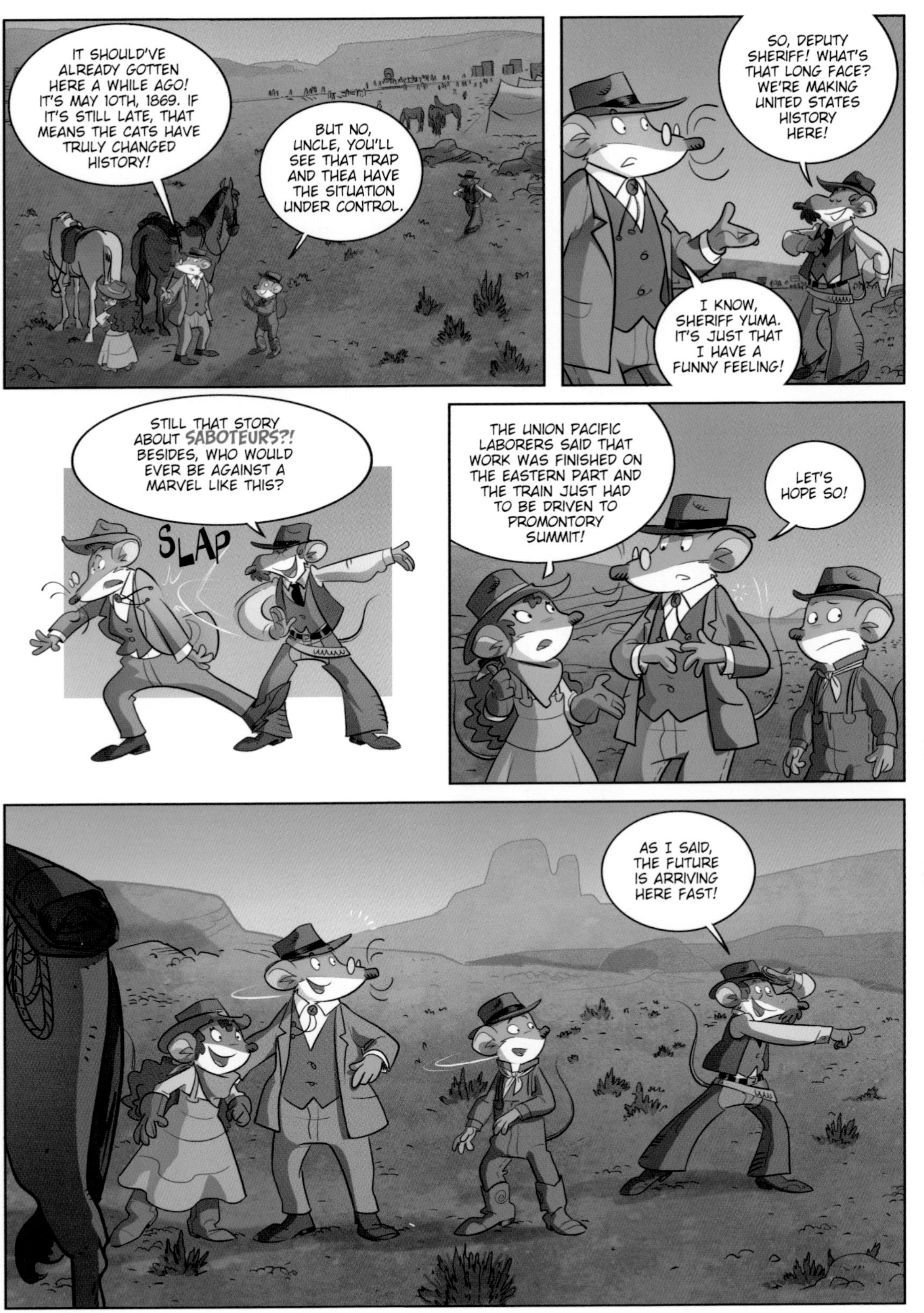
IT SHOULD'VE ALREADY GOTTEN HERE A WHILE AGO! IT'S MAY 10TH, 1869. IF IT'S STILL LATE, THAT MEANS THE CATS HAVE TRULY CHANGED HISTORY!
BUT NO, UNCLE, YOU'LL SEE THAT TRAP AND THEA HAVE THE SITUATION UNDER CONTROL.
SO, DEPUTY SHERIFF! WHAT'S THAT LONG FACE? WE'RE MAKING UNITED STATES HISTORY HERE!
I KNOW, SHERIFF YUMA. IT'S JUST THAT I HAVE A FUNNY FEELING!
STILL THAT STORY ABOUT SABOTEURS?! BESIDES, WHO WOULD EVER BE AGAINST A MARVEL LIKE THIS?
SLAP
THE UNION PACIFIC LABORERS SAID THAT WORK WAS FINISHED ON THE EASTERN PART AND THE TRAIN JUST HAD TO BE DRIVEN TO PROMONTORY SUMMIT!
LET'S HOPE SO!
AS I SAID, THE FUTURE IS ARRIVING HERE FAST!

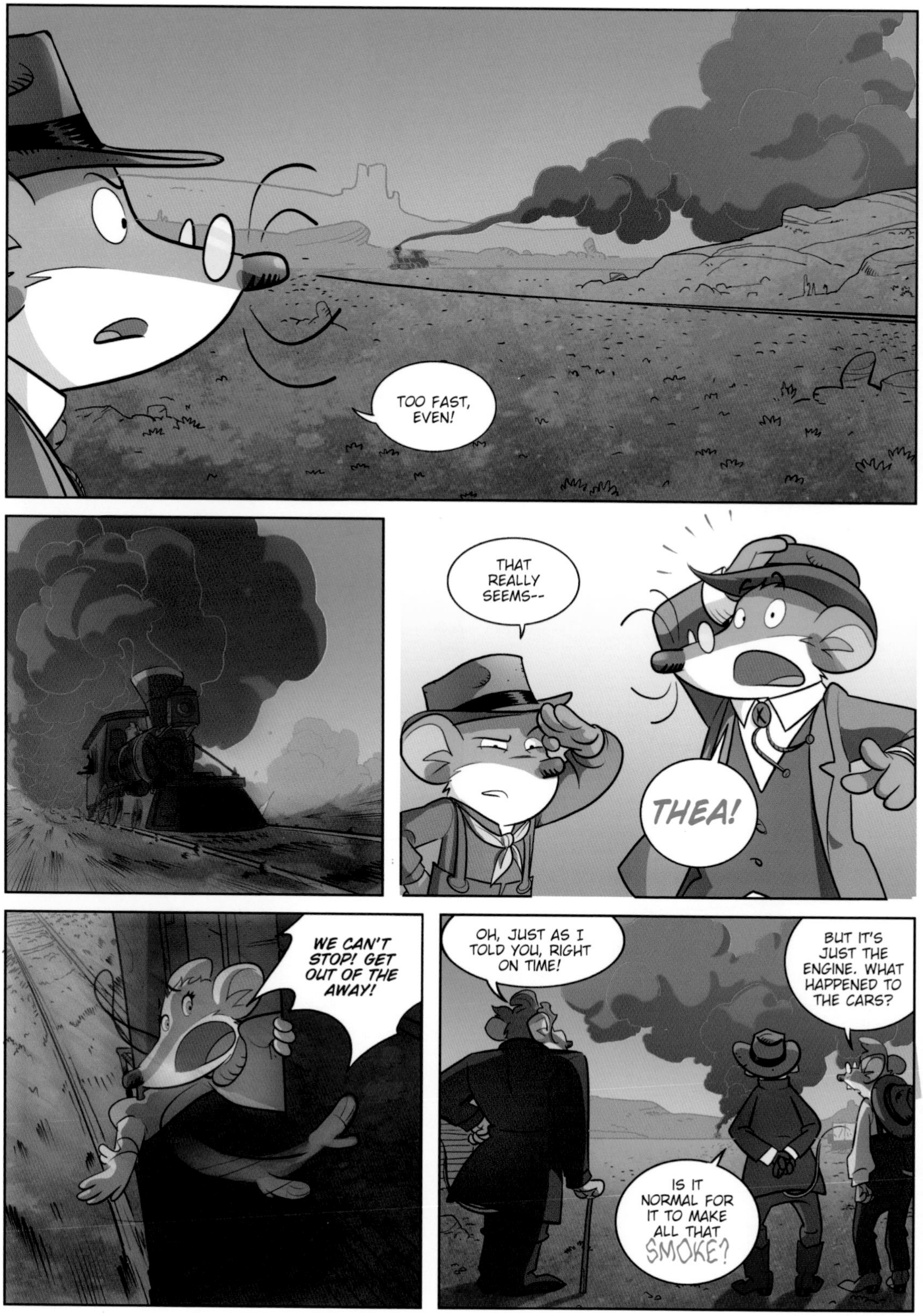

TOO FAST, EVEN!
THAT REALLY SEEMS--
THEA!
WE CAN'T STOP! GET OUT OF THE AWAY!
OH, JUST AS I TOLD YOU, RIGHT ON TIME!
BUT IT'S JUST THE ENGINE. WHAT HAPPENED TO THE CARS?
IS IT NORMAL FOR IT TO MAKE ALL THAT SMOKE?

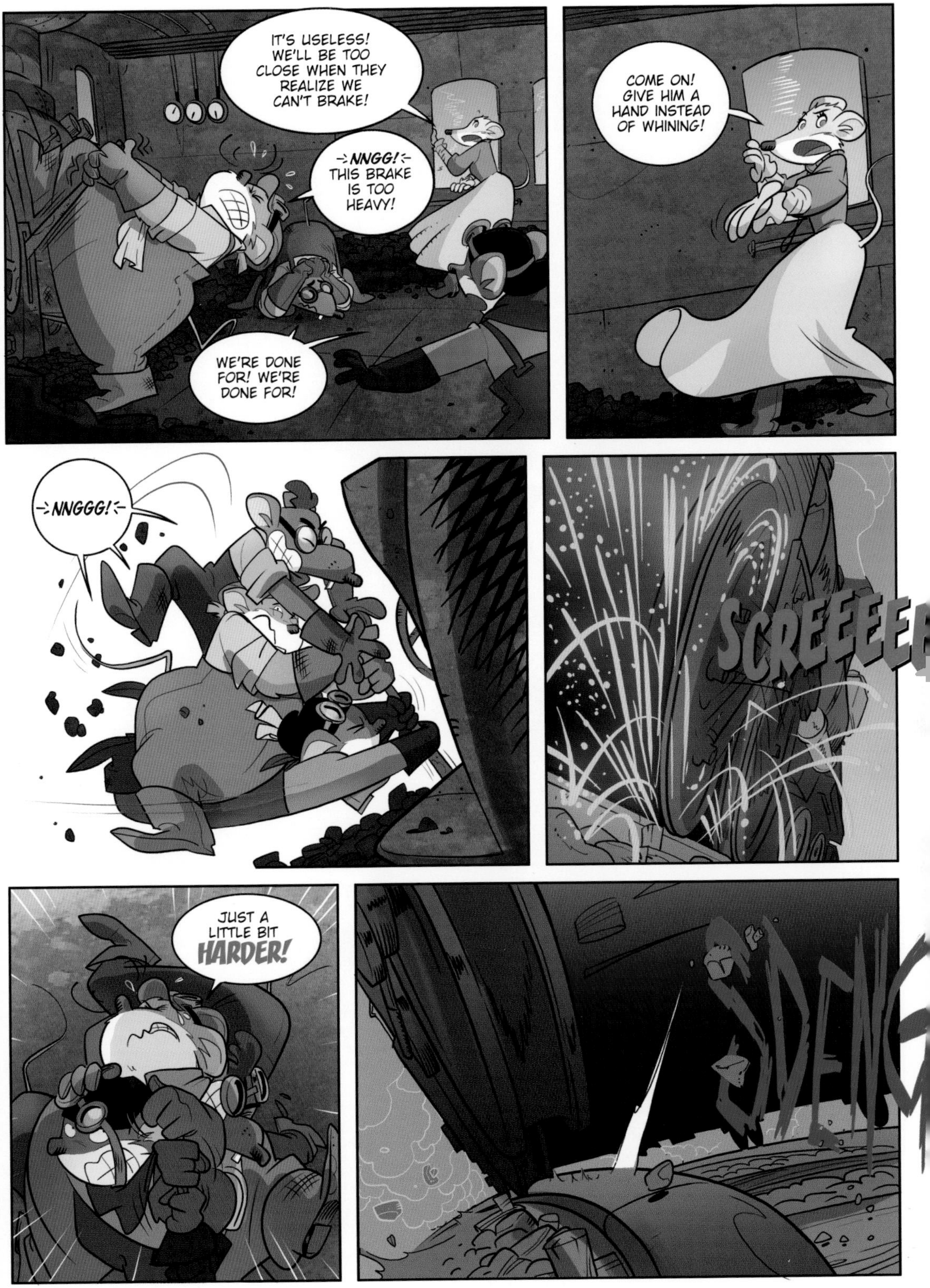
IT'S USELESS! WE'LL BE TOO CLOSE WHEN THEY REALIZE WE CAN'T BRAKE!
-NNGG!- THIS BRAKE IS TOO HEAVY!
WE'RE DONE FOR! WE'RE DONE FOR!
COME ON! GIVE HIM A HAND INSTEAD OF WHINING!
-NNGGG!-
SCREEEEE
JUST A LITTLE BIT HARDER!
SDENG

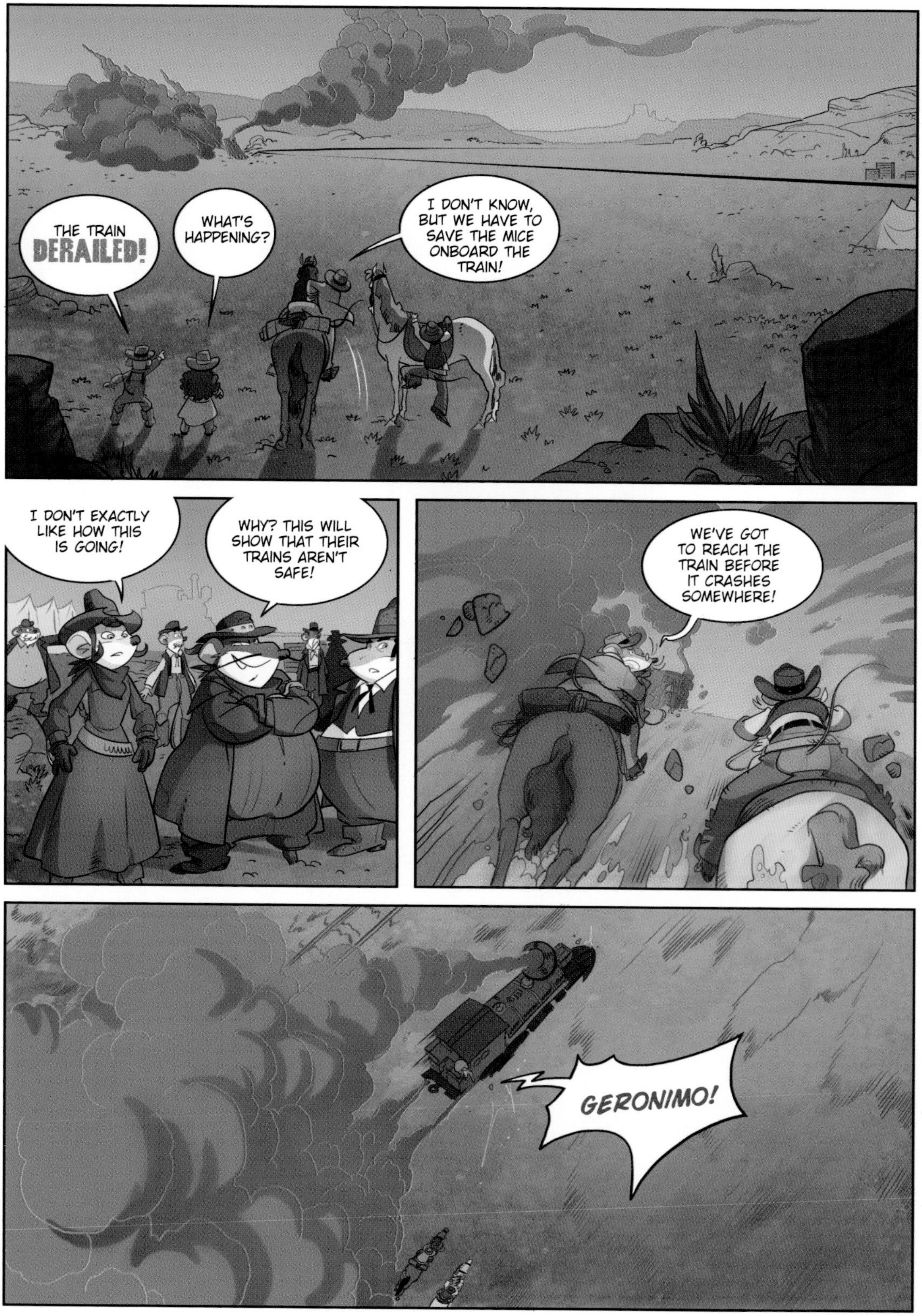
THE TRAIN DERAILED!
WHAT'S HAPPENING?
I DON'T KNOW, BUT WE HAVE TO SAVE THE MICE ONBOARD THE TRAIN!
I DON'T EXACTLY LIKE HOW THIS IS GOING!
WHY? THIS WILL SHOW THAT THEIR TRAINS AREN'T SAFE!
WE'VE GOT TO REACH THE TRAIN BEFORE IT CRASHES SOMEWHERE!
GERONIMO!

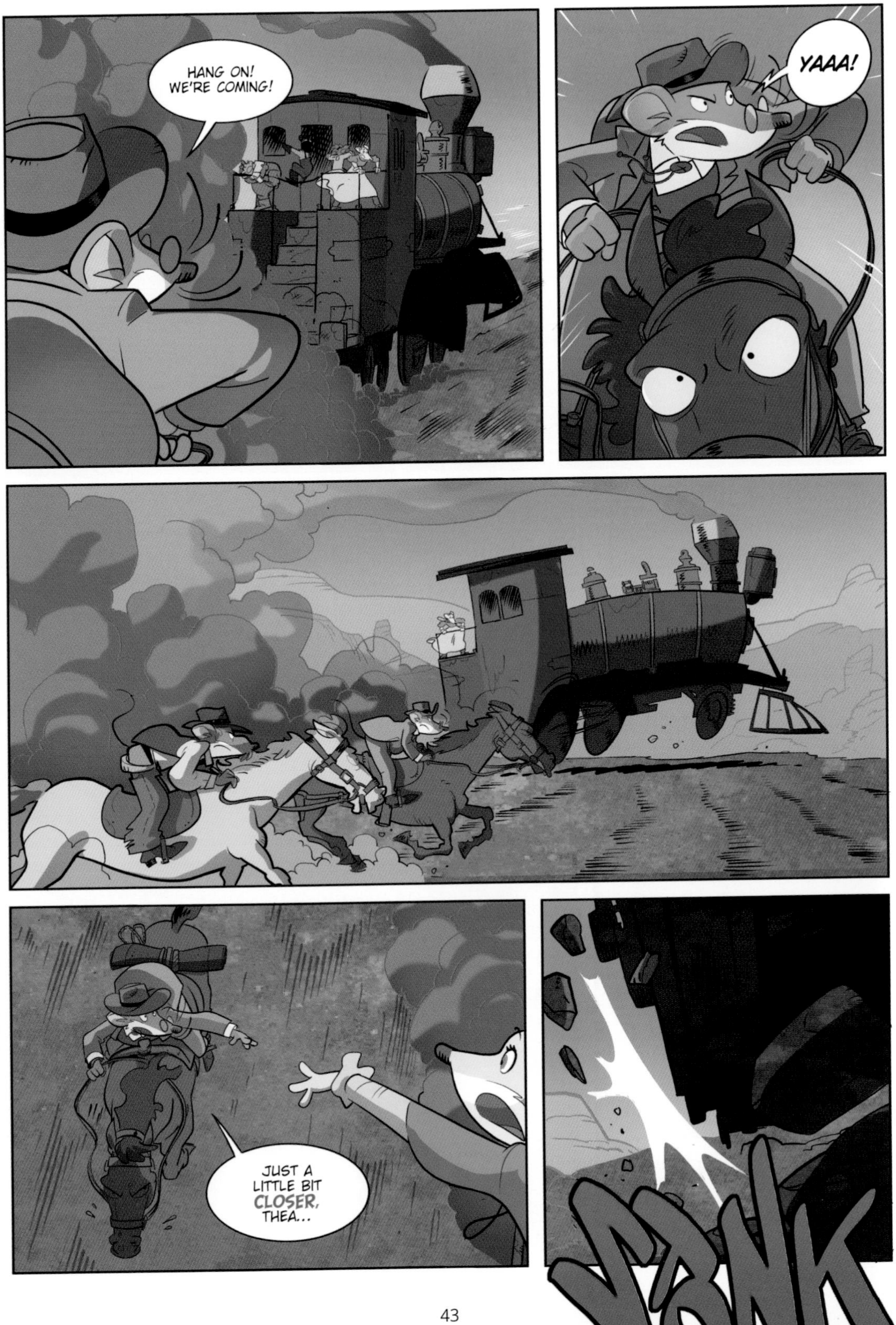
HANG ON! WE'RE COMING!
YAAA!
JUST A LITTLE BIT CLOSER, THEA...
SBONK

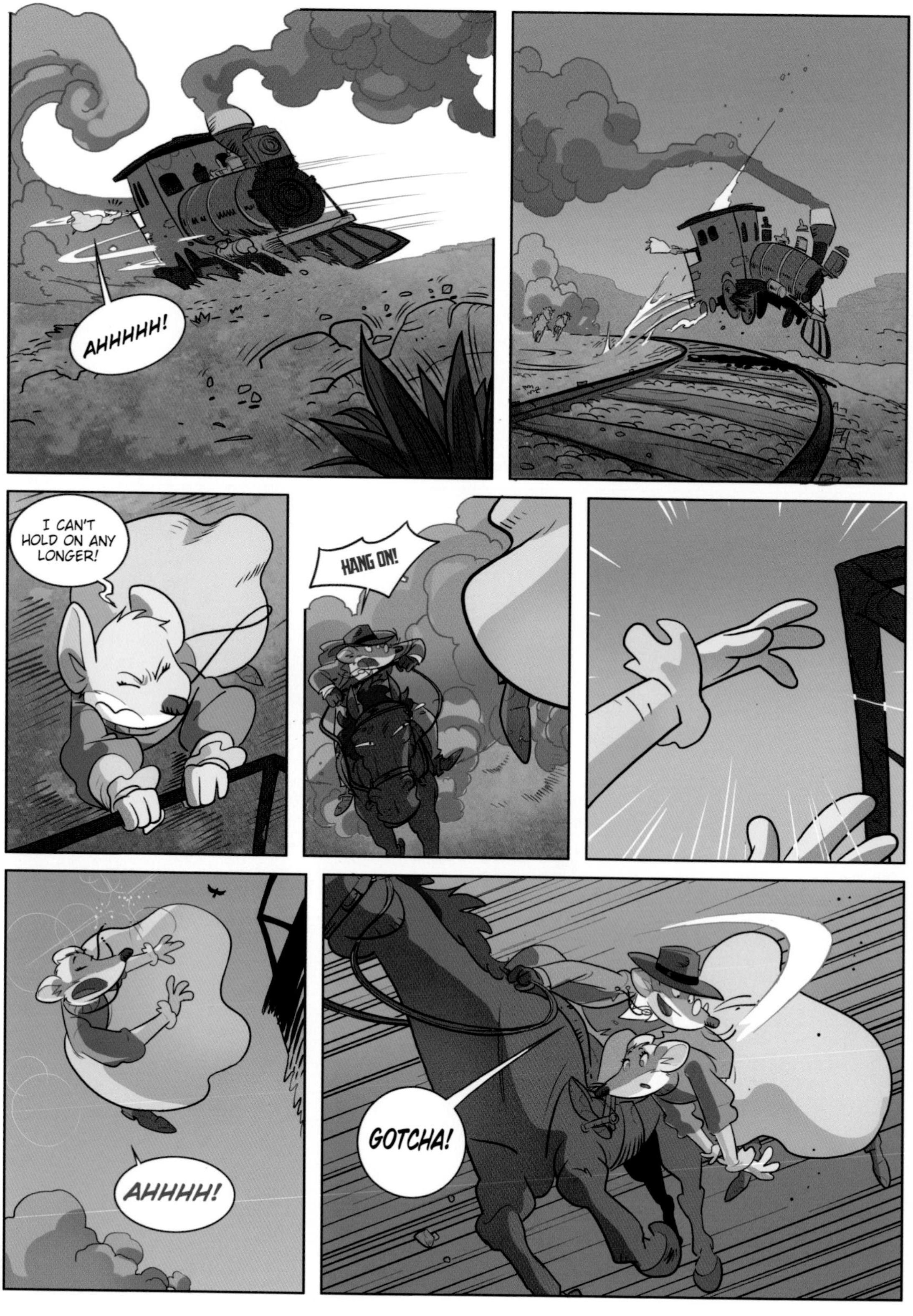
AHHHHH!
I CAN'T HOLD ON ANY LONGER!
HANG ON!
AHHHH!
GOTCHA!

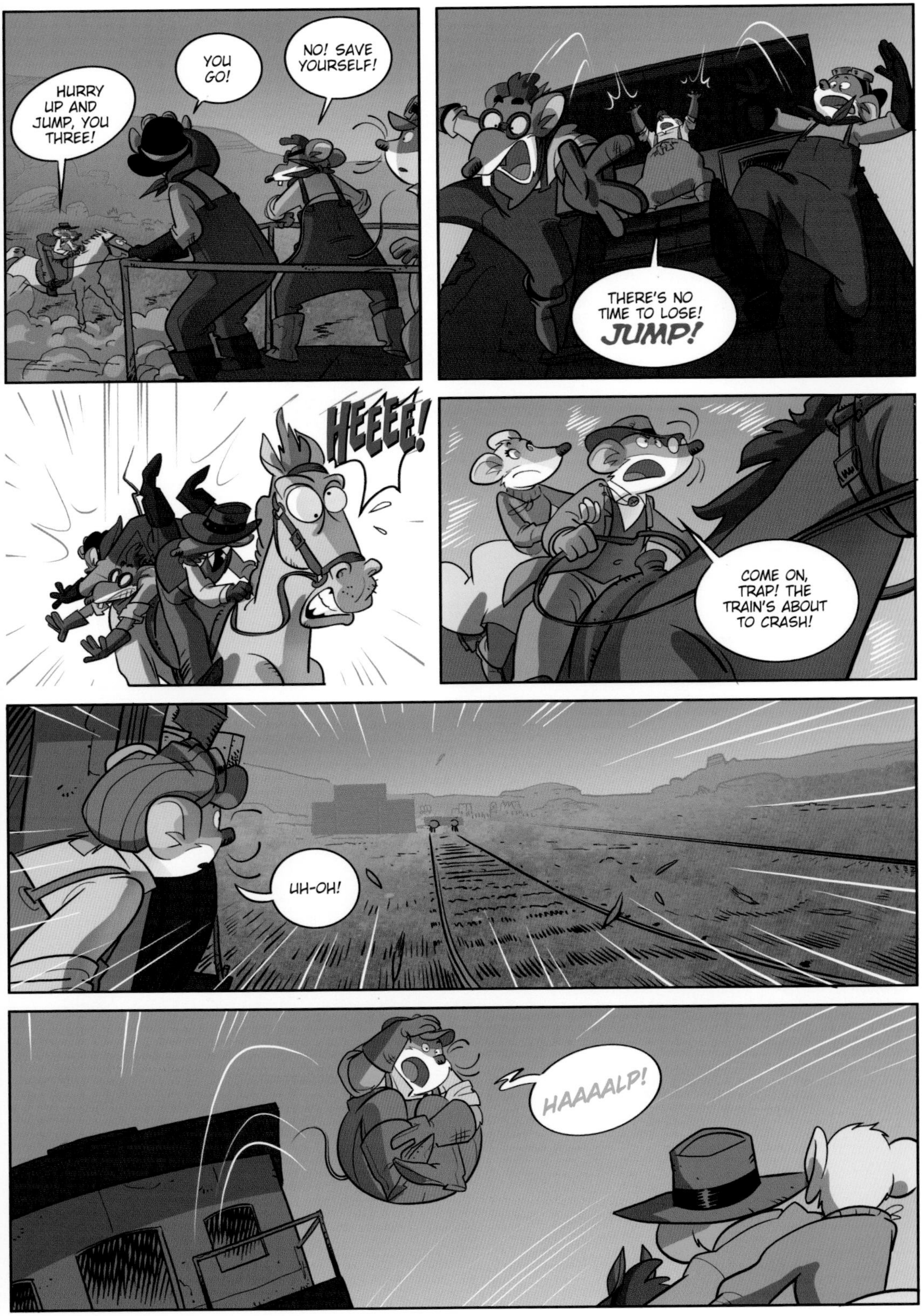
HURRY UP AND JUMP, YOU THREE!
YOU GO!
NO! SAVE YOURSELF!
THERE'S NO TIME TO LOSE! JUMP!
HEEEE!
COME ON, TRAP! THE TRAIN'S ABOUT TO CRASH!
UH-OH!
HAAAALP!

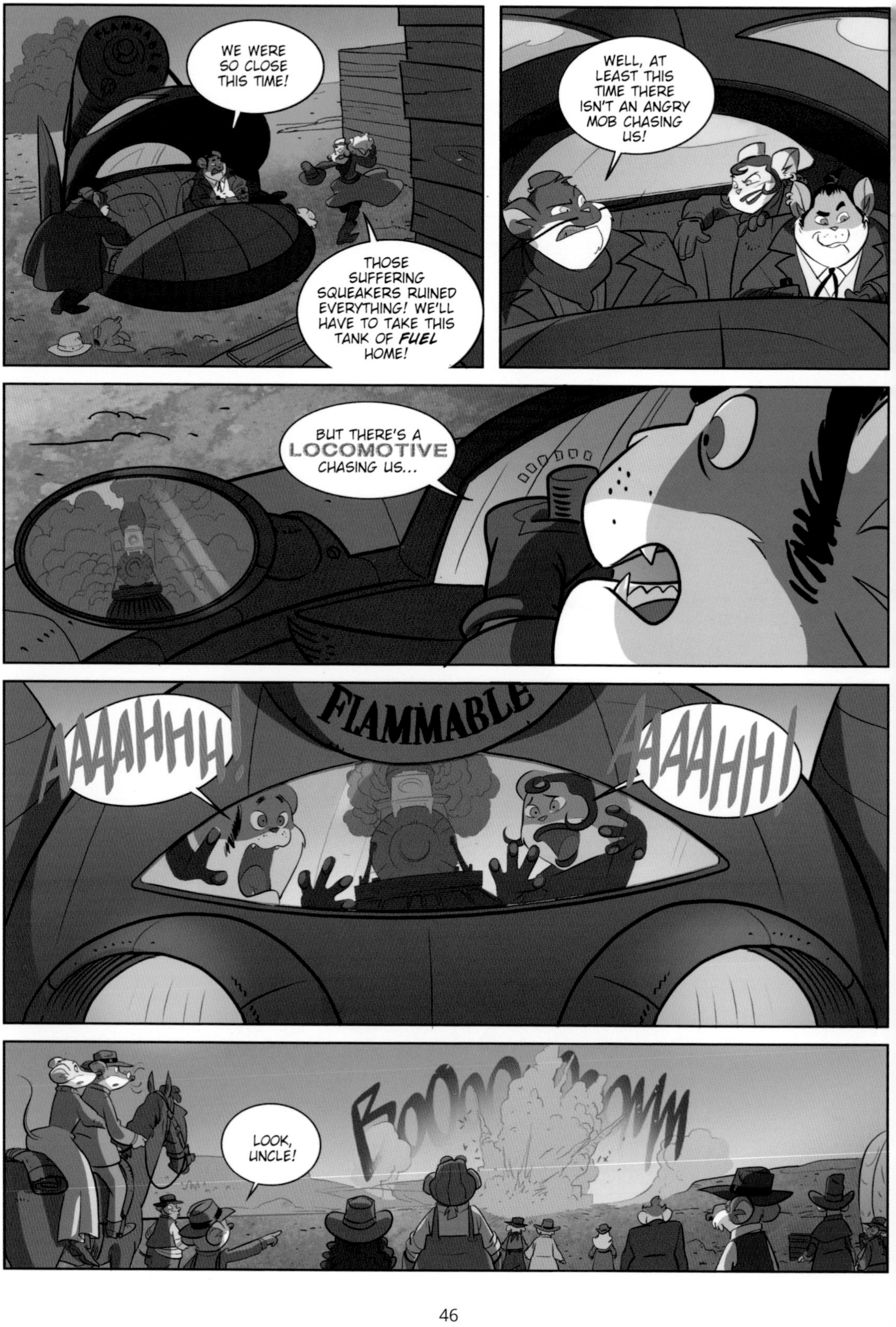
FLAMMABLE
WE WERE SO CLOSE THIS TIME!
THOSE SUFFERING SQUEAKERS RUINED EVERYTHING! WE'LL HAVE TO TAKE THIS TANK OF FUEL HOME!
WELL, AT LEAST THIS TIME THERE ISN'T AN ANGRY MOB CHASING US!
BUT THERE'S A LOCOMOTIVE CHASING US...
FLAMMABLE
AAAAHHH!
AAAAHH!
BOOOOOOOMM
LOOK, UNCLE!

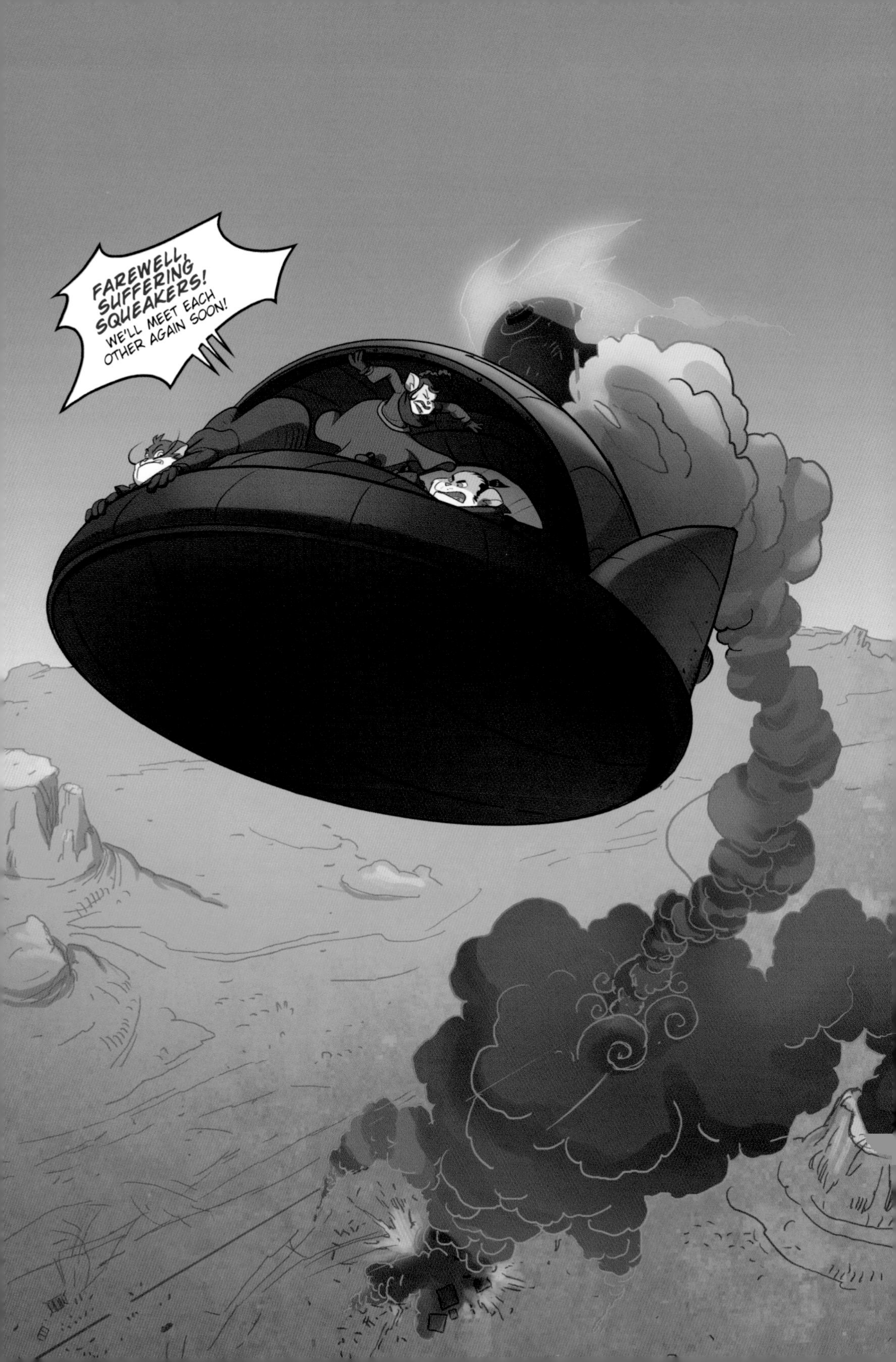
FAREWELL, SUFFERING SQUEAKERS!
WE'LL MEET EACH OTHER AGAIN SOON!

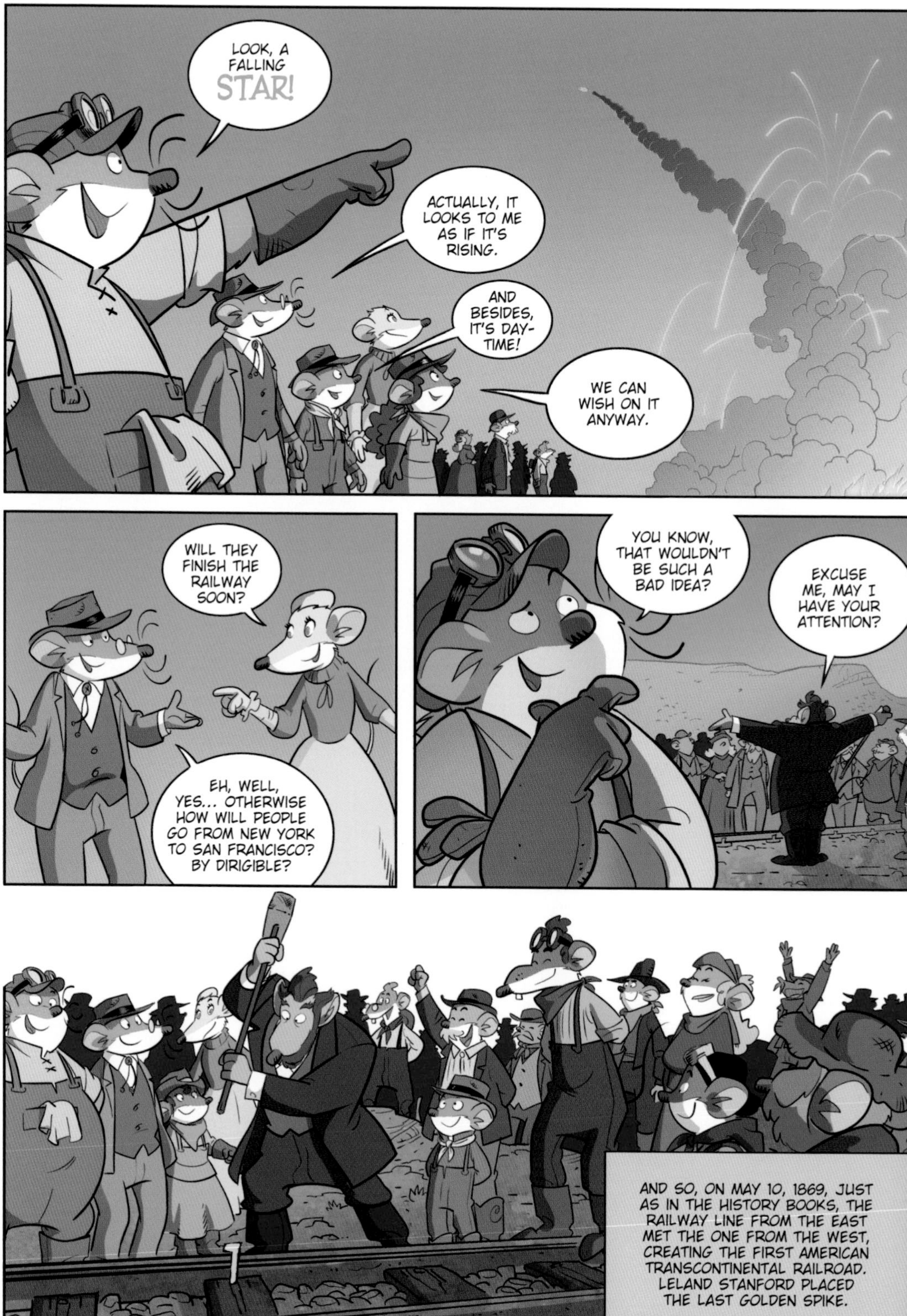
LOOK, A FALLING STAR!
ACTUALLY, IT LOOKS TO ME AS IF IT'S RISING.
AND BESIDES, IT'S DAY-TIME!
WE CAN WISH ON IT ANYWAY.
WILL THEY FINISH THE RAILWAY SOON?
EH, WELL, YES... OTHERWISE HOW WILL PEOPLE GO FROM NEW YORK TO SAN FRANCISCO? BY DIRIGIBLE?
YOU KNOW, THAT WOULDN'T BE SUCH A BAD IDEA?
EXCUSE ME, MAY I HAVE YOUR ATTENTION?
AND SO, ON MAY 10, 1869, JUST AS IN THE HISTORY BOOKS, THE RAILWAY LINE FROM THE EAST MET THE ONE FROM THE WEST, CREATING THE FIRST AMERICAN TRANSCONTINENTAL RAILROAD. LELAND STANFORD PLACED THE LAST GOLDEN SPIKE.

AT PRECISELY THAT MOMENT, A TELEGRAPH MESSAGE WAS SENT TO BOTH ENDS OF THE UNITED STATES, NEW YORK AND SAN FRANCISCO, TO SAY THAT WORK HAD BEEN COMPLETED...

...WHICH WAS CELEBRATED BY THE BELLS TOLLING.

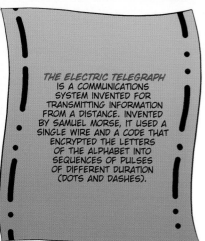

THE ELECTRIC TELEGRAPH IS A COMMUNICATIONS SYSTEM INVENTED FOR TRANSMITTING INFORMATION FROM A DISTANCE. INVENTED BY SAMUEL MORSE, IT USED A SINGLE WIRE AND A CODE THAT ENCRYPTED THE LETTERS OF THE ALPHABET INTO SEQUENCES OF PULSES OF DIFFERENT DURATION (DOTS AND DASHES).

ALL THAT REMAINED FOR US TO DO WAS SAY GOODBYE WHICH WAS MET WITH EVERYONE'S GRATITUDE...

COME ON, GERONIMO, WE'LL BE RUNNING IN JUST A FEW MINUTES!

THANKS, BUT AFTER ALL THAT ACTION, I COULD USE SOME PEACE AND QUIET!

COME ON, KIDS! OUR, —AHEM— RIDE, JUST ARRIVED!

WHIRR

WHIRR

WHIRR

49

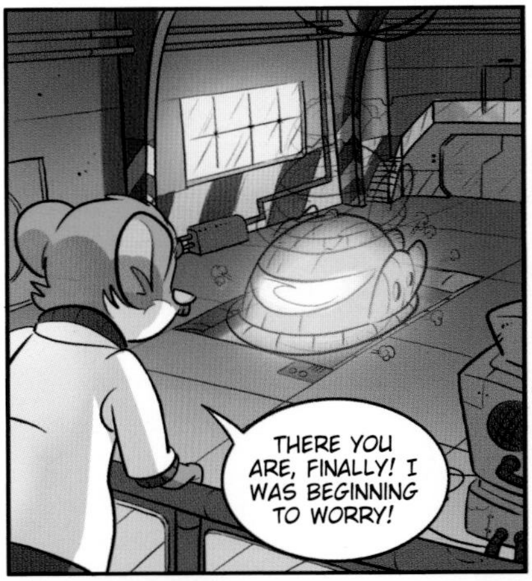
THERE YOU ARE, FINALLY! I WAS BEGINNING TO WORRY!

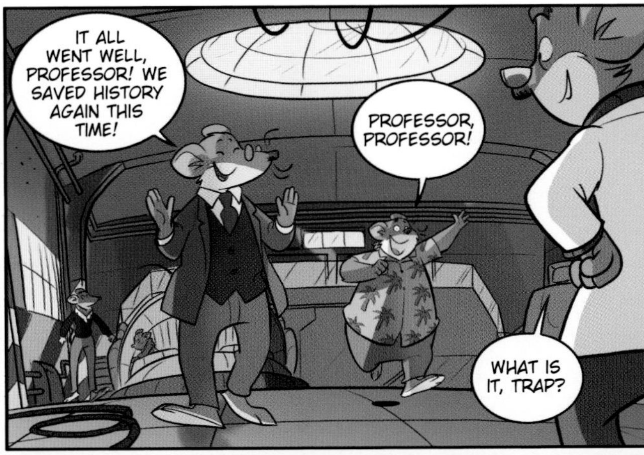
IT ALL WENT WELL, PROFESSOR! WE SAVED HISTORY AGAIN THIS TIME!
PROFESSOR, PROFESSOR!
WHAT IS IT, TRAP?

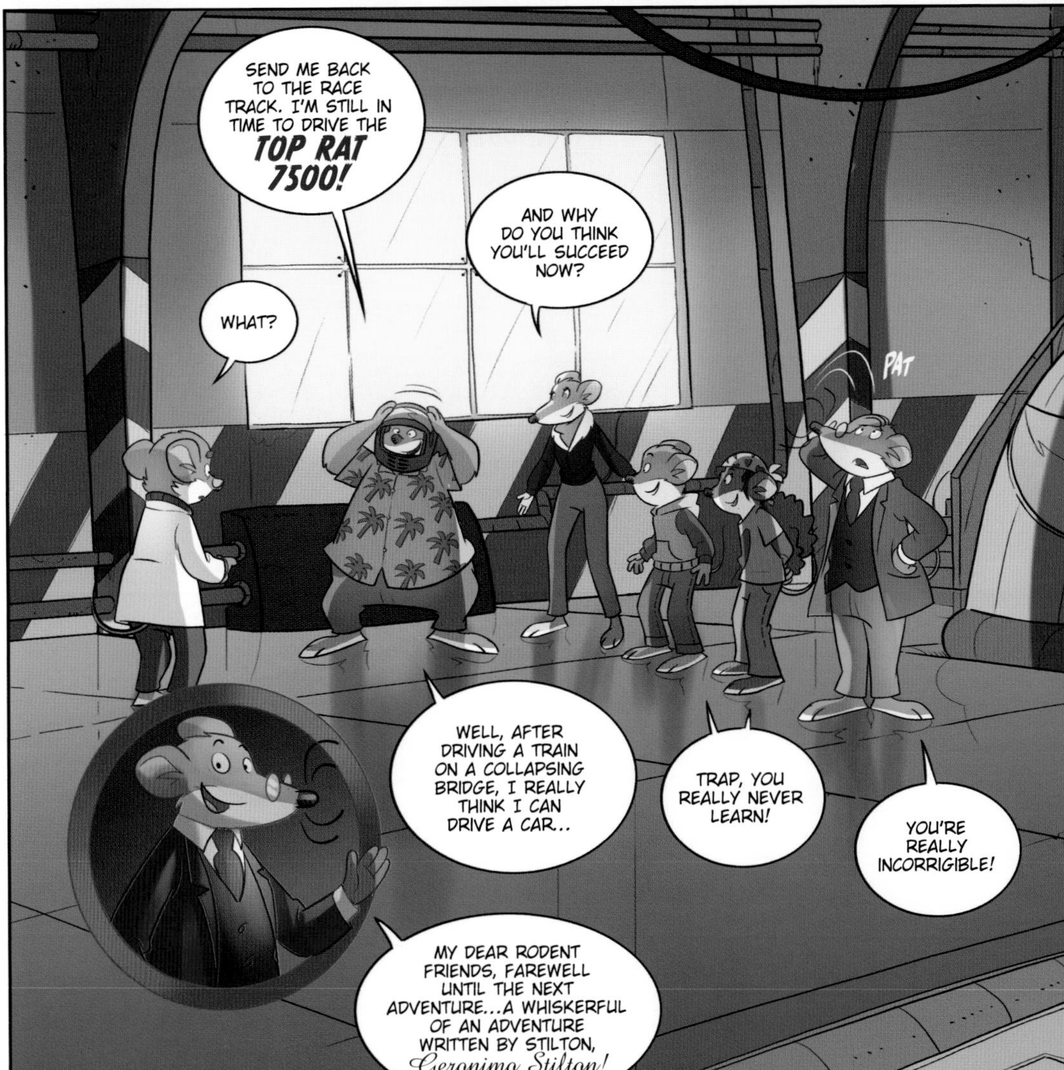
SEND ME BACK TO THE RACE TRACK. I'M STILL IN TIME TO DRIVE THE TOP RAT 7500!
WHAT?
AND WHY DO YOU THINK YOU'LL SUCCEED NOW?
PAT
WELL, AFTER DRIVING A TRAIN ON A COLLAPSING BRIDGE, I REALLY THINK I CAN DRIVE A CAR...
TRAP, YOU REALLY NEVER LEARN!
YOU'RE REALLY INCORRIGIBLE!
MY DEAR RODENT FRIENDS, FAREWELL UNTIL THE NEXT ADVENTURE...A WHISKERFUL OF AN ADVENTURE WRITTEN BY STILTON, Geronimo Stilton!

THE FIRST MOUSE ON THE MOON

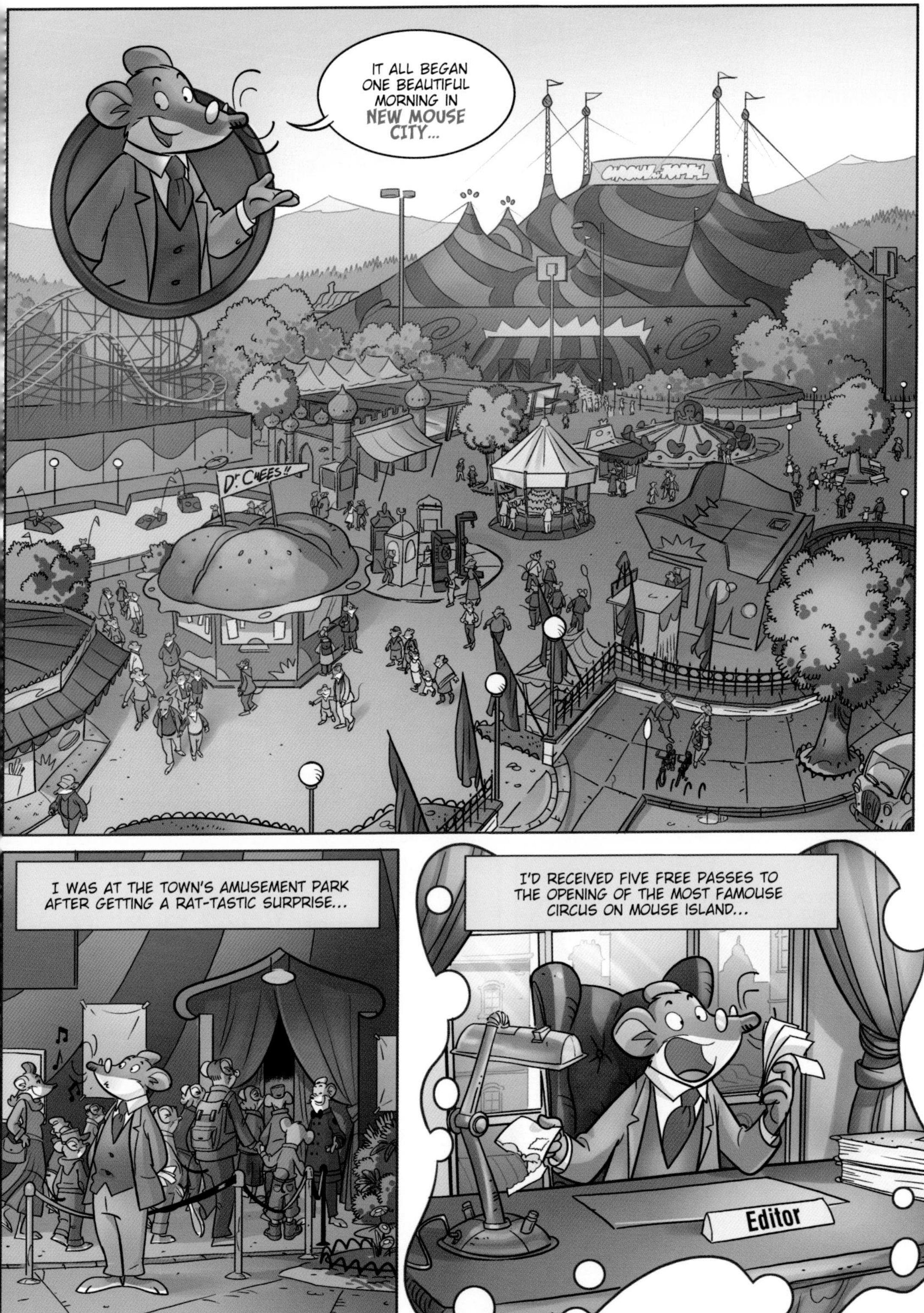
IT ALL BEGAN ONE BEAUTIFUL MORNING IN NEW MOUSE CITY...
I WAS AT THE TOWN'S AMUSEMENT PARK AFTER GETTING A RAT-TASTIC SURPRISE...
I'D RECEIVED FIVE FREE PASSES TO THE OPENING OF THE MOST FAMOUSE CIRCUS ON MOUSE ISLAND...
Editor

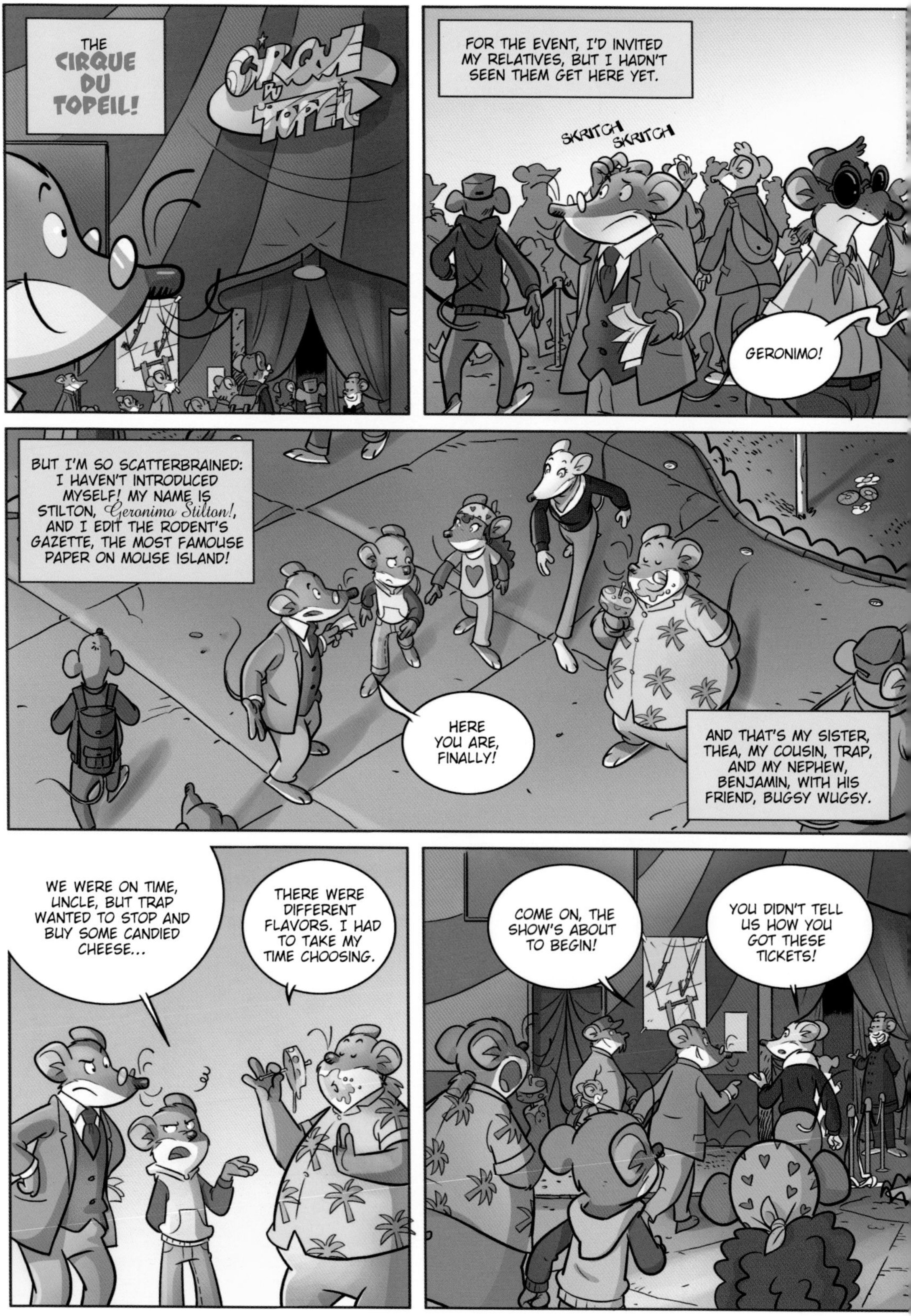
THE CIRQUE DU TOPEIL!
CIRQUE DU TOPEIL
FOR THE EVENT, I'D INVITED MY RELATIVES, BUT I HADN'T SEEN THEM GET HERE YET.
SKRITCH SKRITCH
GERONIMO!
BUT I'M SO SCATTERBRAINED: I HAVEN'T INTRODUCED MYSELF! MY NAME IS STILTON, *Geronimo Stilton!*, AND I EDIT THE RODENT'S GAZETTE, THE MOST FAMOUSE PAPER ON MOUSE ISLAND!
HERE YOU ARE, FINALLY!
AND THAT'S MY SISTER, THEA, MY COUSIN, TRAP, AND MY NEPHEW, BENJAMIN, WITH HIS FRIEND, BUGSY WUGSY.
WE WERE ON TIME, UNCLE, BUT TRAP WANTED TO STOP AND BUY SOME CANDIED CHEESE...
THERE WERE DIFFERENT FLAVORS. I HAD TO TAKE MY TIME CHOOSING.
COME ON, THE SHOW'S ABOUT TO BEGIN!
YOU DIDN'T TELL US HOW YOU GOT THESE TICKETS!

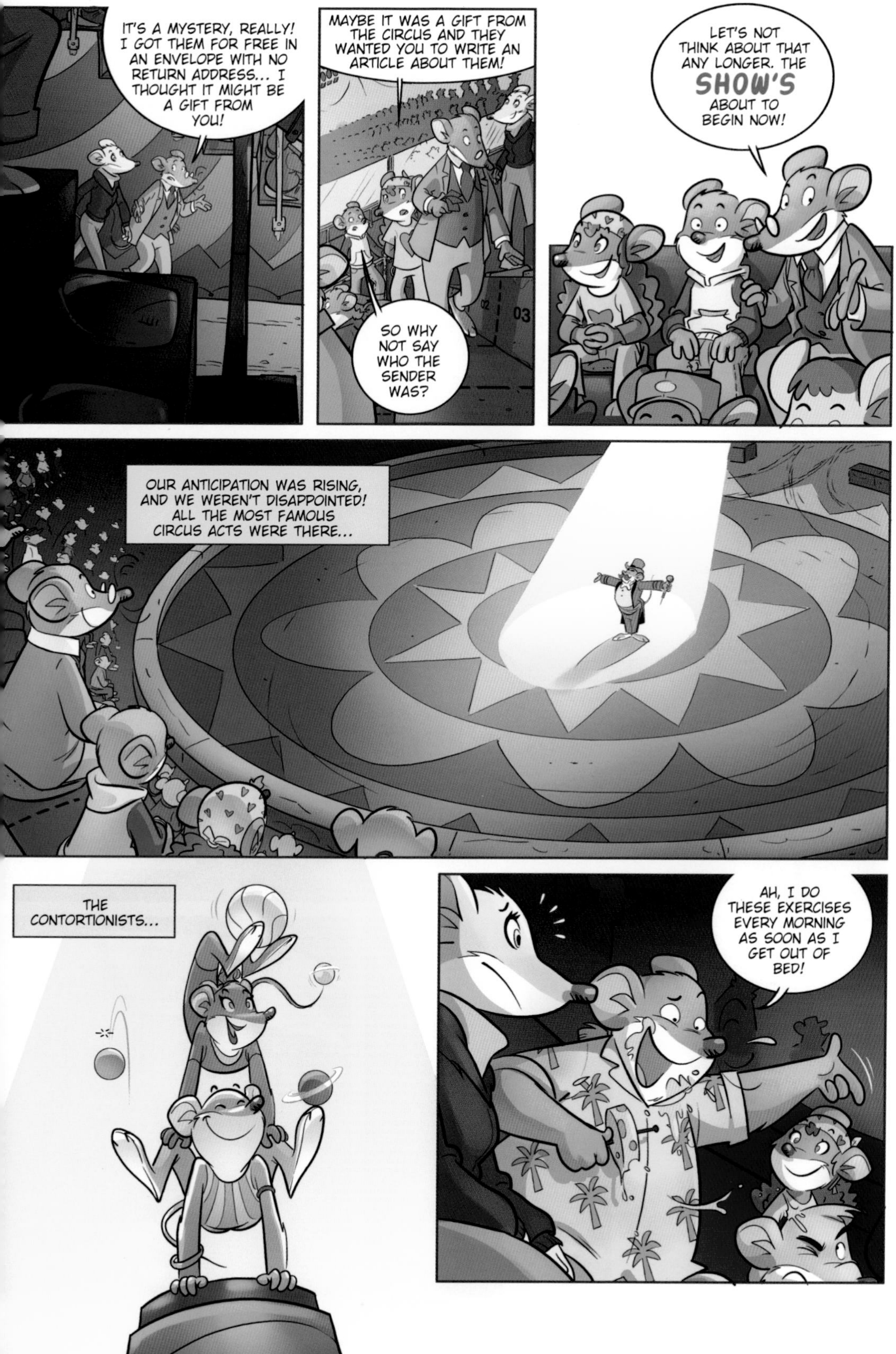
IT'S A MYSTERY, REALLY! I GOT THEM FOR FREE IN AN ENVELOPE WITH NO RETURN ADDRESS... I THOUGHT IT MIGHT BE A GIFT FROM YOU!
MAYBE IT WAS A GIFT FROM THE CIRCUS AND THEY WANTED YOU TO WRITE AN ARTICLE ABOUT THEM!
SO WHY NOT SAY WHO THE SENDER WAS?
LET'S NOT THINK ABOUT THAT ANY LONGER. THE SHOW'S ABOUT TO BEGIN NOW!
OUR ANTICIPATION WAS RISING, AND WE WEREN'T DISAPPOINTED! ALL THE MOST FAMOUS CIRCUS ACTS WERE THERE...
THE CONTORTIONISTS...
AH, I DO THESE EXERCISES EVERY MORNING AS SOON AS I GET OUT OF BED!

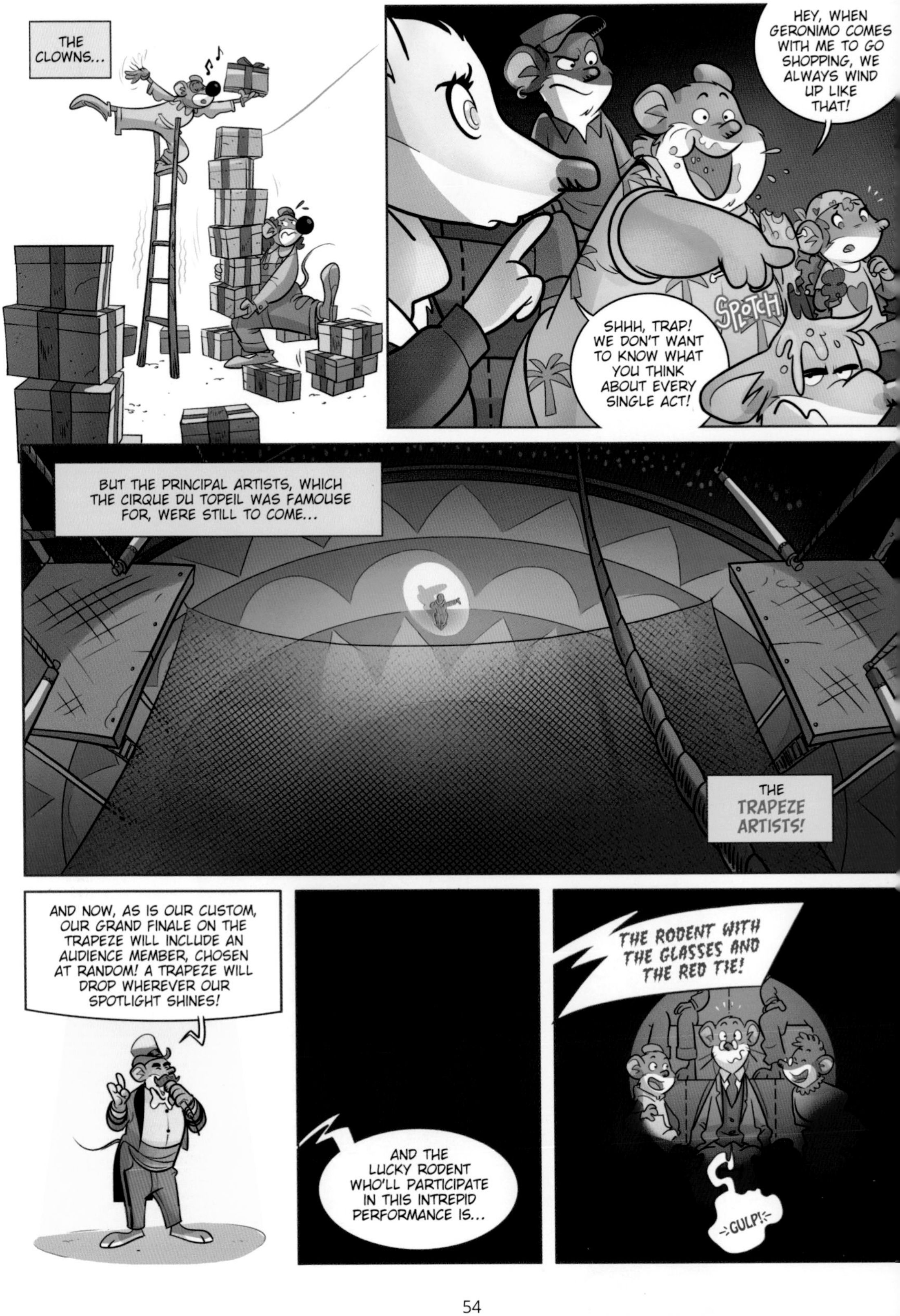
THE CLOWNS...
HEY, WHEN GERONIMO COMES WITH ME TO GO SHOPPING, WE ALWAYS WIND UP LIKE THAT!
SPLOTCH
SHHH, TRAP! WE DON'T WANT TO KNOW WHAT YOU THINK ABOUT EVERY SINGLE ACT!
BUT THE PRINCIPAL ARTISTS, WHICH THE CIRQUE DU TOPEIL WAS FAMOUSE FOR, WERE STILL TO COME...
THE TRAPEZE ARTISTS!
AND NOW, AS IS OUR CUSTOM, OUR GRAND FINALE ON THE TRAPEZE WILL INCLUDE AN AUDIENCE MEMBER, CHOSEN AT RANDOM! A TRAPEZE WILL DROP WHEREVER OUR SPOTLIGHT SHINES!
AND THE LUCKY RODENT WHO'LL PARTICIPATE IN THIS INTREPID PERFORMANCE IS...
THE RODENT WITH THE GLASSES AND THE RED TIE!
GULP!

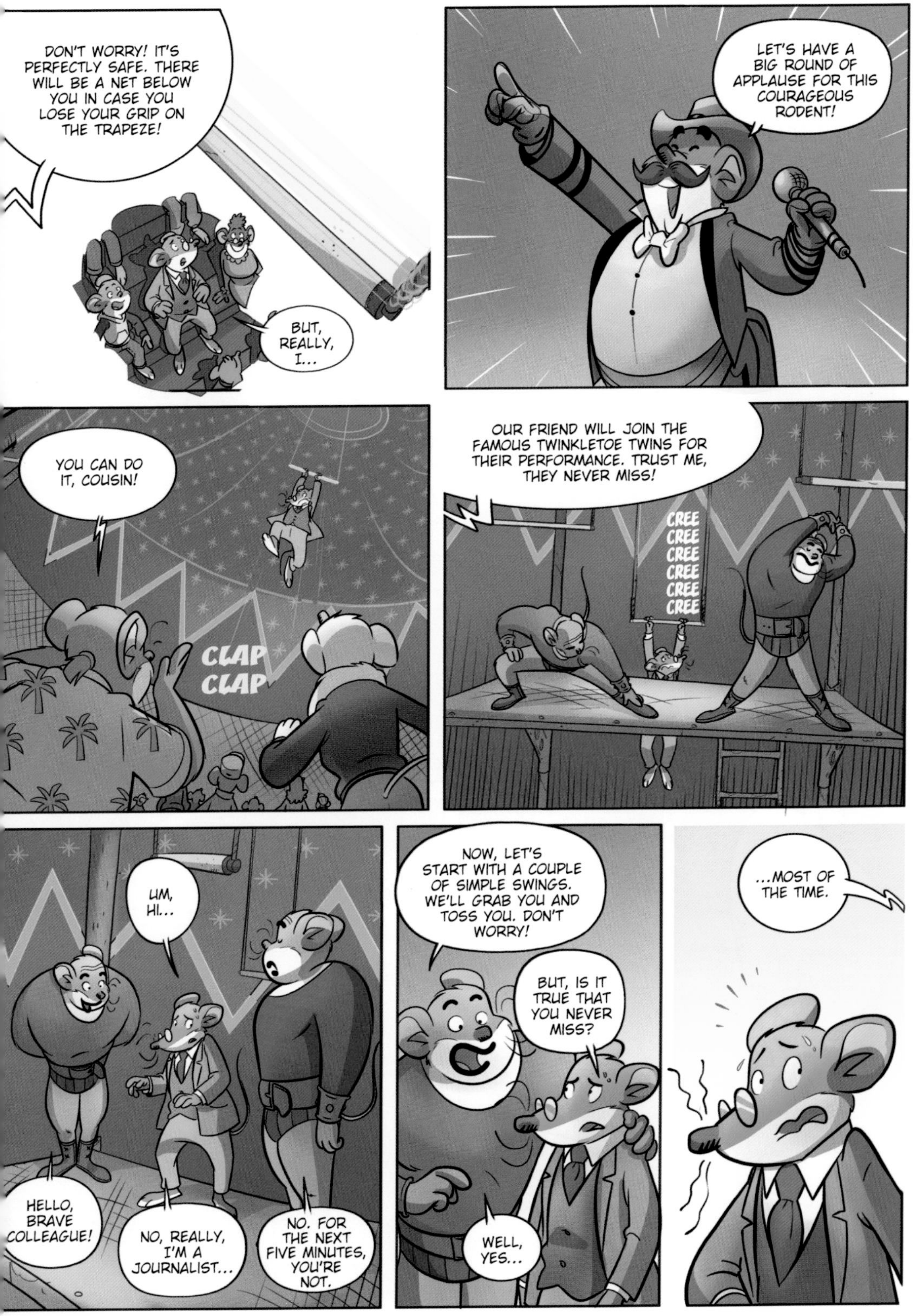
DON'T WORRY! IT'S PERFECTLY SAFE. THERE WILL BE A NET BELOW YOU IN CASE YOU LOSE YOUR GRIP ON THE TRAPEZE!
BUT, REALLY, I...
LET'S HAVE A BIG ROUND OF APPLAUSE FOR THIS COURAGEOUS RODENT!
YOU CAN DO IT, COUSIN!
CLAP CLAP
OUR FRIEND WILL JOIN THE FAMOUS TWINKLETOE TWINS FOR THEIR PERFORMANCE. TRUST ME, THEY NEVER MISS!
CREE CREE CREE CREE CREE CREE
UM, HI...
HELLO, BRAVE COLLEAGUE!
NO, REALLY, I'M A JOURNALIST...
NO. FOR THE NEXT FIVE MINUTES, YOU'RE NOT.
NOW, LET'S START WITH A COUPLE OF SIMPLE SWINGS. WE'LL GRAB YOU AND TOSS YOU. DON'T WORRY!
BUT, IS IT TRUE THAT YOU NEVER MISS?
WELL, YES...
...MOST OF THE TIME.

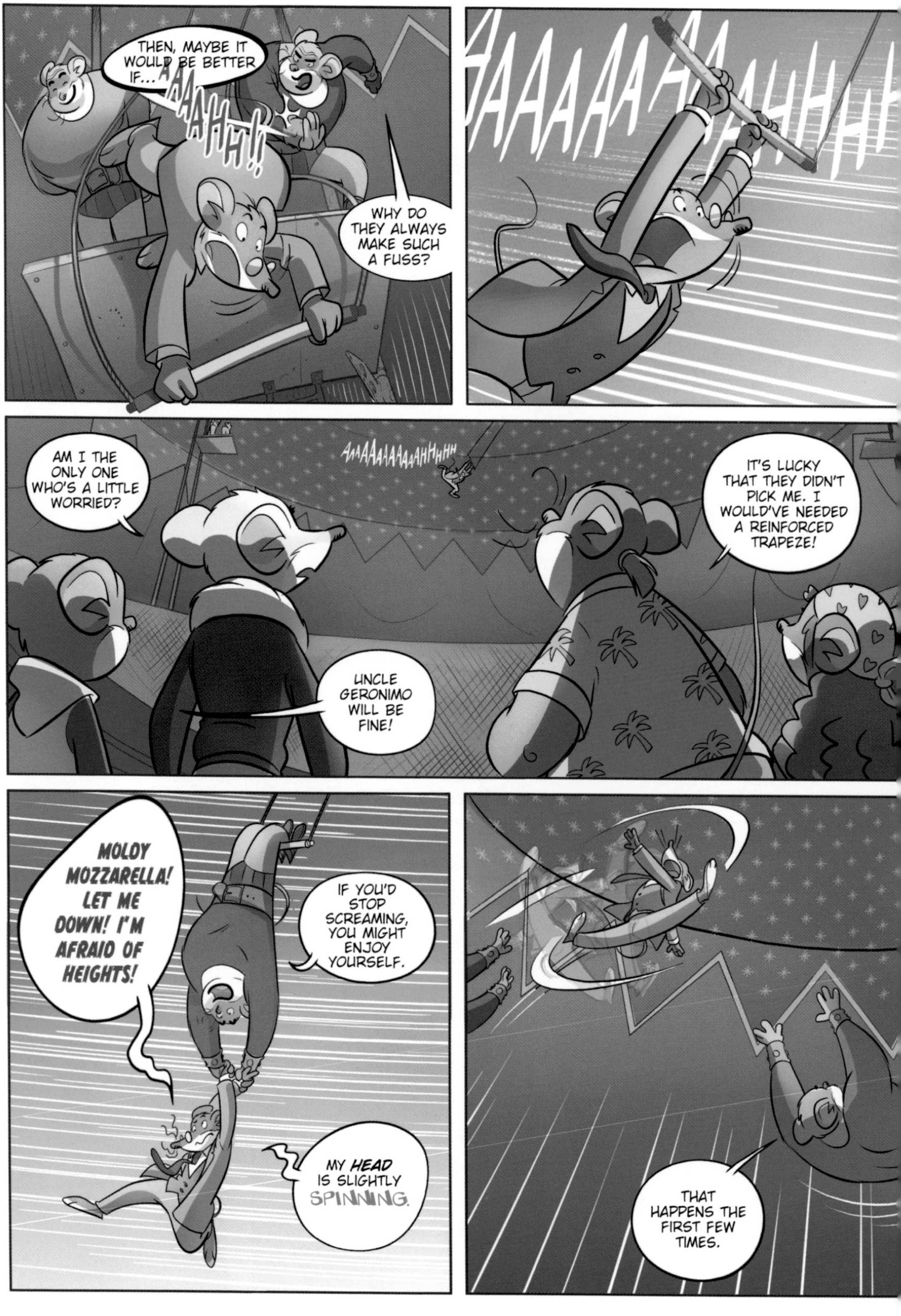
THEN, MAYBE IT WOULD BE BETTER IF...
AAAHHH!!
WHY DO THEY ALWAYS MAKE SUCH A FUSS?
AAAAAAAAAAHHHHH
AM I THE ONLY ONE WHO'S A LITTLE WORRIED?
AAAAAAAAAAAHHHHH
IT'S LUCKY THAT THEY DIDN'T PICK ME. I WOULD'VE NEEDED A REINFORCED TRAPEZE!
UNCLE GERONIMO WILL BE FINE!
MOLDY MOZZARELLA! LET ME DOWN! I'M AFRAID OF HEIGHTS!
IF YOU'D STOP SCREAMING, YOU MIGHT ENJOY YOURSELF.
MY HEAD IS SLIGHTLY SPINNING.
THAT HAPPENS THE FIRST FEW TIMES.

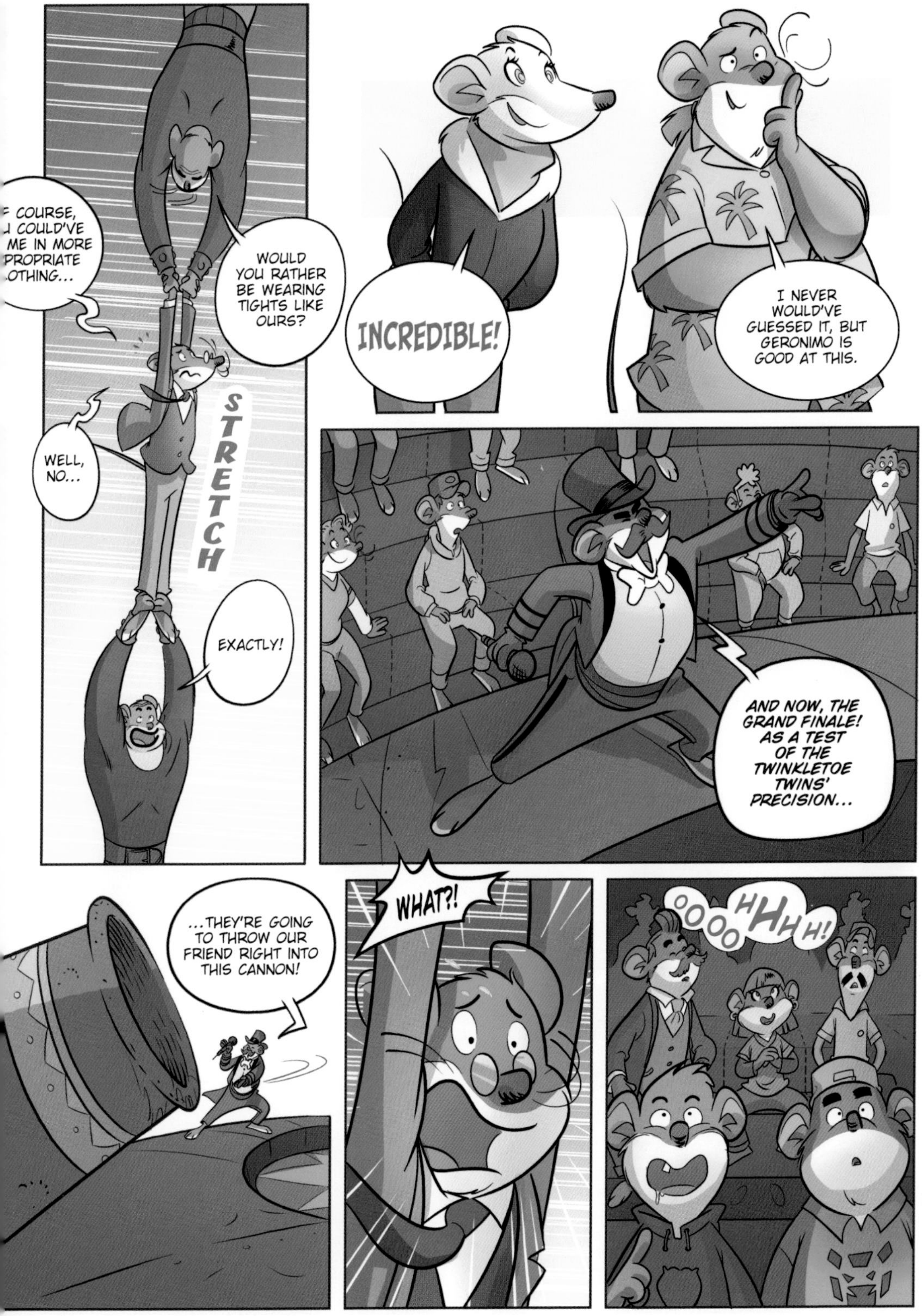
F COURSE, U COULD'VE ME IN MORE PROPRIATE OTHING...
WOULD YOU RATHER BE WEARING TIGHTS LIKE OURS?
WELL, NO...
STRETCH
EXACTLY!
INCREDIBLE!
I NEVER WOULD'VE GUESSED IT, BUT GERONIMO IS GOOD AT THIS.
AND NOW, THE GRAND FINALE! AS A TEST OF THE TWINKLETOE TWINS' PRECISION...
...THEY'RE GOING TO THROW OUR FRIEND RIGHT INTO THIS CANNON!
WHAT?!
OOOOHHHH!

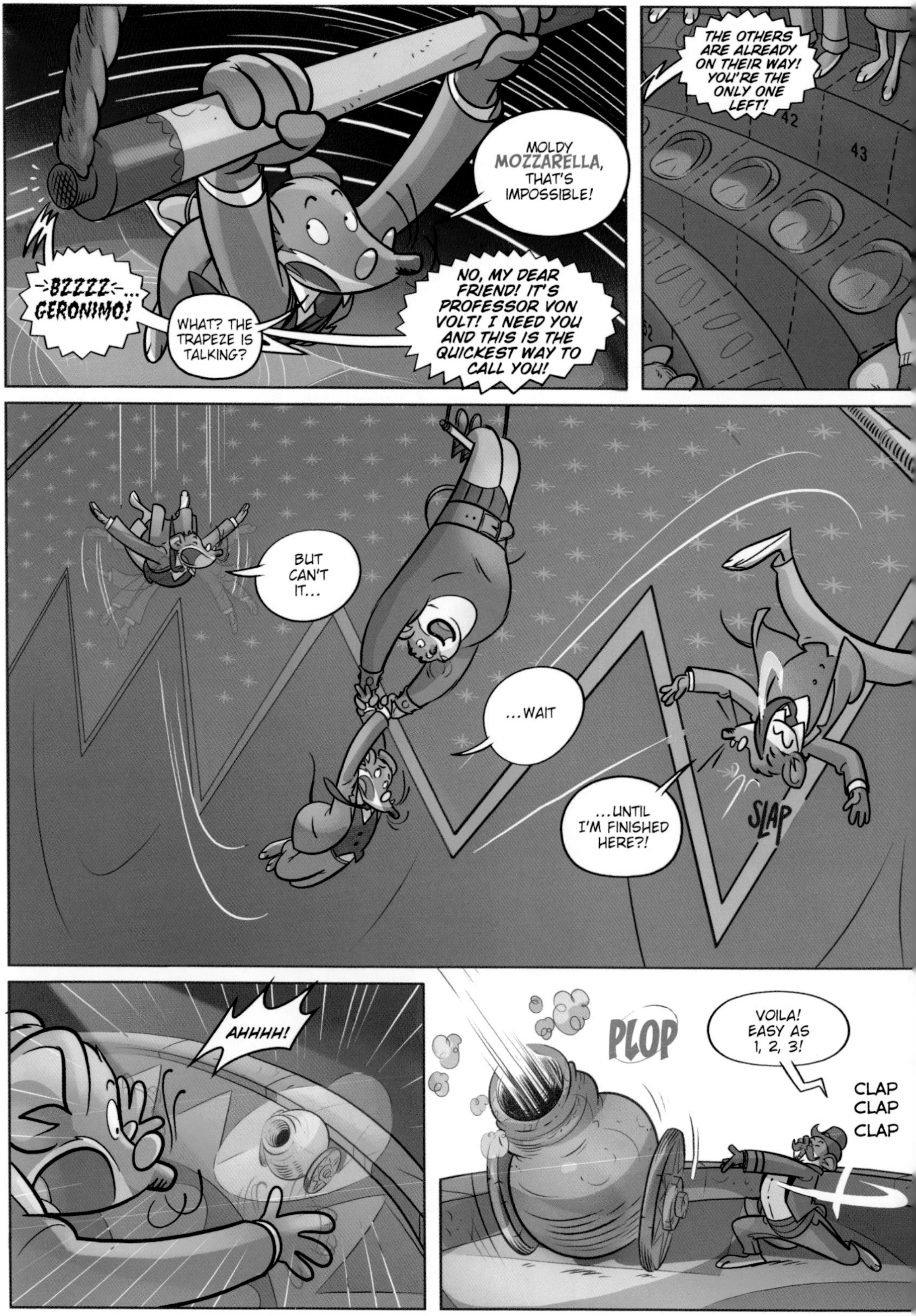
MOLDY MOZZARELLA, THAT'S IMPOSSIBLE!
BZZZZ... GERONIMO!
WHAT? THE TRAPEZE IS TALKING?
NO, MY DEAR FRIEND! IT'S PROFESSOR VON VOLT! I NEED YOU AND THIS IS THE QUICKEST WAY TO CALL YOU!
THE OTHERS ARE ALREADY ON THEIR WAY! YOU'RE THE ONLY ONE LEFT!
42
43
BUT CAN'T IT...
...WAIT
...UNTIL I'M FINISHED HERE?!
SLAP
AHHHH!
PLOP
VOILA! EASY AS 1, 2, 3!
CLAP
CLAP
CLAP

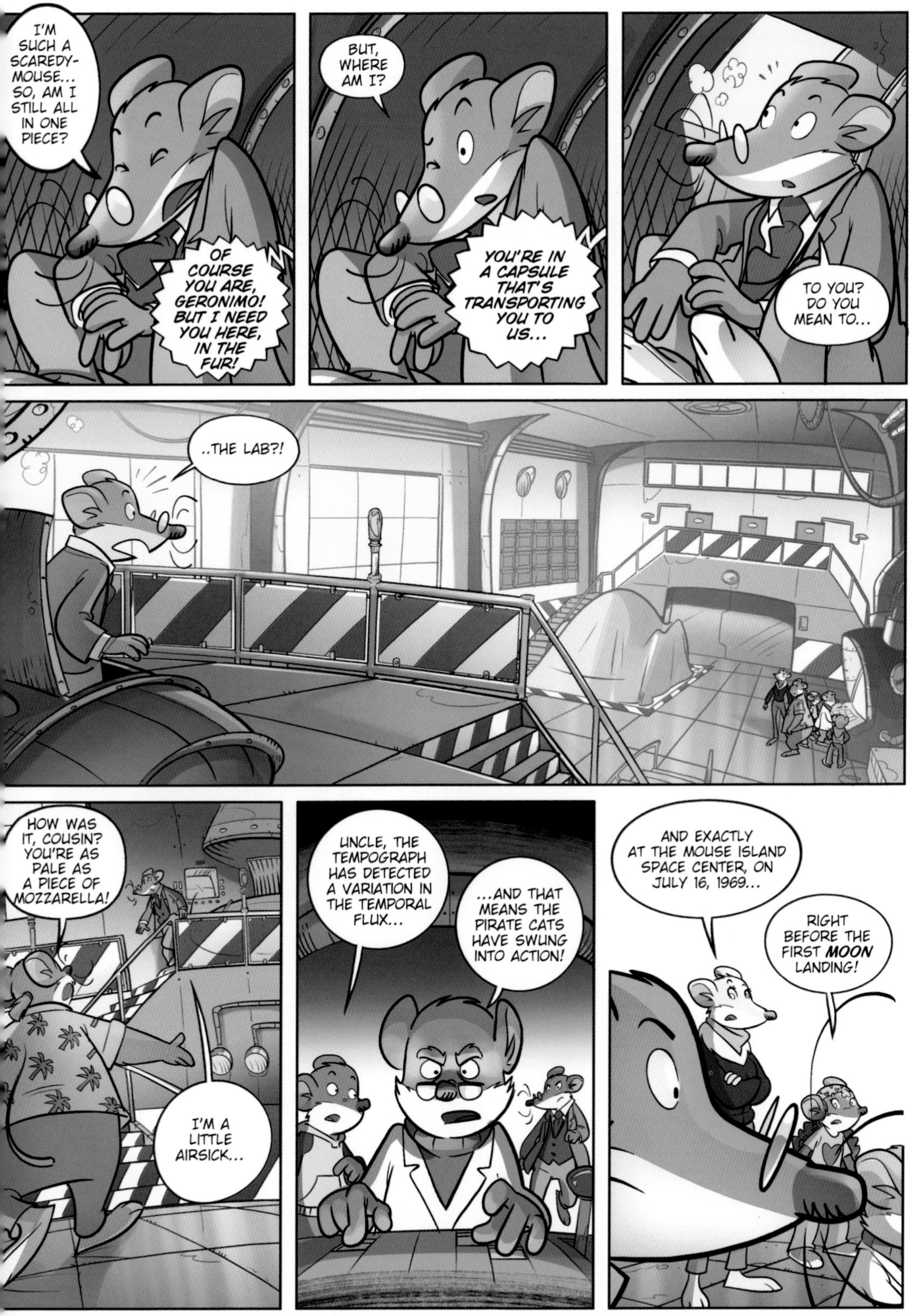
I'M SUCH A SCAREDY-MOUSE... SO, AM I STILL ALL IN ONE PIECE?
OF COURSE YOU ARE, GERONIMO! BUT I NEED YOU HERE, IN THE FUR!
BUT, WHERE AM I?
YOU'RE IN A CAPSULE THAT'S TRANSPORTING YOU TO US...
TO YOU? DO YOU MEAN TO...
..THE LAB?!
HOW WAS IT, COUSIN? YOU'RE AS PALE AS A PIECE OF MOZZARELLA!
I'M A LITTLE AIRSICK...
UNCLE, THE TEMPOGRAPH HAS DETECTED A VARIATION IN THE TEMPORAL FLUX...
...AND THAT MEANS THE PIRATE CATS HAVE SWUNG INTO ACTION!
AND EXACTLY AT THE MOUSE ISLAND SPACE CENTER, ON JULY 16, 1969...
RIGHT BEFORE THE FIRST MOON LANDING!

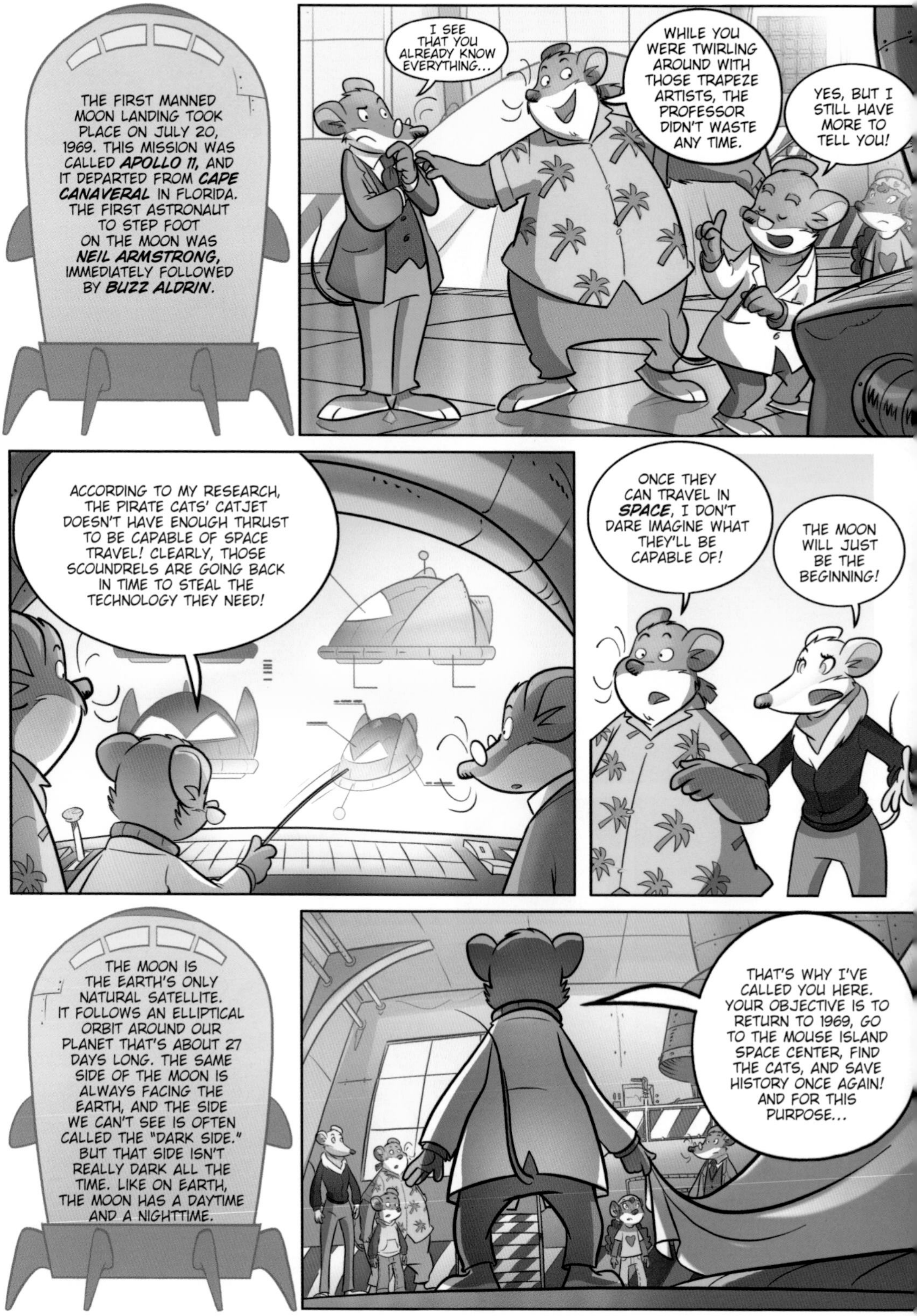
THE FIRST MANNED MOON LANDING TOOK PLACE ON JULY 20, 1969. THIS MISSION WAS CALLED **APOLLO 11,** AND IT DEPARTED FROM **CAPE CANAVERAL** IN FLORIDA. THE FIRST ASTRONAUT TO STEP FOOT ON THE MOON WAS **NEIL ARMSTRONG,** IMMEDIATELY FOLLOWED BY **BUZZ ALDRIN**.
I SEE THAT YOU ALREADY KNOW EVERYTHING...
WHILE YOU WERE TWIRLING AROUND WITH THOSE TRAPEZE ARTISTS, THE PROFESSOR DIDN'T WASTE ANY TIME.
YES, BUT I STILL HAVE MORE TO TELL YOU!
ACCORDING TO MY RESEARCH, THE PIRATE CATS' CATJET DOESN'T HAVE ENOUGH THRUST TO BE CAPABLE OF SPACE TRAVEL! CLEARLY, THOSE SCOUNDRELS ARE GOING BACK IN TIME TO STEAL THE TECHNOLOGY THEY NEED!
ONCE THEY CAN TRAVEL IN **SPACE**, I DON'T DARE IMAGINE WHAT THEY'LL BE CAPABLE OF!
THE MOON WILL JUST BE THE BEGINNING!
THE MOON IS THE EARTH'S ONLY NATURAL SATELLITE. IT FOLLOWS AN ELLIPTICAL ORBIT AROUND OUR PLANET THAT'S ABOUT 27 DAYS LONG. THE SAME SIDE OF THE MOON IS ALWAYS FACING THE EARTH, AND THE SIDE WE CAN'T SEE IS OFTEN CALLED THE "DARK SIDE." BUT THAT SIDE ISN'T REALLY DARK ALL THE TIME. LIKE ON EARTH, THE MOON HAS A DAYTIME AND A NIGHTTIME.
THAT'S WHY I'VE CALLED YOU HERE. YOUR OBJECTIVE IS TO RETURN TO 1969, GO TO THE MOUSE ISLAND SPACE CENTER, FIND THE CATS, AND SAVE HISTORY ONCE AGAIN! AND FOR THIS PURPOSE...

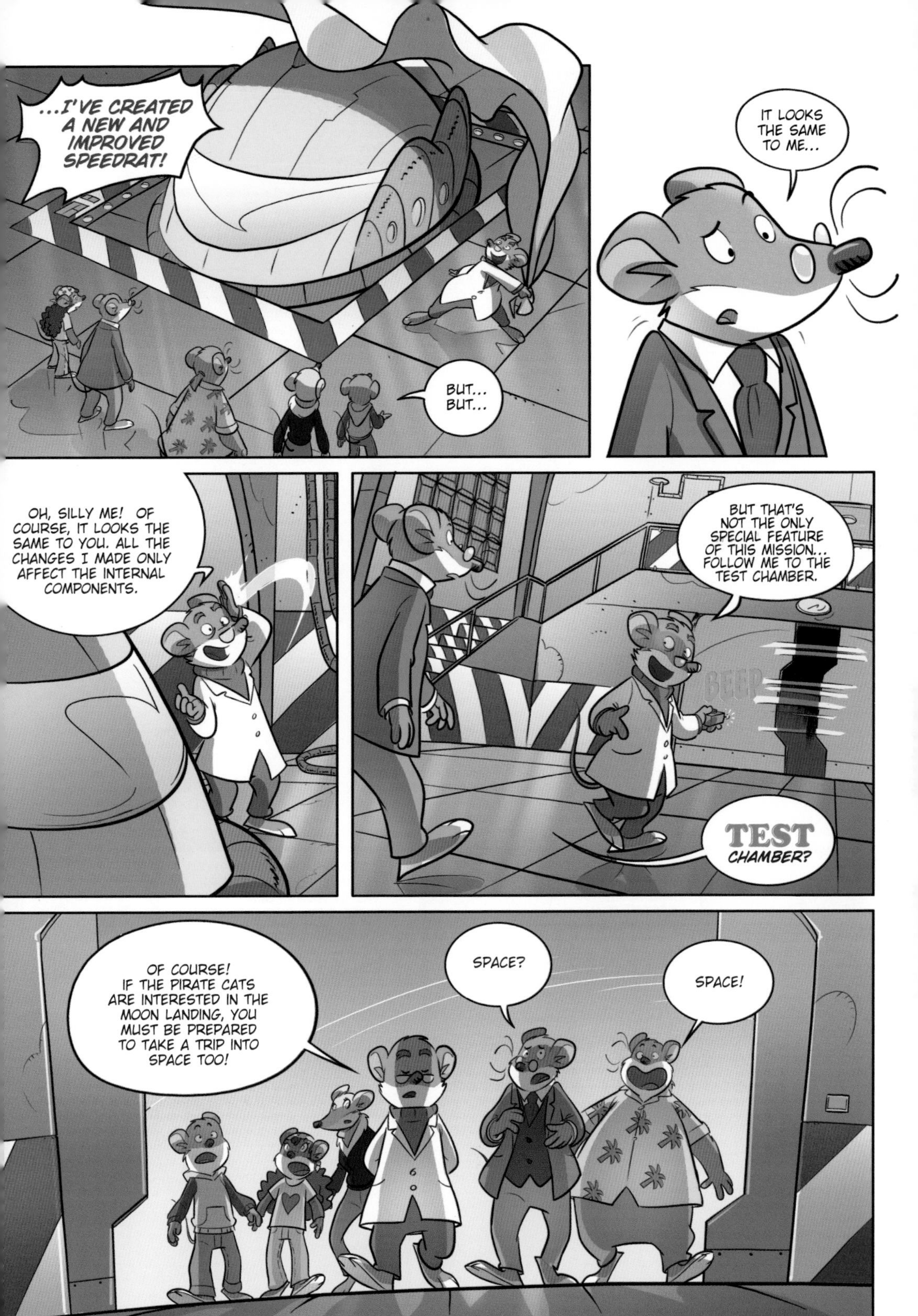
...I'VE CREATED A NEW AND IMPROVED SPEEDRAT!
BUT... BUT...
IT LOOKS THE SAME TO ME...
OH, SILLY ME! OF COURSE, IT LOOKS THE SAME TO YOU. ALL THE CHANGES I MADE ONLY AFFECT THE INTERNAL COMPONENTS.
BUT THAT'S NOT THE ONLY SPECIAL FEATURE OF THIS MISSION... FOLLOW ME TO THE TEST CHAMBER.
BEEP
TEST CHAMBER?
OF COURSE! IF THE PIRATE CATS ARE INTERESTED IN THE MOON LANDING, YOU MUST BE PREPARED TO TAKE A TRIP INTO SPACE TOO!
SPACE?
SPACE!

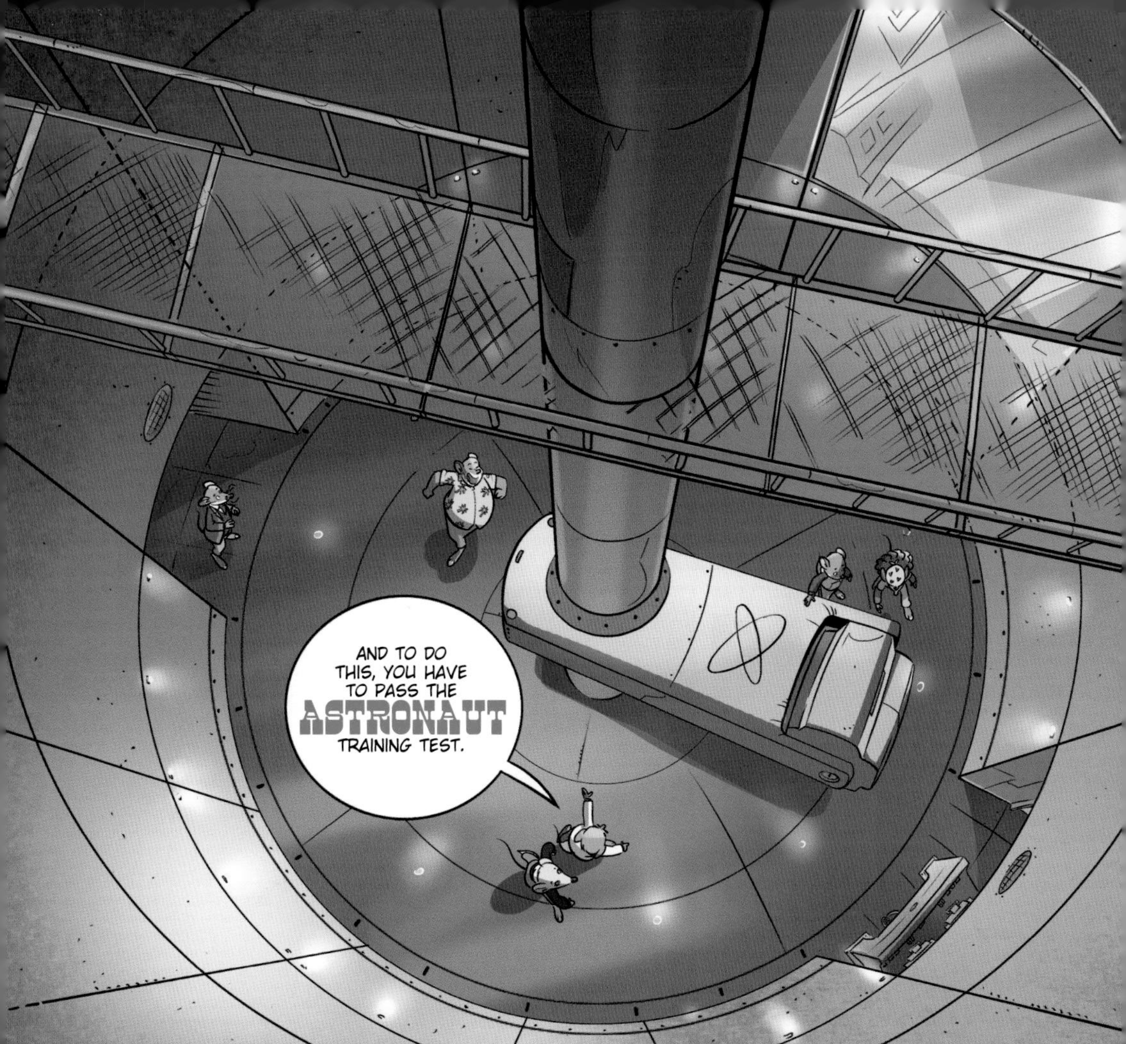
AND TO DO THIS, YOU HAVE TO PASS THE ASTRONAUT TRAINING TEST.

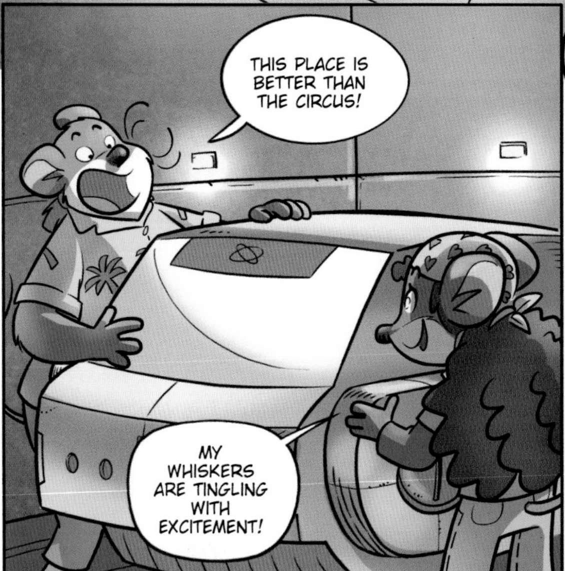
THIS PLACE IS BETTER THAN THE CIRCUS!
MY WHISKERS ARE TINGLING WITH EXCITEMENT!

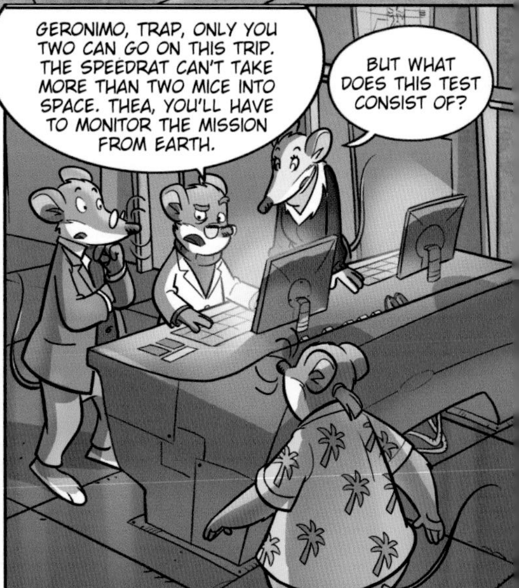
GERONIMO, TRAP, ONLY YOU TWO CAN GO ON THIS TRIP. THE SPEEDRAT CAN'T TAKE MORE THAN TWO MICE INTO SPACE. THEA, YOU'LL HAVE TO MONITOR THE MISSION FROM EARTH.
BUT WHAT DOES THIS TEST CONSIST OF?

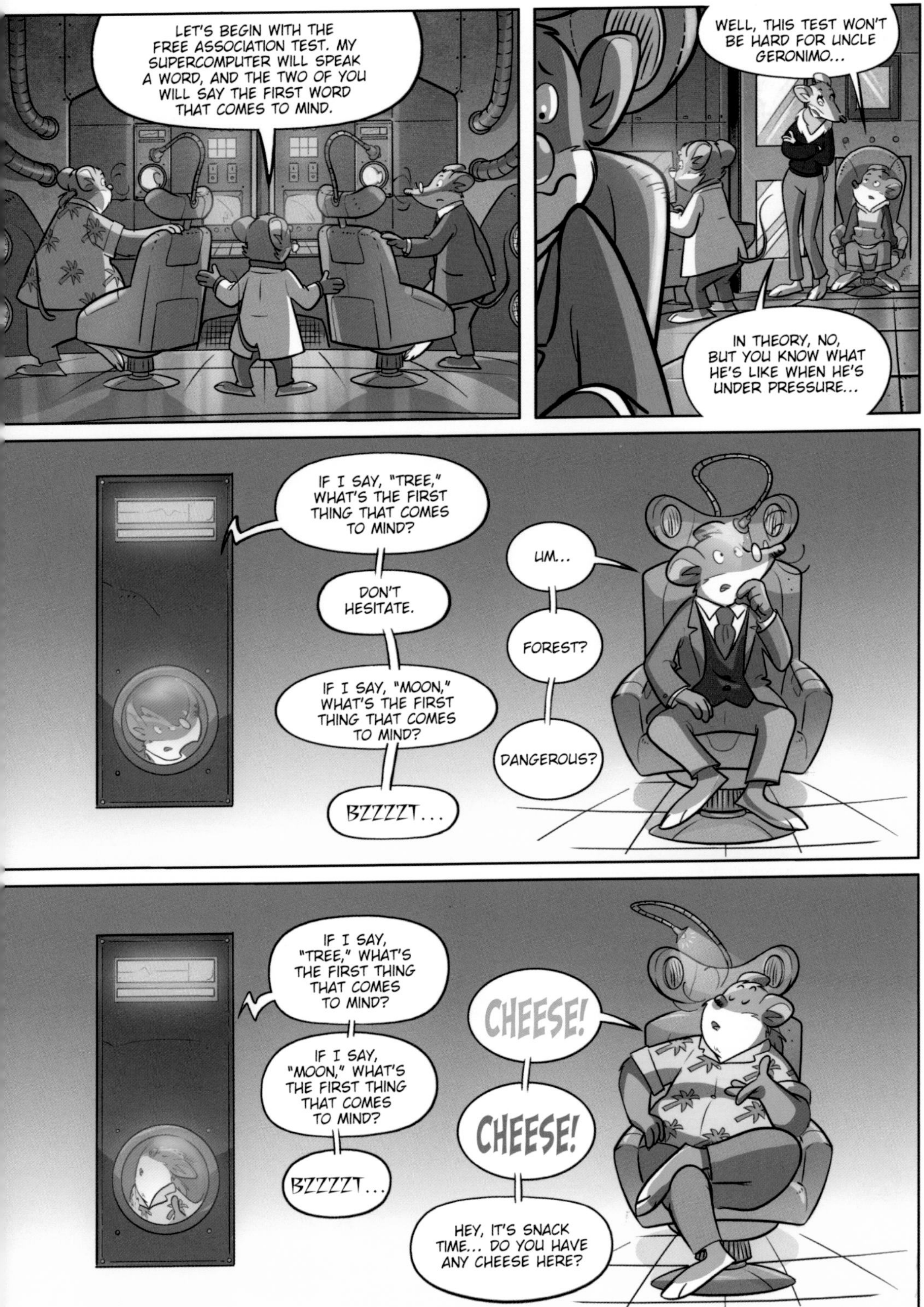
LET'S BEGIN WITH THE FREE ASSOCIATION TEST. MY SUPERCOMPUTER WILL SPEAK A WORD, AND THE TWO OF YOU WILL SAY THE FIRST WORD THAT COMES TO MIND.
WELL, THIS TEST WON'T BE HARD FOR UNCLE GERONIMO...
IN THEORY, NO, BUT YOU KNOW WHAT HE'S LIKE WHEN HE'S UNDER PRESSURE...
IF I SAY, "TREE," WHAT'S THE FIRST THING THAT COMES TO MIND?
UM...
DON'T HESITATE.
FOREST?
IF I SAY, "MOON," WHAT'S THE FIRST THING THAT COMES TO MIND?
DANGEROUS?
BZZZZT...
IF I SAY, "TREE," WHAT'S THE FIRST THING THAT COMES TO MIND?
CHEESE!
IF I SAY, "MOON," WHAT'S THE FIRST THING THAT COMES TO MIND?
CHEESE!
BZZZZT...
HEY, IT'S SNACK TIME... DO YOU HAVE ANY CHEESE HERE?

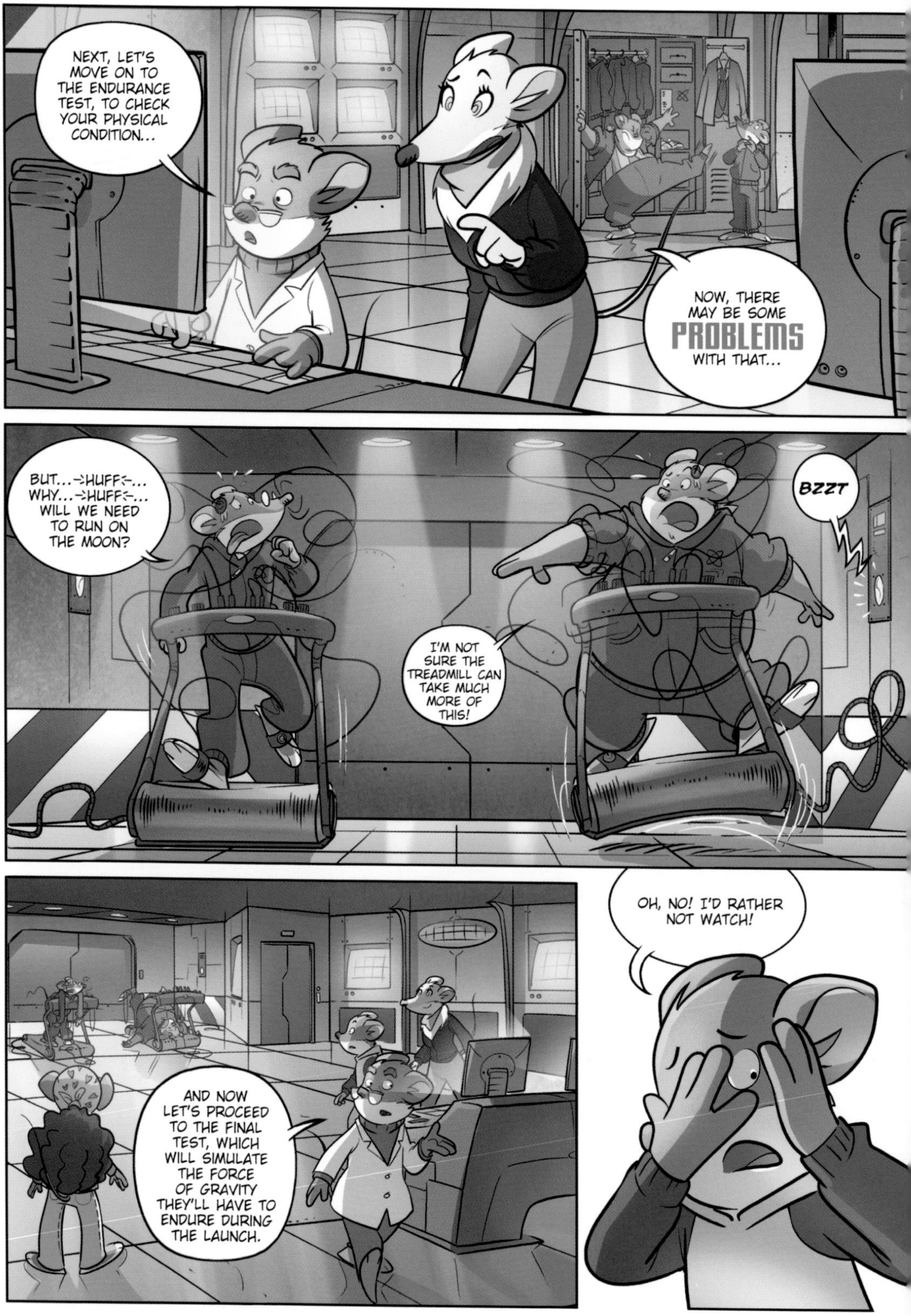
NEXT, LET'S MOVE ON TO THE ENDURANCE TEST, TO CHECK YOUR PHYSICAL CONDITION...
NOW, THERE MAY BE SOME PROBLEMS WITH THAT...
BUT... >HUFF<... WHY... >HUFF<... WILL WE NEED TO RUN ON THE MOON?
I'M NOT SURE THE TREADMILL CAN TAKE MUCH MORE OF THIS!
BZZT
AND NOW LET'S PROCEED TO THE FINAL TEST, WHICH WILL SIMULATE THE FORCE OF GRAVITY THEY'LL HAVE TO ENDURE DURING THE LAUNCH.
OH, NO! I'D RATHER NOT WATCH!

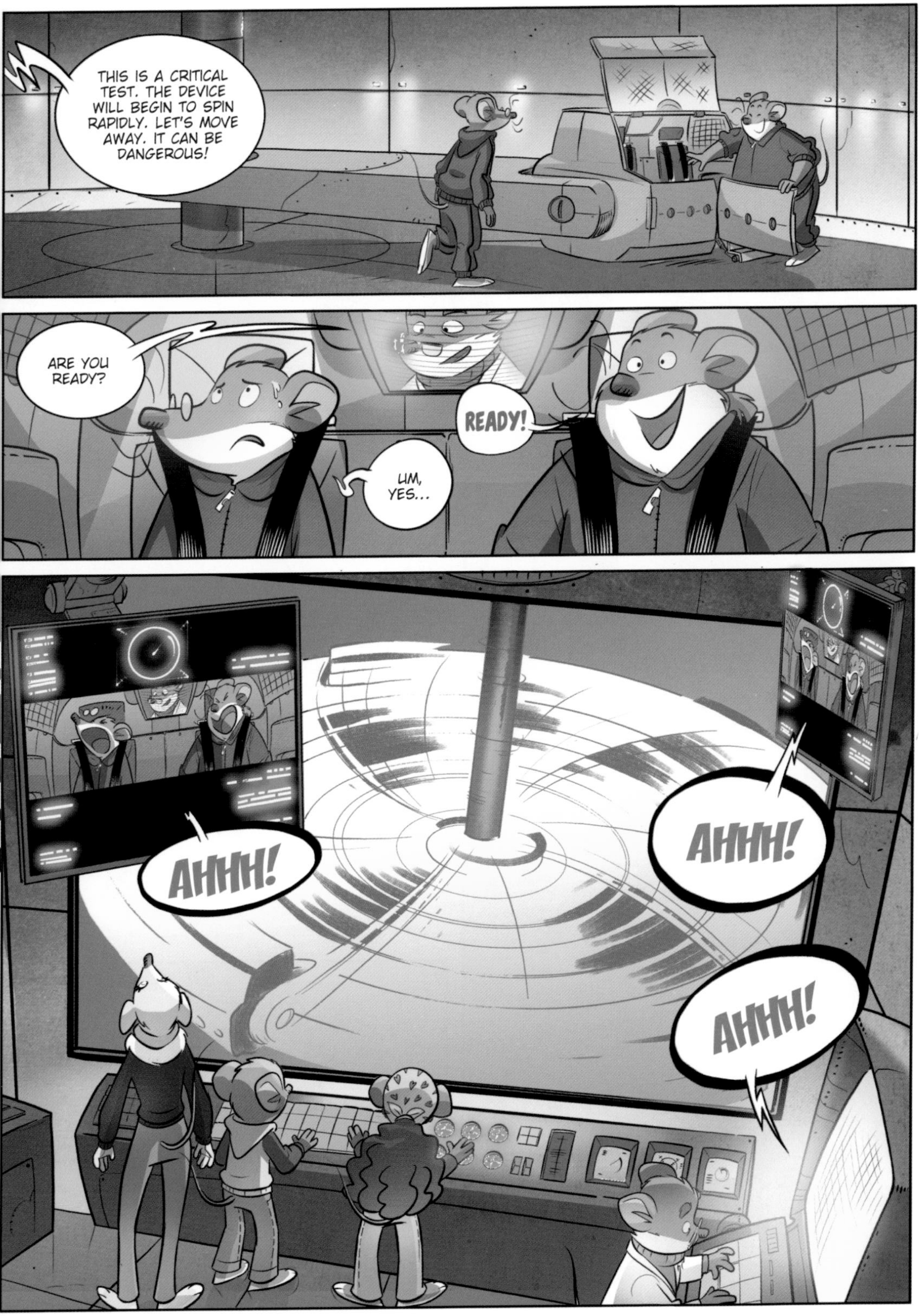
THIS IS A CRITICAL TEST. THE DEVICE WILL BEGIN TO SPIN RAPIDLY. LET'S MOVE AWAY. IT CAN BE DANGEROUS!
ARE YOU READY?
READY!
UM, YES...
AHHH!
AHHH!
AHHH!

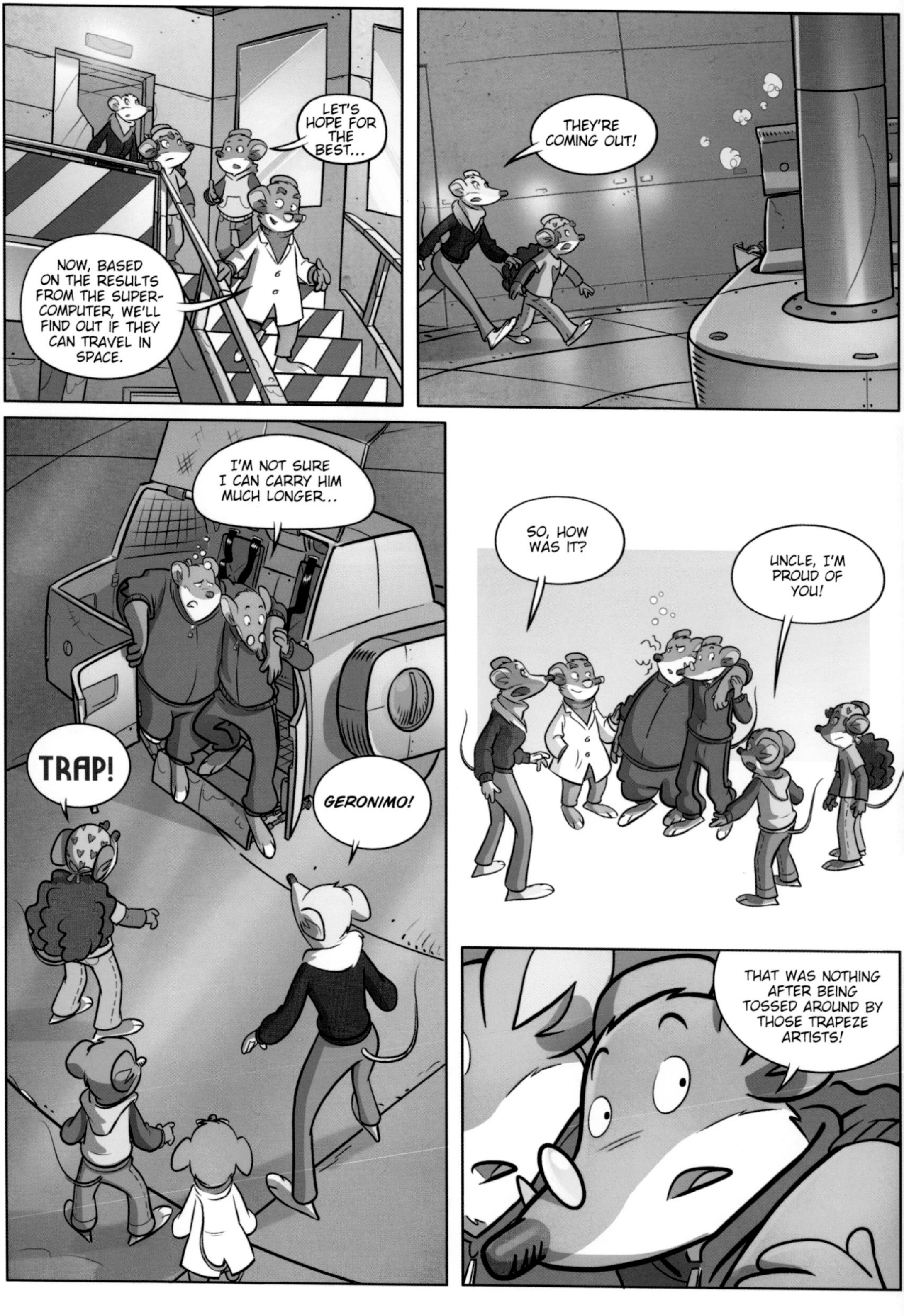
LET'S HOPE FOR THE BEST...
NOW, BASED ON THE RESULTS FROM THE SUPER-COMPUTER, WE'LL FIND OUT IF THEY CAN TRAVEL IN SPACE.
THEY'RE COMING OUT!
I'M NOT SURE I CAN CARRY HIM MUCH LONGER...
TRAP!
GERONIMO!
SO, HOW WAS IT?
UNCLE, I'M PROUD OF YOU!
THAT WAS NOTHING AFTER BEING TOSSED AROUND BY THOSE TRAPEZE ARTISTS!

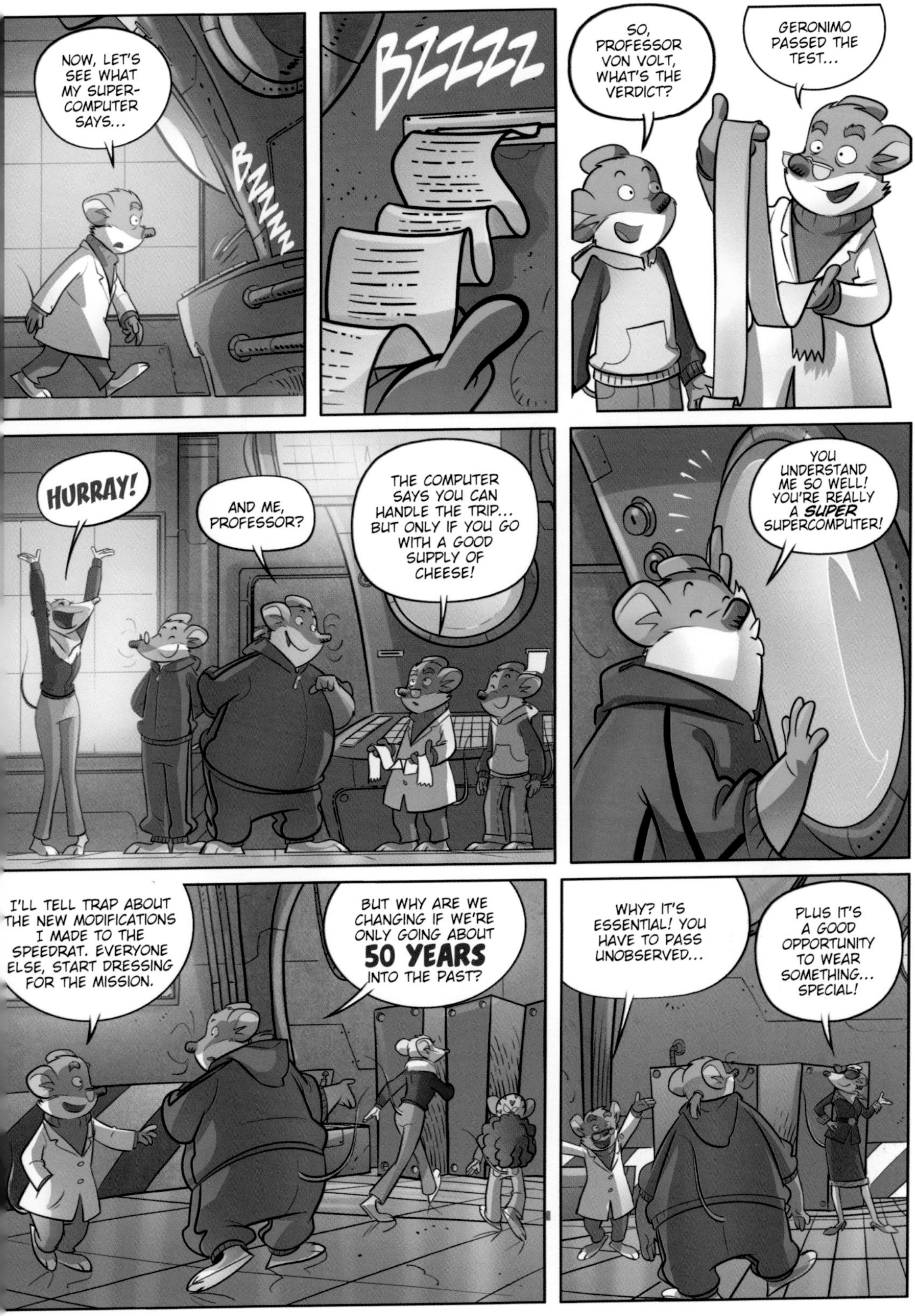
NOW, LET'S SEE WHAT MY SUPER-COMPUTER SAYS...
BZZZZ
BZZZZZ
SO, PROFESSOR VON VOLT, WHAT'S THE VERDICT?
GERONIMO PASSED THE TEST...
HURRAY!
AND ME, PROFESSOR?
THE COMPUTER SAYS YOU CAN HANDLE THE TRIP... BUT ONLY IF YOU GO WITH A GOOD SUPPLY OF CHEESE!
YOU UNDERSTAND ME SO WELL! YOU'RE REALLY A SUPER SUPERCOMPUTER!
I'LL TELL TRAP ABOUT THE NEW MODIFICATIONS I MADE TO THE SPEEDRAT. EVERYONE ELSE, START DRESSING FOR THE MISSION.
BUT WHY ARE WE CHANGING IF WE'RE ONLY GOING ABOUT 50 YEARS INTO THE PAST?
WHY? IT'S ESSENTIAL! YOU HAVE TO PASS UNOBSERVED...
PLUS IT'S A GOOD OPPORTUNITY TO WEAR SOMETHING... SPECIAL!

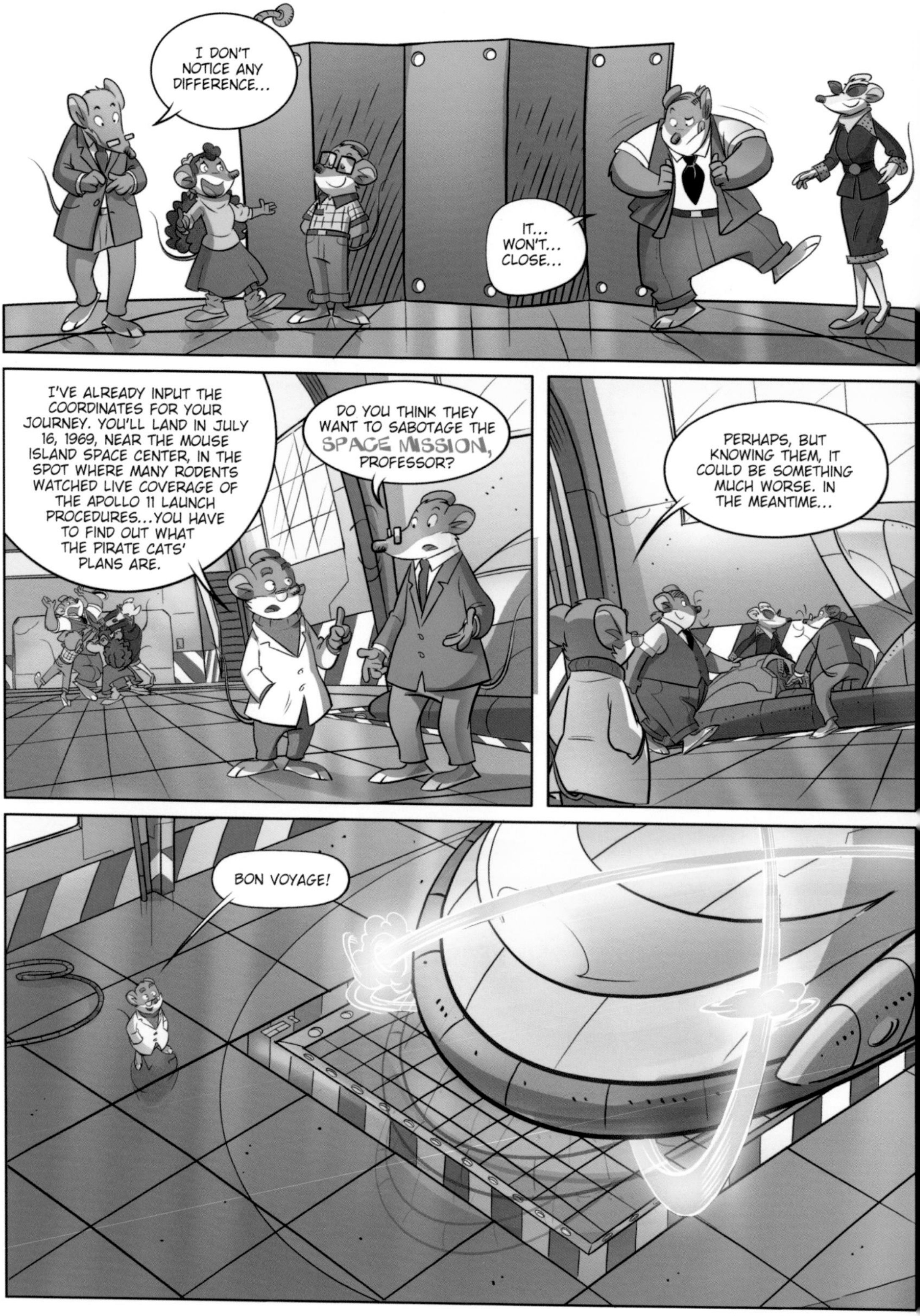
I DON'T NOTICE ANY DIFFERENCE...
IT... WON'T... CLOSE...
I'VE ALREADY INPUT THE COORDINATES FOR YOUR JOURNEY. YOU'LL LAND IN JULY 16, 1969, NEAR THE MOUSE ISLAND SPACE CENTER, IN THE SPOT WHERE MANY RODENTS WATCHED LIVE COVERAGE OF THE APOLLO 11 LAUNCH PROCEDURES...YOU HAVE TO FIND OUT WHAT THE PIRATE CATS' PLANS ARE.
DO YOU THINK THEY WANT TO SABOTAGE THE SPACE MISSION, PROFESSOR?
PERHAPS, BUT KNOWING THEM, IT COULD BE SOMETHING MUCH WORSE. IN THE MEANTIME...
BON VOYAGE!

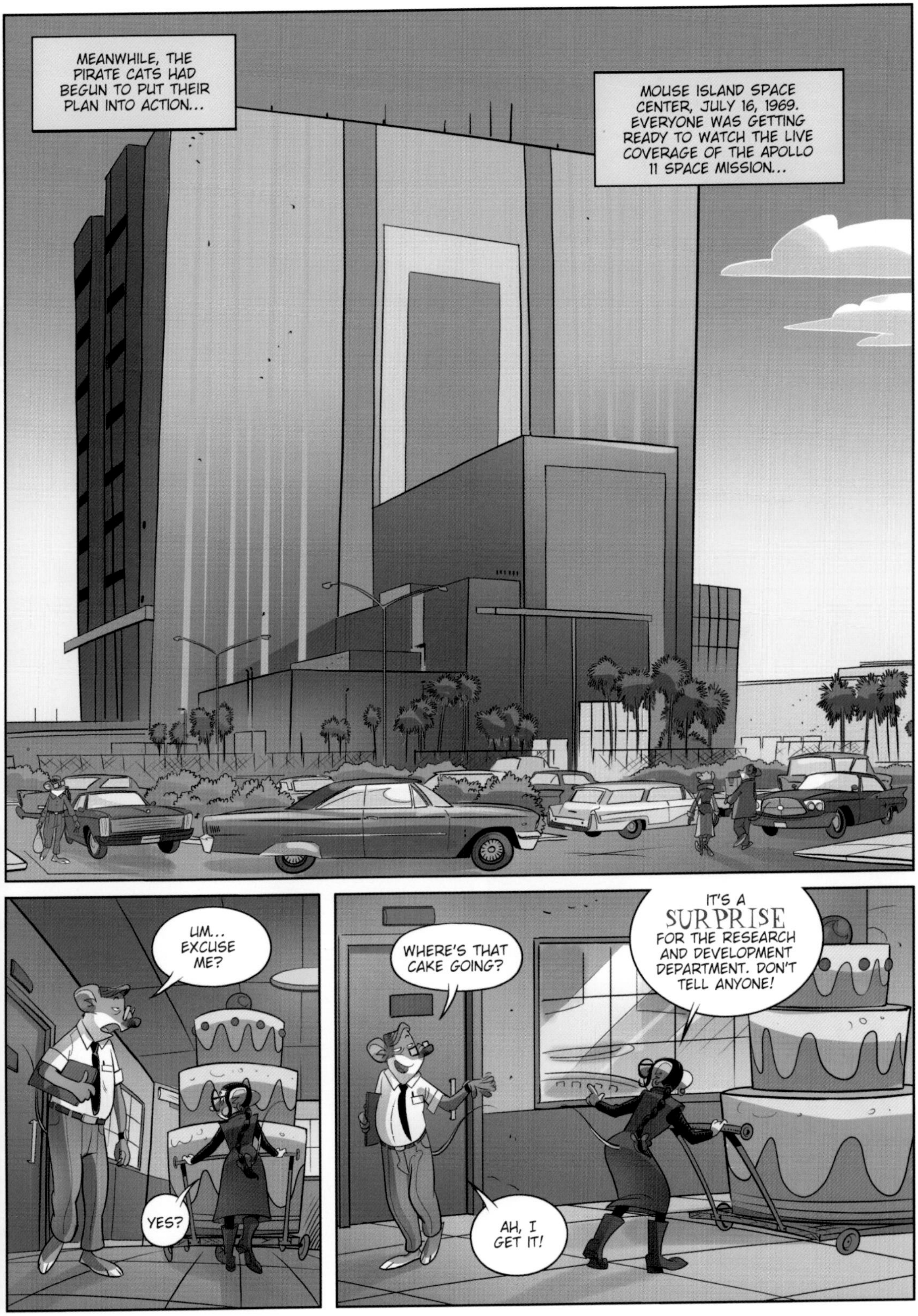
MEANWHILE, THE PIRATE CATS HAD BEGUN TO PUT THEIR PLAN INTO ACTION...
MOUSE ISLAND SPACE CENTER, JULY 16, 1969. EVERYONE WAS GETTING READY TO WATCH THE LIVE COVERAGE OF THE APOLLO 11 SPACE MISSION...
UM... EXCUSE ME?
YES?
WHERE'S THAT CAKE GOING?
IT'S A SURPRISE FOR THE RESEARCH AND DEVELOPMENT DEPARTMENT. DON'T TELL ANYONE!
AH, I GET IT!

YOU ENGINEERS HAVE WORKED VERY HARD SO THE RODENTS OF MOUSE ISLAND CAN WATCH THE LIVE COVERAGE OF TODAY'S LAUNCH. SO, THE MANAGEMENT TEAM WOULD LIKE TO THANK YOU WITH THIS **CAKE!**

YEAH!

A CAKE!

CLAP

CLAP CLAP CLAP

BUT IT'S A VERY SPECIAL CAKE...

BZ ZT

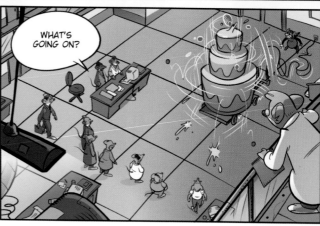

WHAT'S GOING ON?

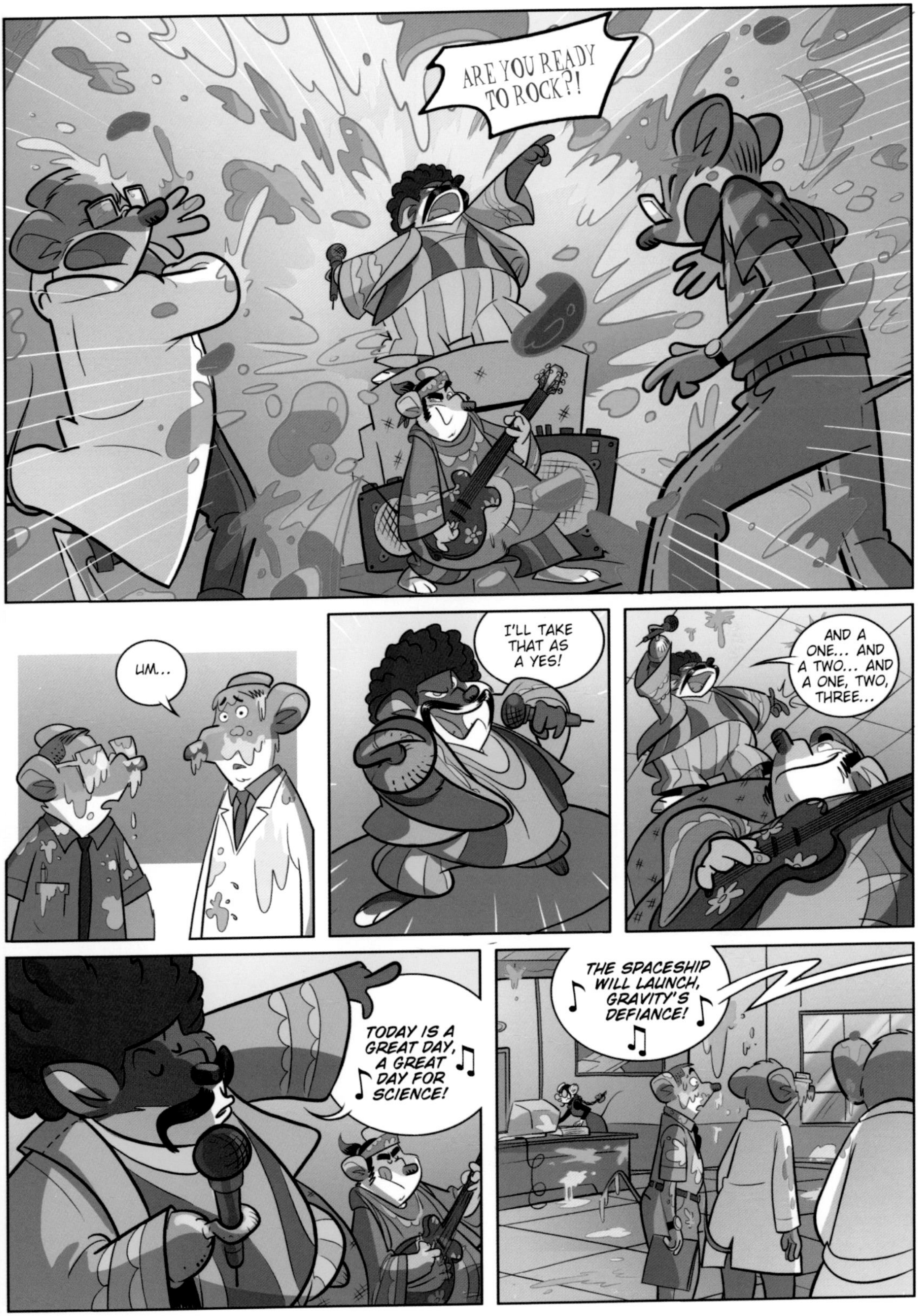
ARE YOU READY TO ROCK?!
UM...
I'LL TAKE THAT AS A YES!
AND A ONE... AND A TWO... AND A ONE, TWO, THREE...
TODAY IS A GREAT DAY, A GREAT DAY FOR SCIENCE!
THE SPACESHIP WILL LAUNCH, GRAVITY'S DEFIANCE!

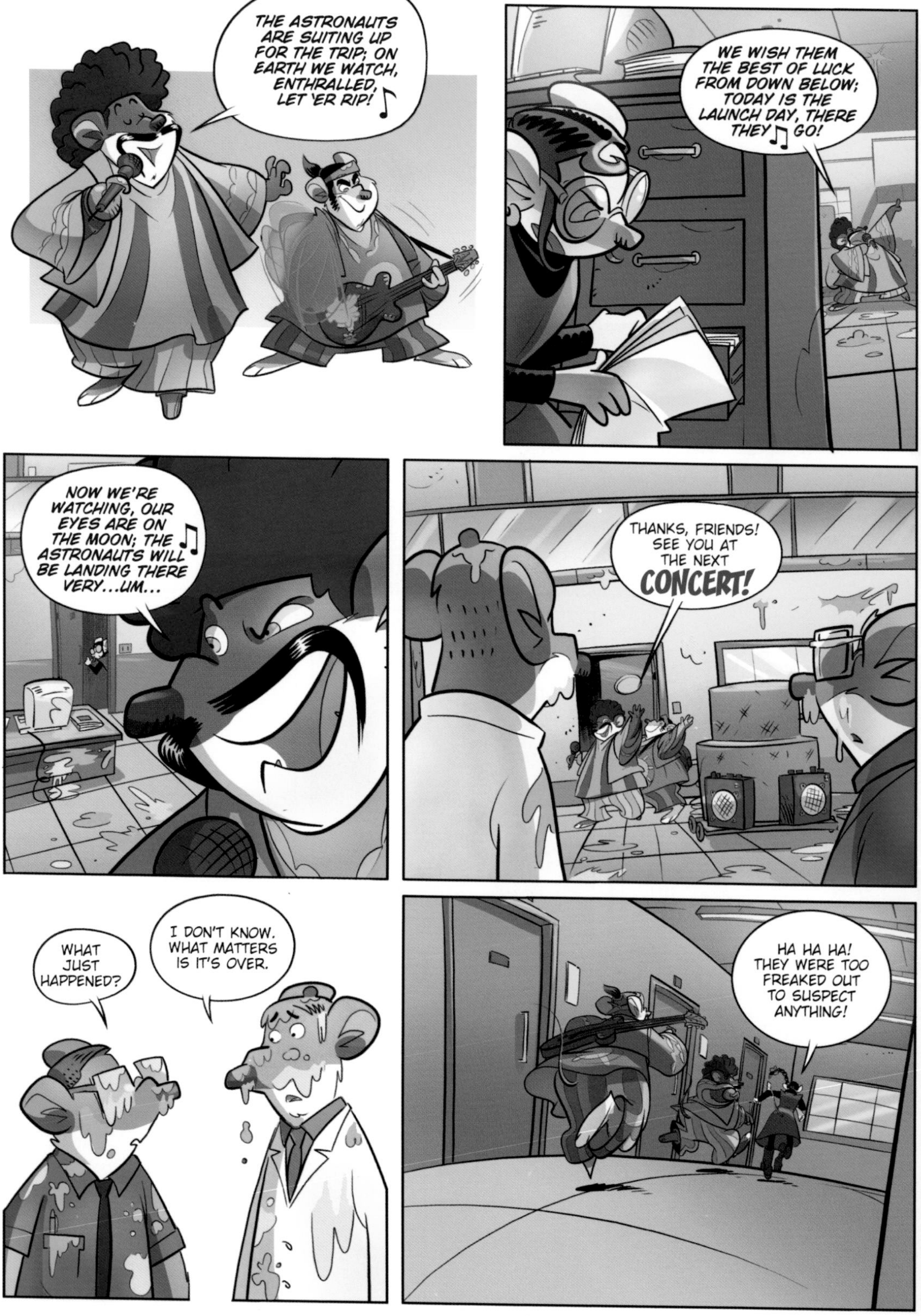
THE ASTRONAUTS ARE SUITING UP FOR THE TRIP; ON EARTH WE WATCH, ENTHRALLED, LET 'ER RIP!
WE WISH THEM THE BEST OF LUCK FROM DOWN BELOW; TODAY IS THE LAUNCH DAY, THERE THEY GO!
NOW WE'RE WATCHING, OUR EYES ARE ON THE MOON; THE ASTRONAUTS WILL BE LANDING THERE VERY...UM...
THANKS, FRIENDS! SEE YOU AT THE NEXT CONCERT!
WHAT JUST HAPPENED?
I DON'T KNOW. WHAT MATTERS IS IT'S OVER.
HA HA HA! THEY WERE TOO FREAKED OUT TO SUSPECT ANYTHING!

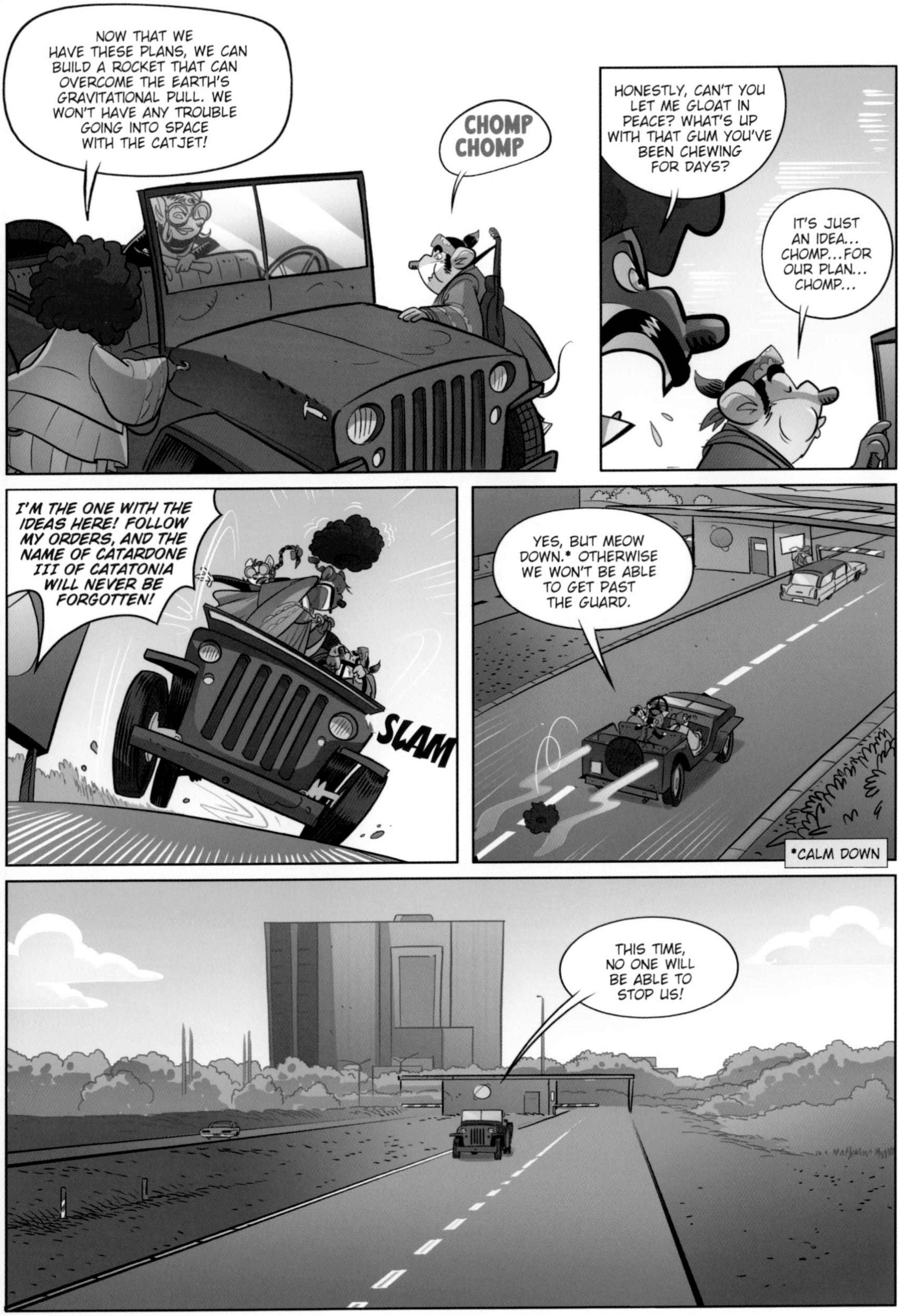
NOW THAT WE HAVE THESE PLANS, WE CAN BUILD A ROCKET THAT CAN OVERCOME THE EARTH'S GRAVITATIONAL PULL. WE WON'T HAVE ANY TROUBLE GOING INTO SPACE WITH THE CATJET!
CHOMP CHOMP
HONESTLY, CAN'T YOU LET ME GLOAT IN PEACE? WHAT'S UP WITH THAT GUM YOU'VE BEEN CHEWING FOR DAYS?
IT'S JUST AN IDEA... CHOMP...FOR OUR PLAN... CHOMP...
I'M THE ONE WITH THE IDEAS HERE! FOLLOW MY ORDERS, AND THE NAME OF CATARDONE III OF CATATONIA WILL NEVER BE FORGOTTEN!
SLAM
YES, BUT MEOW DOWN.* OTHERWISE WE WON'T BE ABLE TO GET PAST THE GUARD.
*CALM DOWN
THIS TIME, NO ONE WILL BE ABLE TO STOP US!

MEANWHILE, WE'D ARRIVED AT THE SPACE CENTER AND LOST NO TIME STARTING OUR INVESTIGATION...

...PROFESSOR VON VOLT HAD GIVEN US PRESS CREDENTIALS TO VISIT THE MOUSE ISLAND SPACE CENTER AND WATCH THE LIVE COVERAGE OF THE APOLLO 11 MISSION.

MEMBERS OF THE PRESS, THANK YOU FOR BEING HERE WITH US TO WITNESS THIS HISTORICAL EVENT. IF YOU'LL FOLLOW ME...

LOOK AT HOW MANY JET HANGARS THERE ARE! I BET THERE ARE A HUNDRED ROCKETS READY TO GO!

ISN'T THE *SPEEDRAT* ENOUGH FOR YOU?

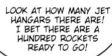

YES, OF COURSE! LET'S HOPE NO ONE SEES IT BEHIND THOSE BUSHES. I WOULDN'T WANT SOMEONE TO FIND IT!

COME IN, PLEASE. ONCE WE'RE INSIDE, WE'LL BEGIN WITH A FEW INTRODUCTORY REMARKS. THEN WE'LL GO TO THE ROOM WHERE WE'LL WATCH THE LIVE MISSION COVERAGE!

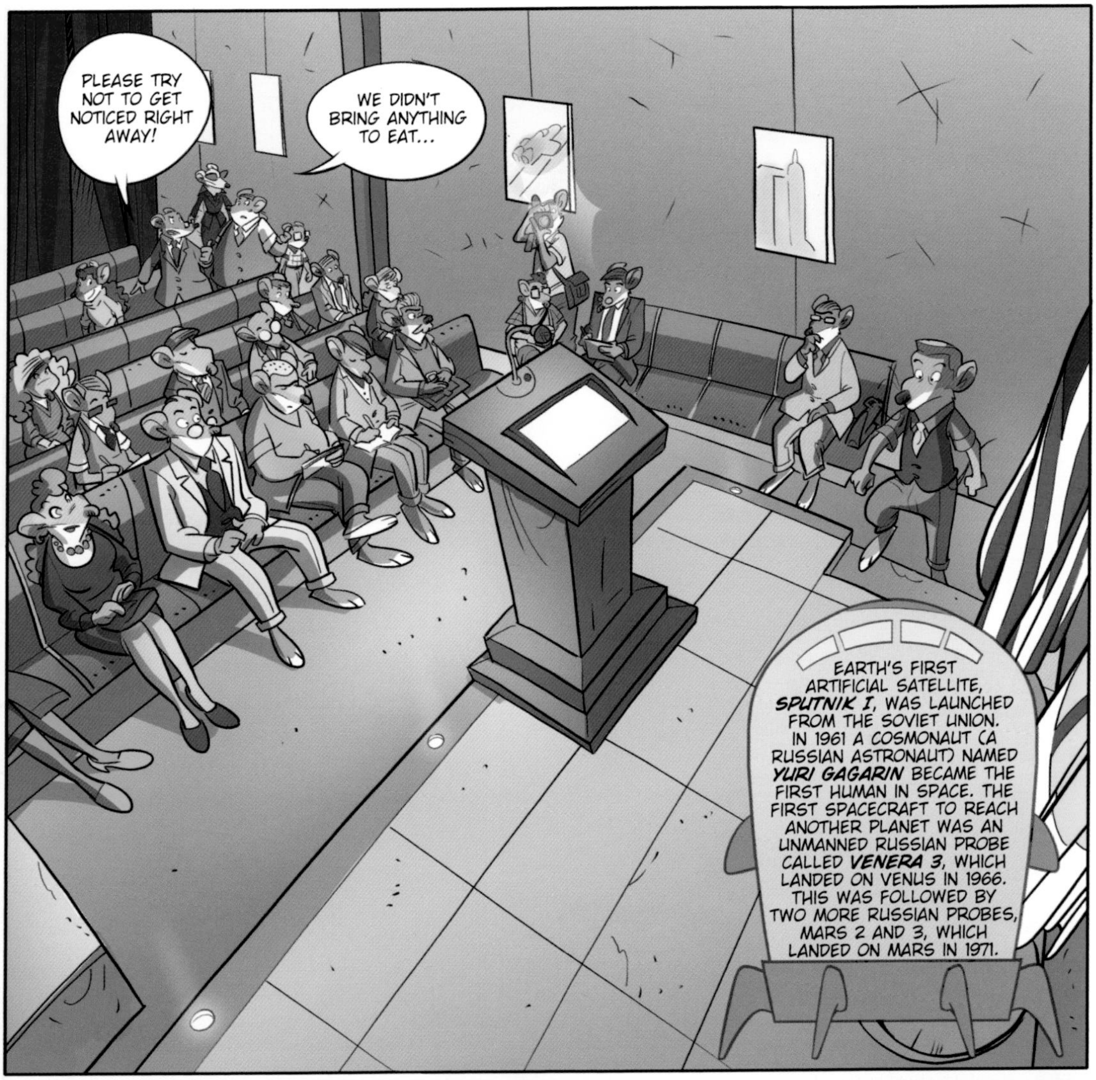
PLEASE TRY NOT TO GET NOTICED RIGHT AWAY!
WE DIDN'T BRING ANYTHING TO EAT...
EARTH'S FIRST ARTIFICIAL SATELLITE, **SPUTNIK I**, WAS LAUNCHED FROM THE SOVIET UNION. IN 1961 A COSMONAUT (A RUSSIAN ASTRONAUT) NAMED **YURI GAGARIN** BECAME THE FIRST HUMAN IN SPACE. THE FIRST SPACECRAFT TO REACH ANOTHER PLANET WAS AN UNMANNED RUSSIAN PROBE CALLED **VENERA 3**, WHICH LANDED ON VENUS IN 1966. THIS WAS FOLLOWED BY TWO MORE RUSSIAN PROBES, MARS 2 AND 3, WHICH LANDED ON MARS IN 1971.

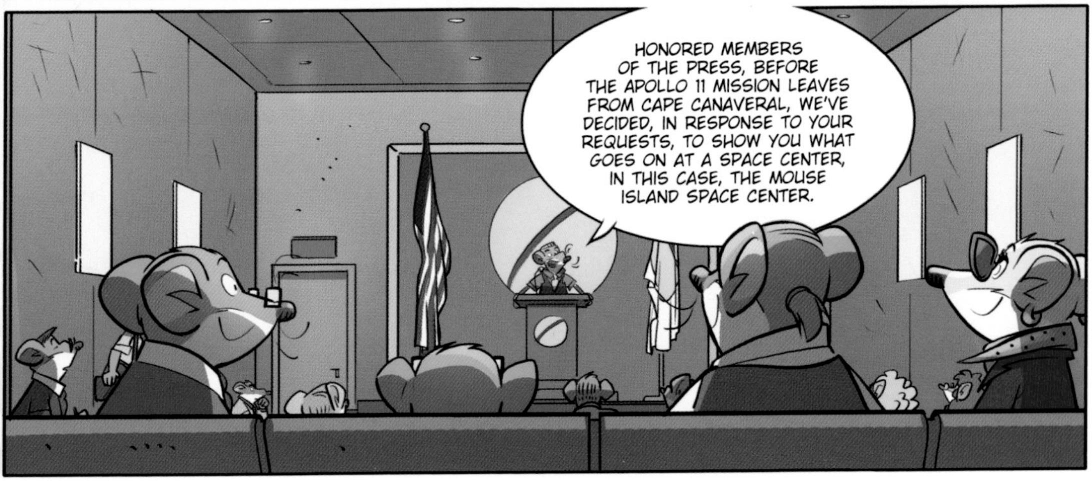
HONORED MEMBERS OF THE PRESS, BEFORE THE APOLLO 11 MISSION LEAVES FROM CAPE CANAVERAL, WE'VE DECIDED, IN RESPONSE TO YOUR REQUESTS, TO SHOW YOU WHAT GOES ON AT A SPACE CENTER, IN THIS CASE, THE MOUSE ISLAND SPACE CENTER.

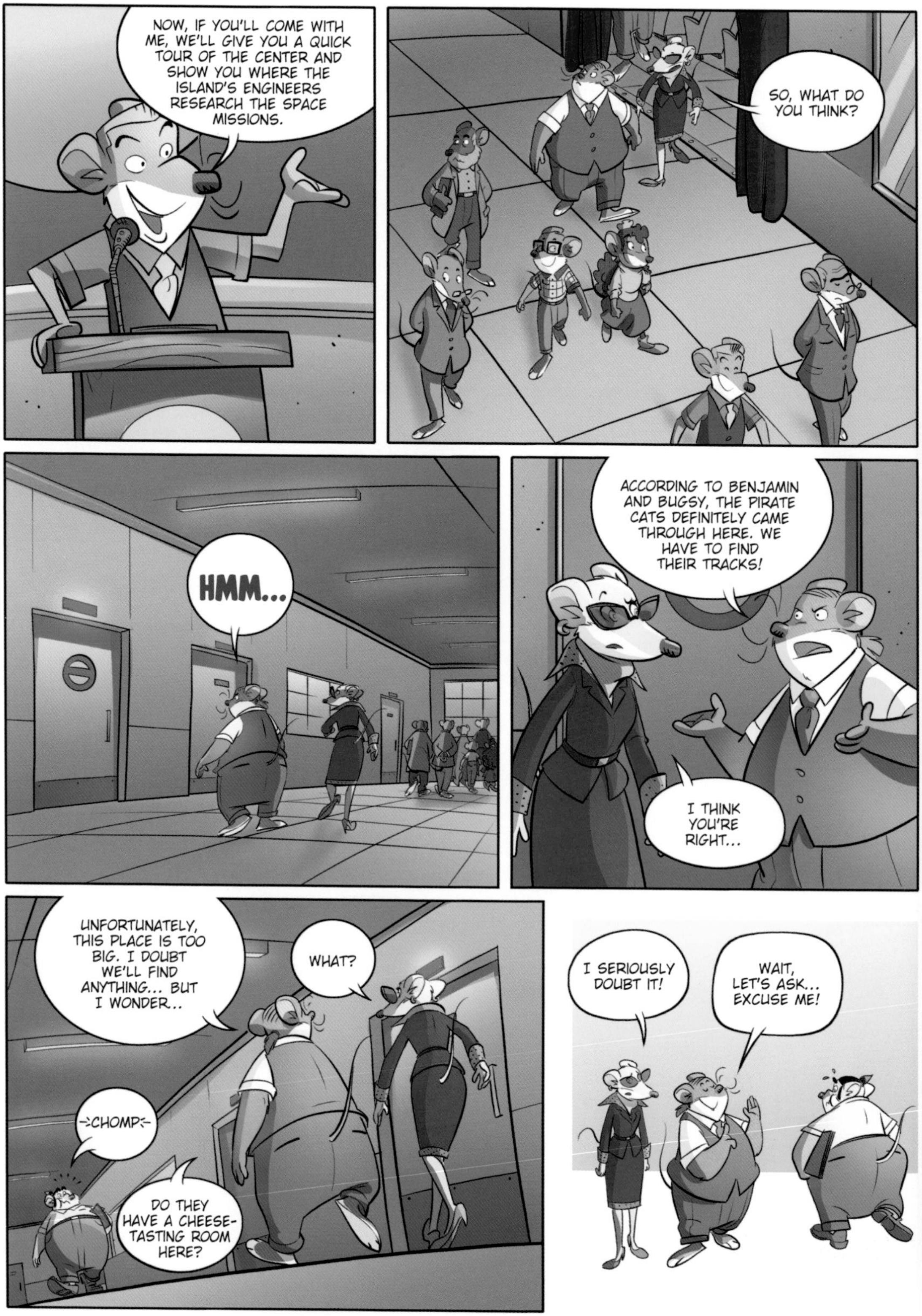
NOW, IF YOU'LL COME WITH ME, WE'LL GIVE YOU A QUICK TOUR OF THE CENTER AND SHOW YOU WHERE THE ISLAND'S ENGINEERS RESEARCH THE SPACE MISSIONS.
SO, WHAT DO YOU THINK?
HMM...
ACCORDING TO BENJAMIN AND BUGSY, THE PIRATE CATS DEFINITELY CAME THROUGH HERE. WE HAVE TO FIND THEIR TRACKS!
I THINK YOU'RE RIGHT...
UNFORTUNATELY, THIS PLACE IS TOO BIG. I DOUBT WE'LL FIND ANYTHING... BUT I WONDER...
WHAT?
CHOMP
DO THEY HAVE A CHEESE-TASTING ROOM HERE?
I SERIOUSLY DOUBT IT!
WAIT, LET'S ASK... EXCUSE ME!

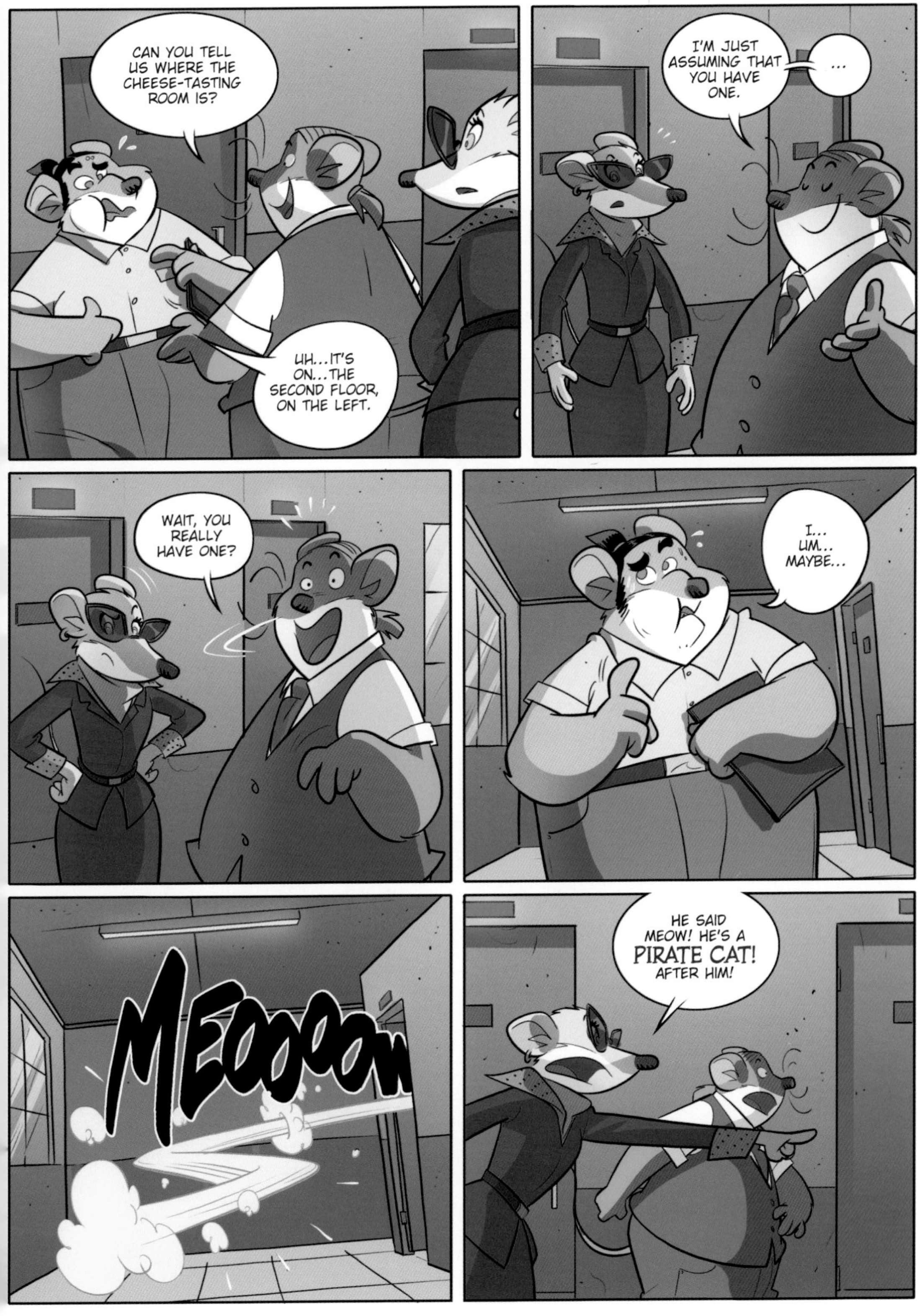
CAN YOU TELL US WHERE THE CHEESE-TASTING ROOM IS?
UH...IT'S ON...THE SECOND FLOOR, ON THE LEFT.
I'M JUST ASSUMING THAT YOU HAVE ONE.
...
WAIT, YOU REALLY HAVE ONE?
I... UM... MAYBE...
MEOOOOOW
HE SAID MEOW! HE'S A PIRATE CAT! AFTER HIM!

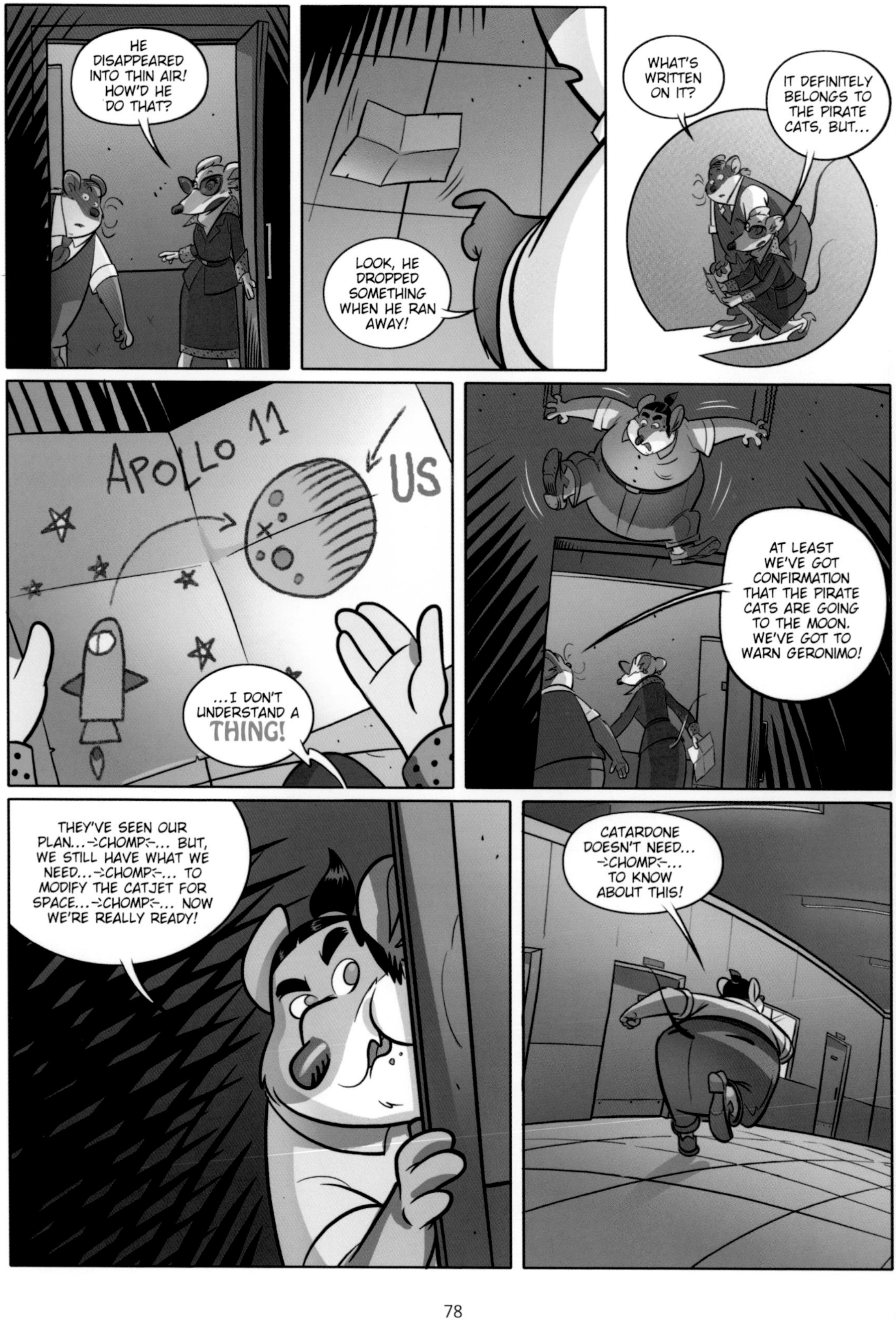
HE DISAPPEARED INTO THIN AIR! HOW'D HE DO THAT?
LOOK, HE DROPPED SOMETHING WHEN HE RAN AWAY!
WHAT'S WRITTEN ON IT?
IT DEFINITELY BELONGS TO THE PIRATE CATS, BUT...
APOLLO 11
US
...I DON'T UNDERSTAND A THING!
AT LEAST WE'VE GOT CONFIRMATION THAT THE PIRATE CATS ARE GOING TO THE MOON. WE'VE GOT TO WARN GERONIMO!
THEY'VE SEEN OUR PLAN... ⇒CHOMP⇐... BUT, WE STILL HAVE WHAT WE NEED... ⇒CHOMP⇐... TO MODIFY THE CATJET FOR SPACE... ⇒CHOMP⇐... NOW WE'RE REALLY READY!
CATARDONE DOESN'T NEED... ⇒CHOMP⇐... TO KNOW ABOUT THIS!

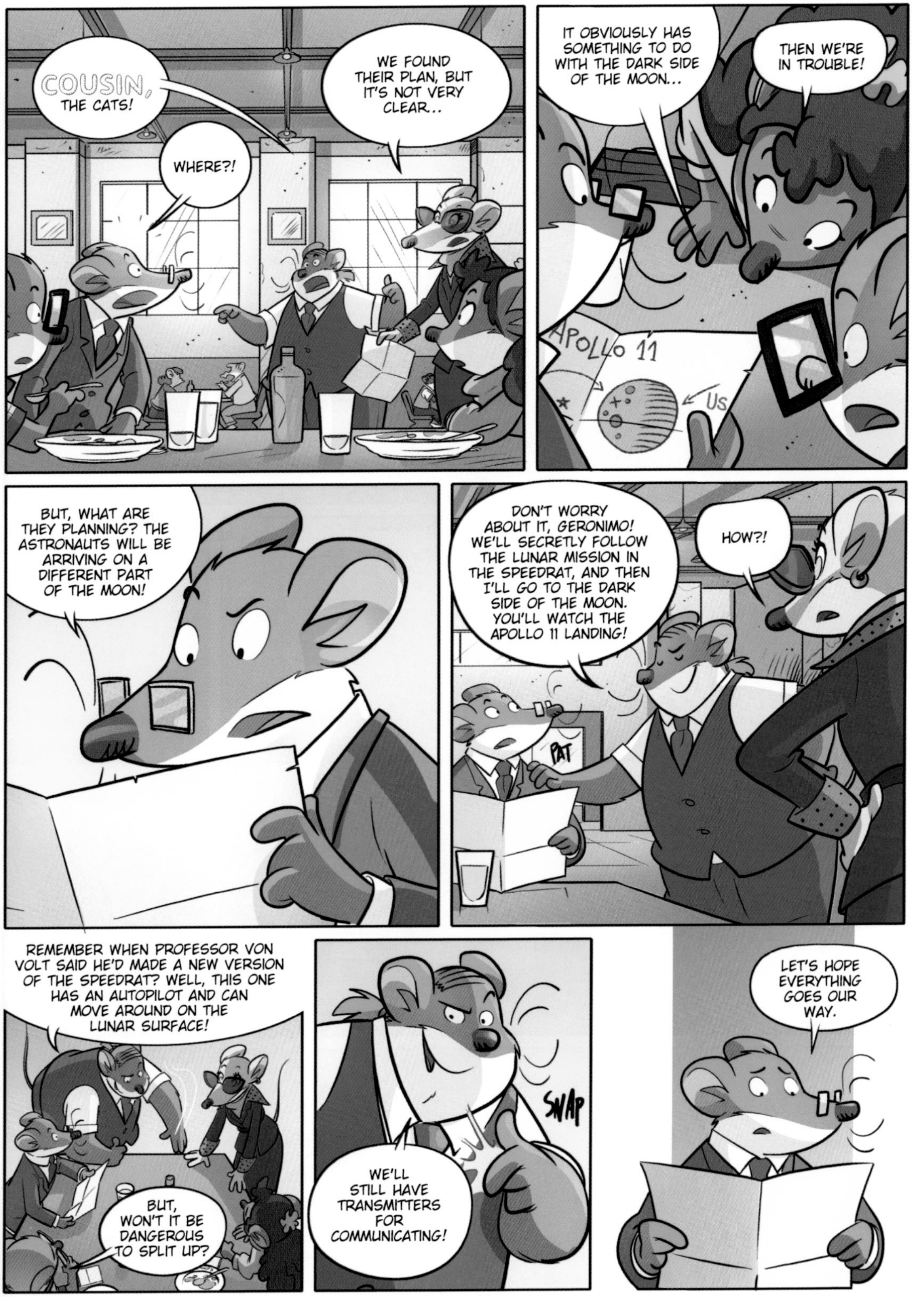
COUSIN, THE CATS!
WHERE?!
WE FOUND THEIR PLAN, BUT IT'S NOT VERY CLEAR...
IT OBVIOUSLY HAS SOMETHING TO DO WITH THE DARK SIDE OF THE MOON...
THEN WE'RE IN TROUBLE!
APOLLO 11
US
BUT, WHAT ARE THEY PLANNING? THE ASTRONAUTS WILL BE ARRIVING ON A DIFFERENT PART OF THE MOON!
DON'T WORRY ABOUT IT, GERONIMO! WE'LL SECRETLY FOLLOW THE LUNAR MISSION IN THE SPEEDRAT, AND THEN I'LL GO TO THE DARK SIDE OF THE MOON. YOU'LL WATCH THE APOLLO 11 LANDING!
HOW?!
PAT
REMEMBER WHEN PROFESSOR VON VOLT SAID HE'D MADE A NEW VERSION OF THE SPEEDRAT? WELL, THIS ONE HAS AN AUTOPILOT AND CAN MOVE AROUND ON THE LUNAR SURFACE!
BUT, WON'T IT BE DANGEROUS TO SPLIT UP?
SNAP
WE'LL STILL HAVE TRANSMITTERS FOR COMMUNICATING!
LET'S HOPE EVERYTHING GOES OUR WAY.

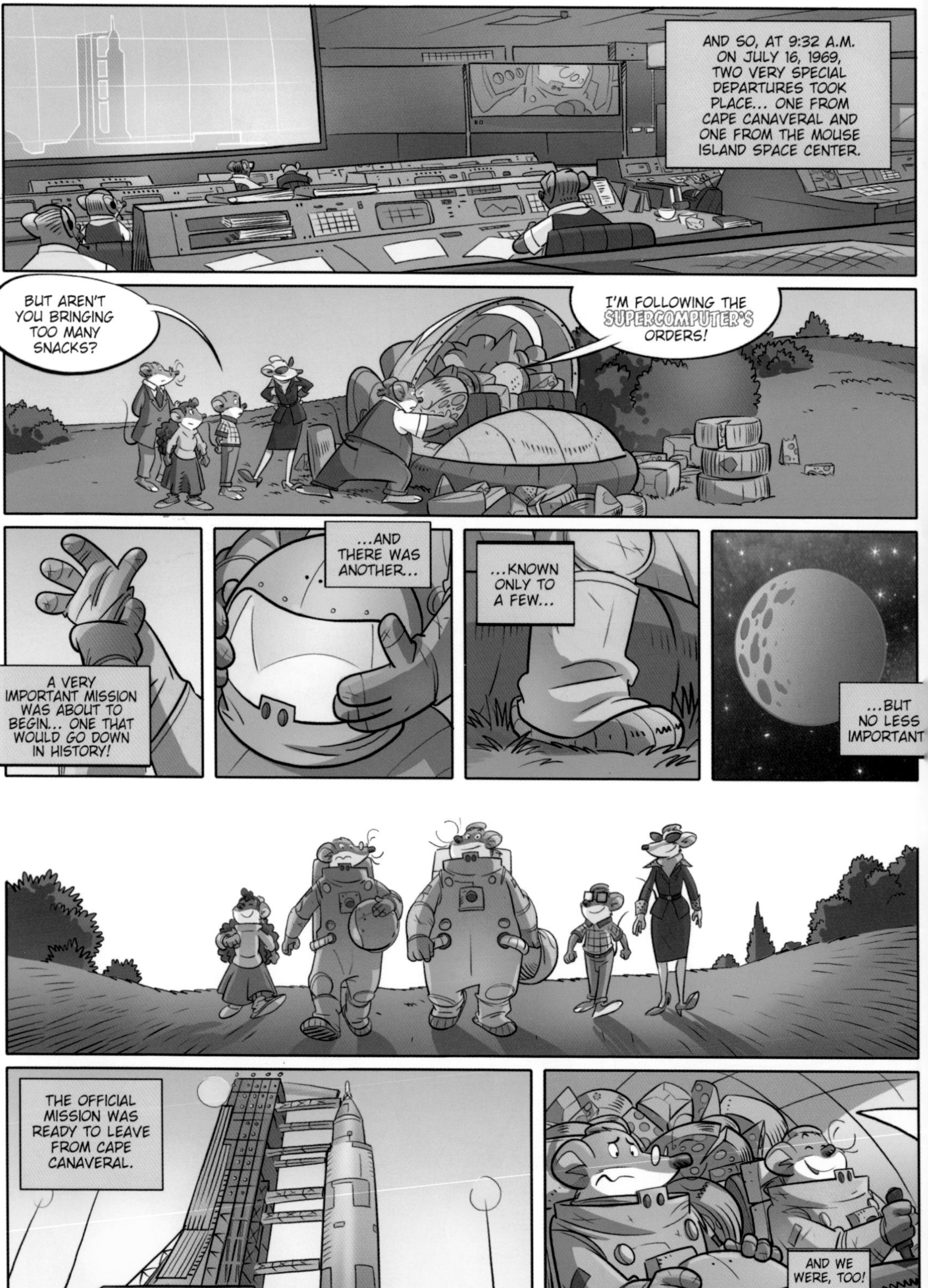
AND SO, AT 9:32 A.M. ON JULY 16, 1969, TWO VERY SPECIAL DEPARTURES TOOK PLACE... ONE FROM CAPE CANAVERAL AND ONE FROM THE MOUSE ISLAND SPACE CENTER.
BUT AREN'T YOU BRINGING TOO MANY SNACKS?
I'M FOLLOWING THE SUPERCOMPUTER'S ORDERS!
A VERY IMPORTANT MISSION WAS ABOUT TO BEGIN... ONE THAT WOULD GO DOWN IN HISTORY!
...AND THERE WAS ANOTHER...
...KNOWN ONLY TO A FEW...
...BUT NO LESS IMPORTANT
THE OFFICIAL MISSION WAS READY TO LEAVE FROM CAPE CANAVERAL.
AND WE WERE, TOO!

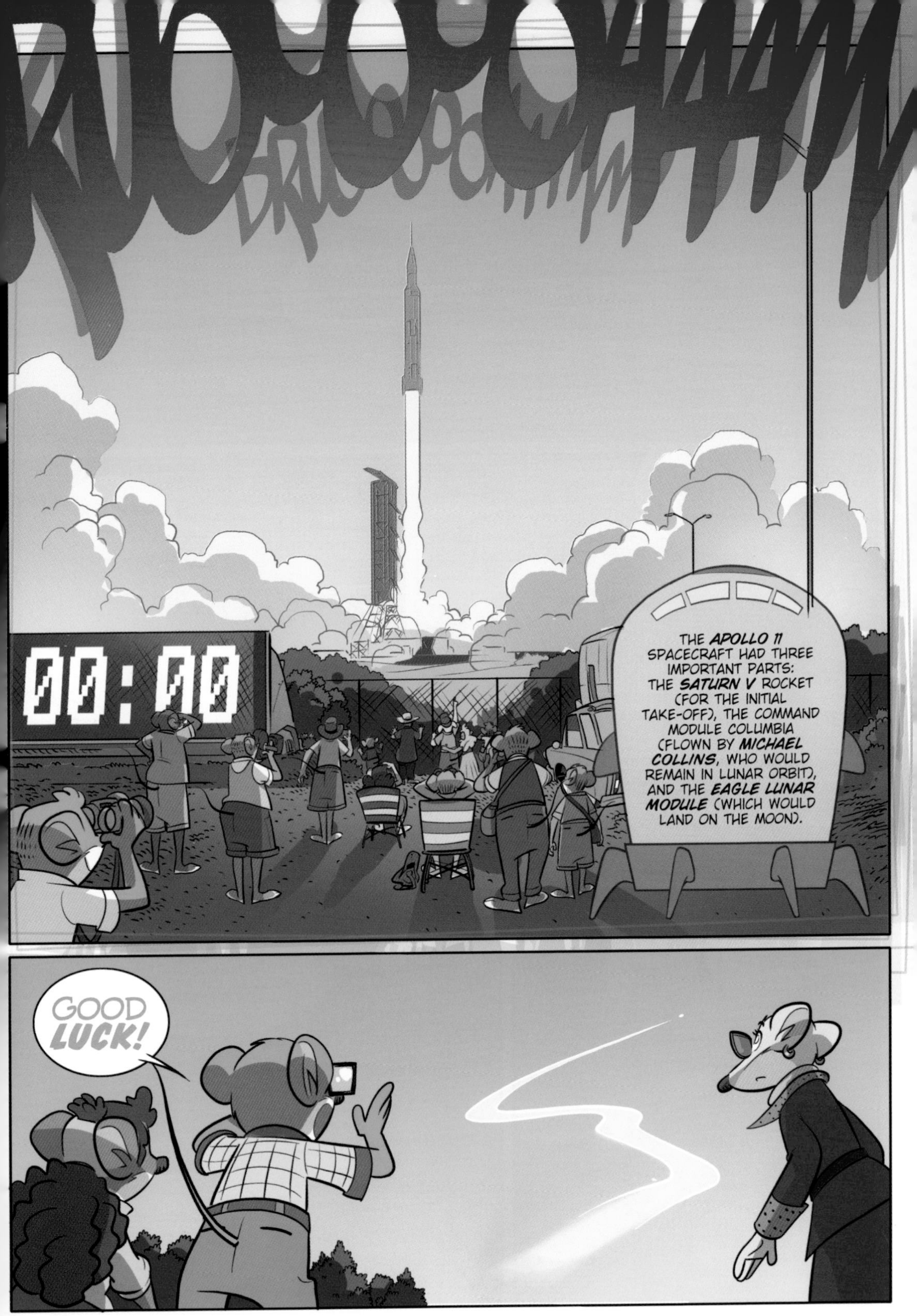
00:00
THE **APOLLO 11** SPACECRAFT HAD THREE IMPORTANT PARTS: THE **SATURN V** ROCKET (FOR THE INITIAL TAKE-OFF), THE COMMAND MODULE COLUMBIA (FLOWN BY **MICHAEL COLLINS**, WHO WOULD REMAIN IN LUNAR ORBIT), AND THE **EAGLE LUNAR MODULE** (WHICH WOULD LAND ON THE MOON).
GOOD **LUCK!**

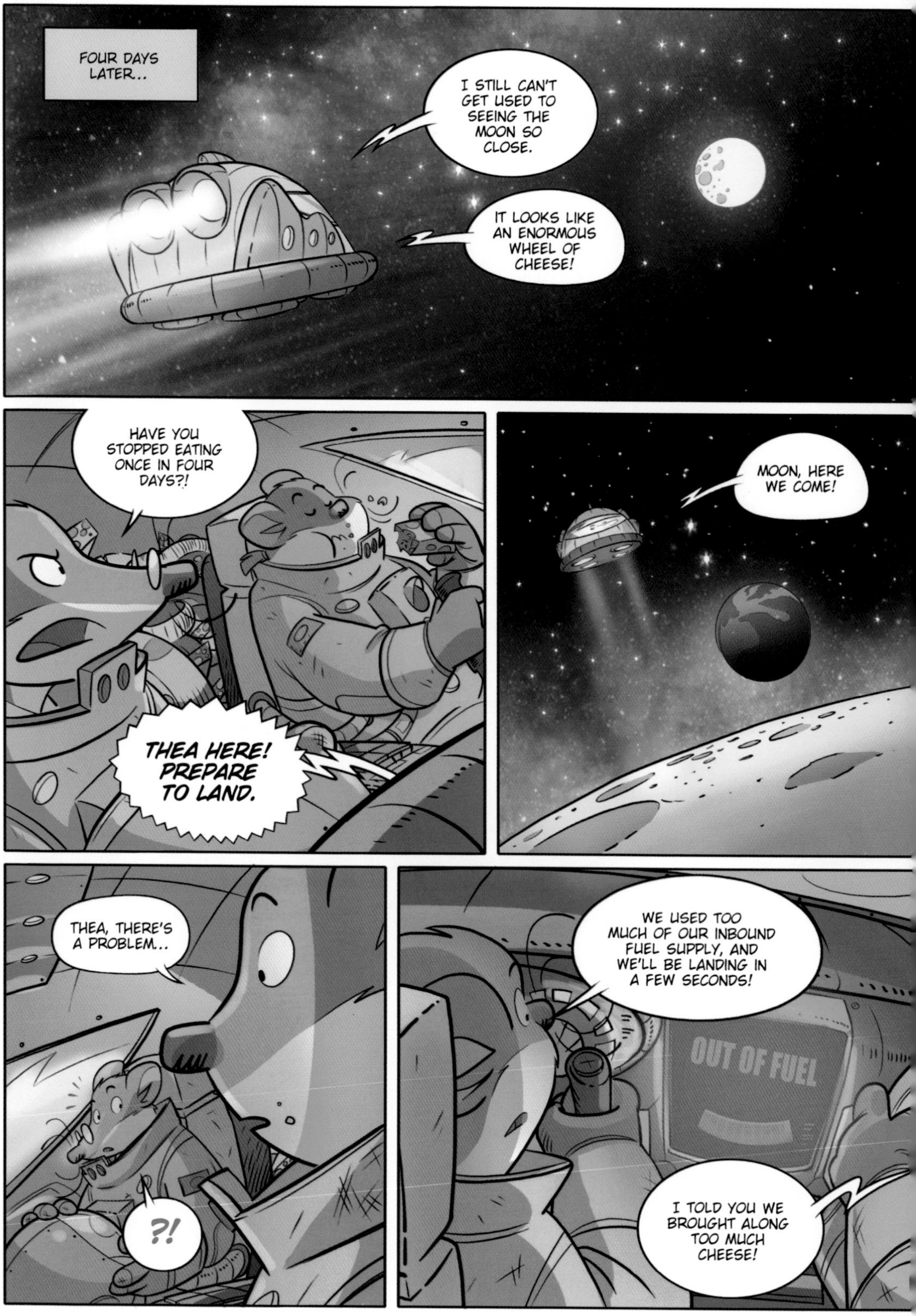
FOUR DAYS LATER...
I STILL CAN'T GET USED TO SEEING THE MOON SO CLOSE.
IT LOOKS LIKE AN ENORMOUS WHEEL OF CHEESE!
HAVE YOU STOPPED EATING ONCE IN FOUR DAYS?!
THEA HERE! PREPARE TO LAND.
MOON, HERE WE COME!
THEA, THERE'S A PROBLEM...
?!
WE USED TOO MUCH OF OUR INBOUND FUEL SUPPLY, AND WE'LL BE LANDING IN A FEW SECONDS!
OUT OF FUEL
I TOLD YOU WE BROUGHT ALONG TOO MUCH CHEESE!

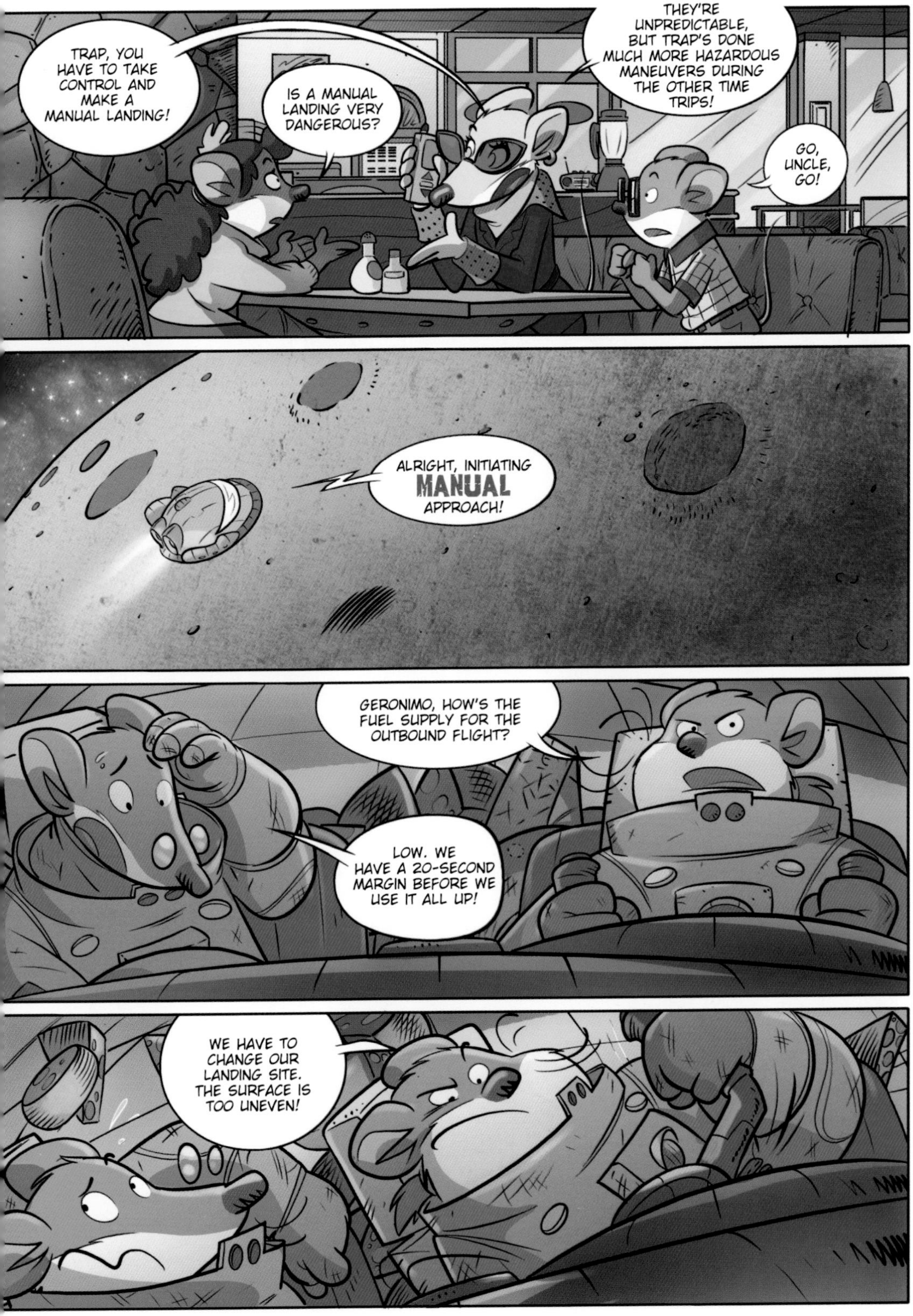
TRAP, YOU HAVE TO TAKE CONTROL AND MAKE A MANUAL LANDING!
IS A MANUAL LANDING VERY DANGEROUS?
THEY'RE UNPREDICTABLE, BUT TRAP'S DONE MUCH MORE HAZARDOUS MANEUVERS DURING THE OTHER TIME TRIPS!
GO, UNCLE, GO!
ALRIGHT, INITIATING MANUAL APPROACH!
GERONIMO, HOW'S THE FUEL SUPPLY FOR THE OUTBOUND FLIGHT?
LOW. WE HAVE A 20-SECOND MARGIN BEFORE WE USE IT ALL UP!
WE HAVE TO CHANGE OUR LANDING SITE. THE SURFACE IS TOO UNEVEN!

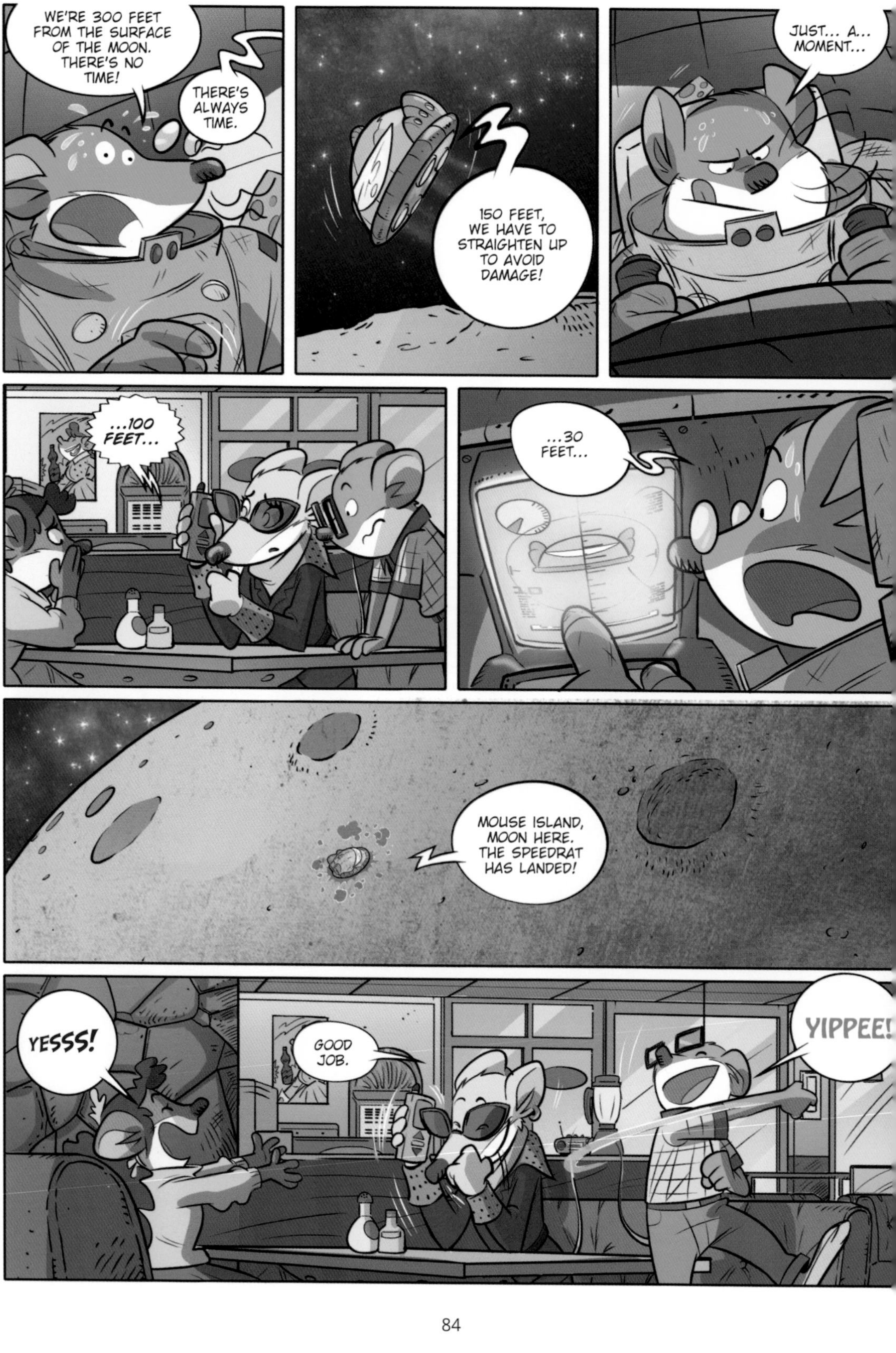
WE'RE 300 FEET FROM THE SURFACE OF THE MOON. THERE'S NO TIME!
THERE'S ALWAYS TIME.
150 FEET, WE HAVE TO STRAIGHTEN UP TO AVOID DAMAGE!
JUST... A... MOMENT...
...100 FEET...
...30 FEET...
MOUSE ISLAND, MOON HERE. THE SPEEDRAT HAS LANDED!
YESSS!
GOOD JOB.
YIPPEE!

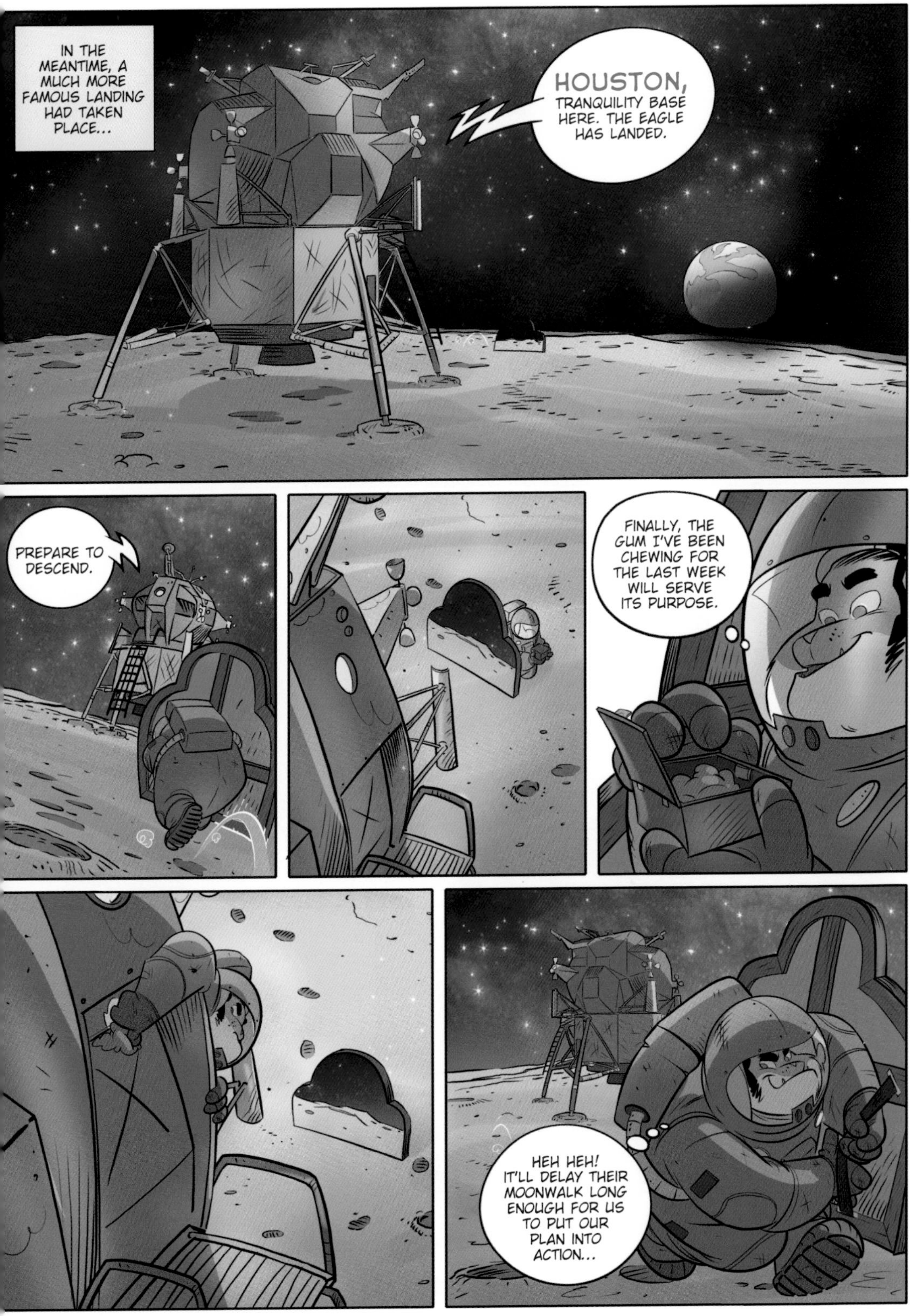
IN THE MEANTIME, A MUCH MORE FAMOUS LANDING HAD TAKEN PLACE...
HOUSTON, TRANQUILITY BASE HERE. THE EAGLE HAS LANDED.
PREPARE TO DESCEND.
FINALLY, THE GUM I'VE BEEN CHEWING FOR THE LAST WEEK WILL SERVE ITS PURPOSE.
HEH HEH! IT'LL DELAY THEIR MOONWALK LONG ENOUGH FOR US TO PUT OUR PLAN INTO ACTION...

THERE'S THE EAGLE. DON'T GET TOO CLOSE. WE CAN'T LET THEM SEE US ON THE **TV CAMERAS!**

THEN, I'LL LEAVE YOU HERE. I'LL GO TO THE DARK SIDE OF THE MOON RIGHT AWAY AND FIND OUT WHAT THE CATS ARE UP TO!

WOW, PROFESSOR VON VOLT'S SUPERCOMPUTER DIDN'T TEACH US HOW TO WALK ON THE MOON!

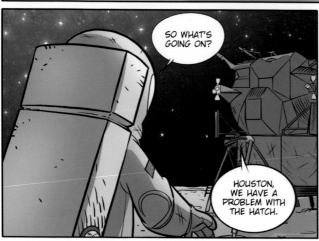

SO WHAT'S GOING ON?

HOUSTON, WE HAVE A PROBLEM WITH THE HATCH.

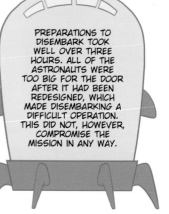

PREPARATIONS TO DISEMBARK TOOK WELL OVER THREE HOURS. ALL OF THE ASTRONAUTS WERE TOO BIG FOR THE DOOR AFTER IT HAD BEEN REDESIGNED, WHICH MADE DISEMBARKING A DIFFICULT OPERATION. THIS DID NOT, HOWEVER, COMPROMISE THE MISSION IN ANY WAY.

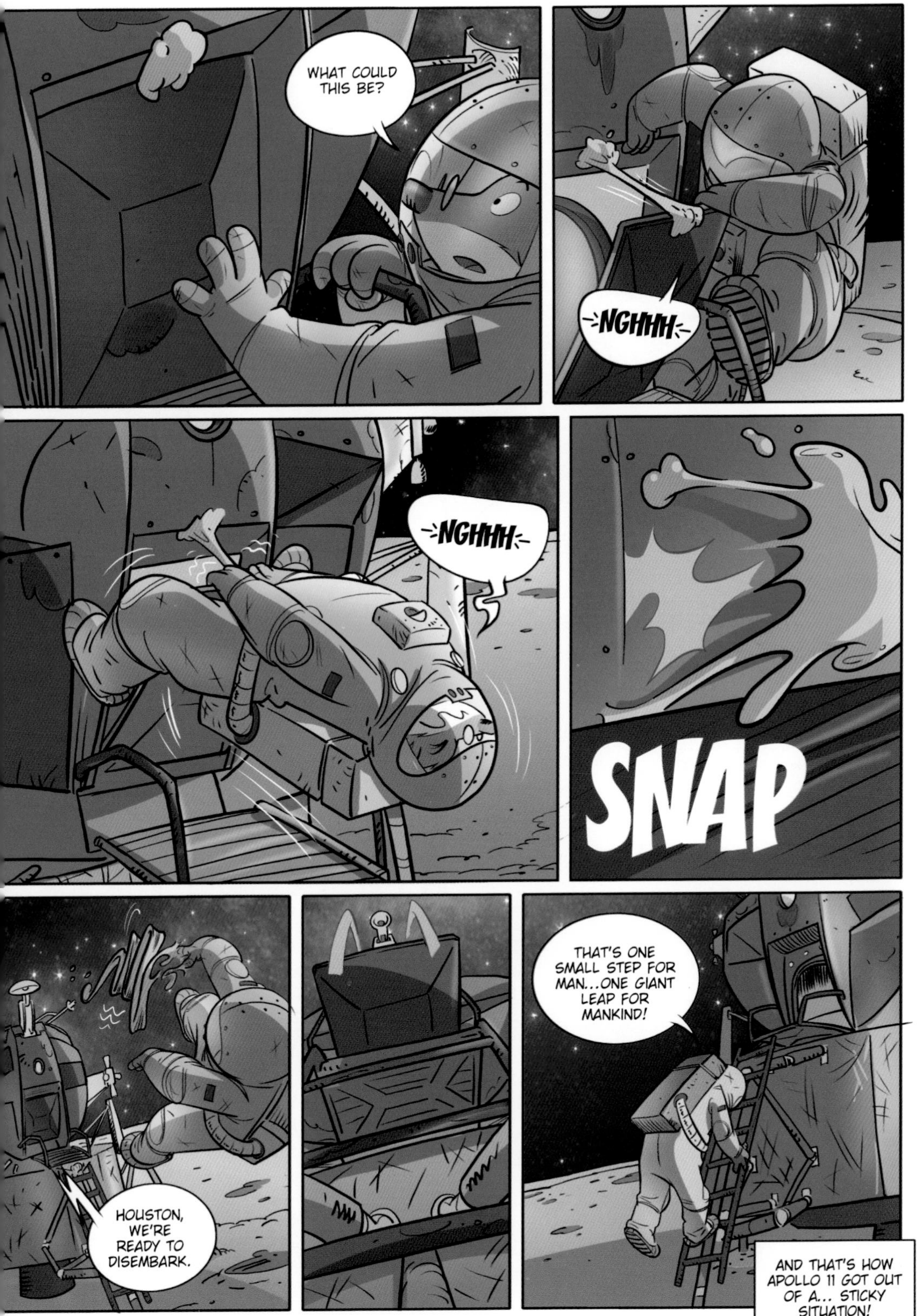
WHAT COULD THIS BE?
NGHHH
NGHHH
SNAP
HOUSTON, WE'RE READY TO DISEMBARK.
THAT'S ONE SMALL STEP FOR MAN...ONE GIANT LEAP FOR MANKIND!
AND THAT'S HOW APOLLO 11 GOT OUT OF A... STICKY SITUATION!

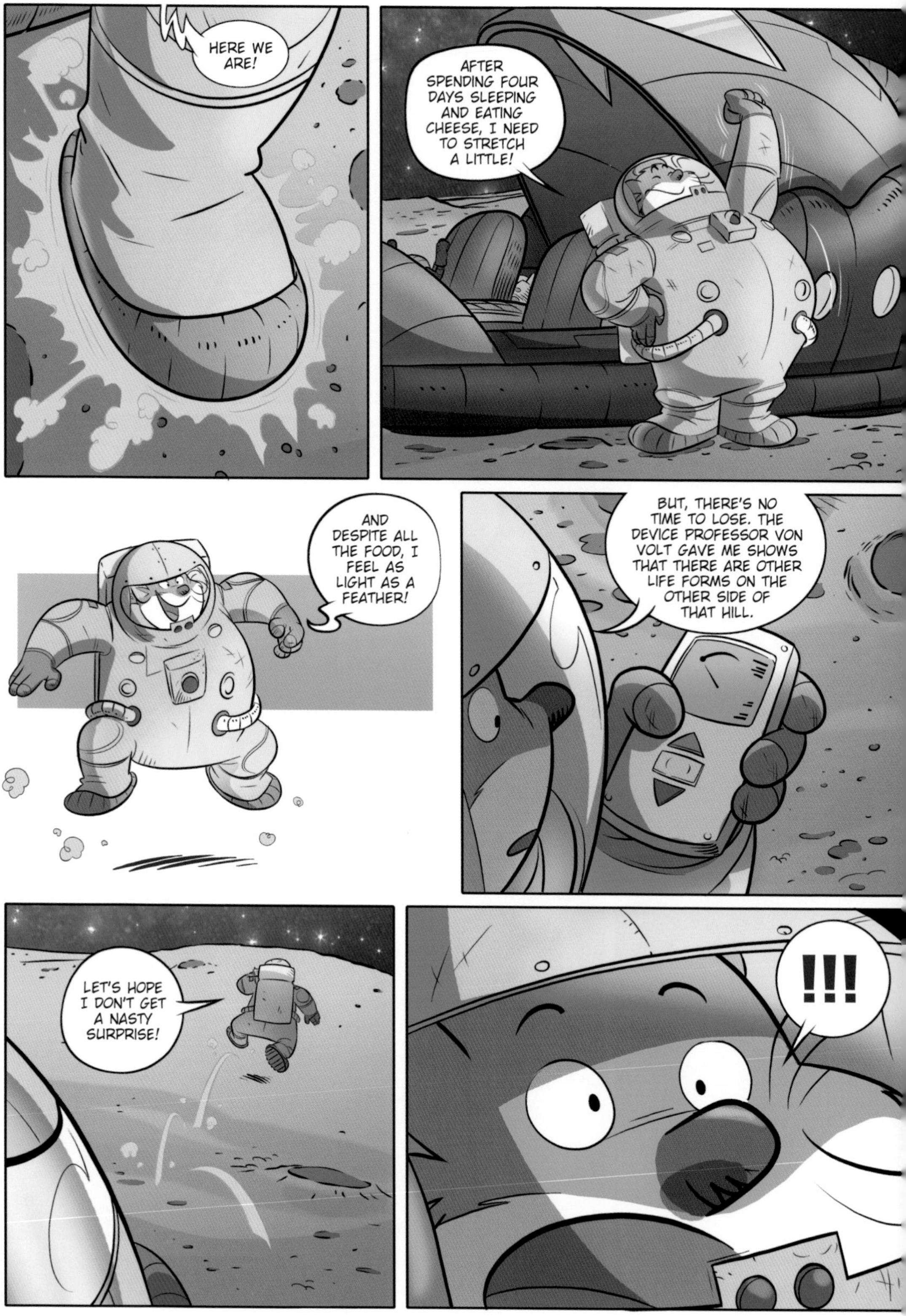
HERE WE ARE!
AFTER SPENDING FOUR DAYS SLEEPING AND EATING CHEESE, I NEED TO STRETCH A LITTLE!
AND DESPITE ALL THE FOOD, I FEEL AS LIGHT AS A FEATHER!
BUT, THERE'S NO TIME TO LOSE. THE DEVICE PROFESSOR VON VOLT GAVE ME SHOWS THAT THERE ARE OTHER LIFE FORMS ON THE OTHER SIDE OF THAT HILL.
LET'S HOPE I DON'T GET A NASTY SURPRISE!
!!!

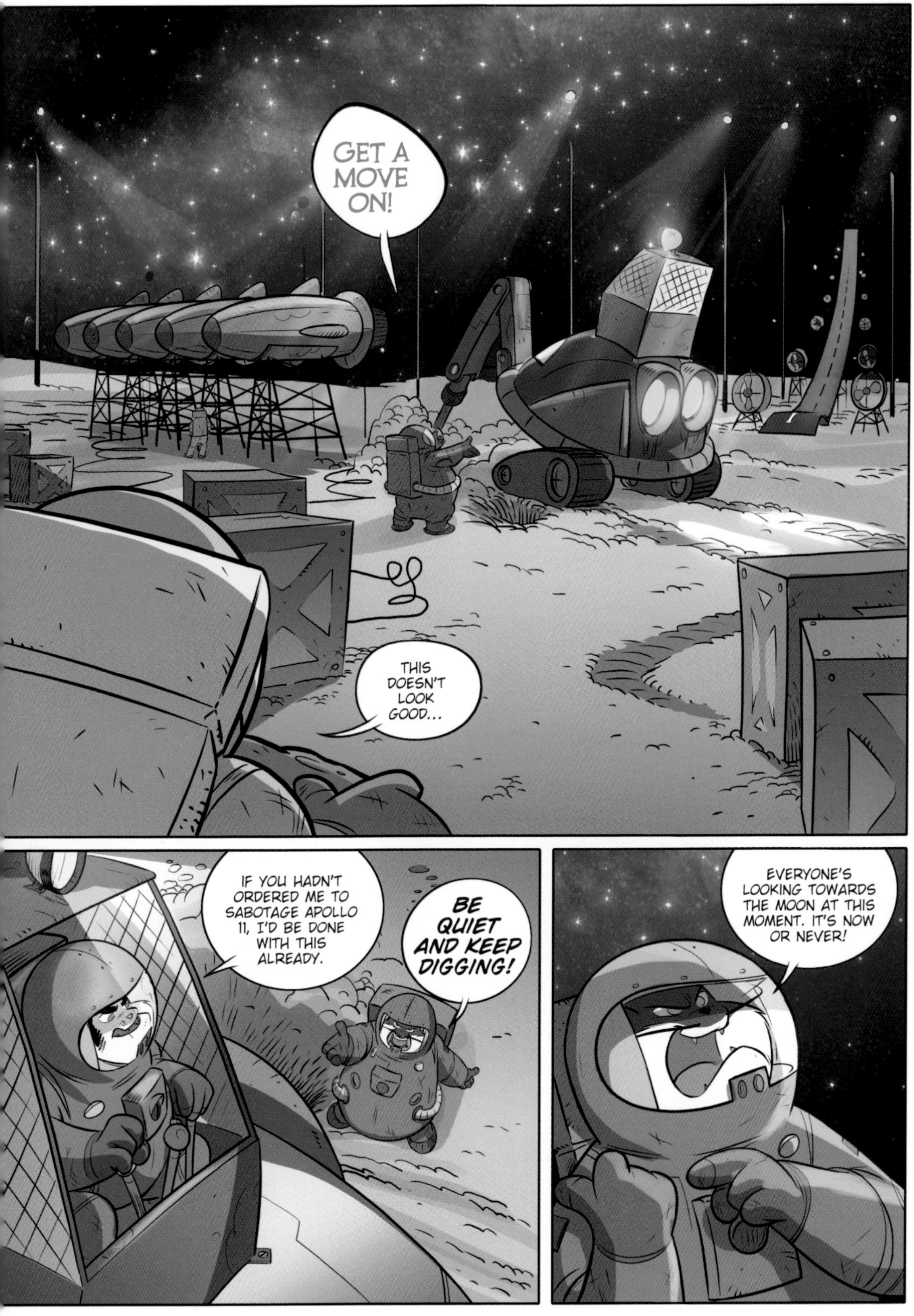
GET A MOVE ON!
THIS DOESN'T LOOK GOOD...
IF YOU HADN'T ORDERED ME TO SABOTAGE APOLLO 11, I'D BE DONE WITH THIS ALREADY.
BE QUIET AND KEEP DIGGING!
EVERYONE'S LOOKING TOWARDS THE MOON AT THIS MOMENT. IT'S NOW OR NEVER!

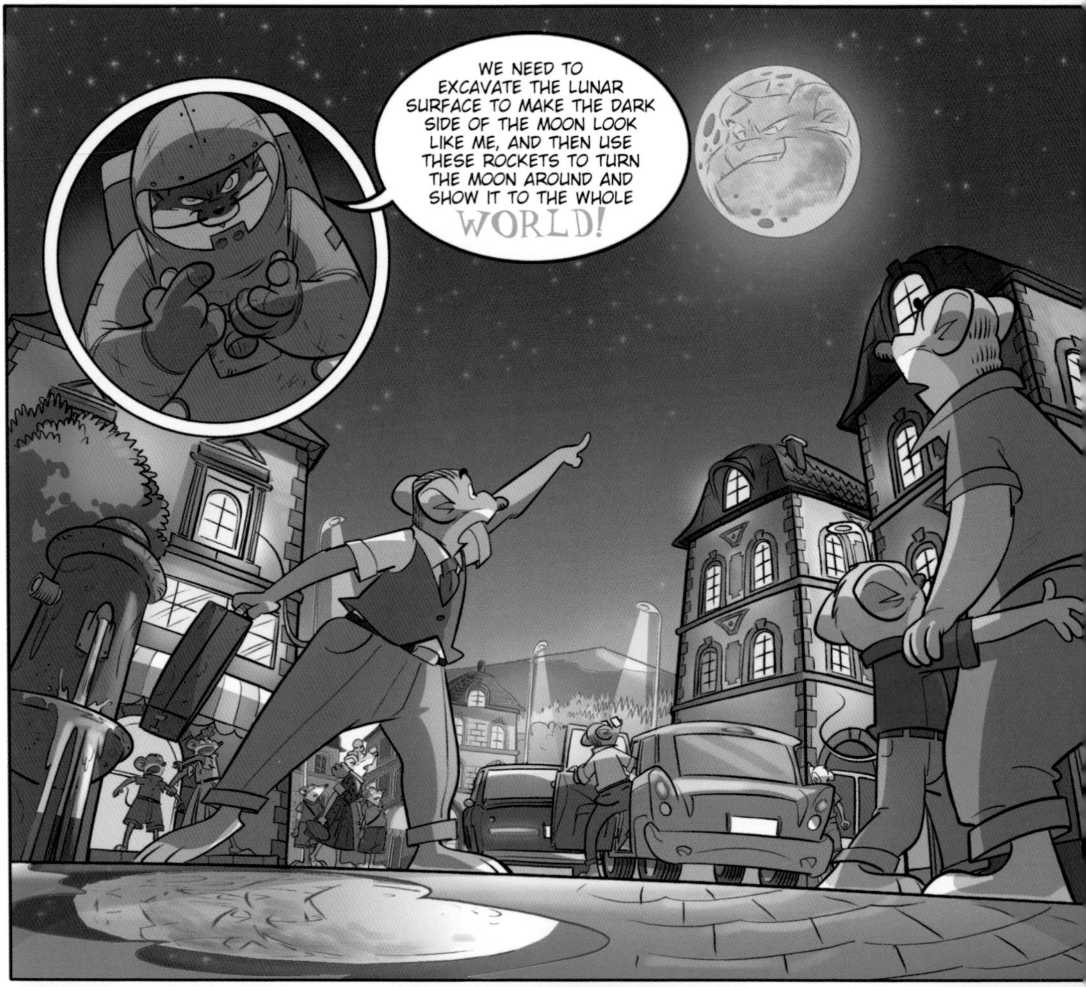
WE NEED TO EXCAVATE THE LUNAR SURFACE TO MAKE THE DARK SIDE OF THE MOON LOOK LIKE ME, AND THEN USE THESE ROCKETS TO TURN THE MOON AROUND AND SHOW IT TO THE WHOLE WORLD!
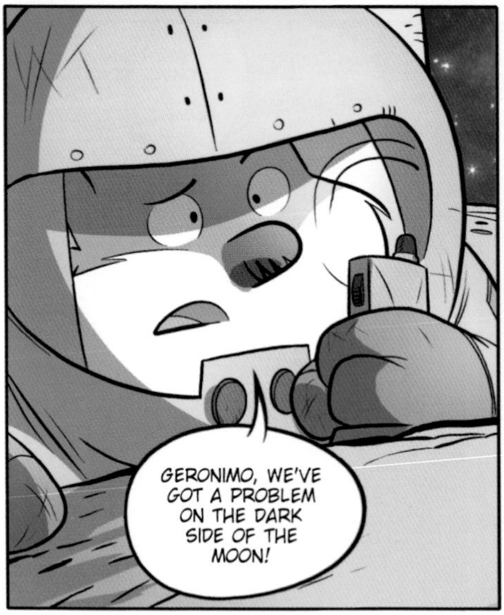
GERONIMO, WE'VE GOT A PROBLEM ON THE DARK SIDE OF THE MOON!
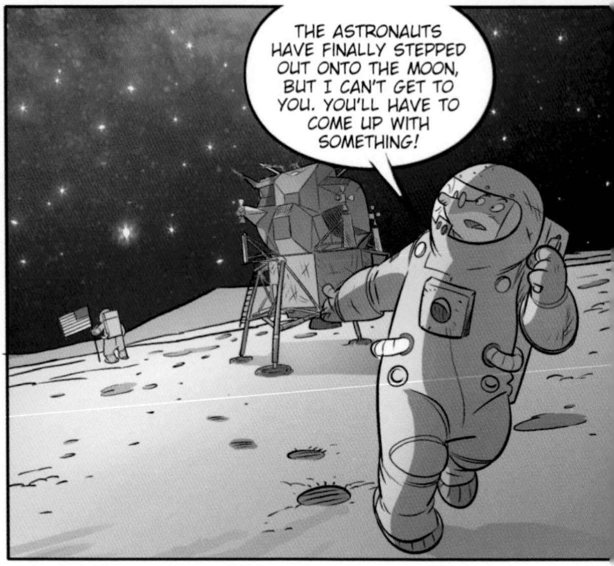
THE ASTRONAUTS HAVE FINALLY STEPPED OUT ONTO THE MOON, BUT I CAN'T GET TO YOU. YOU'LL HAVE TO COME UP WITH SOMETHING!

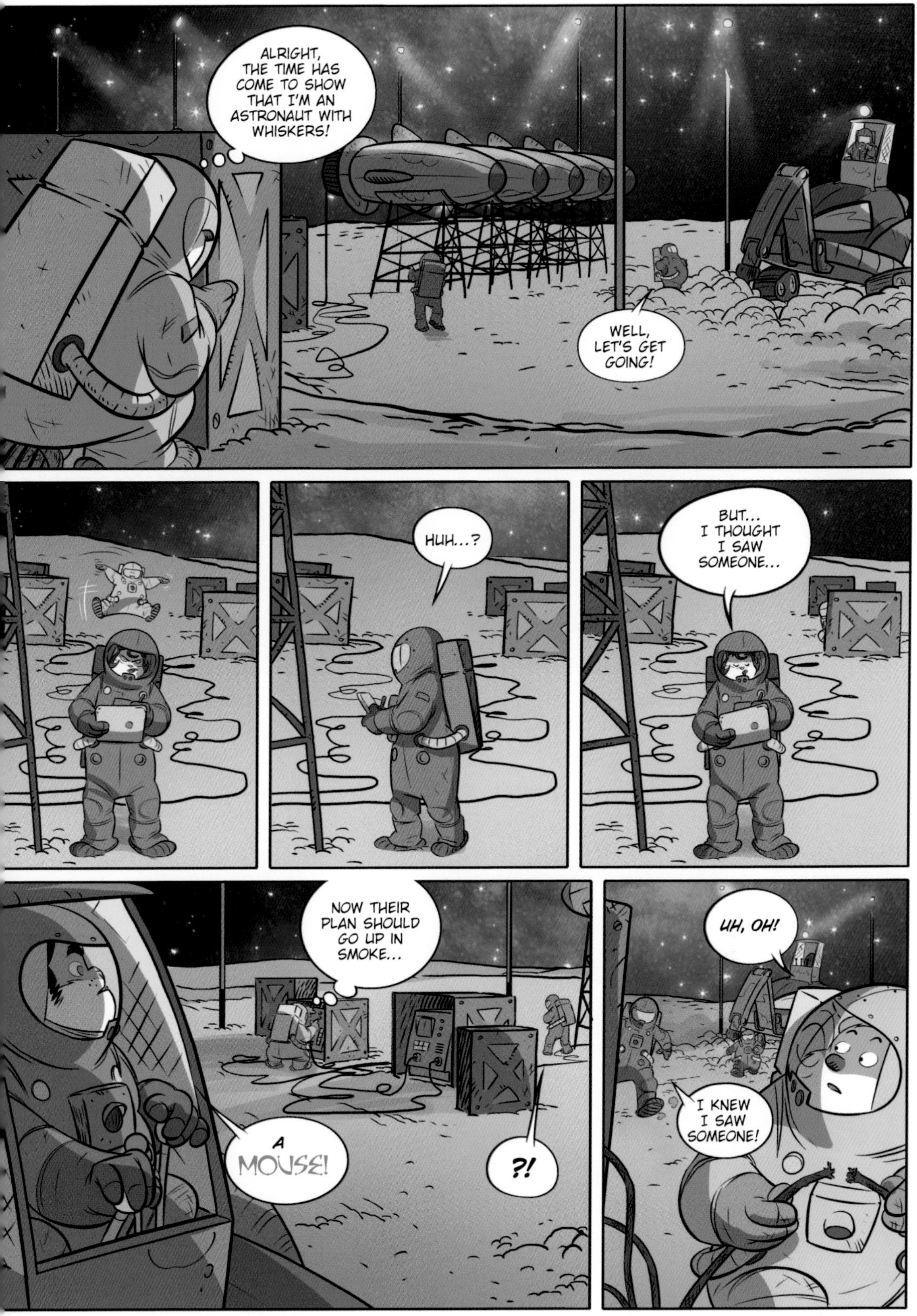
ALRIGHT, THE TIME HAS COME TO SHOW THAT I'M AN ASTRONAUT WITH WHISKERS!
WELL, LET'S GET GOING!
HUH...?
BUT... I THOUGHT I SAW SOMEONE...
NOW THEIR PLAN SHOULD GO UP IN SMOKE...
A MOUSE!
?!
UH, OH!
I KNEW I SAW SOMEONE!

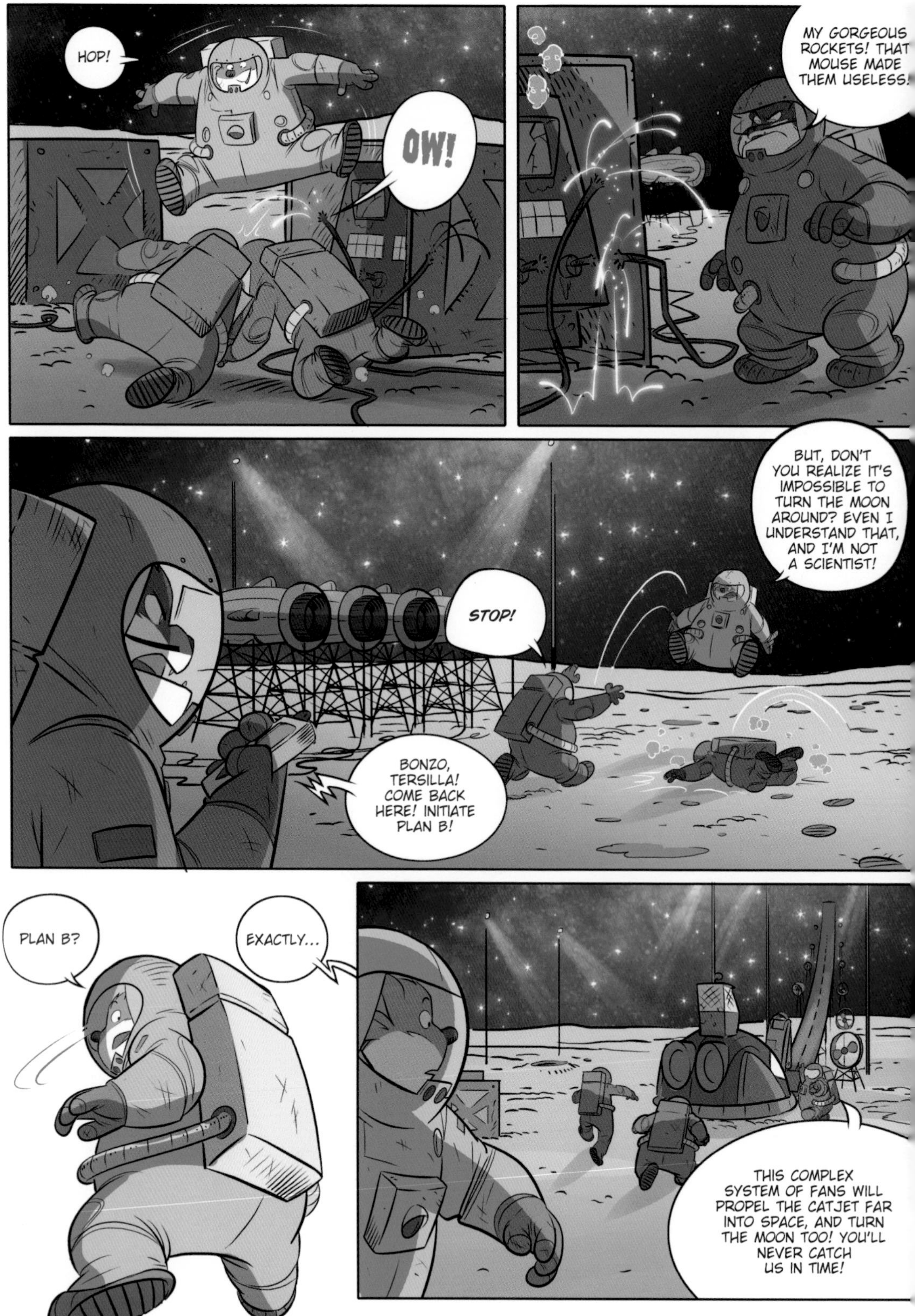
HOP!
OW!
MY GORGEOUS ROCKETS! THAT MOUSE MADE THEM USELESS!
BUT, DON'T YOU REALIZE IT'S IMPOSSIBLE TO TURN THE MOON AROUND? EVEN I UNDERSTAND THAT, AND I'M NOT A SCIENTIST!
STOP!
BONZO, TERSILLA! COME BACK HERE! INITIATE PLAN B!
PLAN B?
EXACTLY...
THIS COMPLEX SYSTEM OF FANS WILL PROPEL THE CATJET FAR INTO SPACE, AND TURN THE MOON TOO! YOU'LL NEVER CATCH US IN TIME!

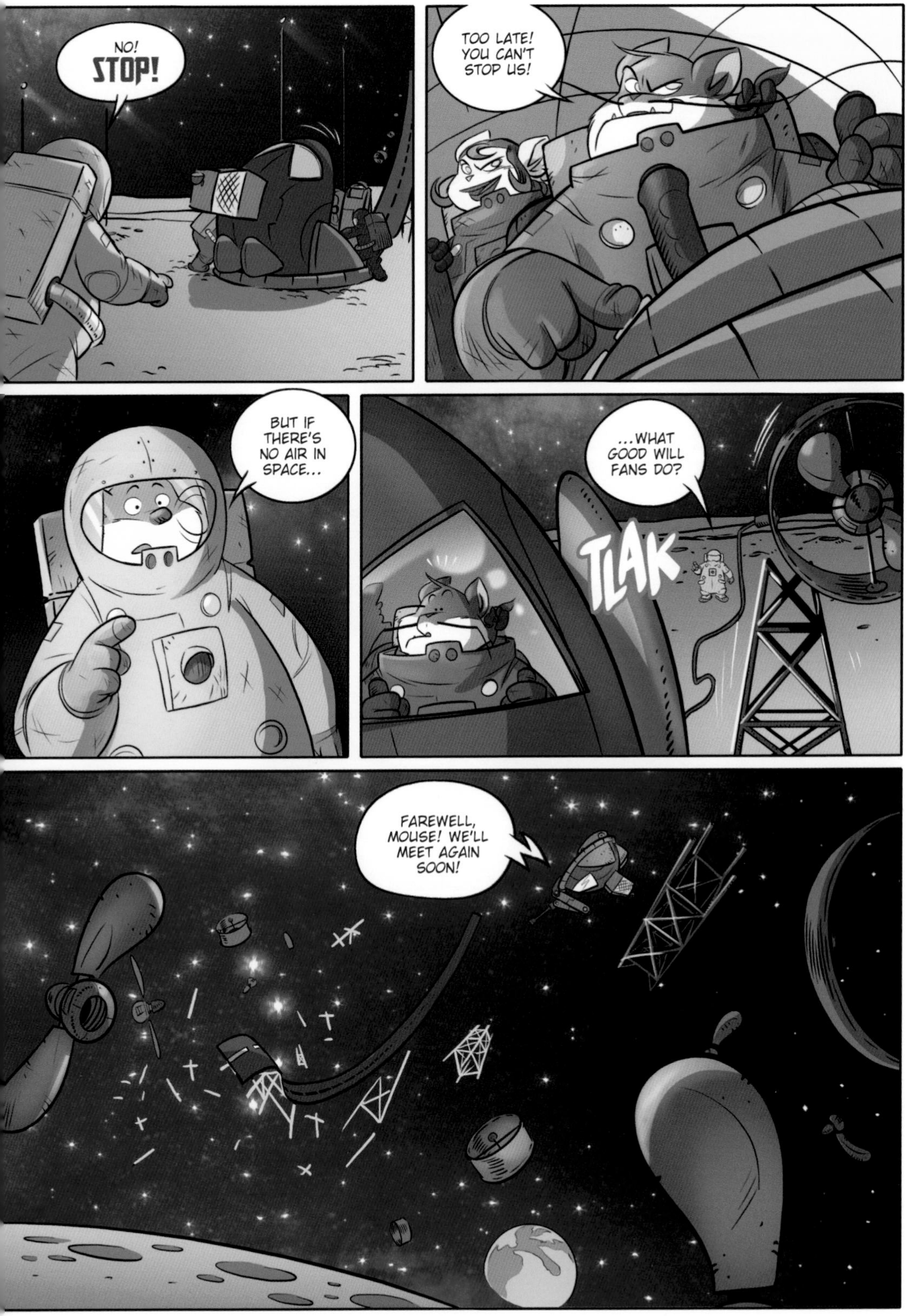
NO! STOP!
TOO LATE! YOU CAN'T STOP US!
BUT IF THERE'S NO AIR IN SPACE...
...WHAT GOOD WILL FANS DO?
TLAK
FAREWELL, MOUSE! WE'LL MEET AGAIN SOON!

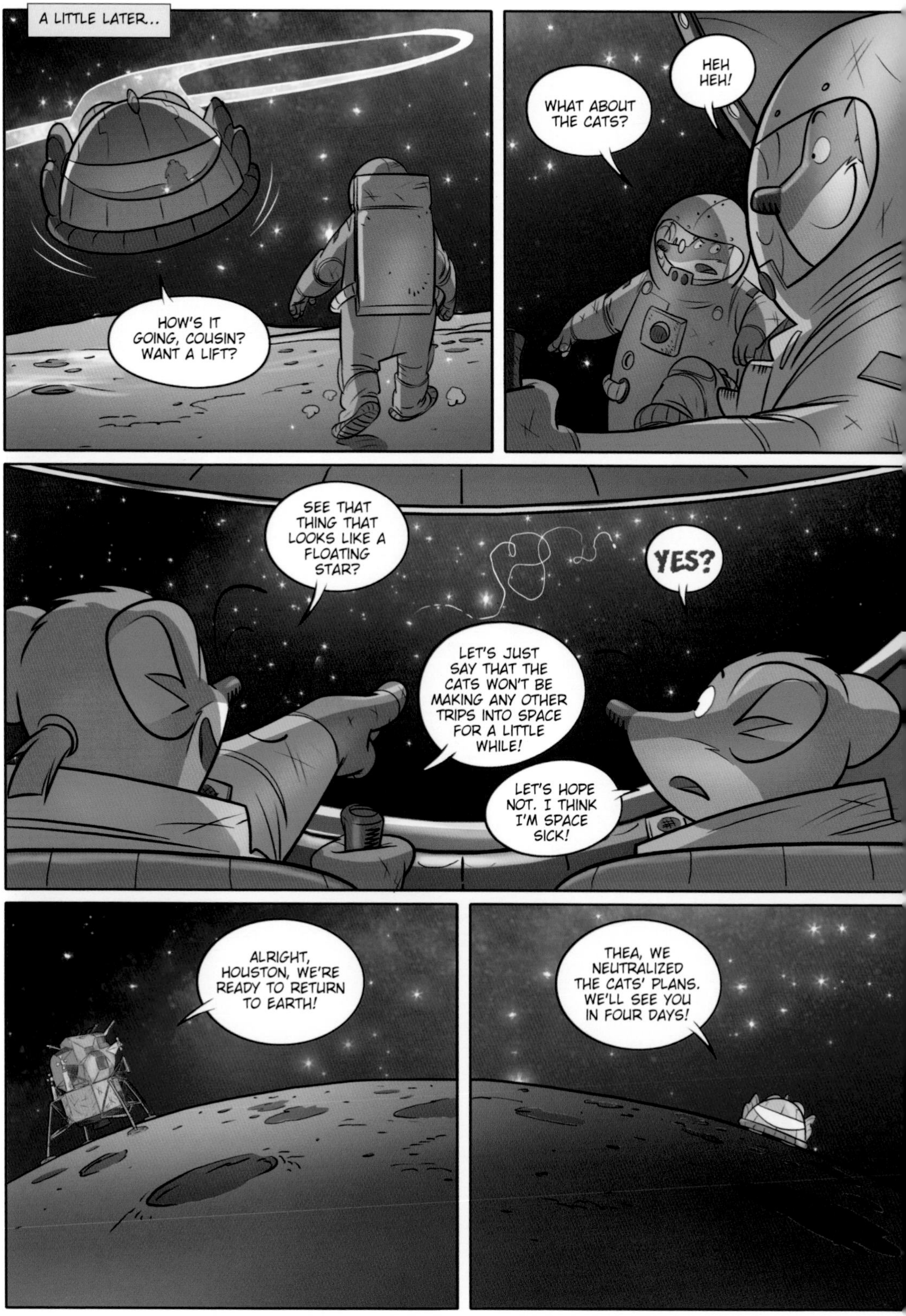
A LITTLE LATER...
HOW'S IT GOING, COUSIN? WANT A LIFT?
WHAT ABOUT THE CATS?
HEH HEH!
SEE THAT THING THAT LOOKS LIKE A FLOATING STAR?
YES?
LET'S JUST SAY THAT THE CATS WON'T BE MAKING ANY OTHER TRIPS INTO SPACE FOR A LITTLE WHILE!
LET'S HOPE NOT. I THINK I'M SPACE SICK!
ALRIGHT, HOUSTON, WE'RE READY TO RETURN TO EARTH!
THEA, WE NEUTRALIZED THE CATS' PLANS. WE'LL SEE YOU IN FOUR DAYS!

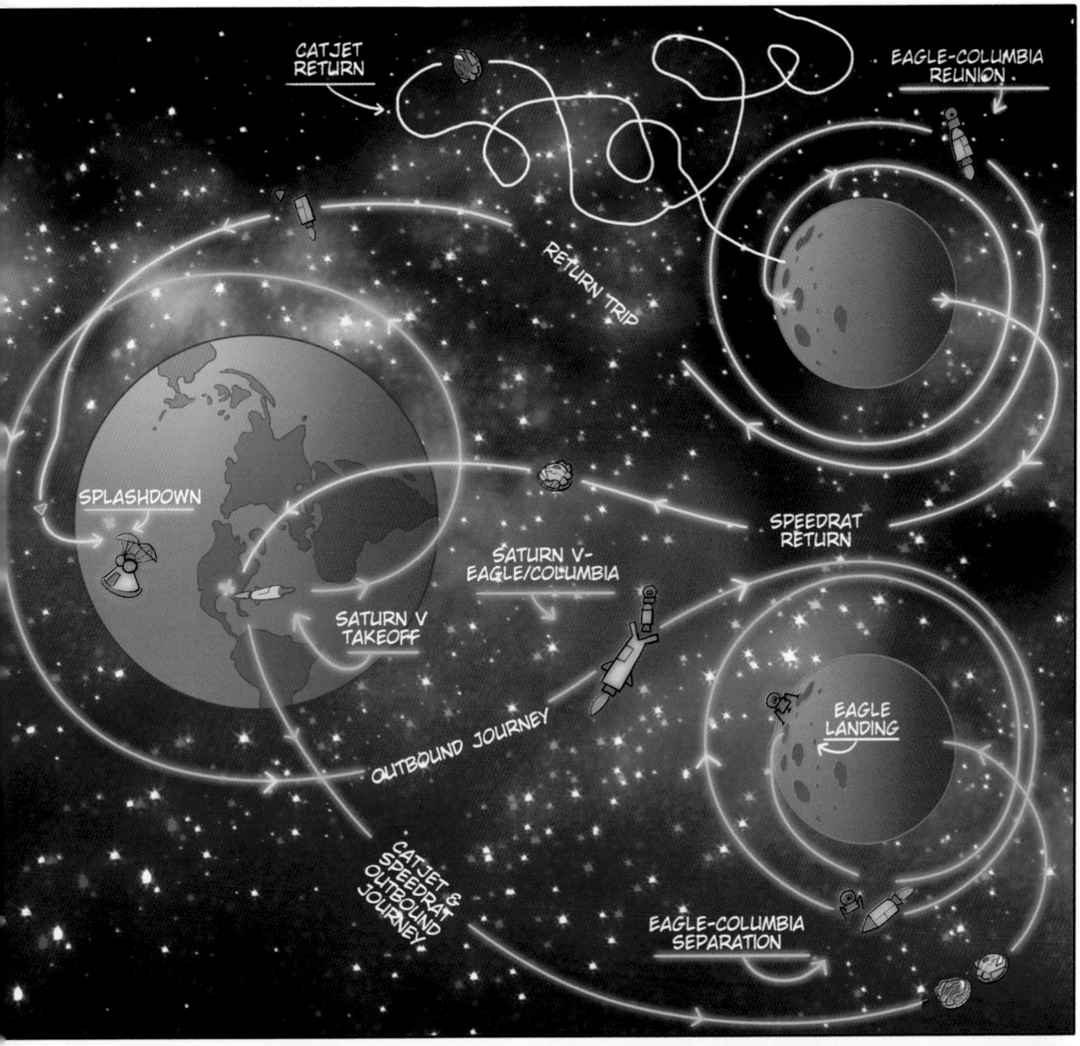
CATJET RETURN
EAGLE-COLUMBIA REUNION
RETURN TRIP
SPLASHDOWN
SPEEDRAT RETURN
SATURN V-EAGLE/COLUMBIA
SATURN V TAKEOFF
OUTBOUND JOURNEY
EAGLE LANDING
CATJET & SPEEDRAT OUTBOUND JOURNEY
EAGLE-COLUMBIA SEPARATION

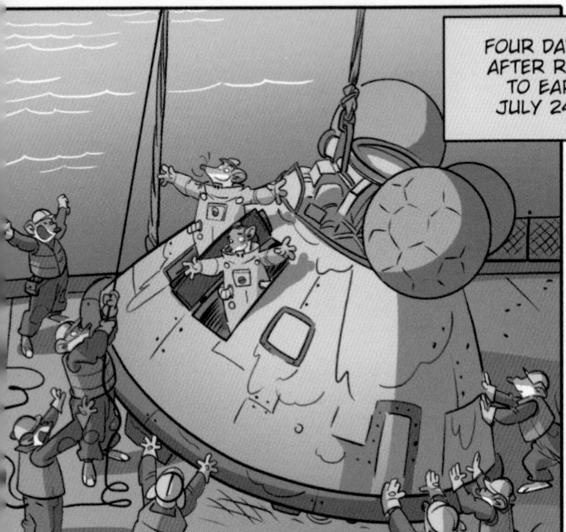
FOUR DAYS LATER, AFTER RETURNING TO EARTH, ON JULY 24, 1969...

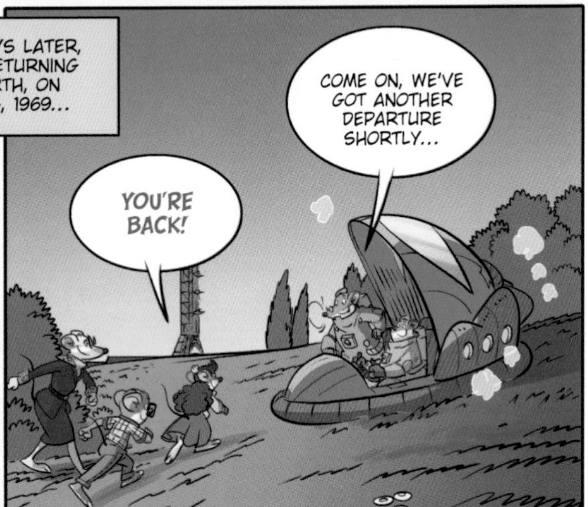
COME ON, WE'VE GOT ANOTHER DEPARTURE SHORTLY...
YOU'RE BACK!

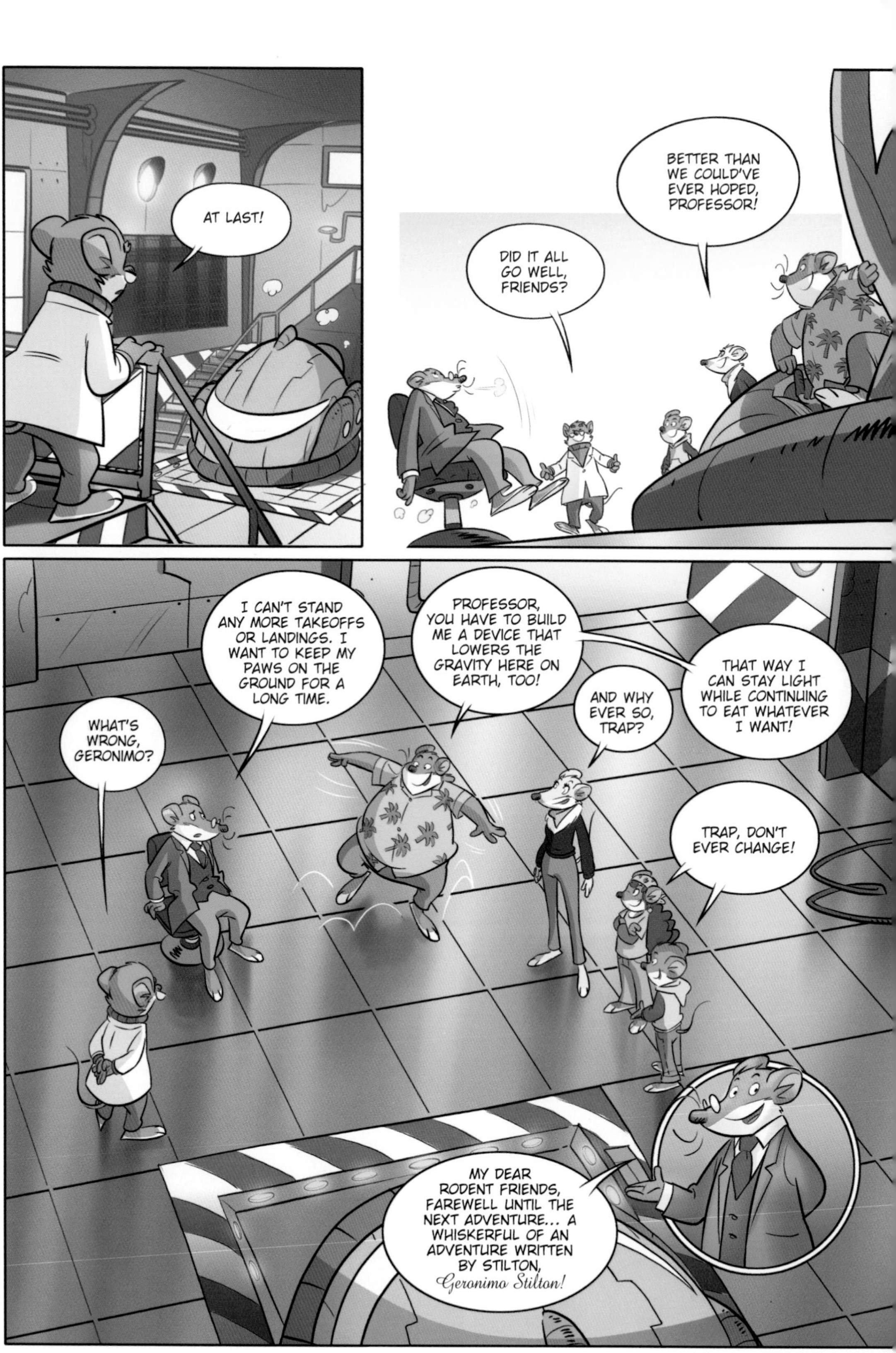
AT LAST!
DID IT ALL GO WELL, FRIENDS?
BETTER THAN WE COULD'VE EVER HOPED, PROFESSOR!
WHAT'S WRONG, GERONIMO?
I CAN'T STAND ANY MORE TAKEOFFS OR LANDINGS. I WANT TO KEEP MY PAWS ON THE GROUND FOR A LONG TIME.
PROFESSOR, YOU HAVE TO BUILD ME A DEVICE THAT LOWERS THE GRAVITY HERE ON EARTH, TOO!
AND WHY EVER SO, TRAP?
THAT WAY I CAN STAY LIGHT WHILE CONTINUING TO EAT WHATEVER I WANT!
TRAP, DON'T EVER CHANGE!
MY DEAR RODENT FRIENDS, FAREWELL UNTIL THE NEXT ADVENTURE... A WHISKERFUL OF AN ADVENTURE WRITTEN BY STILTON, Geronimo Stilton!

ALL FOR STILTON, STILTON FOR ALL!

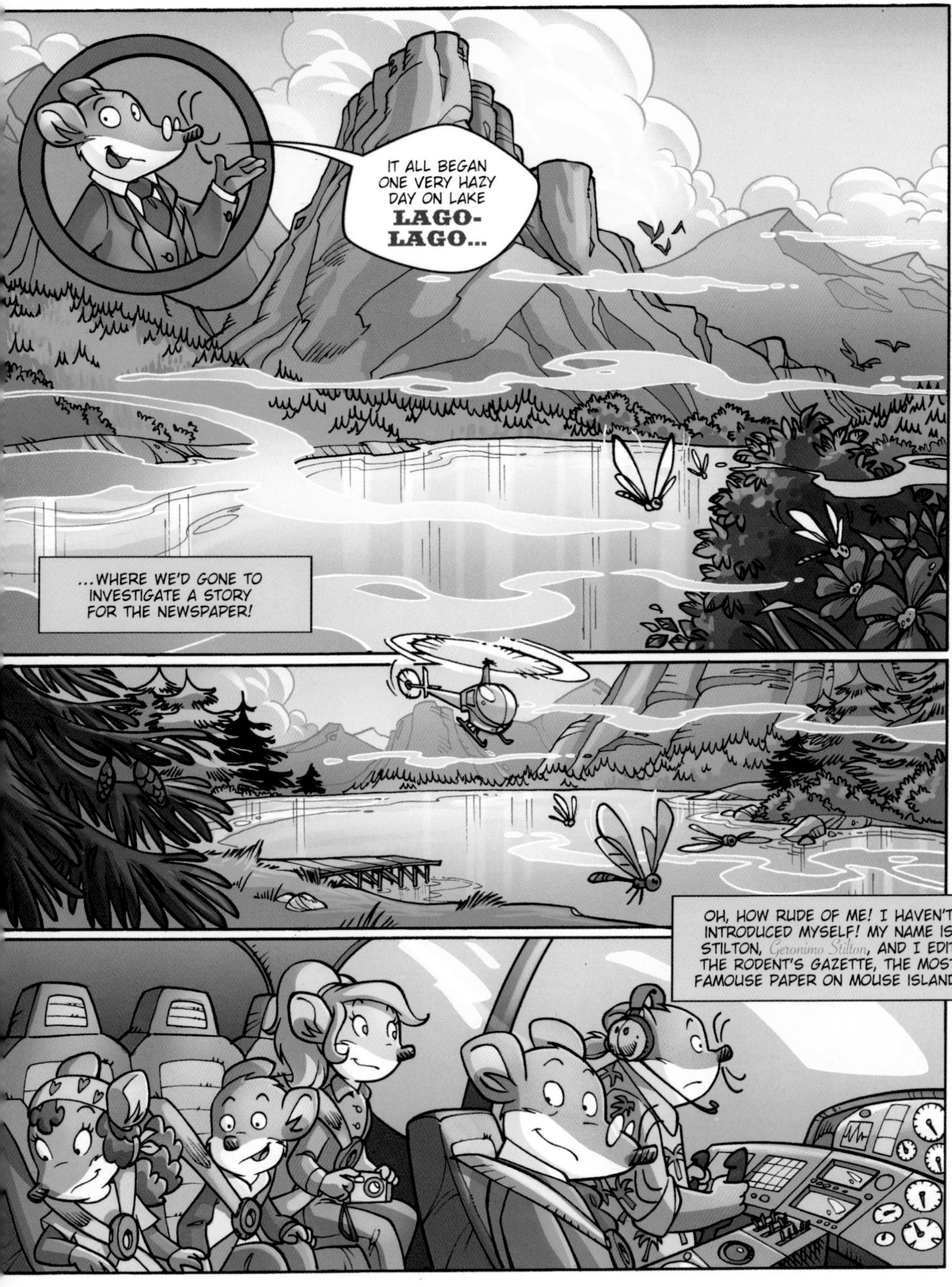
IT ALL BEGAN ONE VERY HAZY DAY ON LAKE **LAGO-LAGO...**
...WHERE WE'D GONE TO INVESTIGATE A STORY FOR THE NEWSPAPER!
OH, HOW RUDE OF ME! I HAVEN'T INTRODUCED MYSELF! MY NAME IS STILTON, *Geronimo Stilton*, AND I EDIT THE RODENT'S GAZETTE, THE MOST FAMOUSE PAPER ON MOUSE ISLAND!

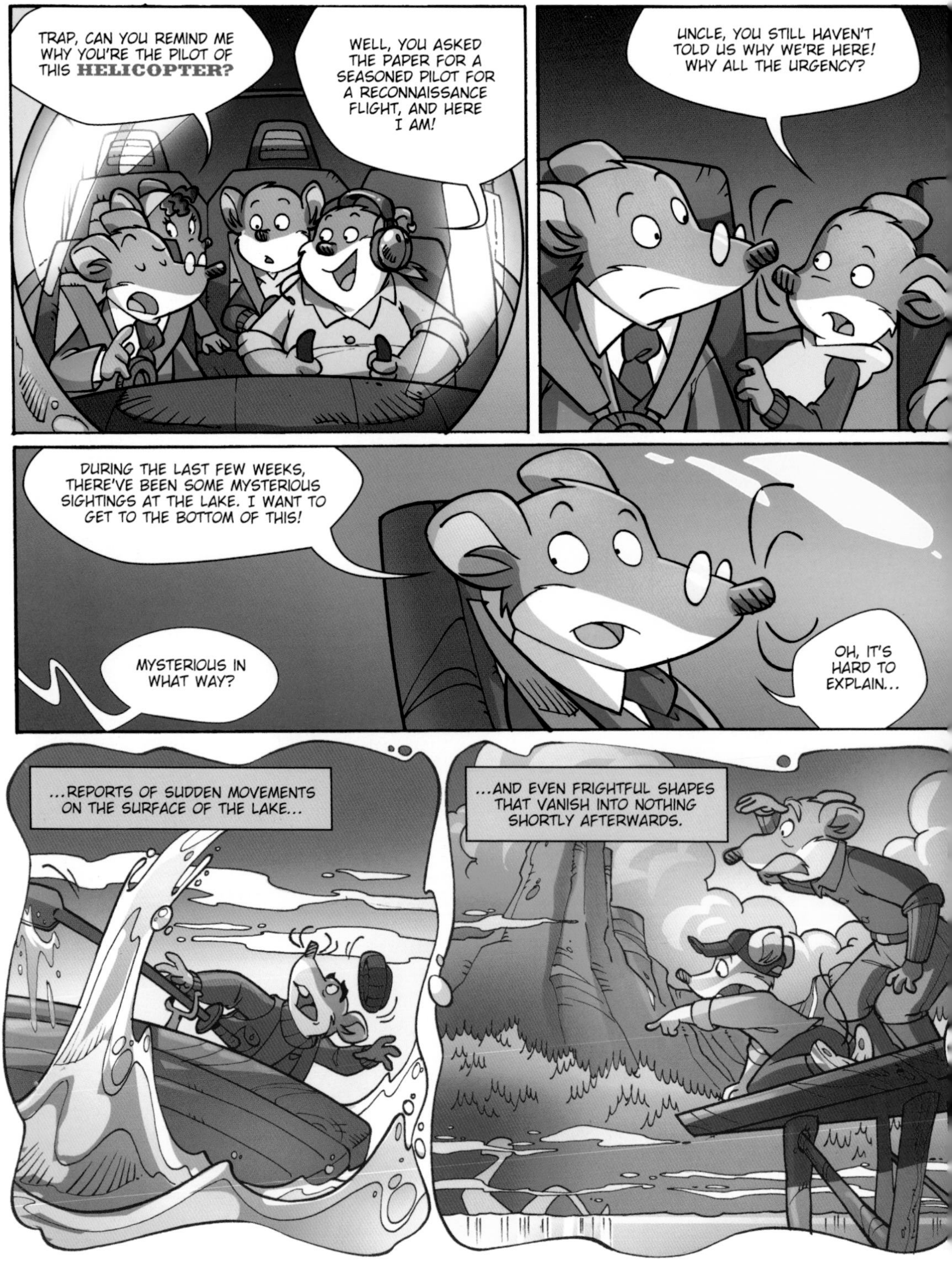

TRAP, CAN YOU REMIND ME WHY YOU'RE THE PILOT OF THIS HELICOPTER?
WELL, YOU ASKED THE PAPER FOR A SEASONED PILOT FOR A RECONNAISSANCE FLIGHT, AND HERE I AM!
UNCLE, YOU STILL HAVEN'T TOLD US WHY WE'RE HERE! WHY ALL THE URGENCY?
DURING THE LAST FEW WEEKS, THERE'VE BEEN SOME MYSTERIOUS SIGHTINGS AT THE LAKE. I WANT TO GET TO THE BOTTOM OF THIS!
MYSTERIOUS IN WHAT WAY?
OH, IT'S HARD TO EXPLAIN...
...REPORTS OF SUDDEN MOVEMENTS ON THE SURFACE OF THE LAKE...
...AND EVEN FRIGHTFUL SHAPES THAT VANISH INTO NOTHING SHORTLY AFTERWARDS.

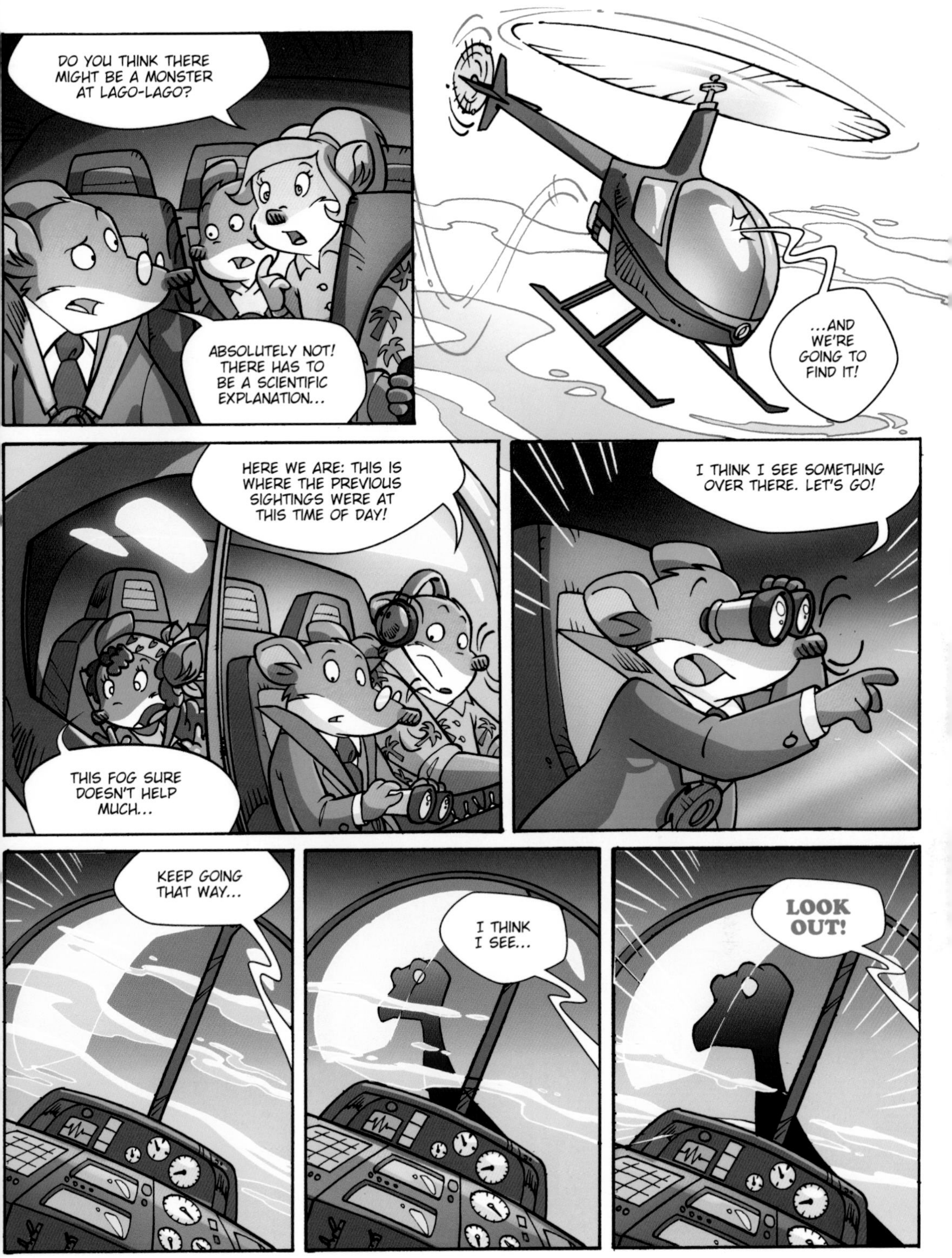
DO YOU THINK THERE MIGHT BE A MONSTER AT LAGO-LAGO?
ABSOLUTELY NOT! THERE HAS TO BE A SCIENTIFIC EXPLANATION...
...AND WE'RE GOING TO FIND IT!
HERE WE ARE: THIS IS WHERE THE PREVIOUS SIGHTINGS WERE AT THIS TIME OF DAY!
THIS FOG SURE DOESN'T HELP MUCH...
I THINK I SEE SOMETHING OVER THERE. LET'S GO!
KEEP GOING THAT WAY...
I THINK I SEE...
LOOK OUT!

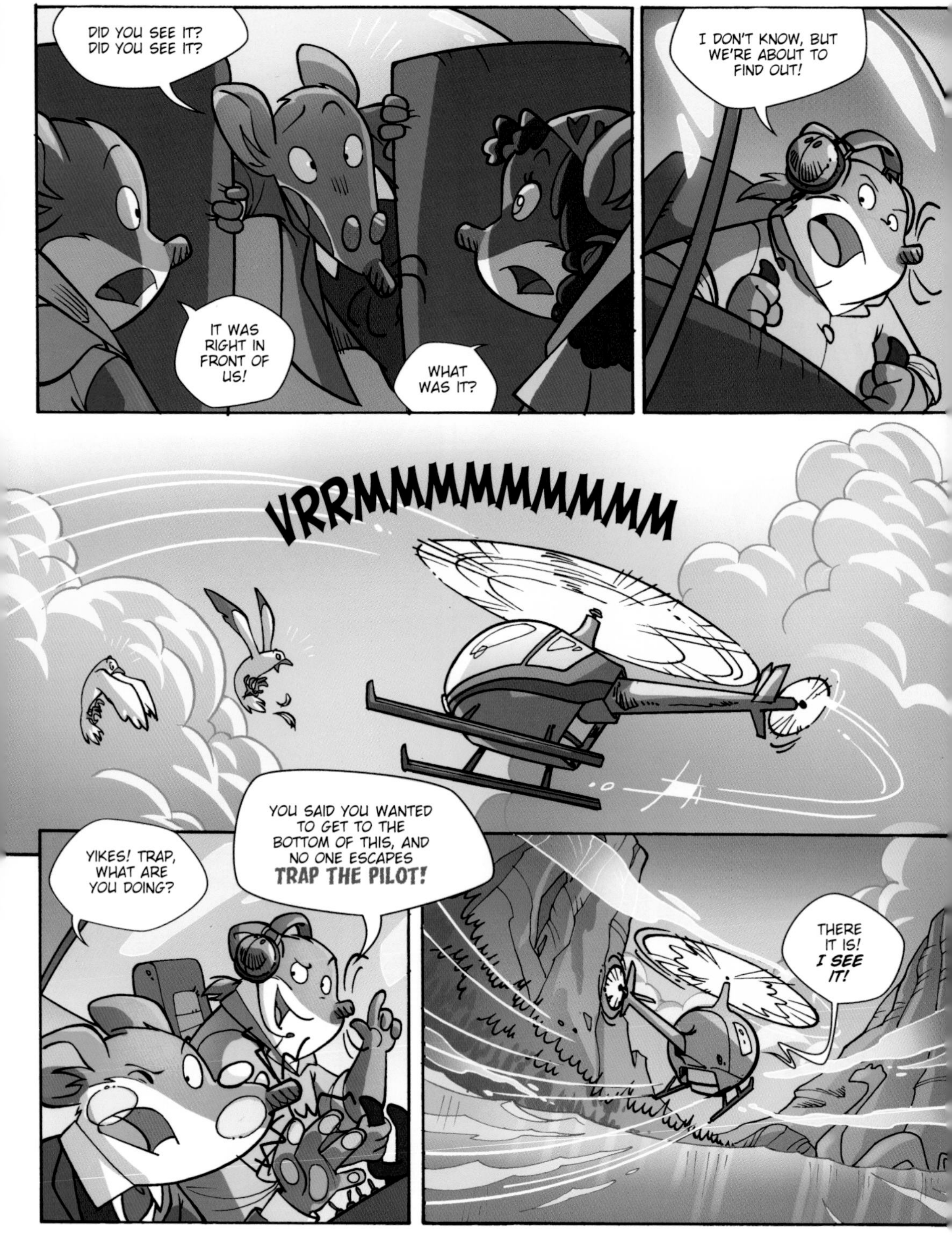
DID YOU SEE IT? DID YOU SEE IT?
IT WAS RIGHT IN FRONT OF US!
WHAT WAS IT?
I DON'T KNOW, BUT WE'RE ABOUT TO FIND OUT!
VRRMMMMMMMMMM
YIKES! TRAP, WHAT ARE YOU DOING?
YOU SAID YOU WANTED TO GET TO THE BOTTOM OF THIS, AND NO ONE ESCAPES TRAP THE PILOT!
THERE IT IS! I SEE IT!

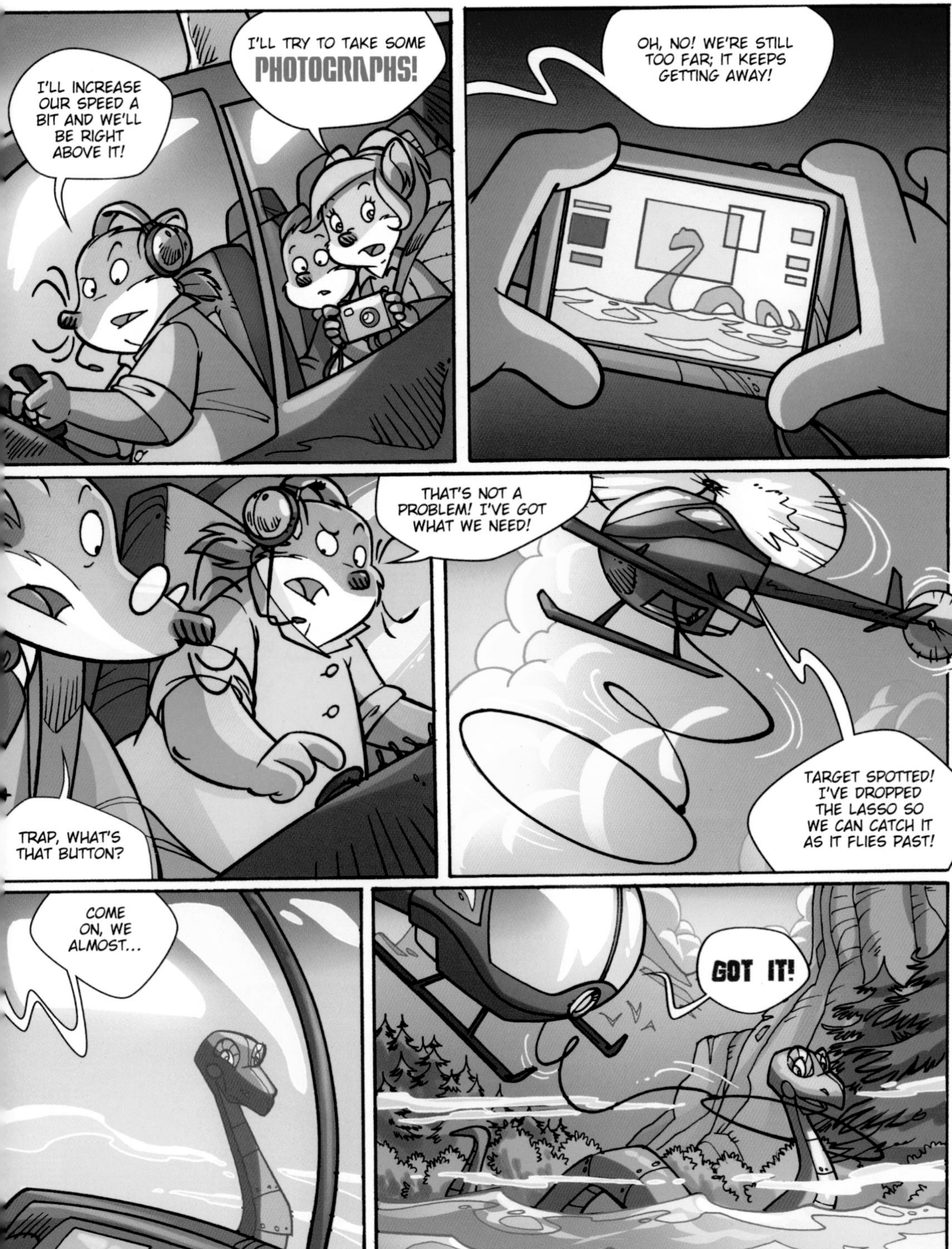
I'LL INCREASE OUR SPEED A BIT AND WE'LL BE RIGHT ABOVE IT!
I'LL TRY TO TAKE SOME PHOTOGRAPHS!
OH, NO! WE'RE STILL TOO FAR; IT KEEPS GETTING AWAY!
THAT'S NOT A PROBLEM! I'VE GOT WHAT WE NEED!
TRAP, WHAT'S THAT BUTTON?
TARGET SPOTTED! I'VE DROPPED THE LASSO SO WE CAN CATCH IT AS IT FLIES PAST!
COME ON, WE ALMOST...
GOT IT!

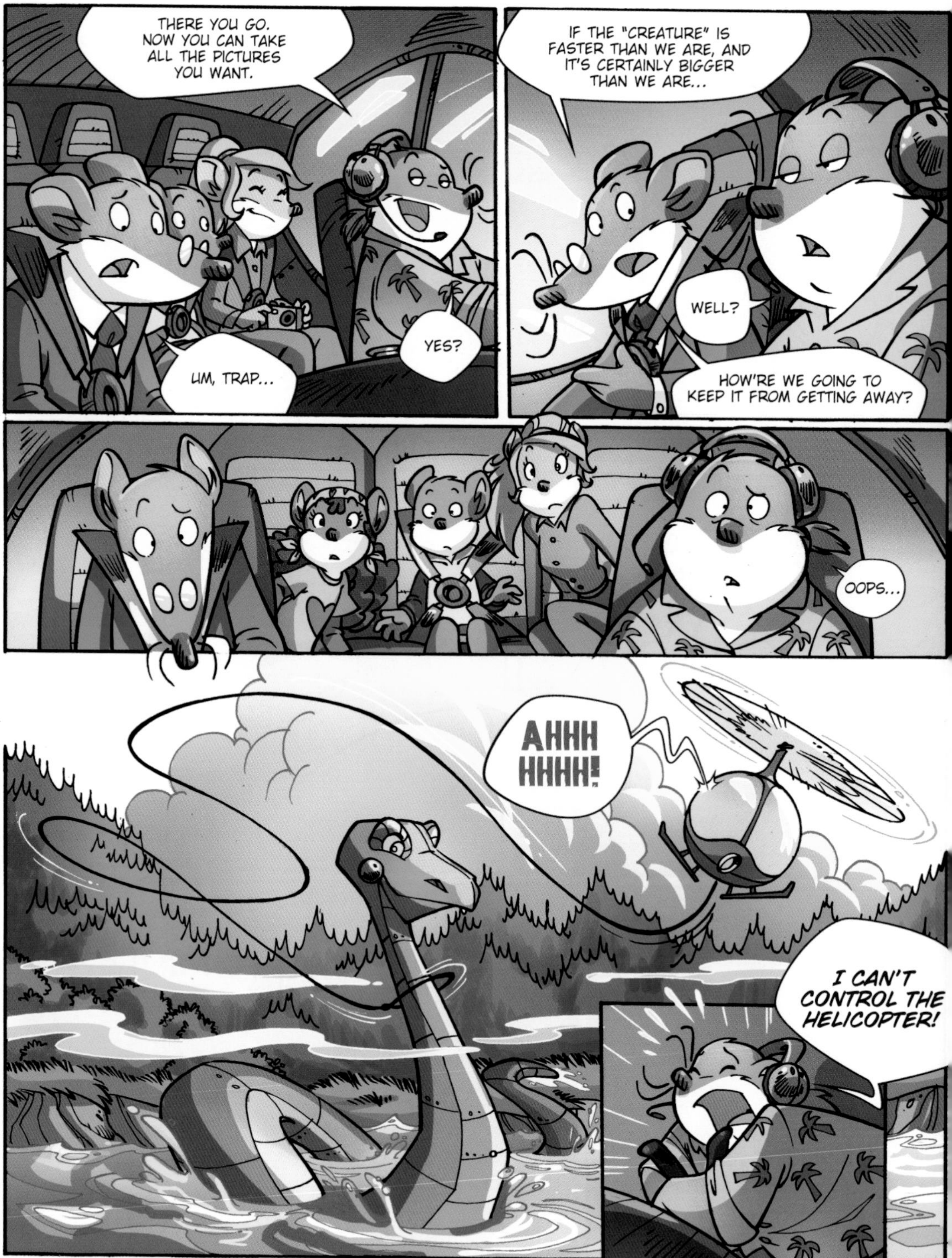
THERE YOU GO. NOW YOU CAN TAKE ALL THE PICTURES YOU WANT.
UM, TRAP...
YES?
IF THE "CREATURE" IS FASTER THAN WE ARE, AND IT'S CERTAINLY BIGGER THAN WE ARE...
WELL?
HOW'RE WE GOING TO KEEP IT FROM GETTING AWAY?
OOPS...
AHHHHHHH!
I CAN'T CONTROL THE HELICOPTER!

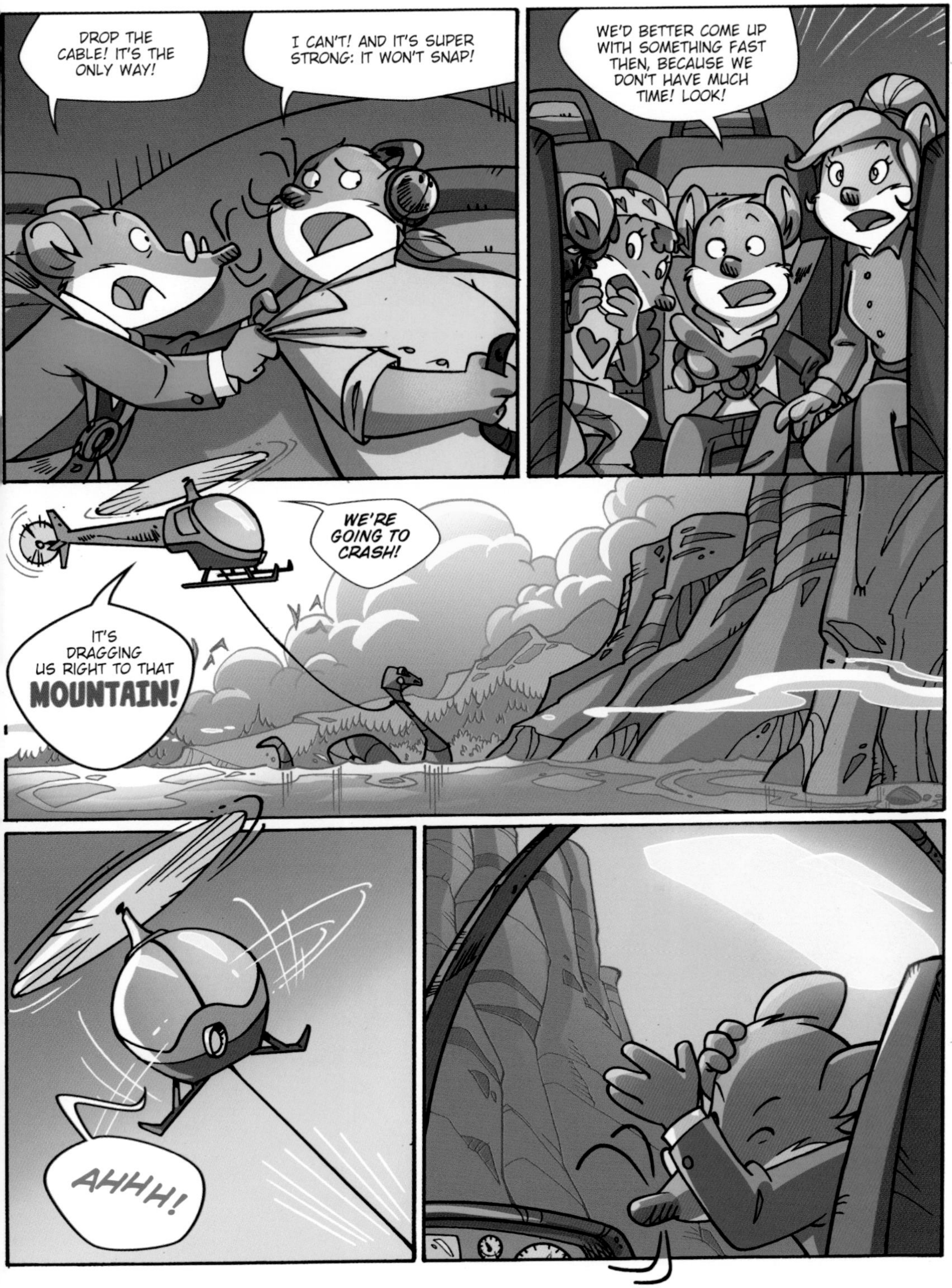
DROP THE CABLE! IT'S THE ONLY WAY!
I CAN'T! AND IT'S SUPER STRONG: IT WON'T SNAP!
WE'D BETTER COME UP WITH SOMETHING FAST THEN, BECAUSE WE DON'T HAVE MUCH TIME! LOOK!
WE'RE GOING TO CRASH!
IT'S DRAGGING US RIGHT TO THAT MOUNTAIN!
AHHHH!

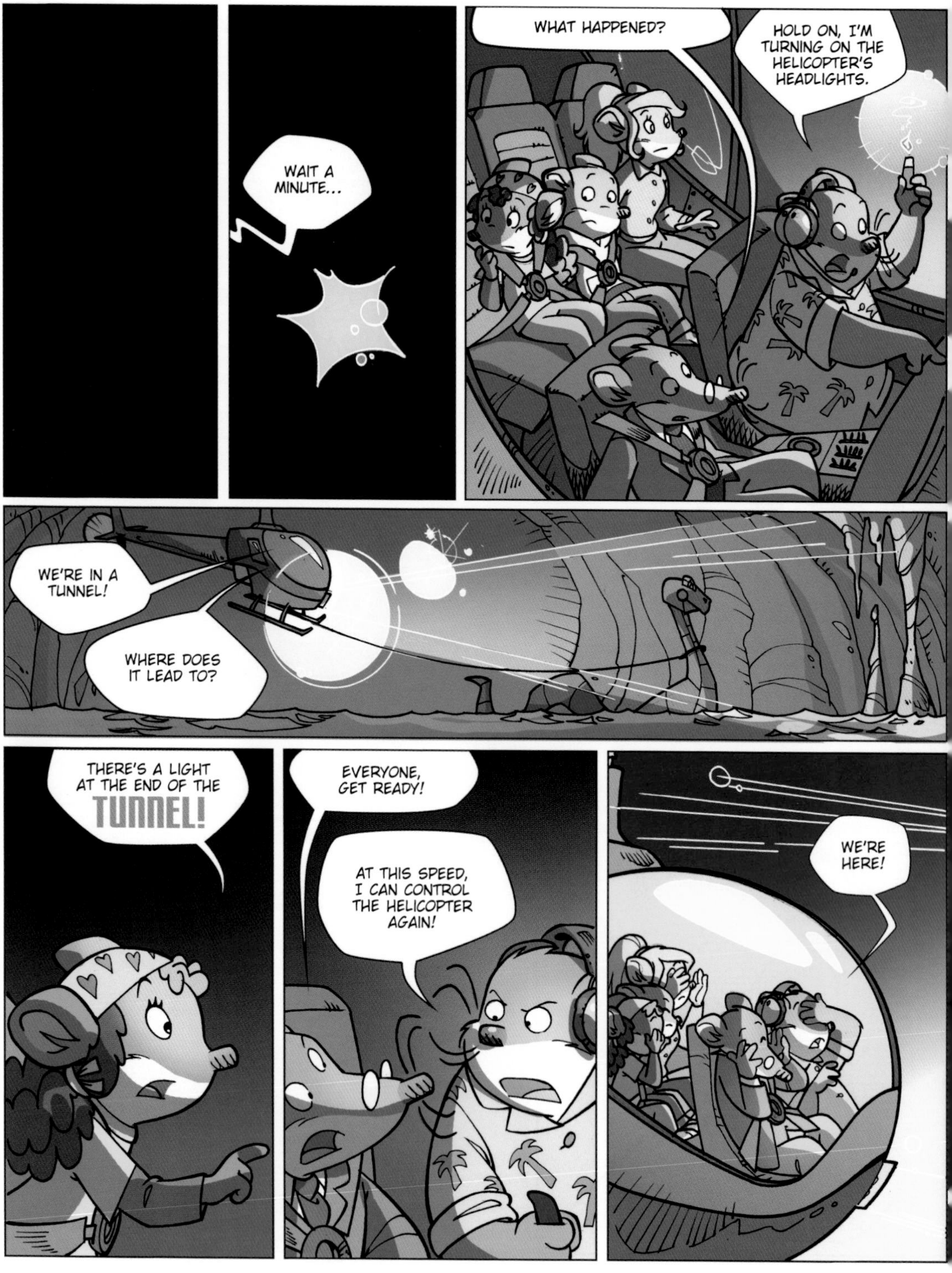
WAIT A MINUTE...
WHAT HAPPENED?
HOLD ON, I'M TURNING ON THE HELICOPTER'S HEADLIGHTS.
WE'RE IN A TUNNEL!
WHERE DOES IT LEAD TO?
THERE'S A LIGHT AT THE END OF THE TUNNEL!
EVERYONE, GET READY!
AT THIS SPEED, I CAN CONTROL THE HELICOPTER AGAIN!
WE'RE HERE!

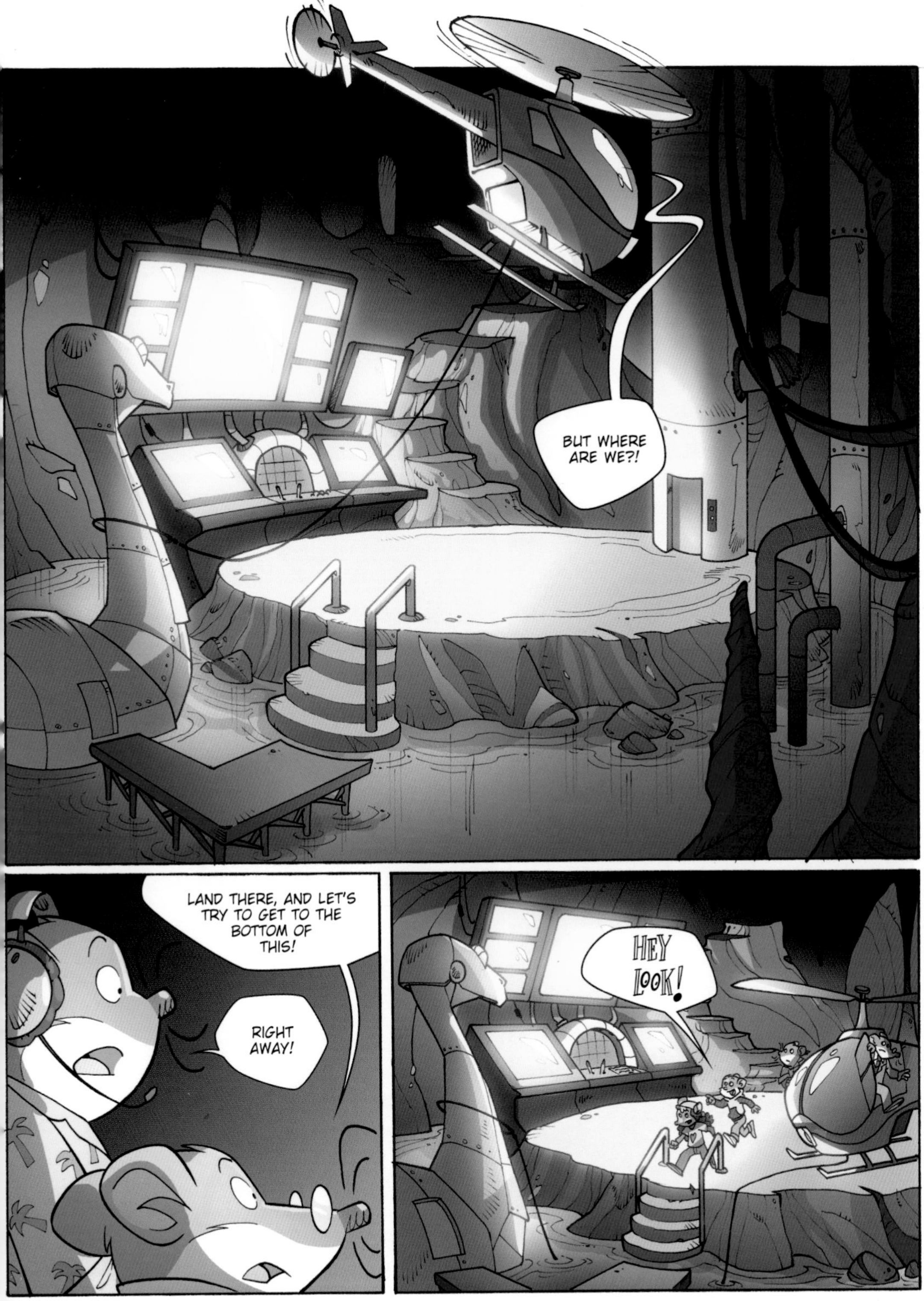
BUT WHERE ARE WE?!
LAND THERE, AND LET'S TRY TO GET TO THE BOTTOM OF THIS!
RIGHT AWAY!
HEY LOOK!

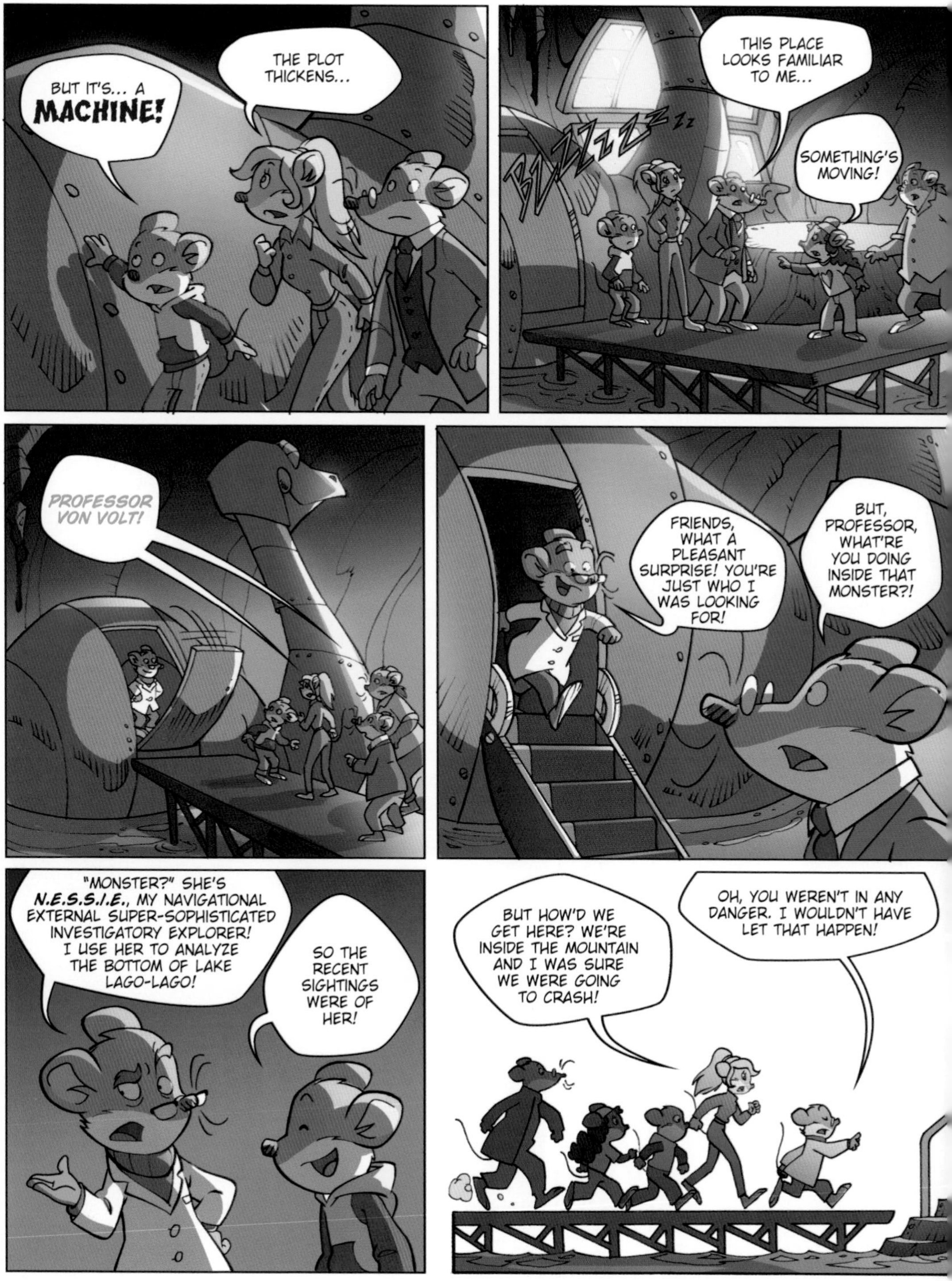

BUT IT'S... A MACHINE!
THE PLOT THICKENS...
THIS PLACE LOOKS FAMILIAR TO ME...
BZZZZZZZZZ
SOMETHING'S MOVING!
PROFESSOR VON VOLT!
FRIENDS, WHAT A PLEASANT SURPRISE! YOU'RE JUST WHO I WAS LOOKING FOR!
BUT, PROFESSOR, WHAT'RE YOU DOING INSIDE THAT MONSTER?!
"MONSTER?" SHE'S N.E.S.S.I.E., MY NAVIGATIONAL EXTERNAL SUPER-SOPHISTICATED INVESTIGATORY EXPLORER! I USE HER TO ANALYZE THE BOTTOM OF LAKE LAGO-LAGO!
SO THE RECENT SIGHTINGS WERE OF HER!
BUT HOW'D WE GET HERE? WE'RE INSIDE THE MOUNTAIN AND I WAS SURE WE WERE GOING TO CRASH!
OH, YOU WEREN'T IN ANY DANGER. I WOULDN'T HAVE LET THAT HAPPEN!

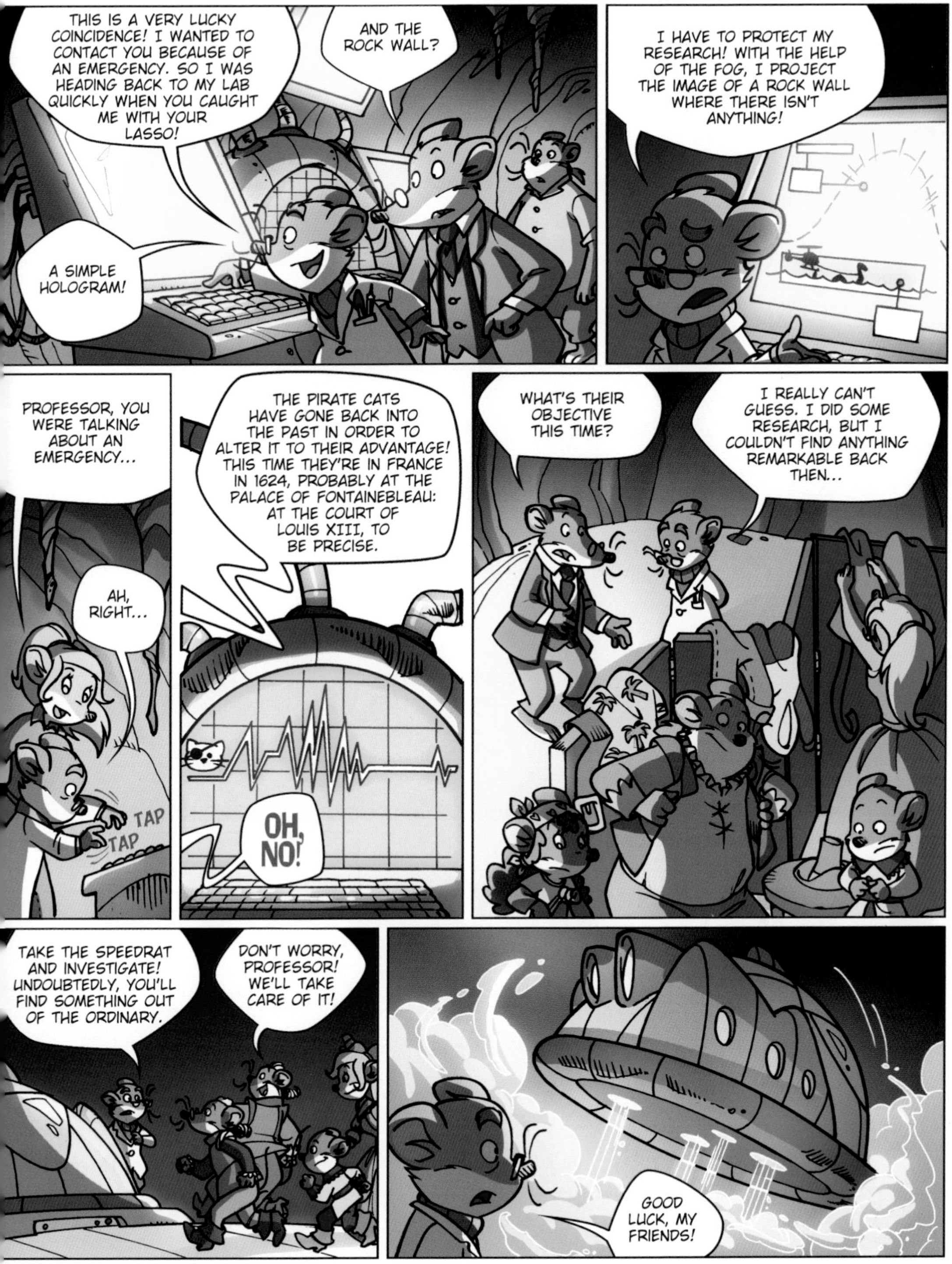
THIS IS A VERY LUCKY COINCIDENCE! I WANTED TO CONTACT YOU BECAUSE OF AN EMERGENCY. SO I WAS HEADING BACK TO MY LAB QUICKLY WHEN YOU CAUGHT ME WITH YOUR LASSO!
AND THE ROCK WALL?
A SIMPLE HOLOGRAM!
I HAVE TO PROTECT MY RESEARCH! WITH THE HELP OF THE FOG, I PROJECT THE IMAGE OF A ROCK WALL WHERE THERE ISN'T ANYTHING!
PROFESSOR, YOU WERE TALKING ABOUT AN EMERGENCY...
AH, RIGHT...
TAP
TAP
THE PIRATE CATS HAVE GONE BACK INTO THE PAST IN ORDER TO ALTER IT TO THEIR ADVANTAGE! THIS TIME THEY'RE IN FRANCE IN 1624, PROBABLY AT THE PALACE OF FONTAINEBLEAU: AT THE COURT OF LOUIS XIII, TO BE PRECISE.
OH, NO!
WHAT'S THEIR OBJECTIVE THIS TIME?
I REALLY CAN'T GUESS. I DID SOME RESEARCH, BUT I COULDN'T FIND ANYTHING REMARKABLE BACK THEN...
TAKE THE SPEEDRAT AND INVESTIGATE! UNDOUBTEDLY, YOU'LL FIND SOMETHING OUT OF THE ORDINARY.
DON'T WORRY, PROFESSOR! WE'LL TAKE CARE OF IT!
GOOD LUCK, MY FRIENDS!

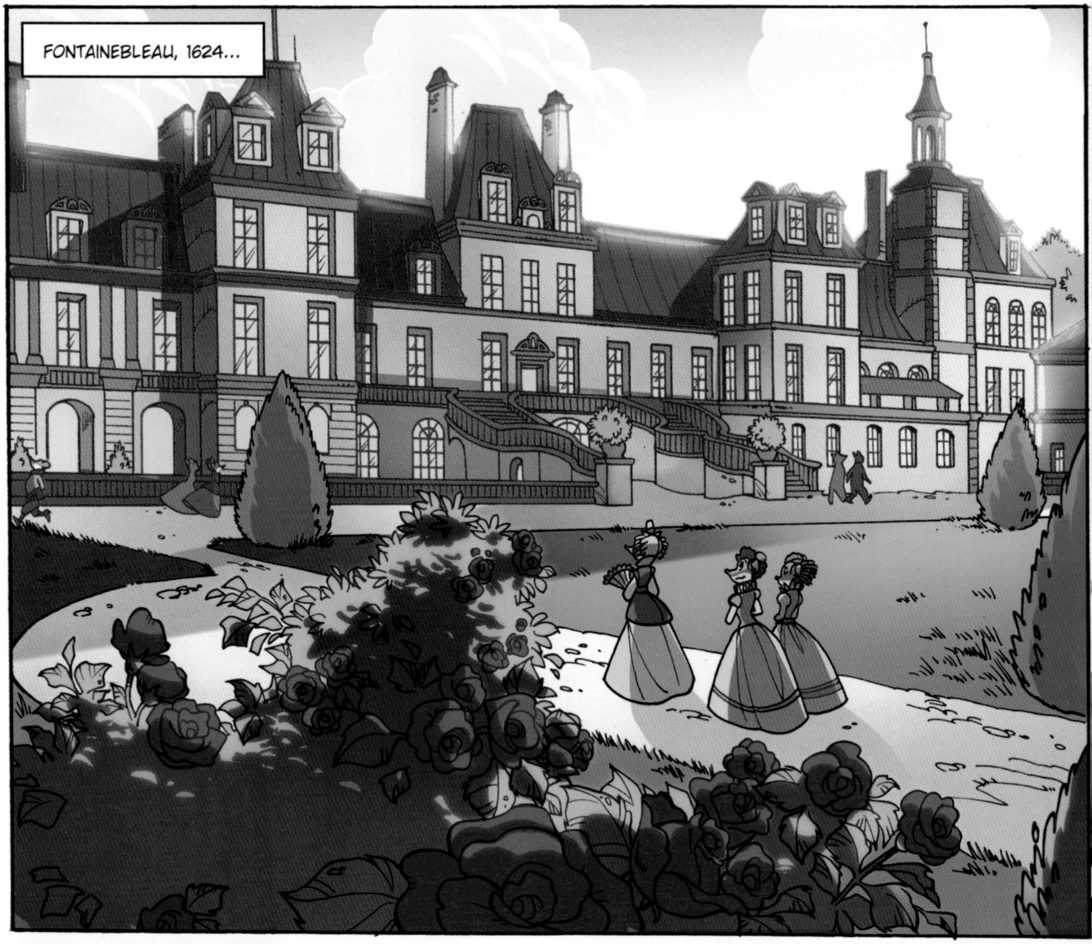
FONTAINEBLEAU, 1624...

THE PALACE OF FONTAINEBLEAU IS A CASTLE LOCATED IN THE SMALL TOWN OF THE SAME NAME-- AS OPPOSED TO THE OTHER FAMOUS FRENCH CASTLE, VERSAILLES. MANY FRENCH MONARCHS CONTRIBUTED TO THE CASTLE, STARTING WITH KING LOUIS VII IN THE 12TH CENTURY. DURING THE RENAISSANCE IT WAS REBUILT BY FRANCIS I. IT FELL OUT OF USE DURING THE FRENCH REVOLUTION, BUT WAS BROUGHT BACK BY NAPOLEON. THE CASTLE IS NOW A UNESCO WORLD HERITAGE SITE AND HOUSES A SCHOOL OF ART, ARCHITECTURE, AND MUSIC.

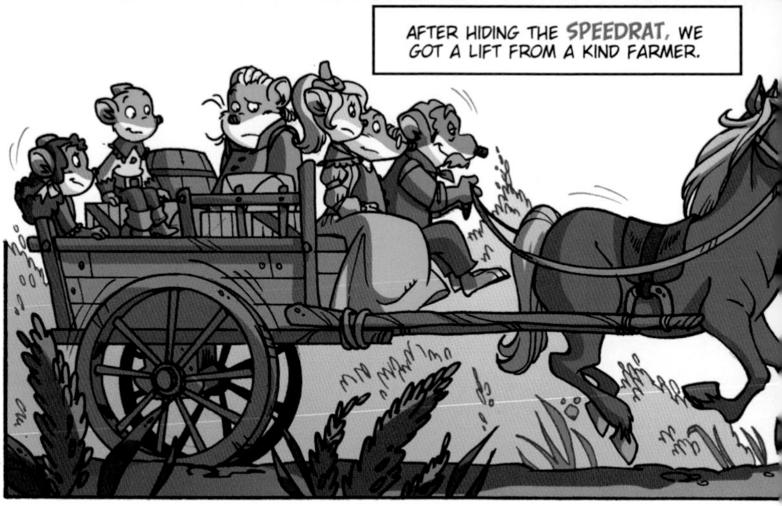
AFTER HIDING THE SPEEDRAT, WE GOT A LIFT FROM A KIND FARMER.

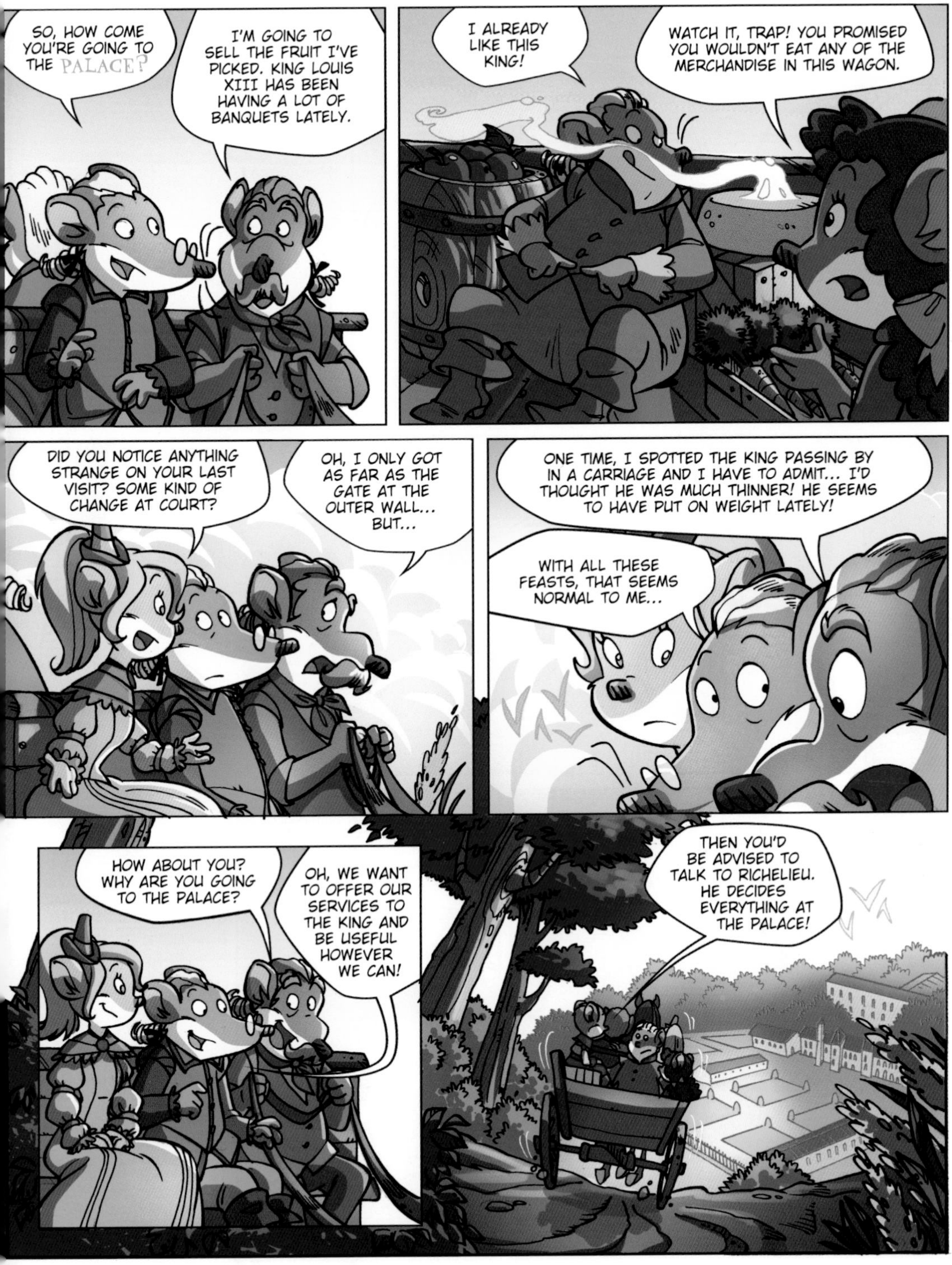
SO, HOW COME YOU'RE GOING TO THE PALACE?
I'M GOING TO SELL THE FRUIT I'VE PICKED. KING LOUIS XIII HAS BEEN HAVING A LOT OF BANQUETS LATELY.
I ALREADY LIKE THIS KING!
WATCH IT, TRAP! YOU PROMISED YOU WOULDN'T EAT ANY OF THE MERCHANDISE IN THIS WAGON.
DID YOU NOTICE ANYTHING STRANGE ON YOUR LAST VISIT? SOME KIND OF CHANGE AT COURT?
OH, I ONLY GOT AS FAR AS THE GATE AT THE OUTER WALL... BUT...
ONE TIME, I SPOTTED THE KING PASSING BY IN A CARRIAGE AND I HAVE TO ADMIT... I'D THOUGHT HE WAS MUCH THINNER! HE SEEMS TO HAVE PUT ON WEIGHT LATELY!
WITH ALL THESE FEASTS, THAT SEEMS NORMAL TO ME...
HOW ABOUT YOU? WHY ARE YOU GOING TO THE PALACE?
OH, WE WANT TO OFFER OUR SERVICES TO THE KING AND BE USEFUL HOWEVER WE CAN!
THEN YOU'D BE ADVISED TO TALK TO RICHELIEU. HE DECIDES EVERYTHING AT THE PALACE!

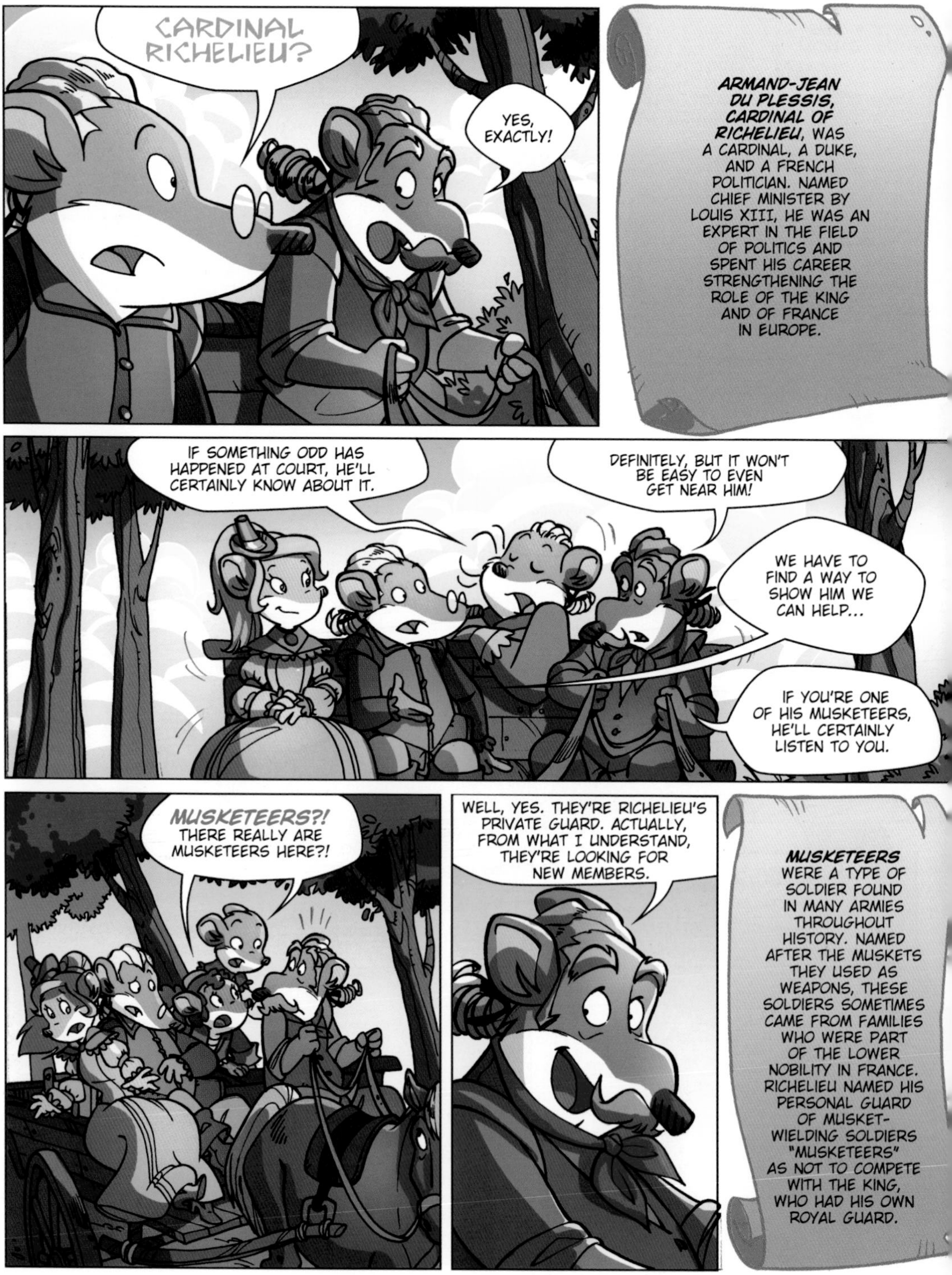
CARDINAL RICHELIEU?
YES, EXACTLY!
ARMAND-JEAN DU PLESSIS, CARDINAL OF RICHELIEU, WAS A CARDINAL, A DUKE, AND A FRENCH POLITICIAN. NAMED CHIEF MINISTER BY LOUIS XIII, HE WAS AN EXPERT IN THE FIELD OF POLITICS AND SPENT HIS CAREER STRENGTHENING THE ROLE OF THE KING AND OF FRANCE IN EUROPE.
IF SOMETHING ODD HAS HAPPENED AT COURT, HE'LL CERTAINLY KNOW ABOUT IT.
DEFINITELY, BUT IT WON'T BE EASY TO EVEN GET NEAR HIM!
WE HAVE TO FIND A WAY TO SHOW HIM WE CAN HELP...
IF YOU'RE ONE OF HIS MUSKETEERS, HE'LL CERTAINLY LISTEN TO YOU.
MUSKETEERS?! THERE REALLY ARE MUSKETEERS HERE?!
WELL, YES. THEY'RE RICHELIEU'S PRIVATE GUARD. ACTUALLY, FROM WHAT I UNDERSTAND, THEY'RE LOOKING FOR NEW MEMBERS.
MUSKETEERS WERE A TYPE OF SOLDIER FOUND IN MANY ARMIES THROUGHOUT HISTORY. NAMED AFTER THE MUSKETS THEY USED AS WEAPONS, THESE SOLDIERS SOMETIMES CAME FROM FAMILIES WHO WERE PART OF THE LOWER NOBILITY IN FRANCE. RICHELIEU NAMED HIS PERSONAL GUARD OF MUSKET-WIELDING SOLDIERS "MUSKETEERS" AS NOT TO COMPETE WITH THE KING, WHO HAD HIS OWN ROYAL GUARD.

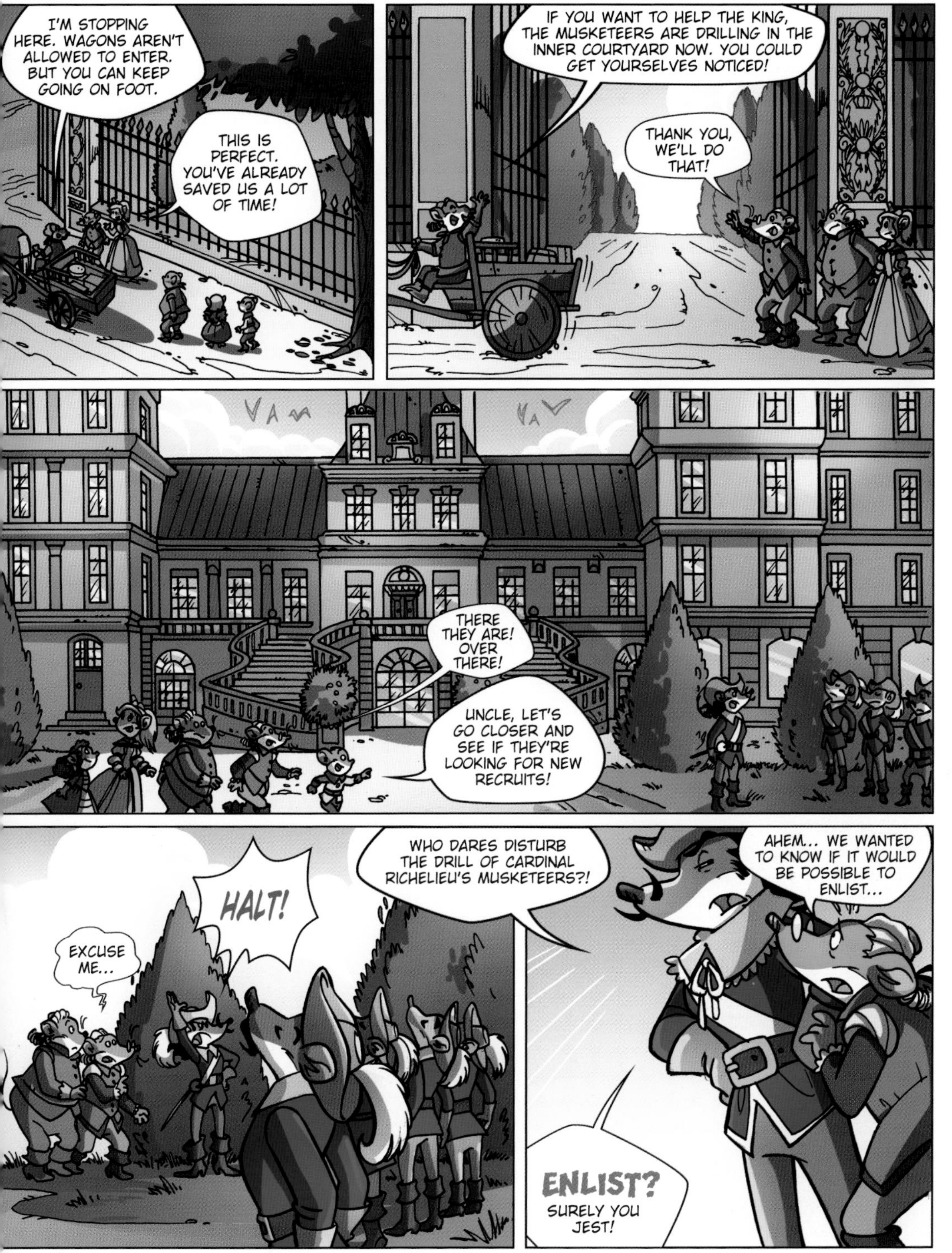
I'M STOPPING HERE. WAGONS AREN'T ALLOWED TO ENTER. BUT YOU CAN KEEP GOING ON FOOT.
THIS IS PERFECT. YOU'VE ALREADY SAVED US A LOT OF TIME!
IF YOU WANT TO HELP THE KING, THE MUSKETEERS ARE DRILLING IN THE INNER COURTYARD NOW. YOU COULD GET YOURSELVES NOTICED!
THANK YOU, WE'LL DO THAT!
THERE THEY ARE! OVER THERE!
UNCLE, LET'S GO CLOSER AND SEE IF THEY'RE LOOKING FOR NEW RECRUITS!
HALT!
EXCUSE ME...
WHO DARES DISTURB THE DRILL OF CARDINAL RICHELIEU'S MUSKETEERS?!
AHEM... WE WANTED TO KNOW IF IT WOULD BE POSSIBLE TO ENLIST...
ENLIST? SURELY YOU JEST!

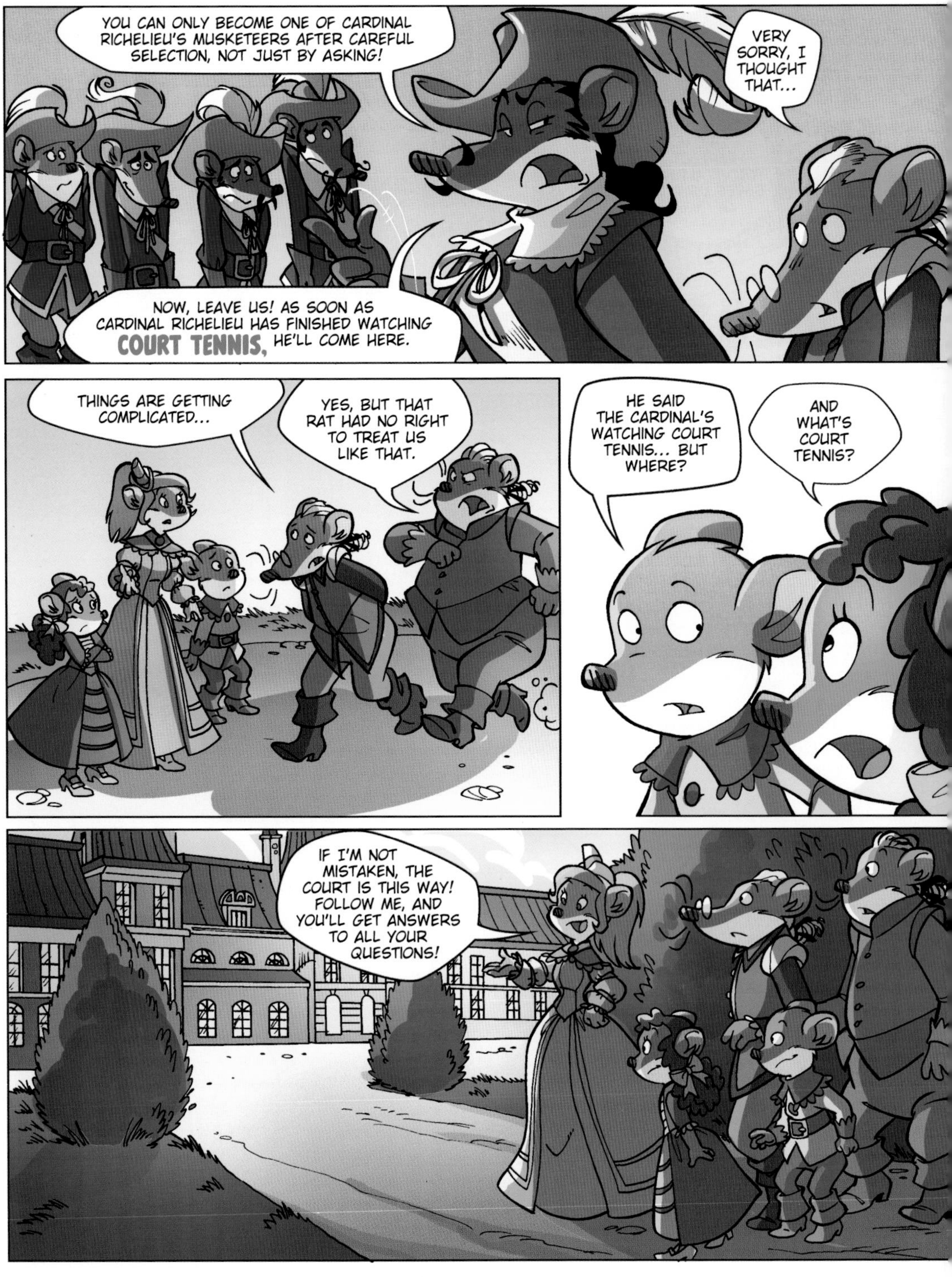
YOU CAN ONLY BECOME ONE OF CARDINAL RICHELIEU'S MUSKETEERS AFTER CAREFUL SELECTION, NOT JUST BY ASKING!
VERY SORRY, I THOUGHT THAT...
NOW, LEAVE US! AS SOON AS CARDINAL RICHELIEU HAS FINISHED WATCHING COURT TENNIS, HE'LL COME HERE.
THINGS ARE GETTING COMPLICATED...
YES, BUT THAT RAT HAD NO RIGHT TO TREAT US LIKE THAT.
HE SAID THE CARDINAL'S WATCHING COURT TENNIS... BUT WHERE?
AND WHAT'S COURT TENNIS?
IF I'M NOT MISTAKEN, THE COURT IS THIS WAY! FOLLOW ME, AND YOU'LL GET ANSWERS TO ALL YOUR QUESTIONS!

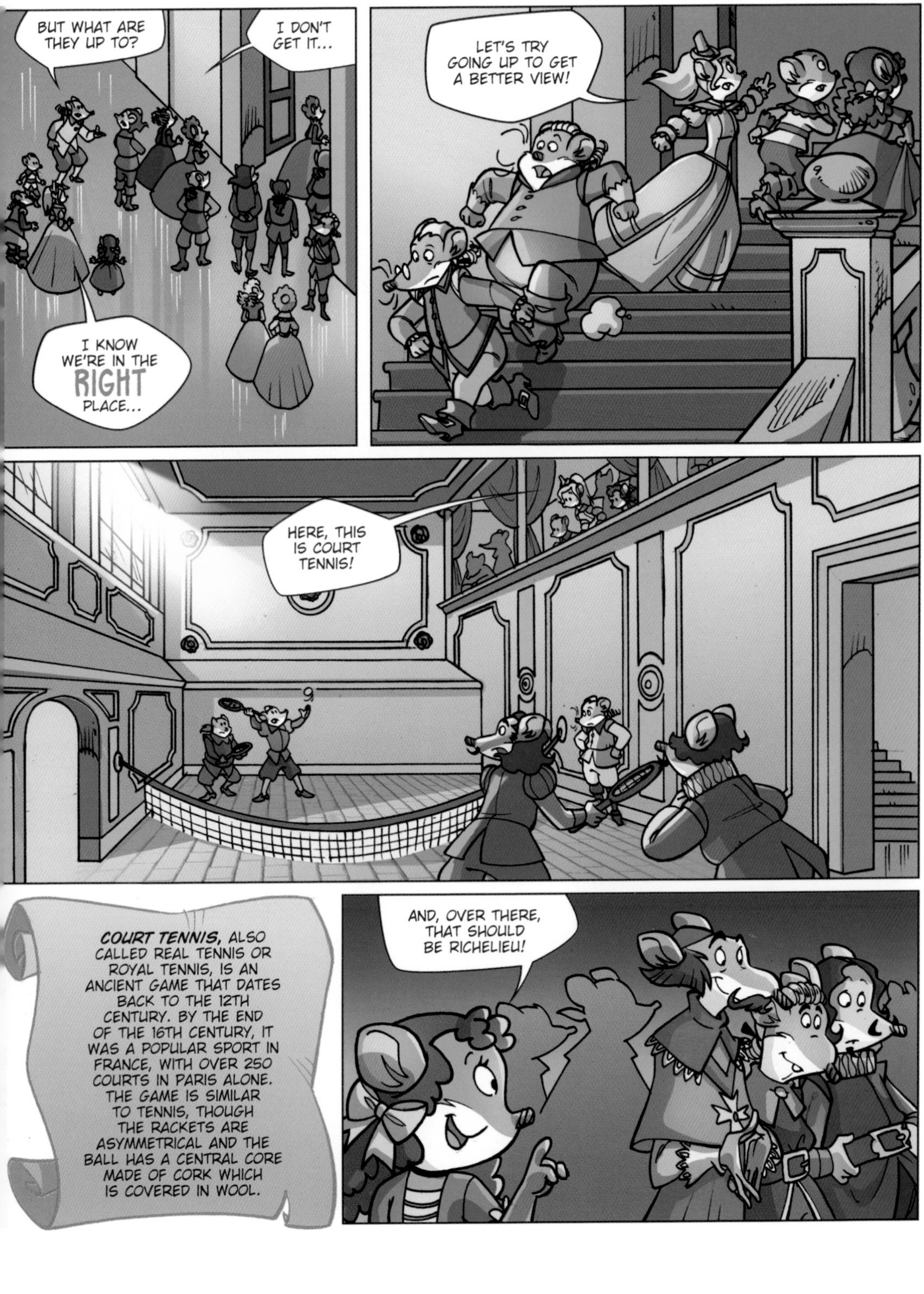

BUT WHAT ARE THEY UP TO?
I DON'T GET IT...
I KNOW WE'RE IN THE RIGHT PLACE...
LET'S TRY GOING UP TO GET A BETTER VIEW!
HERE, THIS IS COURT TENNIS!
COURT TENNIS, ALSO CALLED REAL TENNIS OR ROYAL TENNIS, IS AN ANCIENT GAME THAT DATES BACK TO THE 12TH CENTURY. BY THE END OF THE 16TH CENTURY, IT WAS A POPULAR SPORT IN FRANCE, WITH OVER 250 COURTS IN PARIS ALONE. THE GAME IS SIMILAR TO TENNIS, THOUGH THE RACKETS ARE ASYMMETRICAL AND THE BALL HAS A CENTRAL CORE MADE OF CORK WHICH IS COVERED IN WOOL.
AND, OVER THERE, THAT SHOULD BE RICHELIEU!

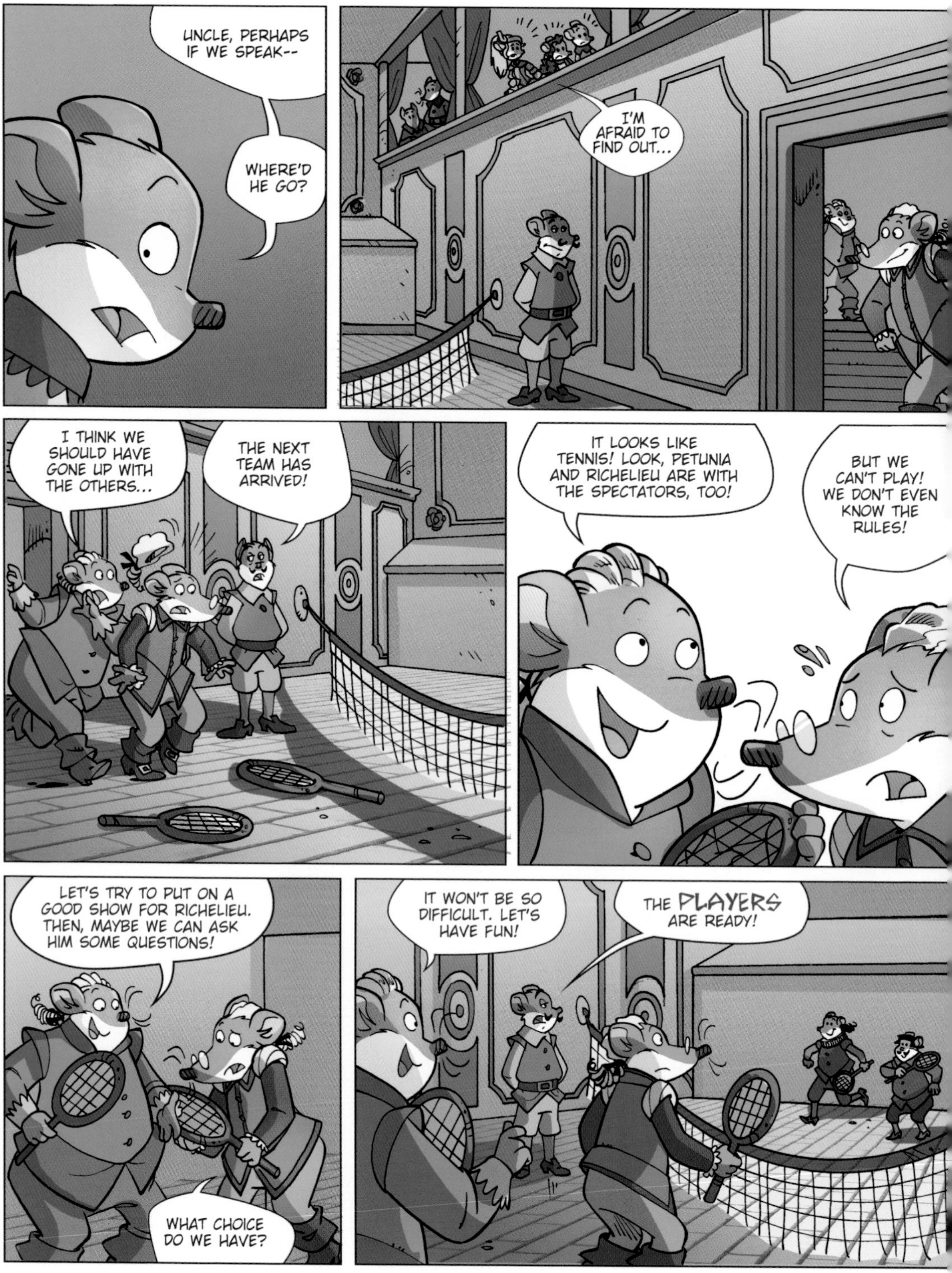
UNCLE, PERHAPS IF WE SPEAK--
WHERE'D HE GO?
I'M AFRAID TO FIND OUT...
I THINK WE SHOULD HAVE GONE UP WITH THE OTHERS...
THE NEXT TEAM HAS ARRIVED!
IT LOOKS LIKE TENNIS! LOOK, PETUNIA AND RICHELIEU ARE WITH THE SPECTATORS, TOO!
BUT WE CAN'T PLAY! WE DON'T EVEN KNOW THE RULES!
LET'S TRY TO PUT ON A GOOD SHOW FOR RICHELIEU. THEN, MAYBE WE CAN ASK HIM SOME QUESTIONS!
WHAT CHOICE DO WE HAVE?
IT WON'T BE SO DIFFICULT. LET'S HAVE FUN!
THE PLAYERS ARE READY!

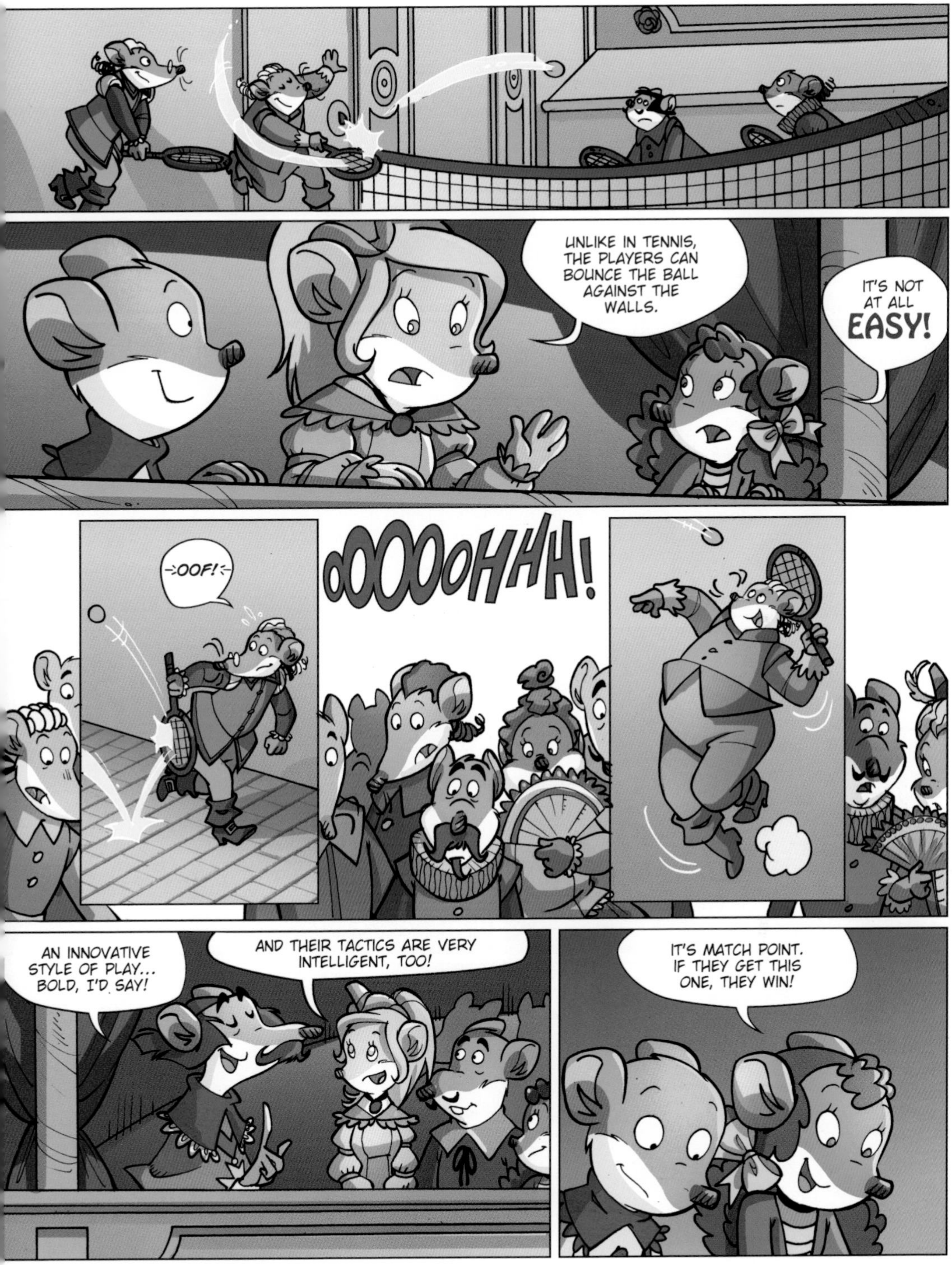
UNLIKE IN TENNIS, THE PLAYERS CAN BOUNCE THE BALL AGAINST THE WALLS.
IT'S NOT AT ALL EASY!
OOF!
OOOOOHHH!
AN INNOVATIVE STYLE OF PLAY... BOLD, I'D SAY!
AND THEIR TACTICS ARE VERY INTELLIGENT, TOO!
IT'S MATCH POINT. IF THEY GET THIS ONE, THEY WIN!

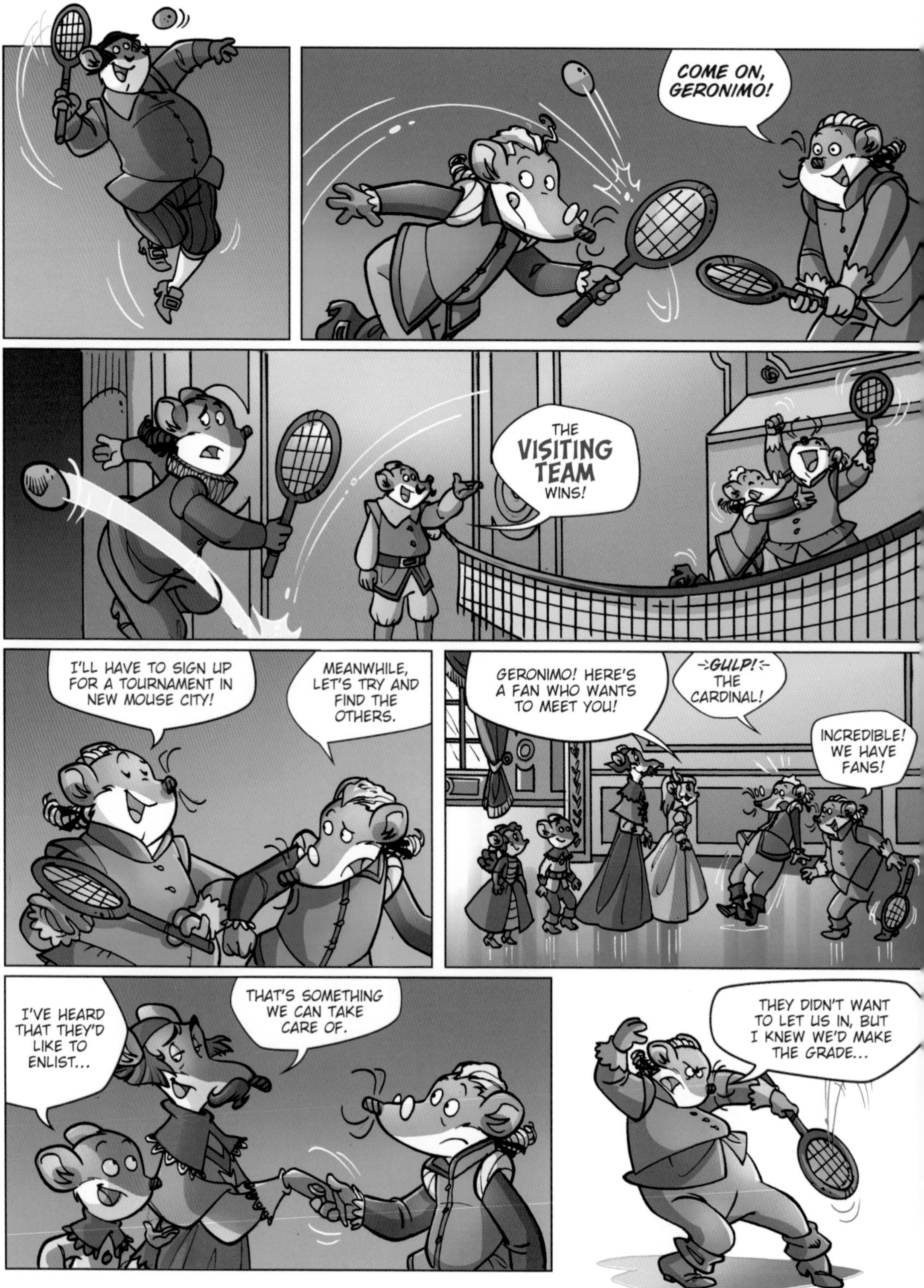

COME ON, GERONIMO!
THE VISITING TEAM WINS!
I'LL HAVE TO SIGN UP FOR A TOURNAMENT IN NEW MOUSE CITY!
MEANWHILE, LET'S TRY AND FIND THE OTHERS.
GERONIMO! HERE'S A FAN WHO WANTS TO MEET YOU!
GULP! THE CARDINAL!
INCREDIBLE! WE HAVE FANS!
I'VE HEARD THAT THEY'D LIKE TO ENLIST...
THAT'S SOMETHING WE CAN TAKE CARE OF.
THEY DIDN'T WANT TO LET US IN, BUT I KNEW WE'D MAKE THE GRADE...

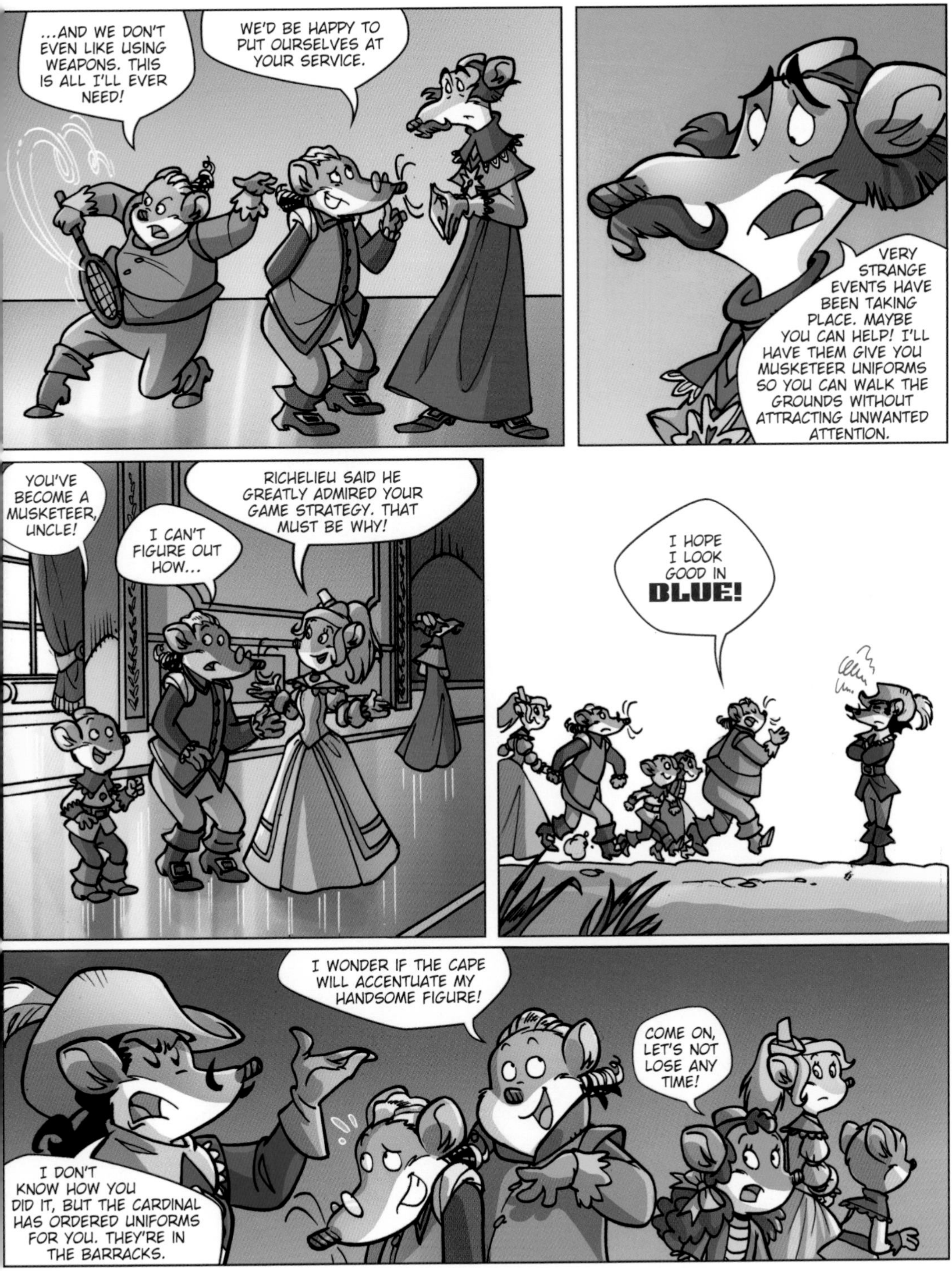

...AND WE DON'T EVEN LIKE USING WEAPONS. THIS IS ALL I'LL EVER NEED!
WE'D BE HAPPY TO PUT OURSELVES AT YOUR SERVICE.
VERY STRANGE EVENTS HAVE BEEN TAKING PLACE. MAYBE YOU CAN HELP! I'LL HAVE THEM GIVE YOU MUSKETEER UNIFORMS SO YOU CAN WALK THE GROUNDS WITHOUT ATTRACTING UNWANTED ATTENTION.
YOU'VE BECOME A MUSKETEER, UNCLE!
I CAN'T FIGURE OUT HOW...
RICHELIEU SAID HE GREATLY ADMIRED YOUR GAME STRATEGY. THAT MUST BE WHY!
I HOPE I LOOK GOOD IN BLUE!
I DON'T KNOW HOW YOU DID IT, BUT THE CARDINAL HAS ORDERED UNIFORMS FOR YOU. THEY'RE IN THE BARRACKS.
I WONDER IF THE CAPE WILL ACCENTUATE MY HANDSOME FIGURE!
COME ON, LET'S NOT LOSE ANY TIME!

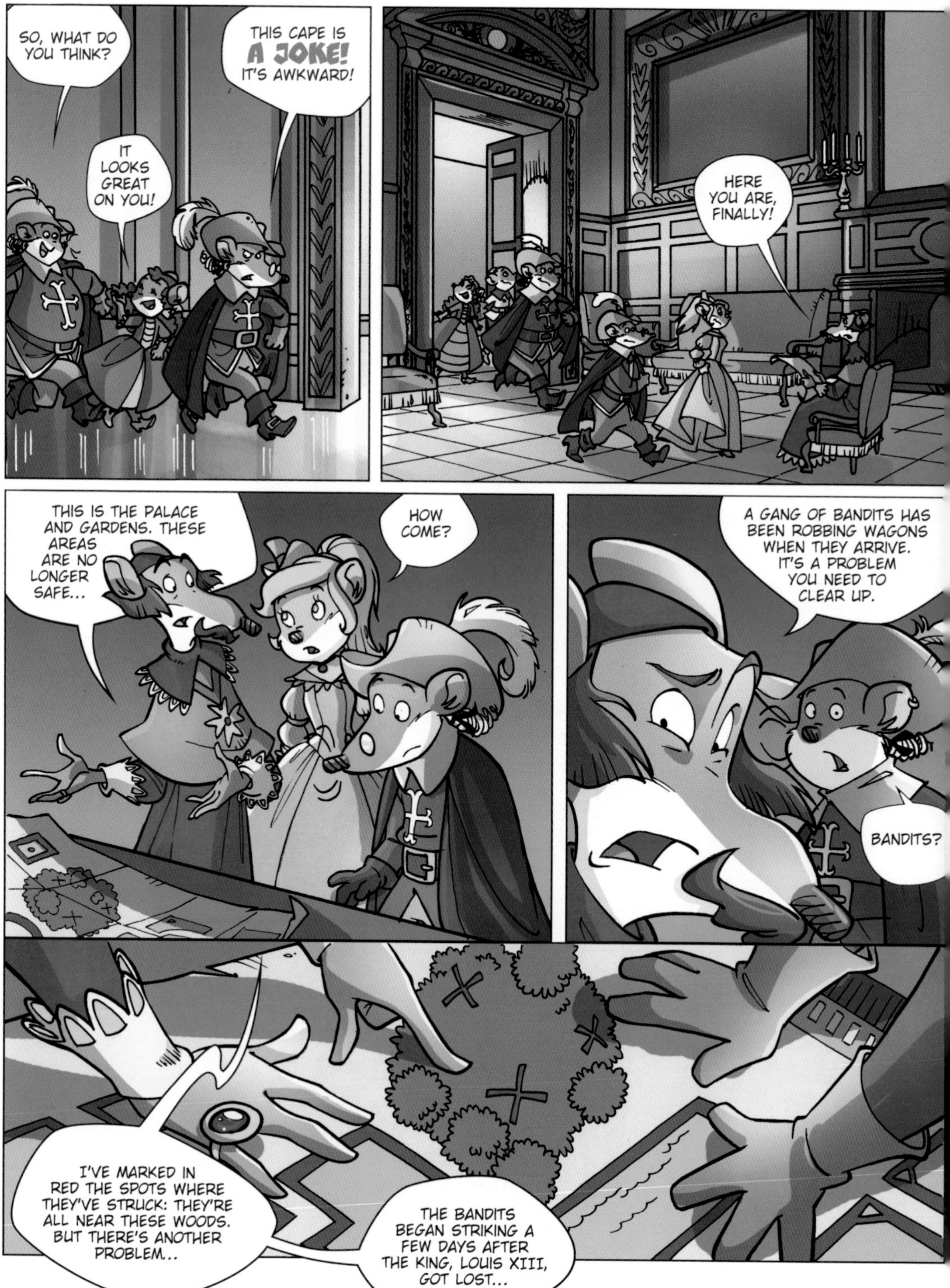
SO, WHAT DO YOU THINK?
THIS CAPE IS A JOKE! IT'S AWKWARD!
IT LOOKS GREAT ON YOU!
HERE YOU ARE, FINALLY!
THIS IS THE PALACE AND GARDENS. THESE AREAS ARE NO LONGER SAFE...
HOW COME?
A GANG OF BANDITS HAS BEEN ROBBING WAGONS WHEN THEY ARRIVE. IT'S A PROBLEM YOU NEED TO CLEAR UP.
BANDITS?
I'VE MARKED IN RED THE SPOTS WHERE THEY'VE STRUCK: THEY'RE ALL NEAR THESE WOODS. BUT THERE'S ANOTHER PROBLEM...
THE BANDITS BEGAN STRIKING A FEW DAYS AFTER THE KING, LOUIS XIII, GOT LOST...

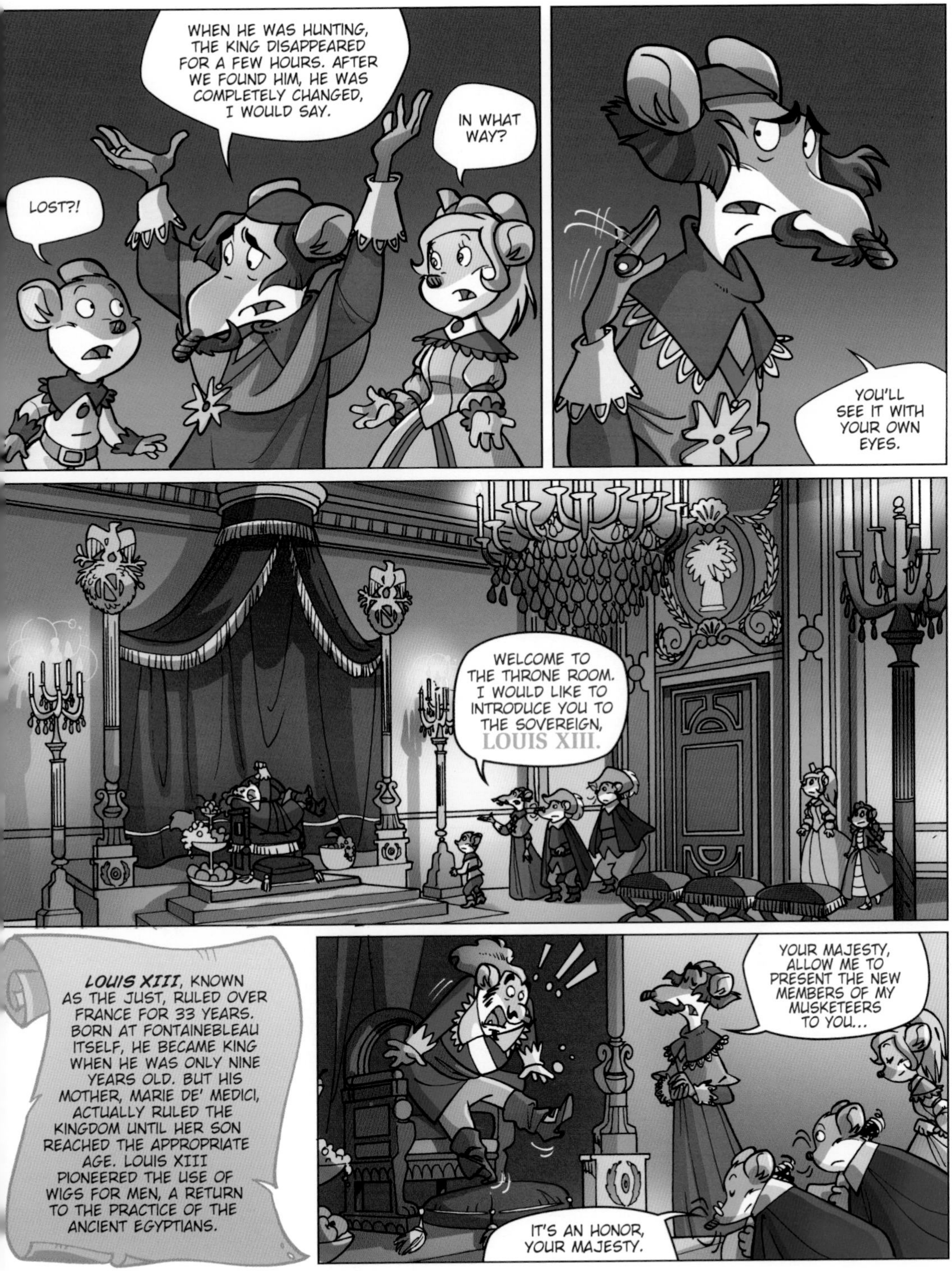
WHEN HE WAS HUNTING, THE KING DISAPPEARED FOR A FEW HOURS. AFTER WE FOUND HIM, HE WAS COMPLETELY CHANGED, I WOULD SAY.
LOST?!
IN WHAT WAY?
YOU'LL SEE IT WITH YOUR OWN EYES.
WELCOME TO THE THRONE ROOM. I WOULD LIKE TO INTRODUCE YOU TO THE SOVEREIGN, LOUIS XIII.
LOUIS XIII, KNOWN AS THE JUST, RULED OVER FRANCE FOR 33 YEARS. BORN AT FONTAINEBLEAU ITSELF, HE BECAME KING WHEN HE WAS ONLY NINE YEARS OLD. BUT HIS MOTHER, MARIE DE' MEDICI, ACTUALLY RULED THE KINGDOM UNTIL HER SON REACHED THE APPROPRIATE AGE. LOUIS XIII PIONEERED THE USE OF WIGS FOR MEN, A RETURN TO THE PRACTICE OF THE ANCIENT EGYPTIANS.
YOUR MAJESTY, ALLOW ME TO PRESENT THE NEW MEMBERS OF MY MUSKETEERS TO YOU...
IT'S AN HONOR, YOUR MAJESTY.

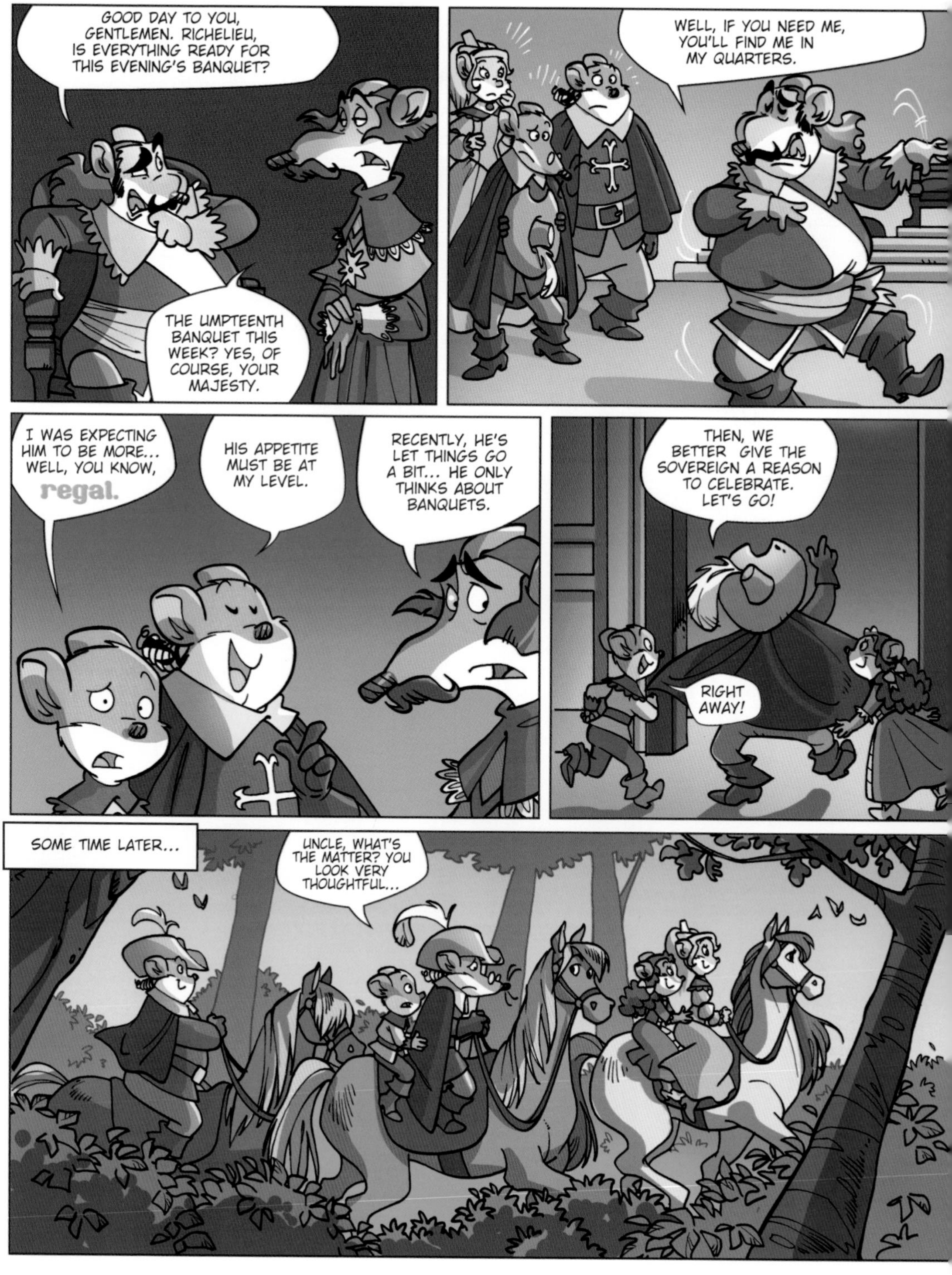
GOOD DAY TO YOU, GENTLEMEN. RICHELIEU, IS EVERYTHING READY FOR THIS EVENING'S BANQUET?
THE UMPTEENTH BANQUET THIS WEEK? YES, OF COURSE, YOUR MAJESTY.
WELL, IF YOU NEED ME, YOU'LL FIND ME IN MY QUARTERS.
I WAS EXPECTING HIM TO BE MORE... WELL, YOU KNOW, regal.
HIS APPETITE MUST BE AT MY LEVEL.
RECENTLY, HE'S LET THINGS GO A BIT... HE ONLY THINKS ABOUT BANQUETS.
THEN, WE BETTER GIVE THE SOVEREIGN A REASON TO CELEBRATE. LET'S GO!
RIGHT AWAY!
SOME TIME LATER...
UNCLE, WHAT'S THE MATTER? YOU LOOK VERY THOUGHTFUL...

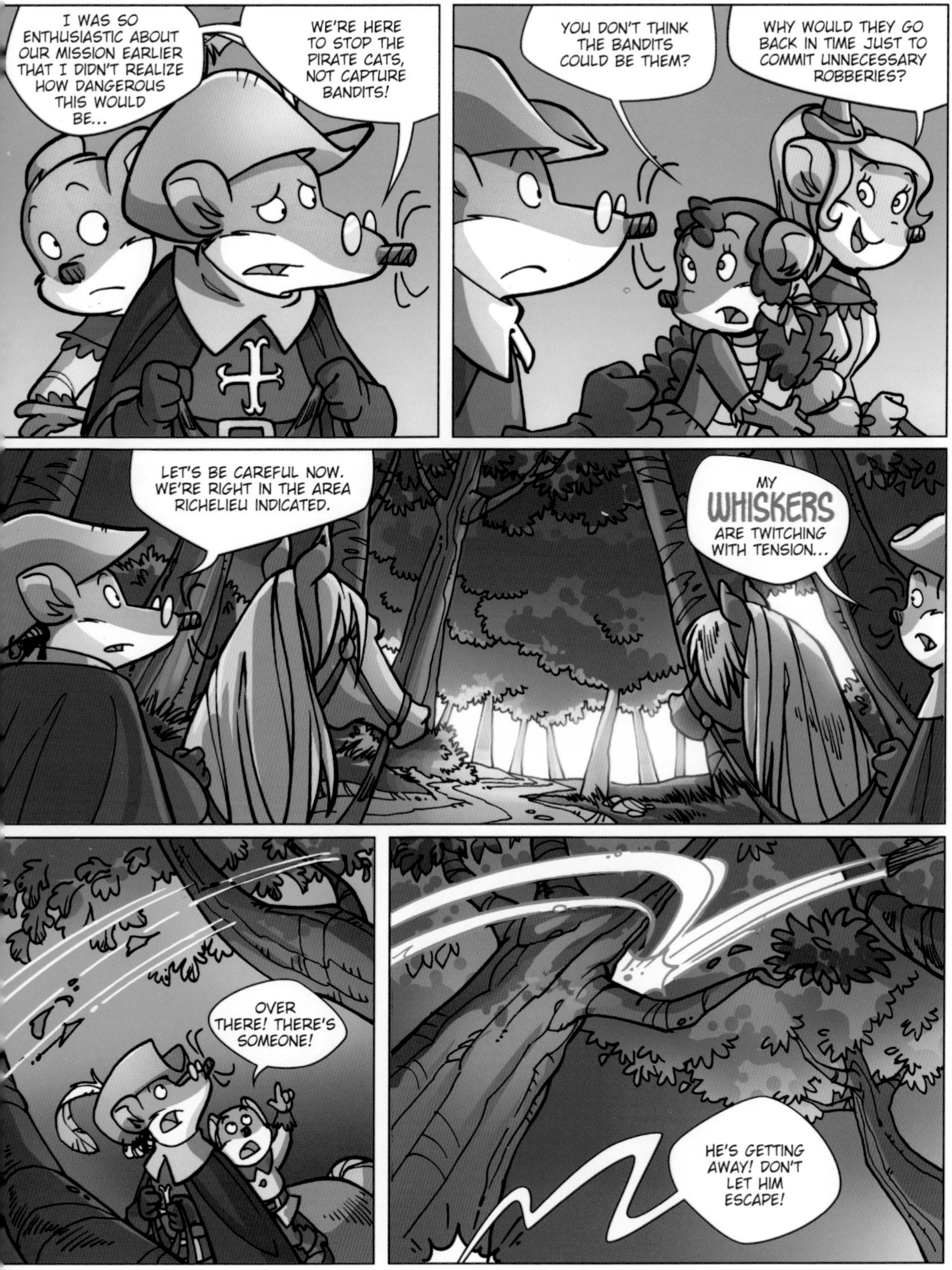

I WAS SO ENTHUSIASTIC ABOUT OUR MISSION EARLIER THAT I DIDN'T REALIZE HOW DANGEROUS THIS WOULD BE...
WE'RE HERE TO STOP THE PIRATE CATS, NOT CAPTURE BANDITS!
YOU DON'T THINK THE BANDITS COULD BE THEM?
WHY WOULD THEY GO BACK IN TIME JUST TO COMMIT UNNECESSARY ROBBERIES?
LET'S BE CAREFUL NOW. WE'RE RIGHT IN THE AREA RICHELIEU INDICATED.
MY WHISKERS ARE TWITCHING WITH TENSION...
OVER THERE! THERE'S SOMEONE!
HE'S GETTING AWAY! DON'T LET HIM ESCAPE!

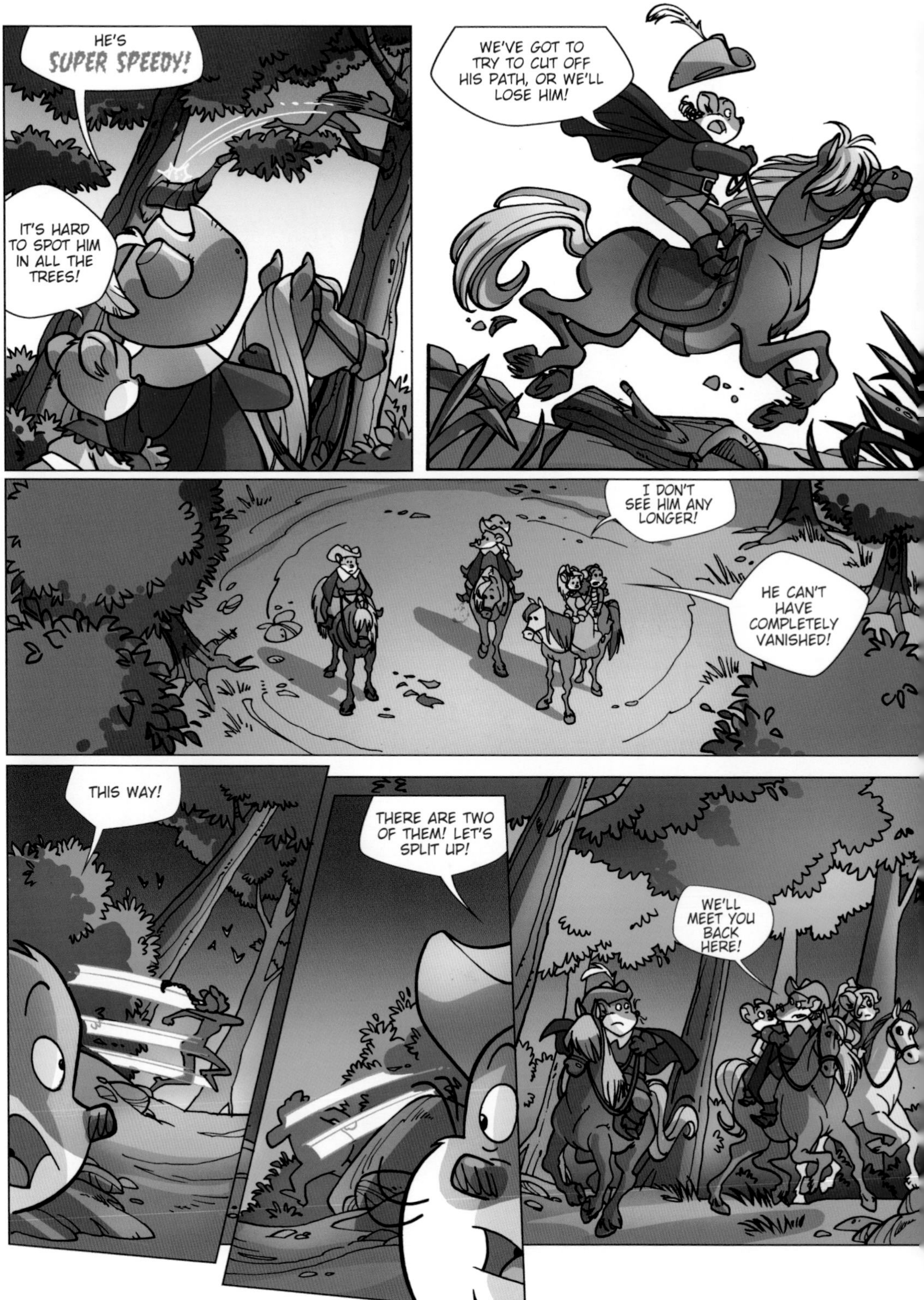
HE'S SUPER SPEEDY!
IT'S HARD TO SPOT HIM IN ALL THE TREES!
WE'VE GOT TO TRY TO CUT OFF HIS PATH, OR WE'LL LOSE HIM!
I DON'T SEE HIM ANY LONGER!
HE CAN'T HAVE COMPLETELY VANISHED!
THIS WAY!
THERE ARE TWO OF THEM! LET'S SPLIT UP!
WE'LL MEET YOU BACK HERE!

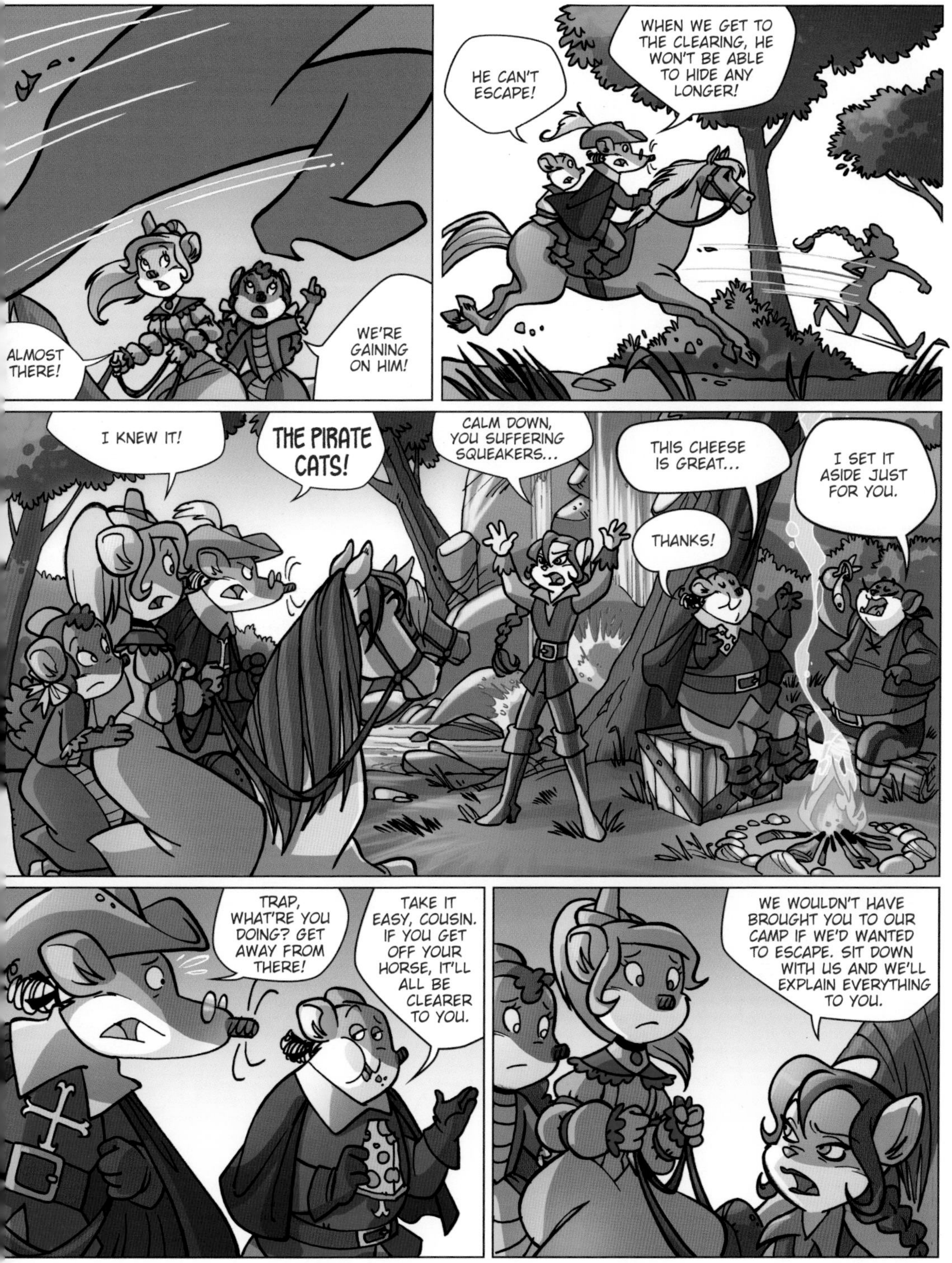
ALMOST THERE!
WE'RE GAINING ON HIM!
HE CAN'T ESCAPE!
WHEN WE GET TO THE CLEARING, HE WON'T BE ABLE TO HIDE ANY LONGER!
I KNEW IT!
THE PIRATE CATS!
CALM DOWN, YOU SUFFERING SQUEAKERS...
THIS CHEESE IS GREAT...
THANKS!
I SET IT ASIDE JUST FOR YOU.
TRAP, WHAT'RE YOU DOING? GET AWAY FROM THERE!
TAKE IT EASY, COUSIN. IF YOU GET OFF YOUR HORSE, IT'LL ALL BE CLEARER TO YOU.
WE WOULDN'T HAVE BROUGHT YOU TO OUR CAMP IF WE'D WANTED TO ESCAPE. SIT DOWN WITH US AND WE'LL EXPLAIN EVERYTHING TO YOU.

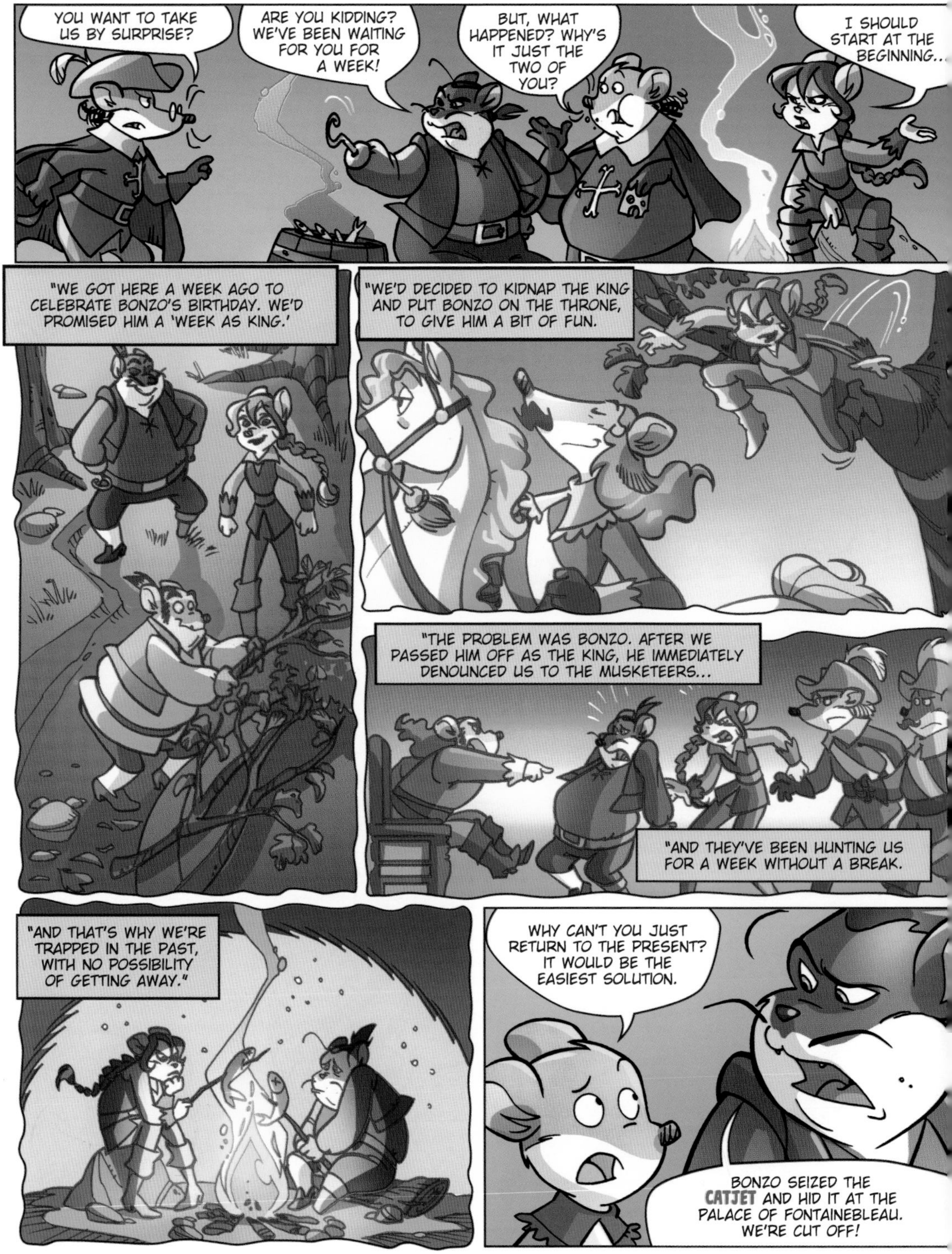
YOU WANT TO TAKE US BY SURPRISE?
ARE YOU KIDDING? WE'VE BEEN WAITING FOR YOU FOR A WEEK!
BUT, WHAT HAPPENED? WHY'S IT JUST THE TWO OF YOU?
I SHOULD START AT THE BEGINNING...
"WE GOT HERE A WEEK AGO TO CELEBRATE BONZO'S BIRTHDAY. WE'D PROMISED HIM A 'WEEK AS KING.'
"WE'D DECIDED TO KIDNAP THE KING AND PUT BONZO ON THE THRONE, TO GIVE HIM A BIT OF FUN.
"THE PROBLEM WAS BONZO. AFTER WE PASSED HIM OFF AS THE KING, HE IMMEDIATELY DENOUNCED US TO THE MUSKETEERS...
"AND THEY'VE BEEN HUNTING US FOR A WEEK WITHOUT A BREAK.
"AND THAT'S WHY WE'RE TRAPPED IN THE PAST, WITH NO POSSIBILITY OF GETTING AWAY."
WHY CAN'T YOU JUST RETURN TO THE PRESENT? IT WOULD BE THE EASIEST SOLUTION.
BONZO SEIZED THE CATJET AND HID IT AT THE PALACE OF FONTAINEBLEAU. WE'RE CUT OFF!

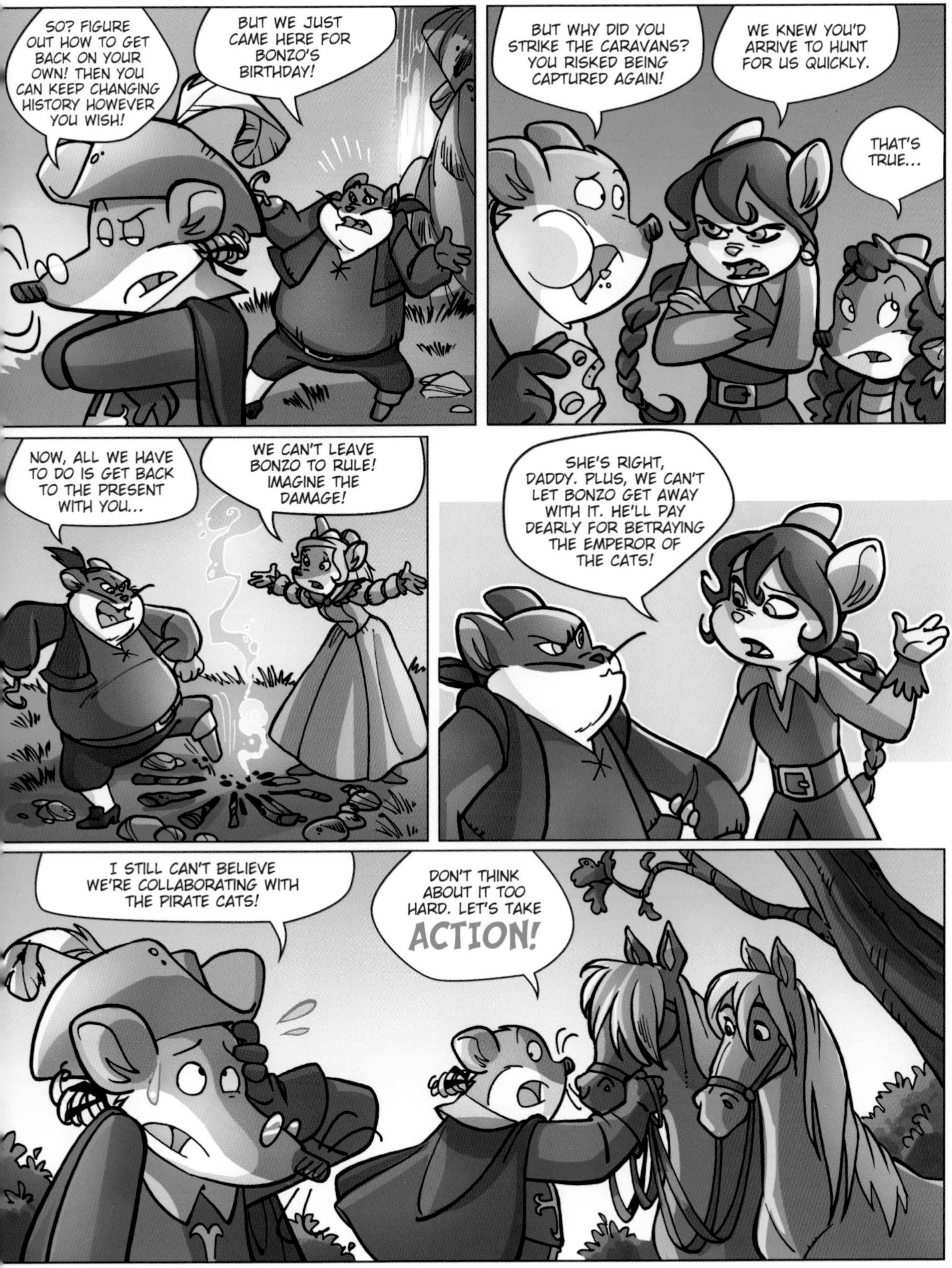
SO? FIGURE OUT HOW TO GET BACK ON YOUR OWN! THEN YOU CAN KEEP CHANGING HISTORY HOWEVER YOU WISH!
BUT WE JUST CAME HERE FOR BONZO'S BIRTHDAY!
BUT WHY DID YOU STRIKE THE CARAVANS? YOU RISKED BEING CAPTURED AGAIN!
WE KNEW YOU'D ARRIVE TO HUNT FOR US QUICKLY.
THAT'S TRUE...
NOW, ALL WE HAVE TO DO IS GET BACK TO THE PRESENT WITH YOU...
WE CAN'T LEAVE BONZO TO RULE! IMAGINE THE DAMAGE!
SHE'S RIGHT, DADDY. PLUS, WE CAN'T LET BONZO GET AWAY WITH IT. HE'LL PAY DEARLY FOR BETRAYING THE EMPEROR OF THE CATS!
I STILL CAN'T BELIEVE WE'RE COLLABORATING WITH THE PIRATE CATS!
DON'T THINK ABOUT IT TOO HARD. LET'S TAKE ACTION!

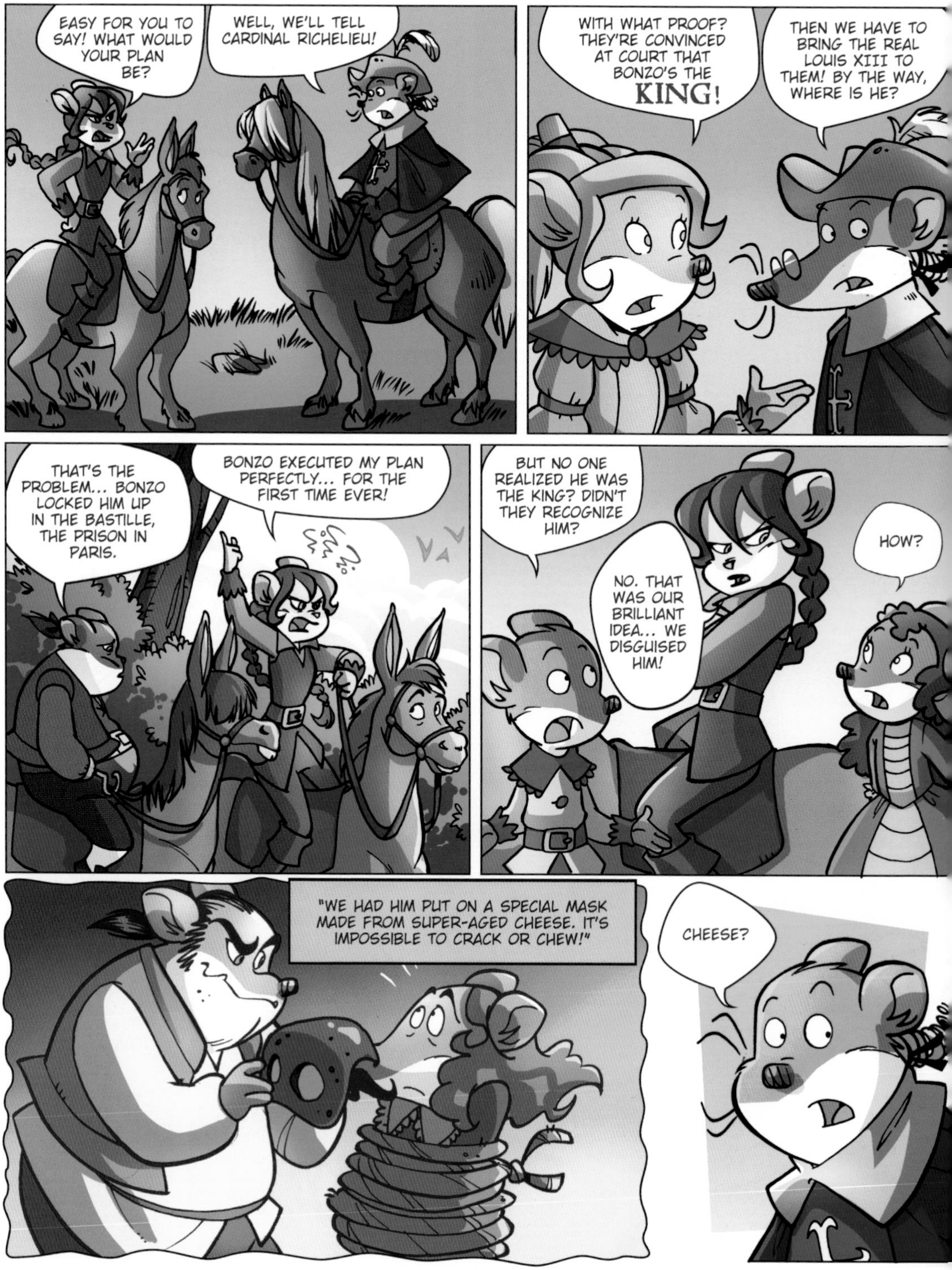
EASY FOR YOU TO SAY! WHAT WOULD YOUR PLAN BE?
WELL, WE'LL TELL CARDINAL RICHELIEU!
WITH WHAT PROOF? THEY'RE CONVINCED AT COURT THAT BONZO'S THE KING!
THEN WE HAVE TO BRING THE REAL LOUIS XIII TO THEM! BY THE WAY, WHERE IS HE?
THAT'S THE PROBLEM... BONZO LOCKED HIM UP IN THE BASTILLE, THE PRISON IN PARIS.
BONZO EXECUTED MY PLAN PERFECTLY... FOR THE FIRST TIME EVER!
BUT NO ONE REALIZED HE WAS THE KING? DIDN'T THEY RECOGNIZE HIM?
NO. THAT WAS OUR BRILLIANT IDEA... WE DISGUISED HIM!
HOW?
"WE HAD HIM PUT ON A SPECIAL MASK MADE FROM SUPER-AGED CHEESE. IT'S IMPOSSIBLE TO CRACK OR CHEW!"
CHEESE?

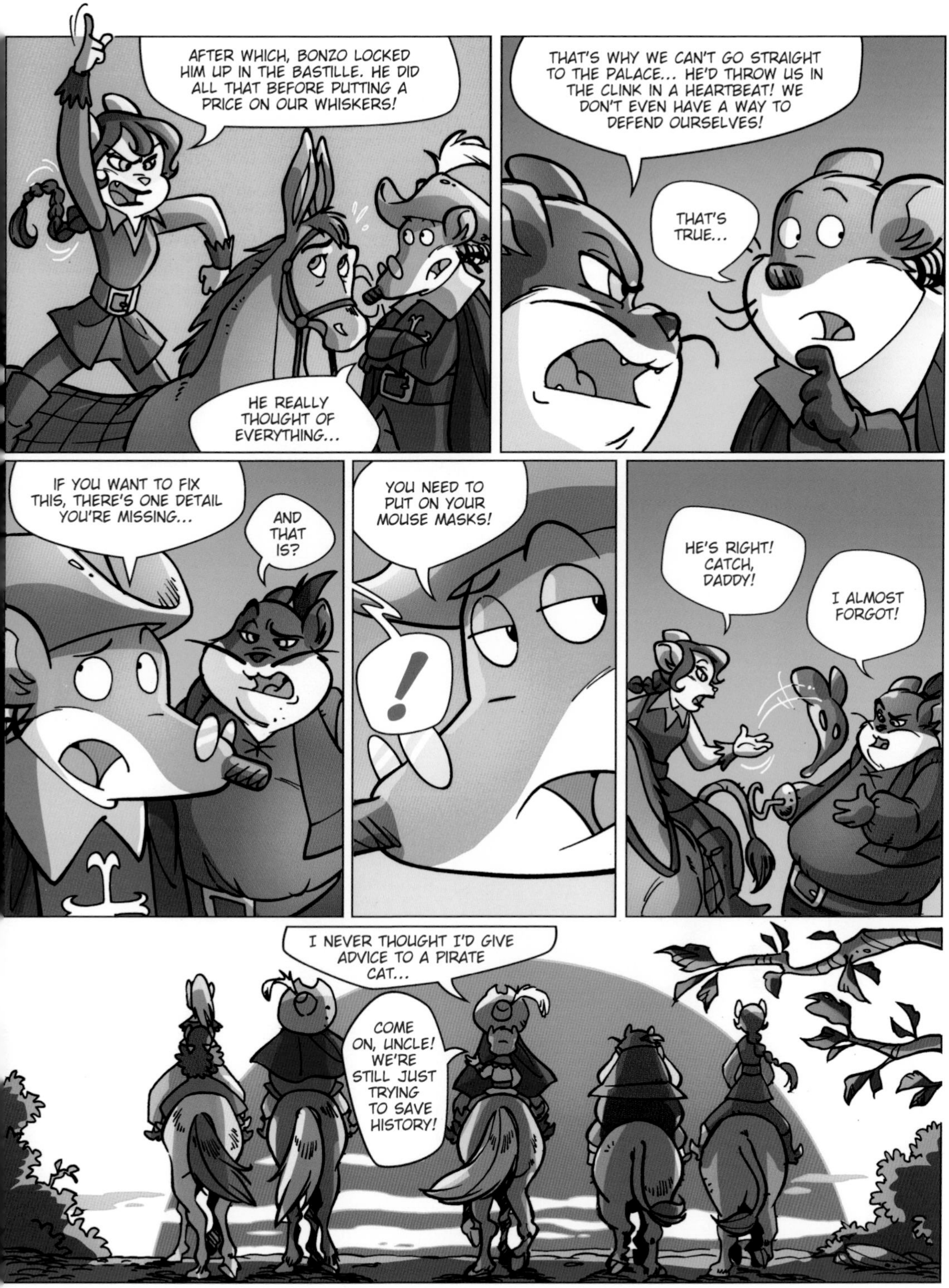
AFTER WHICH, BONZO LOCKED HIM UP IN THE BASTILLE. HE DID ALL THAT BEFORE PUTTING A PRICE ON OUR WHISKERS!
HE REALLY THOUGHT OF EVERYTHING...
THAT'S WHY WE CAN'T GO STRAIGHT TO THE PALACE... HE'D THROW US IN THE CLINK IN A HEARTBEAT! WE DON'T EVEN HAVE A WAY TO DEFEND OURSELVES!
THAT'S TRUE...
IF YOU WANT TO FIX THIS, THERE'S ONE DETAIL YOU'RE MISSING...
AND THAT IS?
YOU NEED TO PUT ON YOUR MOUSE MASKS!
!
HE'S RIGHT! CATCH, DADDY!
I ALMOST FORGOT!
I NEVER THOUGHT I'D GIVE ADVICE TO A PIRATE CAT...
COME ON, UNCLE! WE'RE STILL JUST TRYING TO SAVE HISTORY!

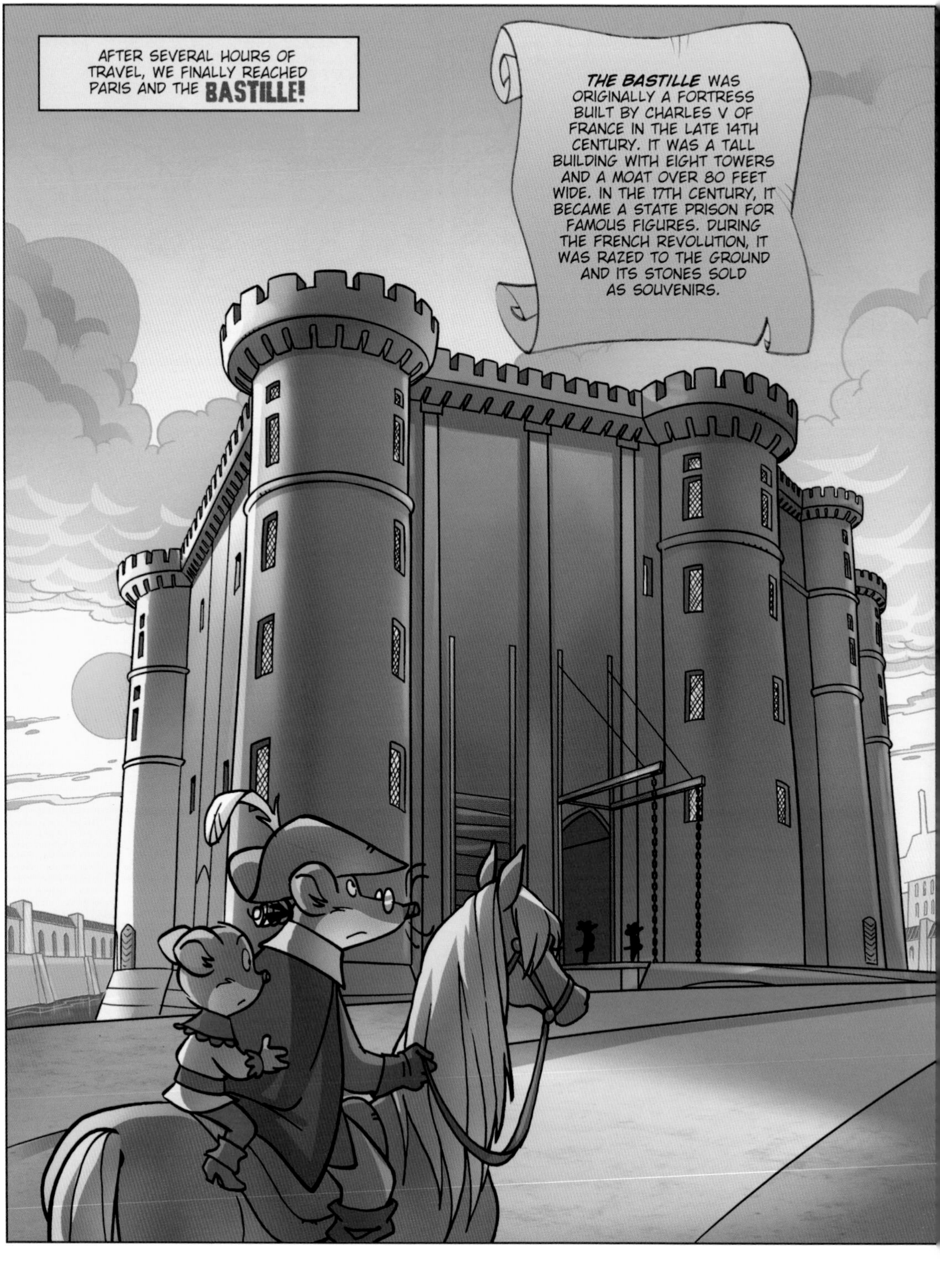
AFTER SEVERAL HOURS OF TRAVEL, WE FINALLY REACHED PARIS AND THE BASTILLE!
THE BASTILLE WAS ORIGINALLY A FORTRESS BUILT BY CHARLES V OF FRANCE IN THE LATE 14TH CENTURY. IT WAS A TALL BUILDING WITH EIGHT TOWERS AND A MOAT OVER 80 FEET WIDE. IN THE 17TH CENTURY, IT BECAME A STATE PRISON FOR FAMOUS FIGURES. DURING THE FRENCH REVOLUTION, IT WAS RAZED TO THE GROUND AND ITS STONES SOLD AS SOUVENIRS.

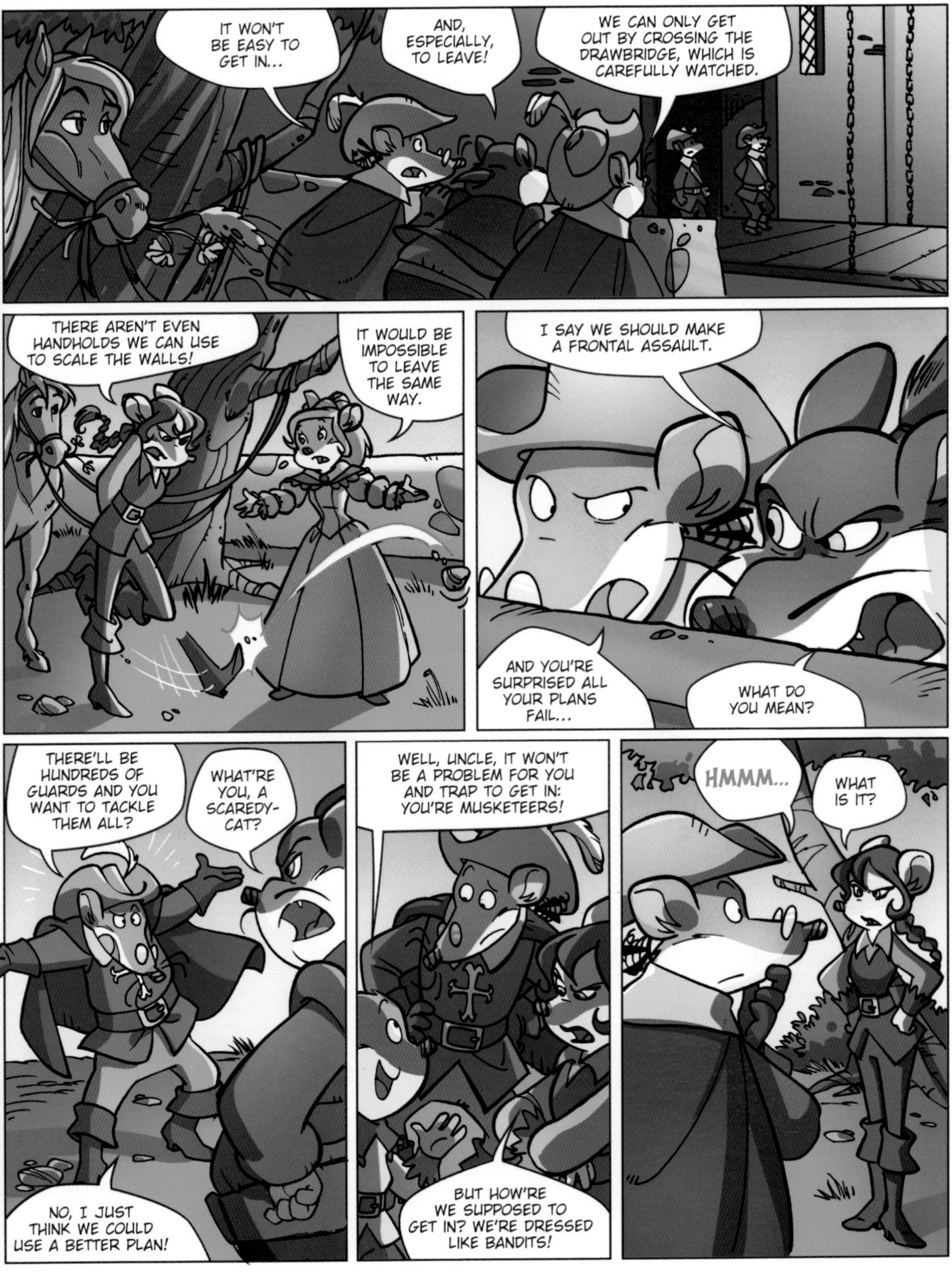
IT WON'T BE EASY TO GET IN...
AND, ESPECIALLY, TO LEAVE!
WE CAN ONLY GET OUT BY CROSSING THE DRAWBRIDGE, WHICH IS CAREFULLY WATCHED.
THERE AREN'T EVEN HANDHOLDS WE CAN USE TO SCALE THE WALLS!
IT WOULD BE IMPOSSIBLE TO LEAVE THE SAME WAY.
I SAY WE SHOULD MAKE A FRONTAL ASSAULT.
AND YOU'RE SURPRISED ALL YOUR PLANS FAIL...
WHAT DO YOU MEAN?
THERE'LL BE HUNDREDS OF GUARDS AND YOU WANT TO TACKLE THEM ALL?
WHAT'RE YOU, A SCAREDY-CAT?
NO, I JUST THINK WE COULD USE A BETTER PLAN!
WELL, UNCLE, IT WON'T BE A PROBLEM FOR YOU AND TRAP TO GET IN: YOU'RE MUSKETEERS!
BUT HOW'RE WE SUPPOSED TO GET IN? WE'RE DRESSED LIKE BANDITS!
HMMM...
WHAT IS IT?

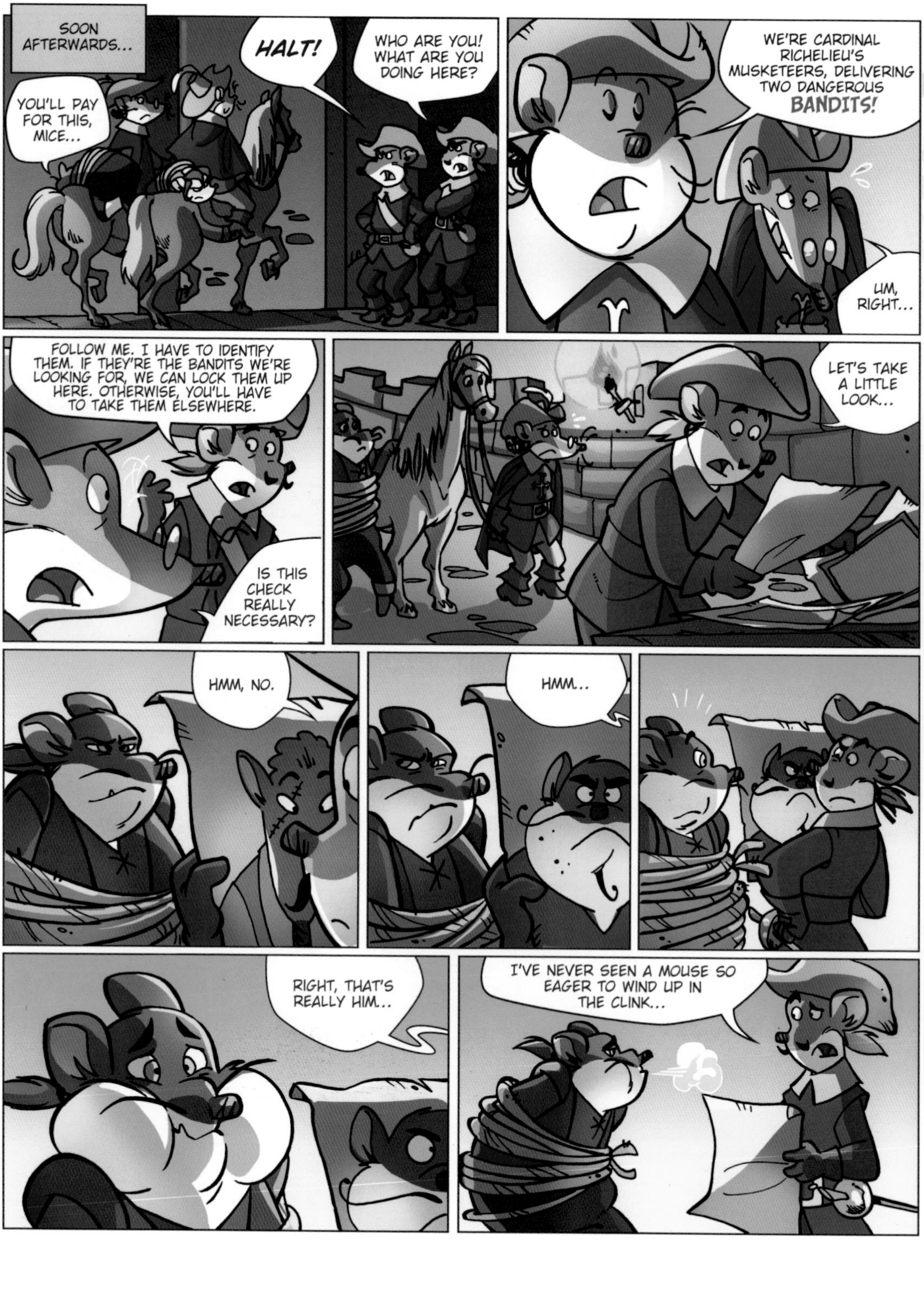
SOON AFTERWARDS...
YOU'LL PAY FOR THIS, MICE...
HALT!
WHO ARE YOU! WHAT ARE YOU DOING HERE?
WE'RE CARDINAL RICHELIEU'S MUSKETEERS, DELIVERING TWO DANGEROUS BANDITS!
UM, RIGHT...
FOLLOW ME. I HAVE TO IDENTIFY THEM. IF THEY'RE THE BANDITS WE'RE LOOKING FOR, WE CAN LOCK THEM UP HERE. OTHERWISE, YOU'LL HAVE TO TAKE THEM ELSEWHERE.
IS THIS CHECK REALLY NECESSARY?
LET'S TAKE A LITTLE LOOK...
HMM, NO.
HMM...
RIGHT, THAT'S REALLY HIM...
I'VE NEVER SEEN A MOUSE SO EAGER TO WIND UP IN THE CLINK...

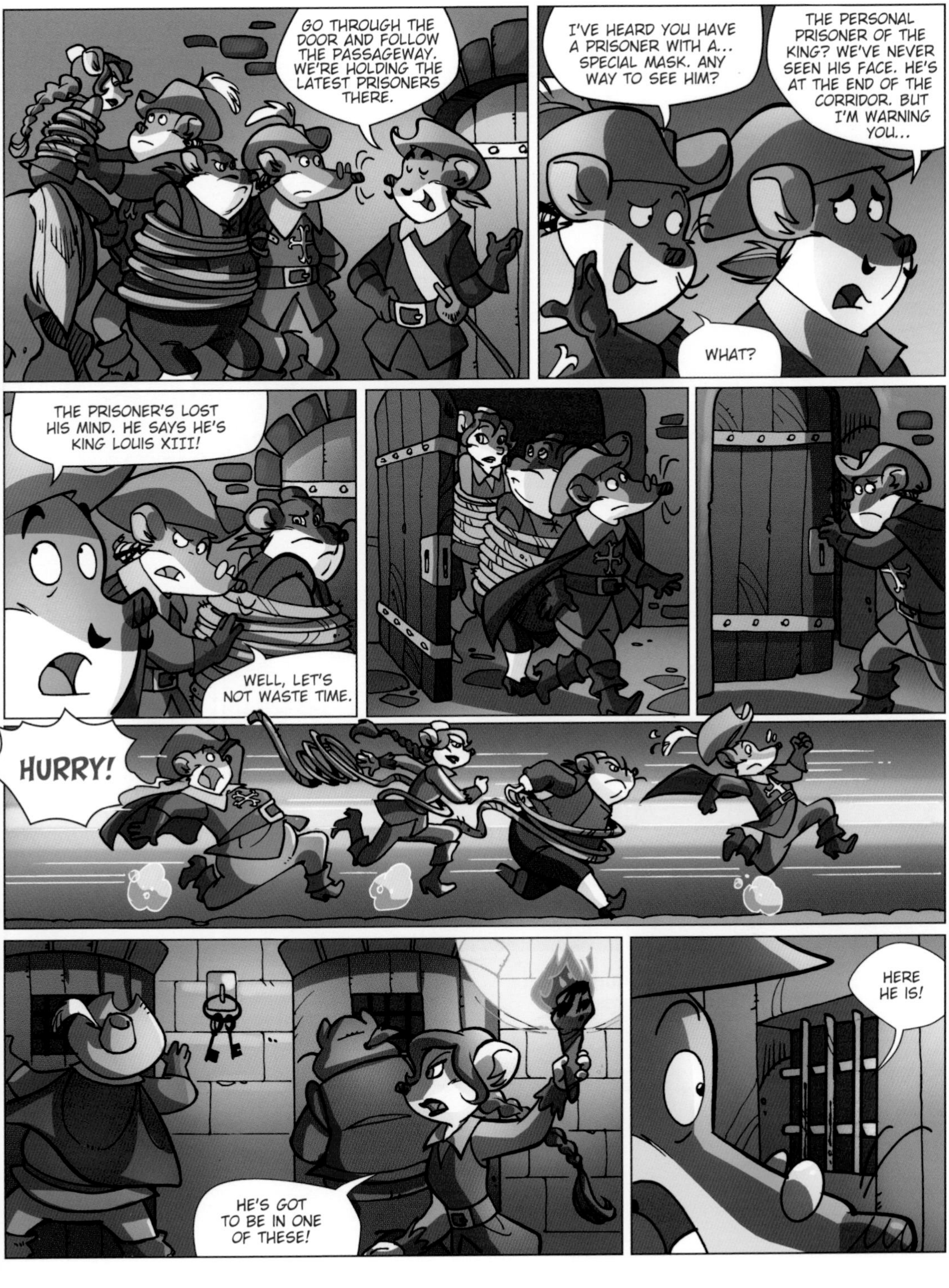
GO THROUGH THE DOOR AND FOLLOW THE PASSAGEWAY. WE'RE HOLDING THE LATEST PRISONERS THERE.
I'VE HEARD YOU HAVE A PRISONER WITH A... SPECIAL MASK. ANY WAY TO SEE HIM?
THE PERSONAL PRISONER OF THE KING? WE'VE NEVER SEEN HIS FACE. HE'S AT THE END OF THE CORRIDOR. BUT I'M WARNING YOU...
WHAT?
THE PRISONER'S LOST HIS MIND. HE SAYS HE'S KING LOUIS XIII!
WELL, LET'S NOT WASTE TIME.
HURRY!
HE'S GOT TO BE IN ONE OF THESE!
HERE HE IS!

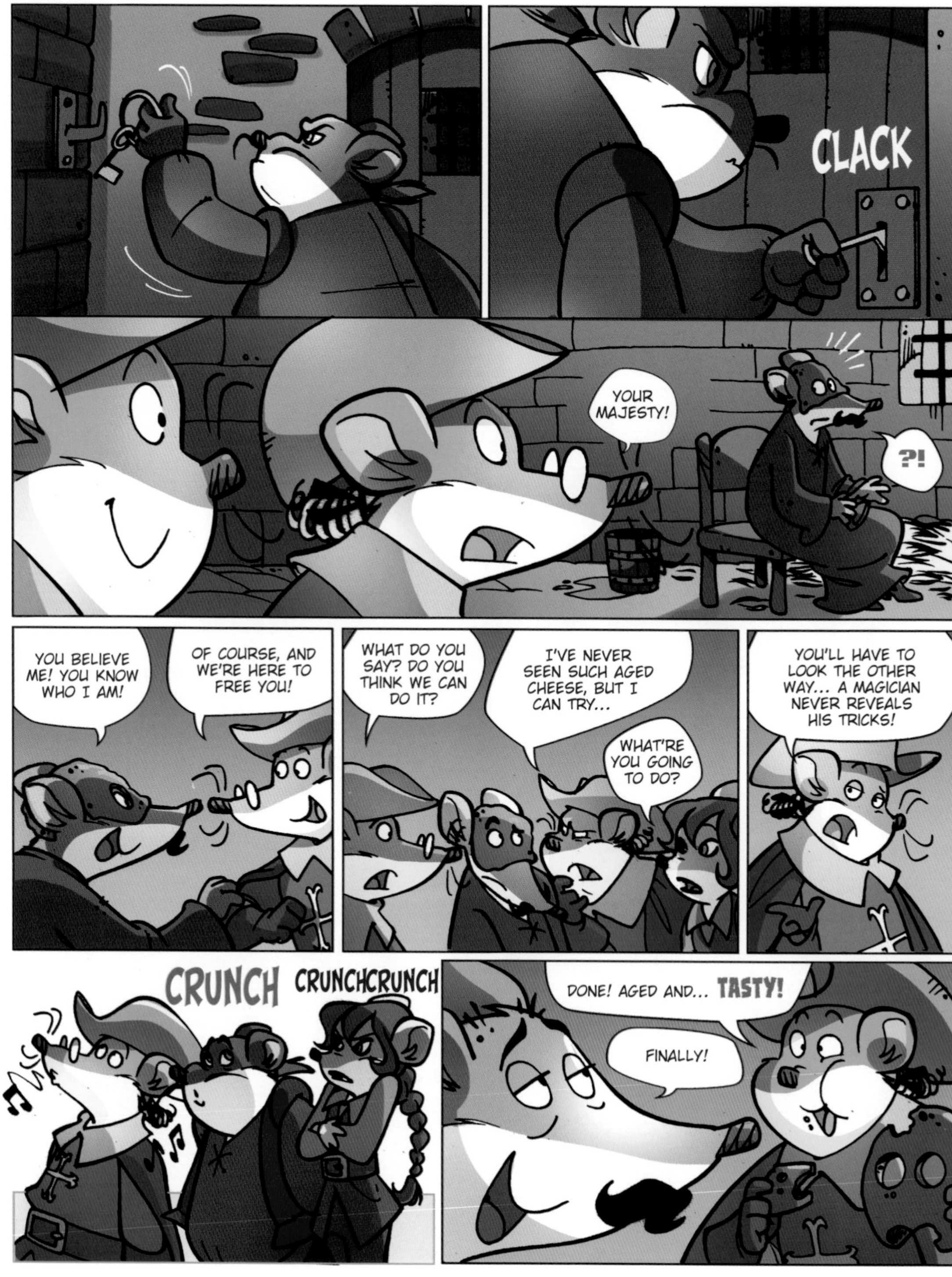
CLACK
YOUR MAJESTY!
?!
YOU BELIEVE ME! YOU KNOW WHO I AM!
OF COURSE, AND WE'RE HERE TO FREE YOU!
WHAT DO YOU SAY? DO YOU THINK WE CAN DO IT?
I'VE NEVER SEEN SUCH AGED CHEESE, BUT I CAN TRY...
WHAT'RE YOU GOING TO DO?
YOU'LL HAVE TO LOOK THE OTHER WAY... A MAGICIAN NEVER REVEALS HIS TRICKS!
CRUNCH
CRUNCHCRUNCH
DONE! AGED AND... TASTY!
FINALLY!

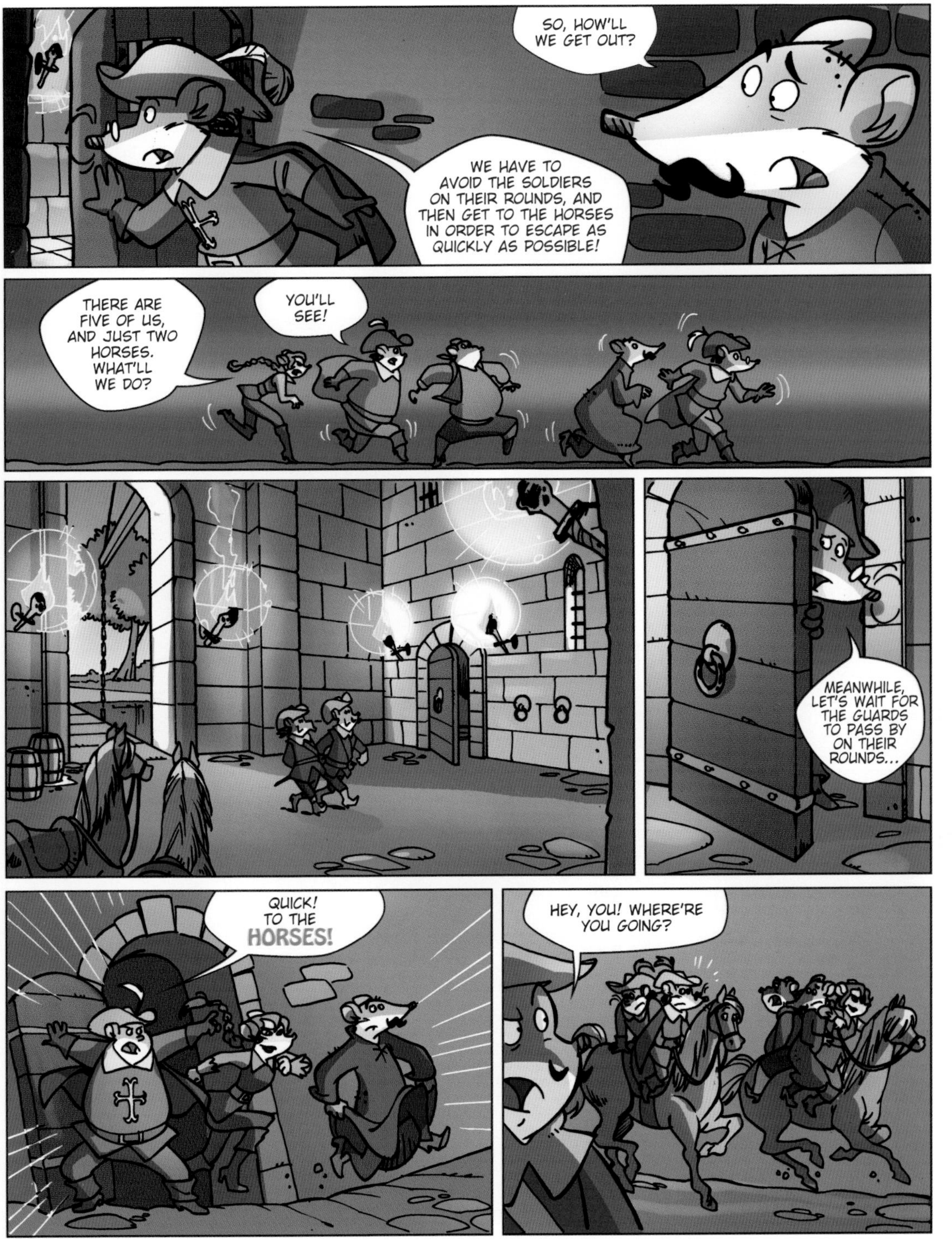
SO, HOW'LL WE GET OUT?
WE HAVE TO AVOID THE SOLDIERS ON THEIR ROUNDS, AND THEN GET TO THE HORSES IN ORDER TO ESCAPE AS QUICKLY AS POSSIBLE!
THERE ARE FIVE OF US, AND JUST TWO HORSES. WHAT'LL WE DO?
YOU'LL SEE!
MEANWHILE, LET'S WAIT FOR THE GUARDS TO PASS BY ON THEIR ROUNDS...
QUICK! TO THE HORSES!
HEY, YOU! WHERE'RE YOU GOING?

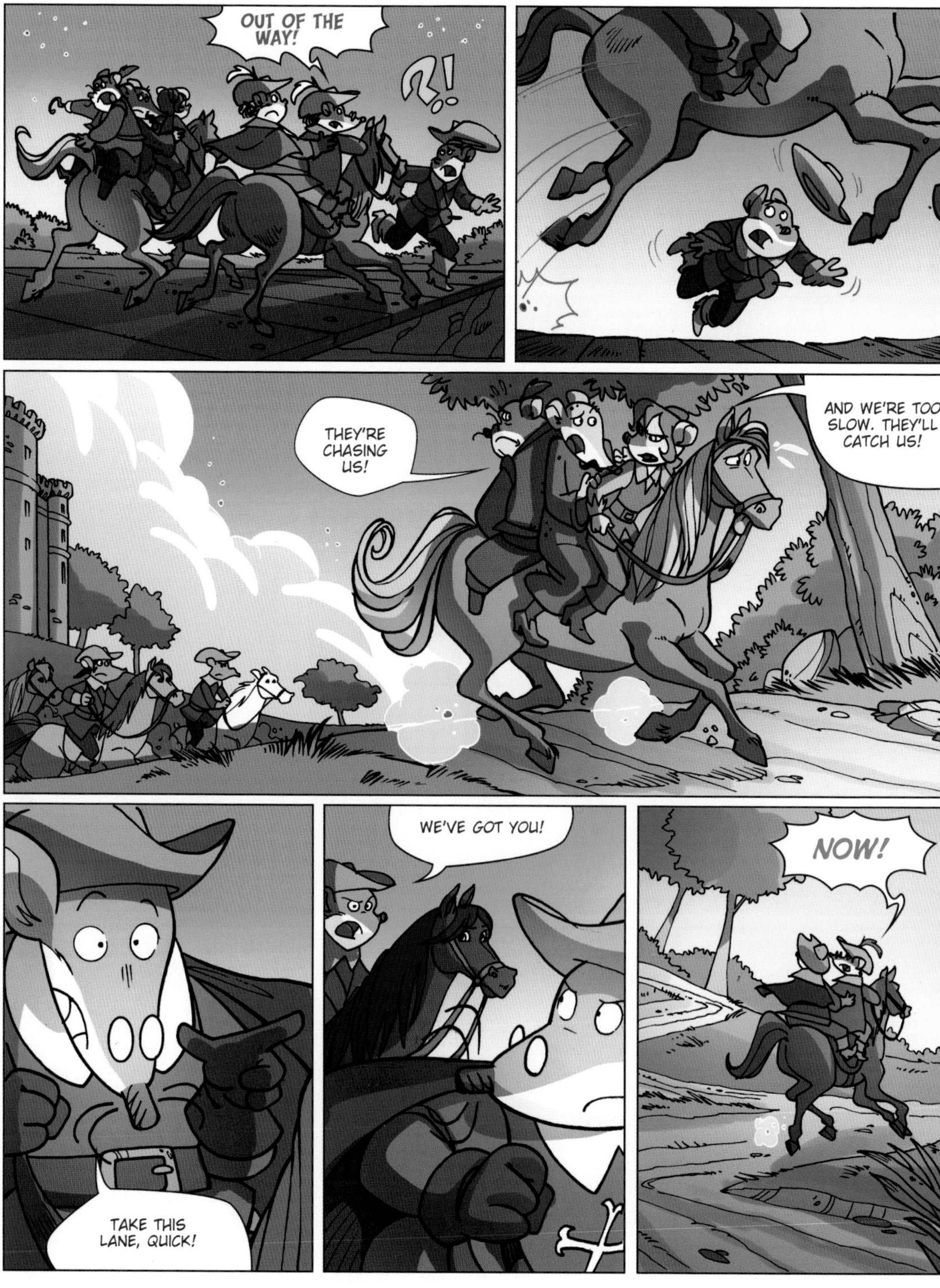
OUT OF THE WAY!
?!
THEY'RE CHASING US!
AND WE'RE TOO SLOW. THEY'LL CATCH US!
TAKE THIS LANE, QUICK!
WE'VE GOT YOU!
NOW!

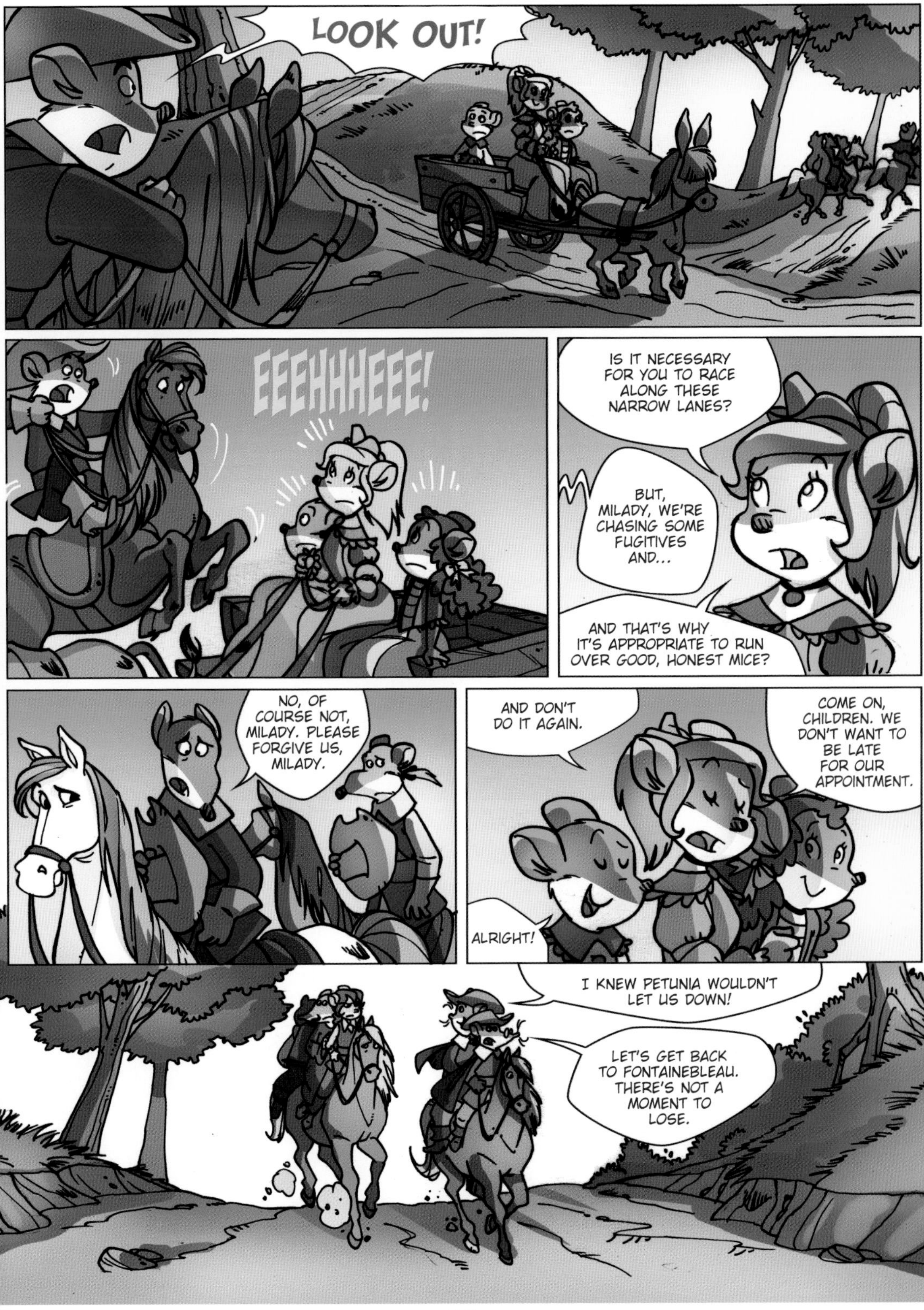
LOOK OUT!
EEEHHHEEE!
IS IT NECESSARY FOR YOU TO RACE ALONG THESE NARROW LANES?
BUT, MILADY, WE'RE CHASING SOME FUGITIVES AND...
AND THAT'S WHY IT'S APPROPRIATE TO RUN OVER GOOD, HONEST MICE?
NO, OF COURSE NOT, MILADY. PLEASE FORGIVE US, MILADY.
AND DON'T DO IT AGAIN.
COME ON, CHILDREN. WE DON'T WANT TO BE LATE FOR OUR APPOINTMENT.
ALRIGHT!
I KNEW PETUNIA WOULDN'T LET US DOWN!
LET'S GET BACK TO FONTAINEBLEAU. THERE'S NOT A MOMENT TO LOSE.

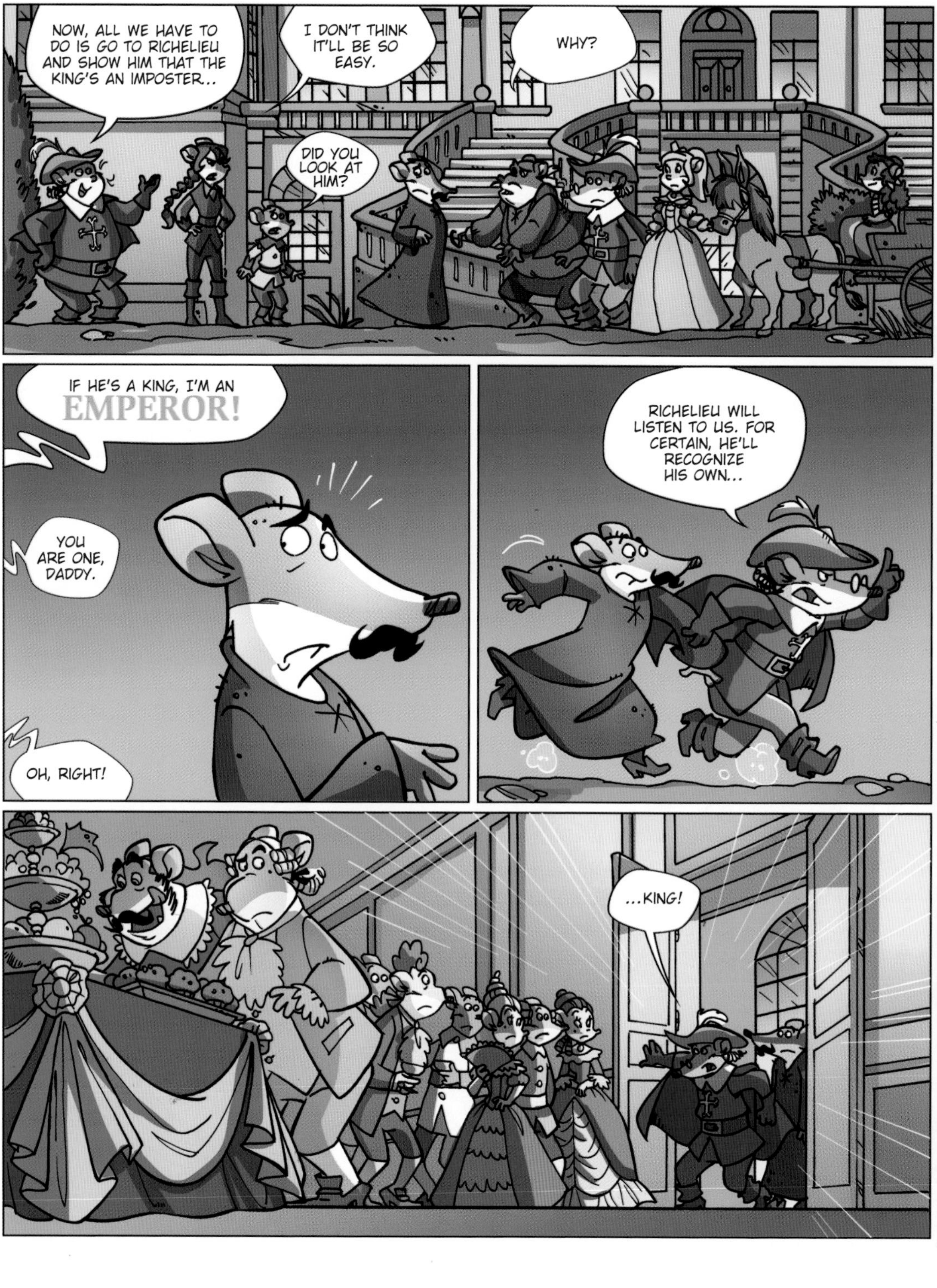
NOW, ALL WE HAVE TO DO IS GO TO RICHELIEU AND SHOW HIM THAT THE KING'S AN IMPOSTER...
I DON'T THINK IT'LL BE SO EASY.
WHY?
DID YOU LOOK AT HIM?
IF HE'S A KING, I'M AN EMPEROR!
YOU ARE ONE, DADDY.
OH, RIGHT!
RICHELIEU WILL LISTEN TO US. FOR CERTAIN, HE'LL RECOGNIZE HIS OWN...
...KING!

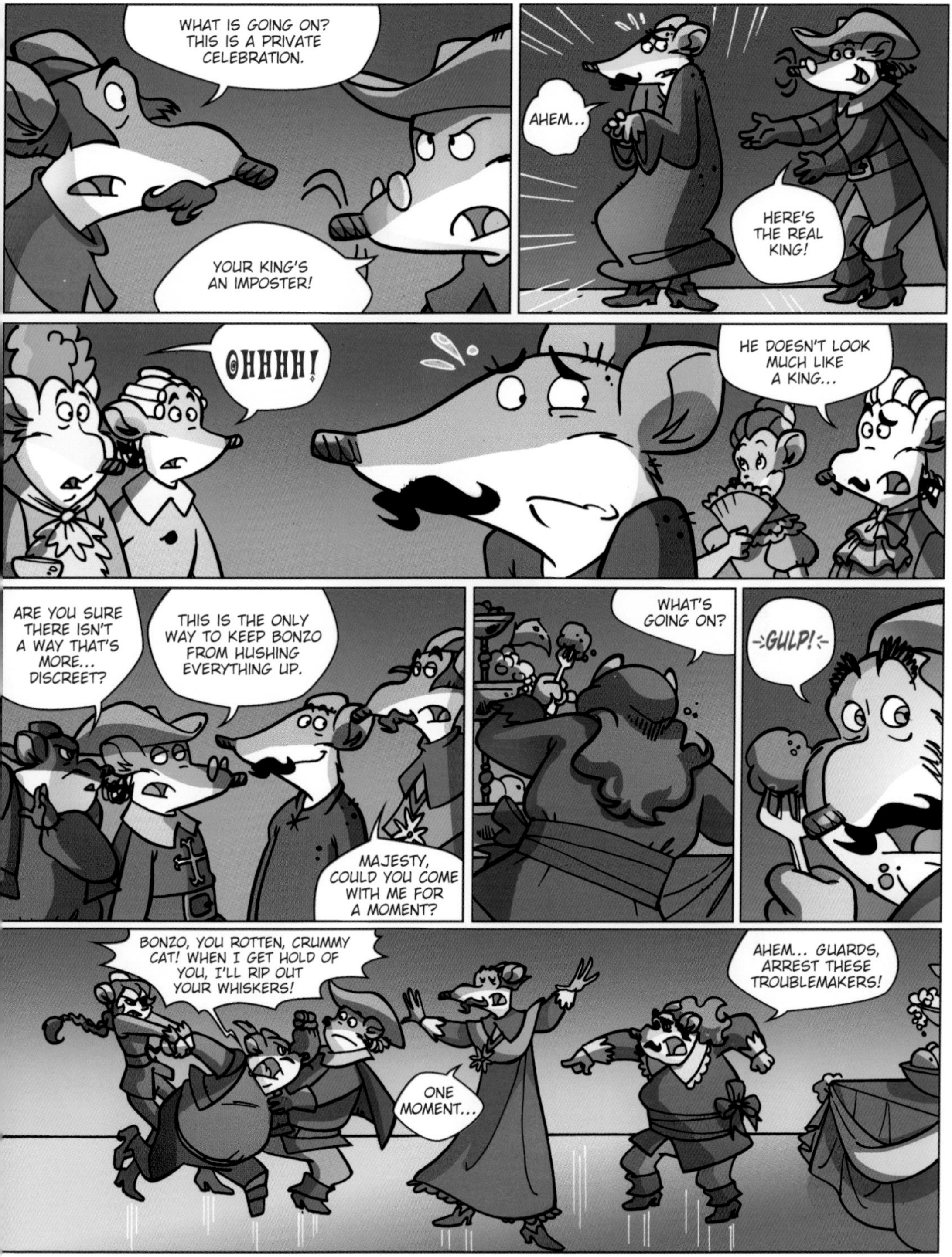
WHAT IS GOING ON? THIS IS A PRIVATE CELEBRATION.
YOUR KING'S AN IMPOSTER!
AHEM...
HERE'S THE REAL KING!
OHHHH!
HE DOESN'T LOOK MUCH LIKE A KING...
ARE YOU SURE THERE ISN'T A WAY THAT'S MORE... DISCREET?
THIS IS THE ONLY WAY TO KEEP BONZO FROM HUSHING EVERYTHING UP.
MAJESTY, COULD YOU COME WITH ME FOR A MOMENT?
WHAT'S GOING ON?
GULP!
BONZO, YOU ROTTEN, CRUMMY CAT! WHEN I GET HOLD OF YOU, I'LL RIP OUT YOUR WHISKERS!
ONE MOMENT...
AHEM... GUARDS, ARREST THESE TROUBLEMAKERS!

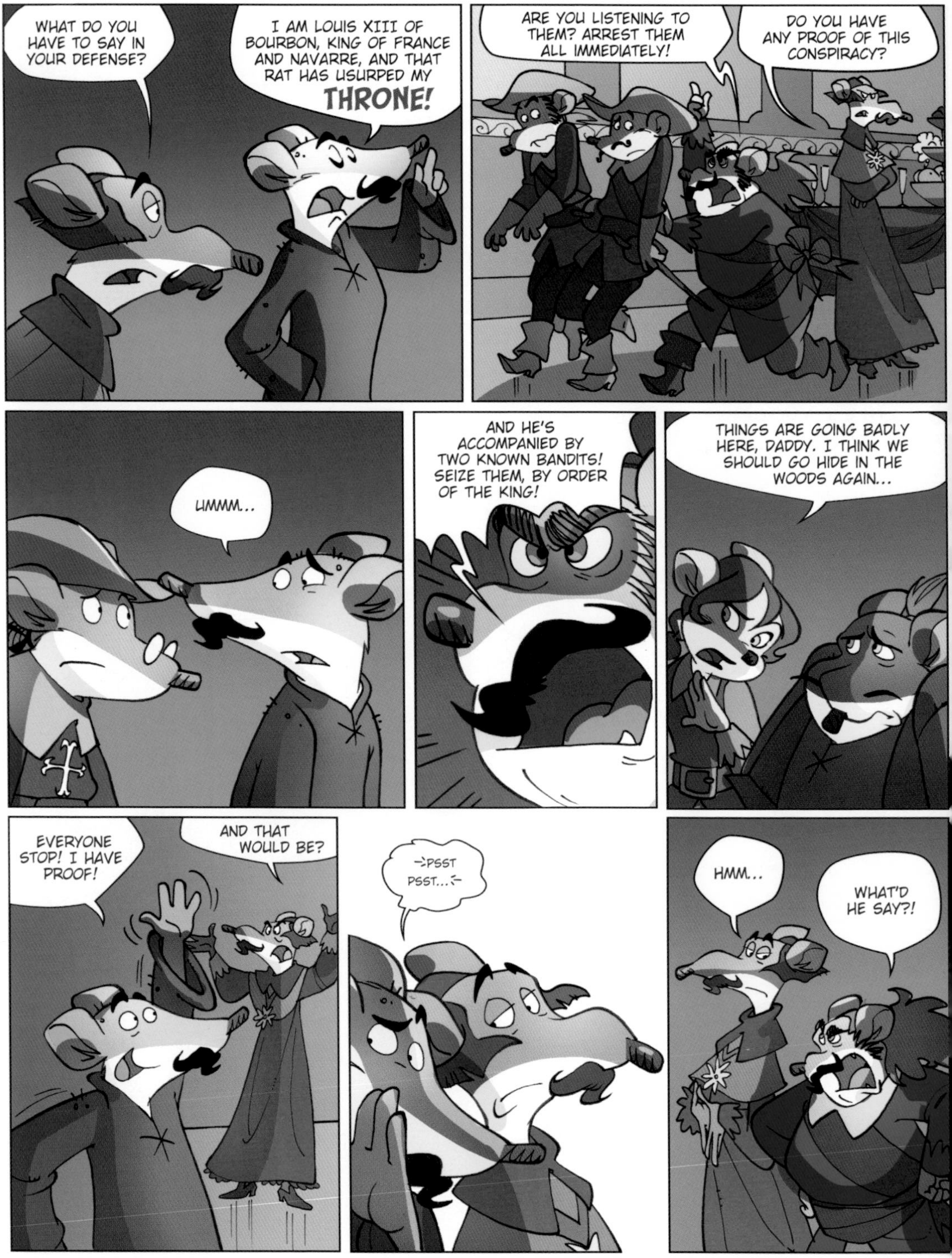
WHAT DO YOU HAVE TO SAY IN YOUR DEFENSE?
I AM LOUIS XIII OF BOURBON, KING OF FRANCE AND NAVARRE, AND THAT RAT HAS USURPED MY THRONE!
ARE YOU LISTENING TO THEM? ARREST THEM ALL IMMEDIATELY!
DO YOU HAVE ANY PROOF OF THIS CONSPIRACY?
UMMM...
AND HE'S ACCOMPANIED BY TWO KNOWN BANDITS! SEIZE THEM, BY ORDER OF THE KING!
THINGS ARE GOING BADLY HERE, DADDY. I THINK WE SHOULD GO HIDE IN THE WOODS AGAIN...
EVERYONE STOP! I HAVE PROOF!
AND THAT WOULD BE?
PSST PSST...
HMM...
WHAT'D HE SAY?!

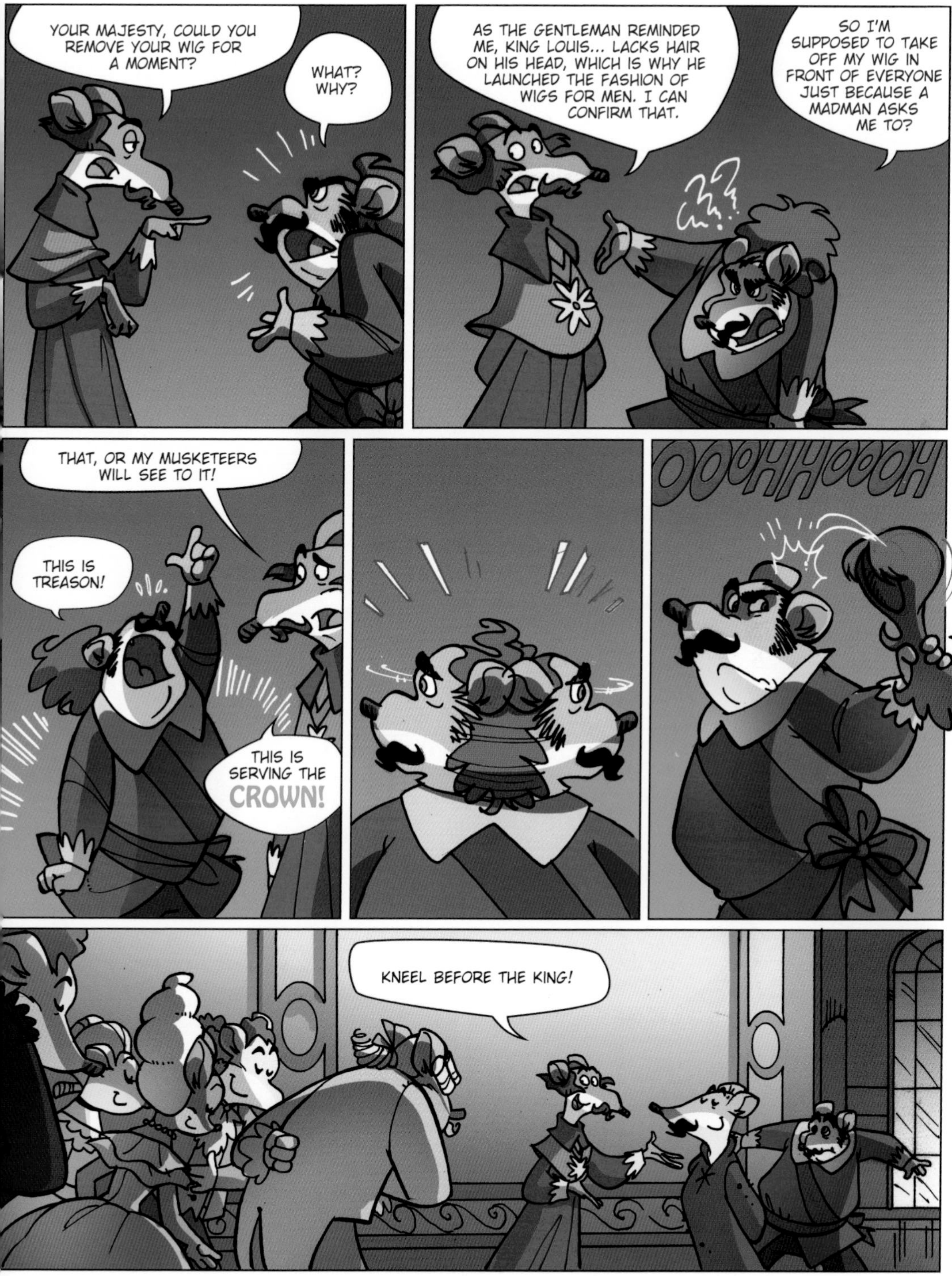
YOUR MAJESTY, COULD YOU REMOVE YOUR WIG FOR A MOMENT?
WHAT? WHY?
AS THE GENTLEMAN REMINDED ME, KING LOUIS... LACKS HAIR ON HIS HEAD, WHICH IS WHY HE LAUNCHED THE FASHION OF WIGS FOR MEN. I CAN CONFIRM THAT.
SO I'M SUPPOSED TO TAKE OFF MY WIG IN FRONT OF EVERYONE JUST BECAUSE A MADMAN ASKS ME TO?
THAT, OR MY MUSKETEERS WILL SEE TO IT!
THIS IS TREASON!
THIS IS SERVING THE CROWN!
OOOHHOOOH
KNEEL BEFORE THE KING!

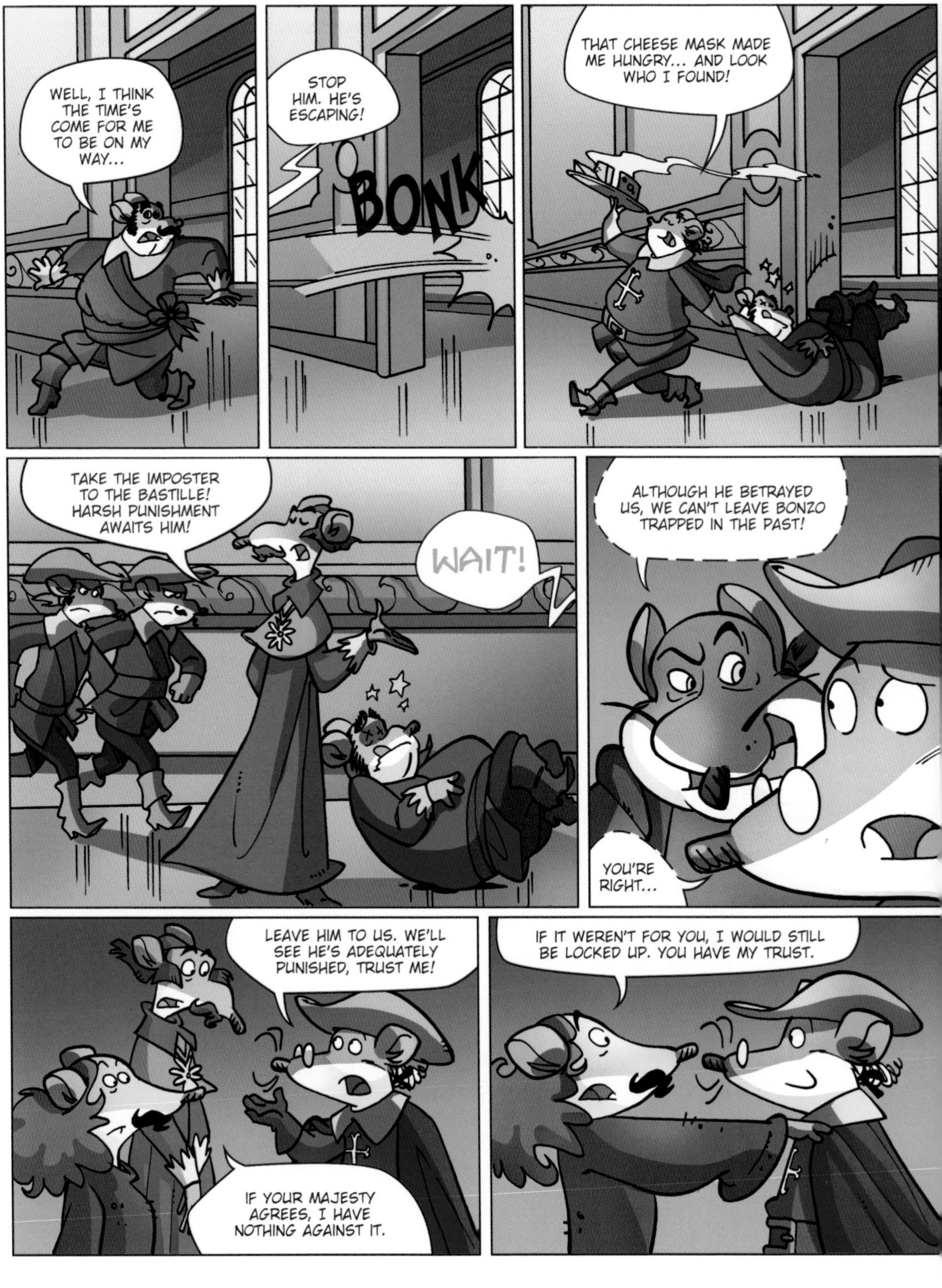
WELL, I THINK THE TIME'S COME FOR ME TO BE ON MY WAY...
STOP HIM. HE'S ESCAPING!
BONK
THAT CHEESE MASK MADE ME HUNGRY... AND LOOK WHO I FOUND!
TAKE THE IMPOSTER TO THE BASTILLE! HARSH PUNISHMENT AWAITS HIM!
WAIT!
ALTHOUGH HE BETRAYED US, WE CAN'T LEAVE BONZO TRAPPED IN THE PAST!
YOU'RE RIGHT...
LEAVE HIM TO US. WE'LL SEE HE'S ADEQUATELY PUNISHED, TRUST ME!
IF YOUR MAJESTY AGREES, I HAVE NOTHING AGAINST IT.
IF IT WEREN'T FOR YOU, I WOULD STILL BE LOCKED UP. YOU HAVE MY TRUST.

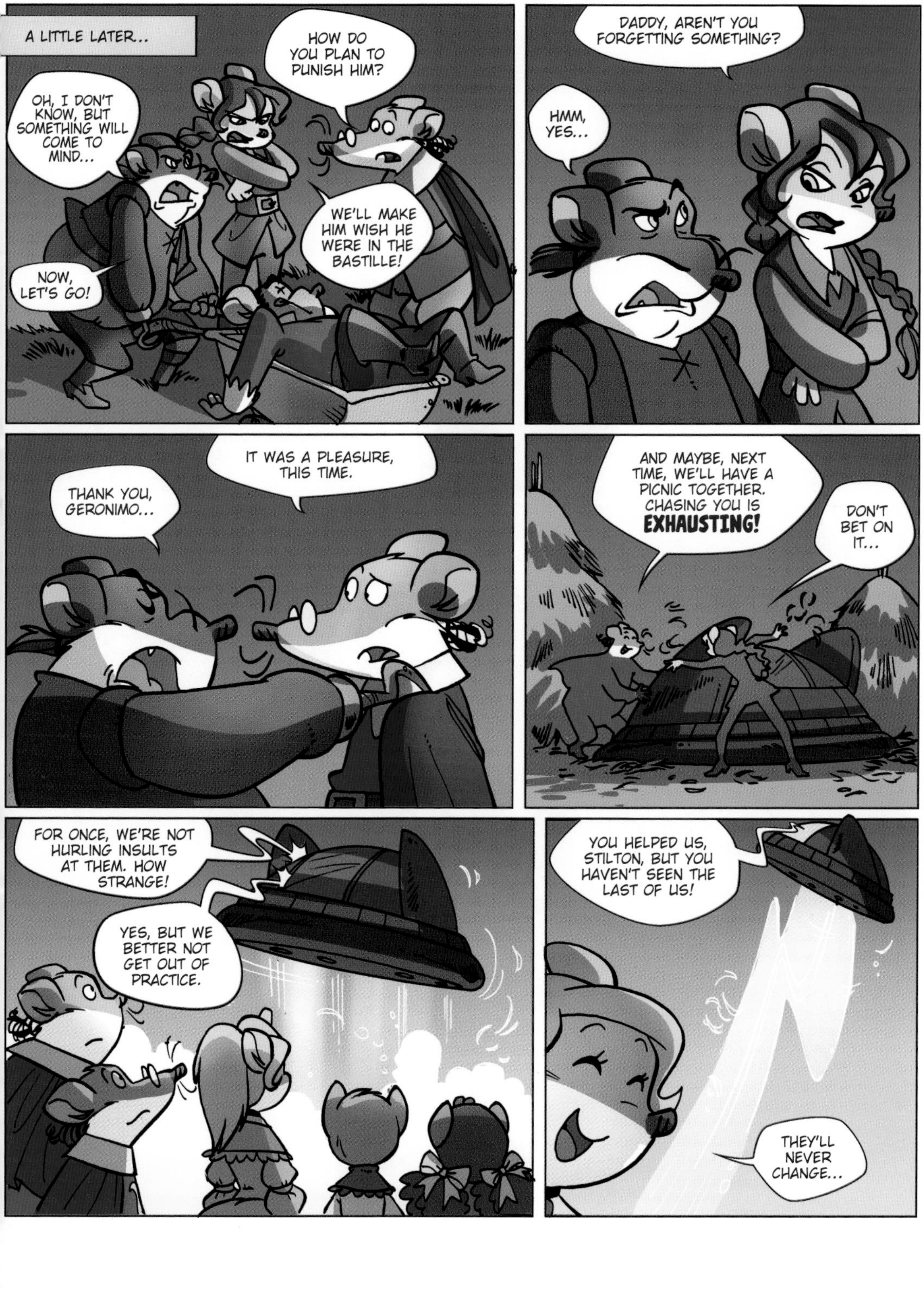
A LITTLE LATER...
HOW DO YOU PLAN TO PUNISH HIM?
OH, I DON'T KNOW, BUT SOMETHING WILL COME TO MIND...
WE'LL MAKE HIM WISH HE WERE IN THE BASTILLE!
NOW, LET'S GO!
DADDY, AREN'T YOU FORGETTING SOMETHING?
HMM, YES...
THANK YOU, GERONIMO...
IT WAS A PLEASURE, THIS TIME.
AND MAYBE, NEXT TIME, WE'LL HAVE A PICNIC TOGETHER. CHASING YOU IS EXHAUSTING!
DON'T BET ON IT...
FOR ONCE, WE'RE NOT HURLING INSULTS AT THEM. HOW STRANGE!
YES, BUT WE BETTER NOT GET OUT OF PRACTICE.
YOU HELPED US, STILTON, BUT YOU HAVEN'T SEEN THE LAST OF US!
THEY'LL NEVER CHANGE...

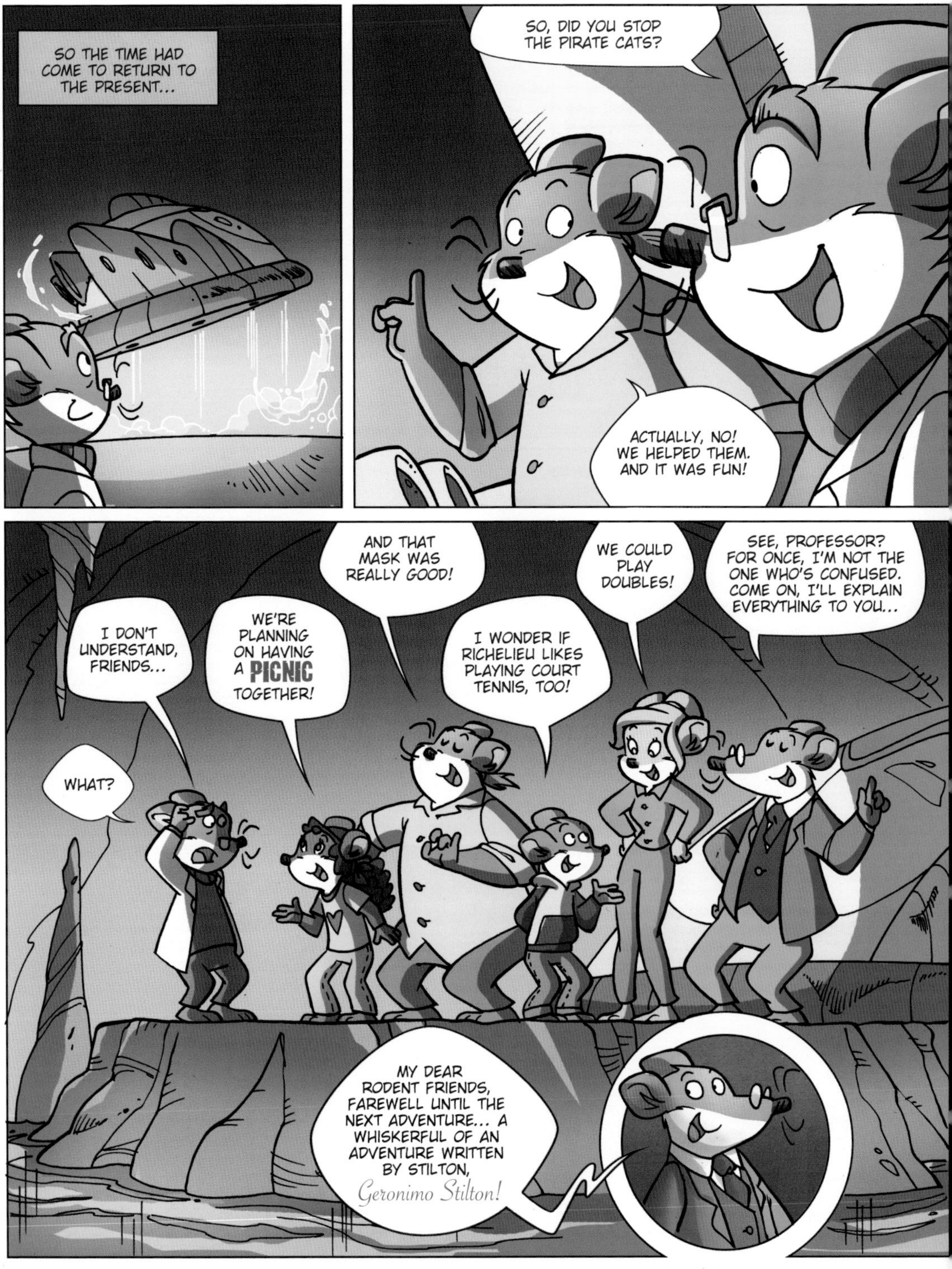
SO THE TIME HAD COME TO RETURN TO THE PRESENT...
SO, DID YOU STOP THE PIRATE CATS?
ACTUALLY, NO! WE HELPED THEM. AND IT WAS FUN!
WHAT?
I DON'T UNDERSTAND, FRIENDS...
WE'RE PLANNING ON HAVING A PICNIC TOGETHER!
AND THAT MASK WAS REALLY GOOD!
I WONDER IF RICHELIEU LIKES PLAYING COURT TENNIS, TOO!
WE COULD PLAY DOUBLES!
SEE, PROFESSOR? FOR ONCE, I'M NOT THE ONE WHO'S CONFUSED. COME ON, I'LL EXPLAIN EVERYTHING TO YOU...
MY DEAR RODENT FRIENDS, FAREWELL UNTIL THE NEXT ADVENTURE... A WHISKERFUL OF AN ADVENTURE WRITTEN BY STILTON, Geronimo Stilton!

Watch Out For PAPERCUTZ

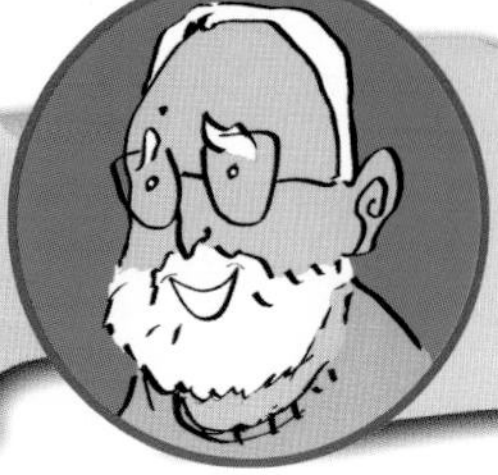

Welcome to the fifth time-travelling GERONIMO STILTON 3 IN 1 graphic novel, collecting three great GERONIMO STILTON graphic novels: "The Fastest Train in the West," "The First Mouse on the Moon and "All for Stilton, Stilton for All!," from Papercutz—that cheesy crew dedicated to publishing great graphic novels for all ages. Oh, and I'm Salicrup, *Jim Salicrup*, the Editor-in-Chief and Sometimes the Only Person on the Seventh Floor, here to talk about mice...

But before I let the cat out of the bag, so to speak, I should mention that Papercutz has published so many graphic novels featuring cats, that we joke about changing our name to Papercatz. But when it comes to publishing graphic novels about mice, there haven't been as many. The obvious exception has been GERONIMO STILTON. Over the years Papercutz has published the original GERONIMO STILTON graphic novel series that is being collected here in GERONIMO STILTON 3 IN 1, as well as the slightly confusing THEA STILTON series. Confusing because the series featured the Thea Sisters, five college students that were studying to become journalists like their idol, Thea Stilton. But Thea did appear in the series too.

In fact, Papercutz briefly published graphic novels starring perhaps the most well-known mice in the world—Mickey and Minnie Mouse. My favorite was "Mickey's Inferno," which was an all-star parody of "Dante's Inferno." Unfortunately, it's no longer available from Papercutz, but if you're lucky, you may find a copy either at your local public library or at your favorite Used Bookstore.

And of course, we're currently publishing GERONIMO STILTON REPORTER, which features adaptations of the animated GERONIMO STILTON TV series. That Geronimo—he's a star of chapter books, graphic novels, and cartoons!

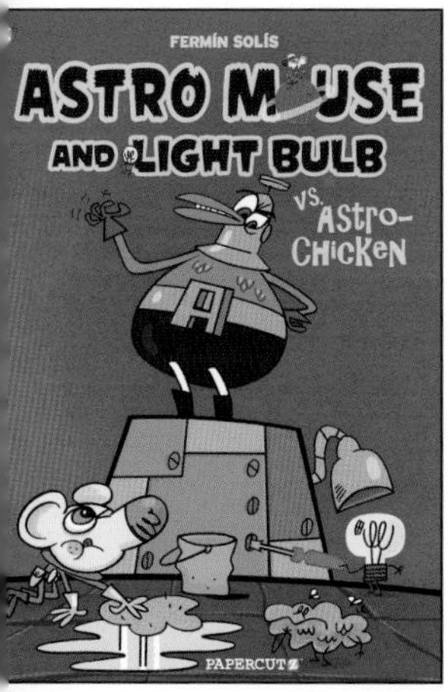

FERMÍN SOLÍS
ASTRO MOUSE AND LIGHT BULB
VS. ASTRO-CHICKEN
PAPERCUTZ

But recently, Papercutz started publishing the adventures of another mouse—ASTRO MOUSE (and his sidekick, LIGHT BULB). Unlike "The First Mouse on the Moon," which mixes science and fantasy, ASTRO MOUSE AND LIGHT BULB is all fantasy. Funny adventure fantasy to be more specific. Created, written, and drawn by the incredibly talented Fermín Solís, ASTRO MOUSE AND LIGHT BULB are sort of silly super-heroes in space encountering such strange characters as Potatoator, Astro Chicken, not to mention, The Troublesome Four—Captain Fastidious, Skunk Girl, Meduso, and Arkade. In case you're wondering, LIGHT BULB really is a sentient (that means it can think) light bulb. You never know what's going to happen next in their surprising adventures, but it's always fun in its own weird way. So, check out ASTRO MOUSE AND LIGHT BULB. If you enjoy DOG-MAN, we suspect you'll also enjoy this Dysfunctional Duo too!

And don't forget to pick up the next volumes of GERONIMO STILTON REPORTER and GERONIMO STILTON 3 IN 1—the next volume features "Lights, Camera, Stilton!," "The Mystery of the Pirate Ship," and "First to the Last Place on Earth." So see you in the future for more fun journeys into the past!

Thanks,
JIM

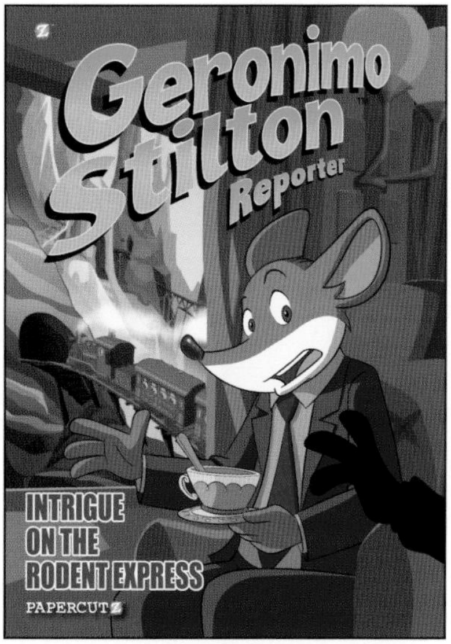

Geronimo Stilton Reporter
INTRIGUE ON THE RODENT EXPRESS
PAPERCUTZ

STAY IN TOUCH!

EMAIL:	salicrup@papercutz.com
WEB:	papercutz.com
TWITTER:	@papercutzgn
INSTAGRAM:	@papercutzgn
FACEBOOK:	PAPERCUTZGRAPHICNOVELS
SNAIL MAIL:	Papercutz, 160 Broadway, Suite 700, East Wing, New York, NY 10038

Go to papercutz.com and sign up for the free Papercutz e-newsletter!